M000236568

A R D I S

B O O K   O N E

A LIFE ON WATER

. . . is a genre-blending novel about a marine biologist's tour of duty as an Allied spy in Portugal. Under the cover of turtle research, Ardis Lowney's mission takes her to Lisbon's sophisticated salons, rustic villages, and sunny beach towns. Just when her cover no longer holds water, she makes an extraordinary discovery at sea, yet comes face-to-face with her would-be lover, staring down the barrel of his luger. The narrative soars with sublime moments that clash with the absurd facades of Fatima, war, and romance.

ARDIS
BOOK ONE

A LIFE ON WATER

A novel by

TIMOTHY PALECZNY

Cavalarico Books

A Life on Water

Copyright © 2023 by Timothy Paleczny

All rights reserved.

No part of this book may be used or reproduced in any manner whatsoever without the prior written permission of the publisher, except in the case of brief quotations embodied in reviews.

This novel's story and characters are fictitious. Names, characters, businesses, events, and incidents are the products of the author's imagination. Space and time have been rearranged to suit the convenience of the book. With the exception of public figures, any resemblance to people living or dead is coincidental. The opinions expressed are those of the characters and should not be confused with the author's.

Published by Cavalarico Books Ltd. located in Barrie, Ontario, Canada

Publisher's website: cavalarico.com

You can purchase the products of Cavalarico Books, including printed books and e-books, online through Amazon Books.

Author's website: timpaleczny.com

Library and Archives Canada Cataloguing in Publication

Title: A Life on Water : a novel / Timothy Paleczny.

Names: Paleczny, Timothy Arthur, 1955- author.

Identifiers:

Canadian (print) ISBN 978-1-7386433-2-5

Canadian (ebook) ISBN 978-1-7386433-3-2

TIMOTHY PALECZNY

For Aidan & Olivia

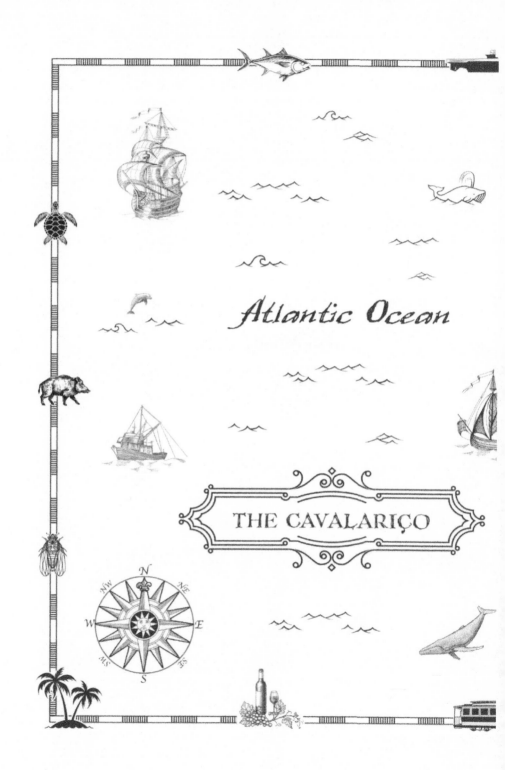

Atlantic Ocean

THE CAVALARIÇO

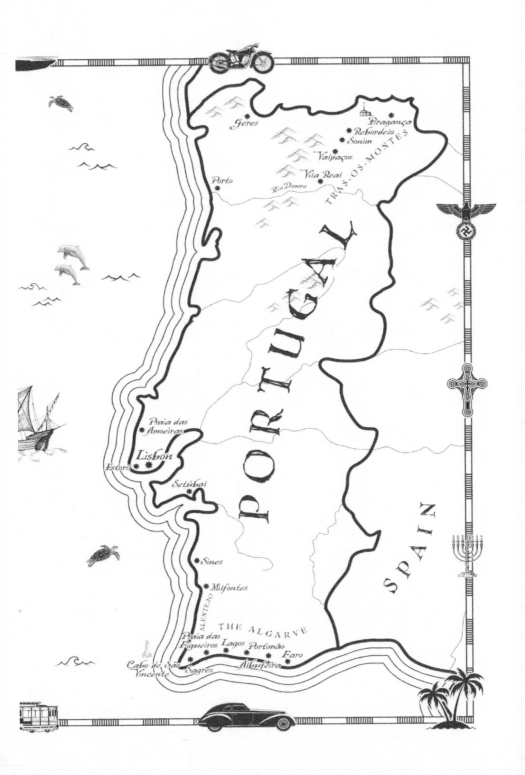

A LIFE ON WATER

ALSO BY TIMOTHY PALECZNY

THE TALE OF INDIGO (2022), POETRY

EXPLORES OUR MOST-ENDURING MYTH AND THE GREAT
ISSUES OF OUR TIME—
GREED, WAR WITH PATHOGENS,
AND CLIMATE CHANGE

TIMOTHY PALECZNY

A LIFE ON
WATER

Part One, 1941 and Earlier

Ardis

1. She Ought to Have Fins

C *harging through crystal-clear water with the lightning surge of a fork-tailed tuna . . . from the edge of tide pools in the sun to depths where light cannot penetrate . . . over deep troughs, ridges, and beds of thriving coral . . . through shafts of sunlight illuminating clouds of fish in every colour, shape, and size—an endless array of immaculate beings astonishing in their individual right to shimmer, quiver, and swim in the dazzling green and blue—*

Her eyelids blinked then opened. She rolled onto her back.

This green and blue was the sea.

Ardis looked beyond the ceiling. She had had a glimpse of the fluid world beneath the surface. Its enormity exceeded what she had seen in books, and anything she could conjure in her wildest imagining.

She sprang out of bed.

Now I know what I want.

She pulled on a pair of slacks. In front of a mirror, she buttoned a blouse with a tiny flower print on a deep chocolate background and tucked it in. She didn't brush her messy bed head. The curls would have fallen where they wanted anyway.

At twenty-five, her complexion was clear. Ardis was lightly freckled and her blue eyes shone like the ocean.

In the kitchen, she filled the kettle and plugged it in. She put two scoops of ground coffee in a carafe, and looked out the window. Sunlight slanted through lofty conifers to brighten her yard. Around this time four years ago, she went with her parents to visit friends in New Jersey. They were all in the kitchen having morning coffee. A radio was on in the background. Ardis heard the announcer introduce a program that featured aquatic life and their underwater communities.

"Hey Dad, turn it up."

Her father liked stations with big bands. That day, he happened to neglect the radio when Ardis, whose hearing was sharper than his, focused in on the conversation that was low in the background.

"Dad, it's about to start."

He adjusted the volume and everyone ceased conversation to listen to the radio, an experience that was novel to them all.

"Welcome to *Romance Under the Waters* with Rachel Carson." It was a radio program about a sea turtle growing up with her family in a lagoon filled with a variety of sea creatures and their challenges to survive in the face of increasing threats from humankind.

Rachel Carson, the show's creator, was a marine biologist.

Here is a woman who gets it.

That was 1935.

Ardis poured the boiling water over the coffee and turned on the radio. "Good morning, Vancouver!" She lowered the volume and turned another dial, looking for music. There were three radio stations in Vancouver and one of them would be playing music. She skipped past "Over the Rainbow," the new hit song from *The Wizard of Oz*, which she had seen, and settled on "Moonlight Serenade," the instrumental sensation from the Glenn Miller Orchestra. She turned up the volume.

She trapped the grounds with the wire mesh, filled her mug, added milk, and took it out to the garden. The kitchen screen door banged shut behind her, reminding her of her parent's cottage on Lake Huron where she spent every summer of her childhood. She didn't realize it when she rented the flat but now she was convinced the screen door was the reason she fell in love with this place—the screen door and this garden.

Besides, this bungalow was close to the campus on Point Grey.

Her second priority that morning was her thesis. She left the warmth of her bed to check the calendar on her desk, a safety measure borne from her drive to complete months of assignments, essays, and exams.

Free at last. For the first time in how long.

Well, not entirely free.

Ardis placed her mug on the arm of the garden chair and slid back into the curves of the wood slats, admiring a flowering wisteria that commanded that corner of garden. Instantly, she fell into a lazy stare with eyes focused yet unfocused. Thinking but not thinking.

It had taken her four years to get into the program and finish it. Now a new problem was nattering at her every quiet moment. *What will I do when I graduate?*

Where do I want to be? How will I get there?

***

She looked at the clothing strewn haphazardly around her. *Right, catch up with laundry and tidy up. In the afternoon, Pete.*

How she met Pete was Caroline's doing. It had begun on campus. Ardis sat at a long table in the library concourse, a cavernous hall beneath the wood trusses of its Gothic edifice. Light emanating from large, amber windows illuminated creamy-yellow walls of limestone that came from Caen, in northwest France.

"Ardis Lowney."

Ardis looked up from the page. It was Caroline.

"Coming to the movies tonight?"

Ardis closed her book. "I wouldn't miss a new release."

"Who are you kidding?" Caroline took pleasure in provoking Ardis's repartee. "I don't know anyone in our class who is as devoted to studying as you are."

"You're right. I have priorities." Ardis gave up nothing even when conceding. "What's showing?"

"The guys"—Caroline's boyfriend, Max, and his friend, Pete— "want to see *Angels with Dirty Faces*, starring James Cagney. It's playing at the Hollywood."

The Hollywood had been showing a string of film noir movies that tended to have serious plots dealing with the criminal underworld of America. There were lighter offerings at the Lux on West Hastings, the Capital on Granville, and the Allen on West Georgia. But being students at the university, they all lived within walking distance of the Hollywood on West Broadway—including Max, who occupied the top floor of the coach house at his parents' oceanfront estate. So they saw yet another gangster movie, which was fine with Ardis, who was fascinated with the bad guy's smooth-talking lawyer played by Humphrey Bogart. She had noticed him in another movie in that kind of supporting role.

"Bogart should have had the lead," she said to the guys exiting the theatre. But they would have none of that. They were Cagney fans.

Why, one would wonder.

They stopped at a soda bar for floats. Max talked about the Sandy DeSantis Orchestra, a swing band he had seen in the Commodore Ballroom at Georgia and Granville. The dance bands were small, he explained, with five to ten pieces: a cornet or trumpet, saxophone, violin, piano, tuba or stand-up string bass, and drums. Other bands led by Lafe Cassidy, Len Chamberlain, Les Crane, Harry Pryce, and others, fit this mold, he insisted, but the band at the Commodore was exceptional. "The bands are getting bigger," Max crowed.

Even Caroline rolled her eyes.

Max went on about a show coming up—Stan Patton's reed and rhythm band on a cruise offered by Union Steamship Lines. "I want to hear them play 'Moonlight Serenade.' It will be romantic, if not serene." He showed the flyer his father brought home from the yacht club.

"It will be a black-tie affair." Caroline frowned.

"Yeah, so? It would be fun." Max was determined to secure a date.

Caroline dismissed the idea. She wanted to say, I don't have a dress.

Max smiled; he was intuitive because he understood the issues. He would take Caroline shopping, soon.

In the lull when Caroline and Max were talking about dresses, Pete asked Ardis how things were going.

She shrugged. "I have been buried in biology textbooks."

Pete was an indigenous student in forestry management. He kept his grades up, although he would not let on as much to Max.

"I study in case his father changes his mind." He looked in her eyes.

"Why? What is so important you want to accomplish?"

He didn't hesitate. "I want to help my Squamish community."

She imagined him applying sustainable forestry practices to maintain old growth forests on Squamish traditional lands.

"Why would you even work for Max's father?"

Max's father had a reputation for producing the most lumber and employing the most men. There had been issues with its clear-cutting practices, blighting the landscape as far as the eye could see.

"To learn the business. Our coursework doesn't cover operations, equipment, land leasing, and labour management. In just a couple of years I can learn a lot."

All but Ardis were intending to work at the firm owned by Max's father, which was the main reason Max and Caroline were not so concerned with their grades.

Ardis did not think highly of their attitude toward education and she didn't agree with this strategy, but she had no right to say anything. She imagined the Fraser River where it opened wide to meet the sea.

Pete looked at her. "What will you do?"

His angular nose and jaw, bright eyes, and white teeth distracted her. "I want to make newsreels, like the kind we see at the movies," Ardis revealed an idea she had not yet investigated, "about marine life." She nodded as if to convince herself.

"There are lots of seals on Point Grey that you could film."

"I know! I went there with my class. The waves on the rocks would be amazing, too—if only I had a movie camera."

Max, who had been listening, cut in. "You're a mermaid, who grew legs to live among us. You just act like a student."

Caroline seized the opening. "If she's a fish she ought to have fins."

"I'm sorry." Ardis looked down at the menu she was rolling in her hands. "Helping marine life is what I want–"

"No!" Max jolted her reverie. "Not until you show us your gills."

"Ahhhh!" She blushed deeply as she swatted him with the rolled-up menu, which made her friends laugh even more.

"All in good fun, right guys?" Caroline chirped in, protecting her.

It was no wonder the guys enjoyed kidding her—she would have been a trophy catch. Beneath the lustre of her God-given features, Ardis was ordinary and plain. She wore calico dresses and her blonde hair fell on her shoulders. She didn't use make-up; most women didn't. Other than going out to the movies, she wasn't active socially. Going out among the islands was another matter. Scanning for sea life was what she did when she wasn't writing papers and preparing for exams.

"What makes you think you can even do this?" Max scrunched his eyes and held his hands open in front of him.

Max could be so dramatic. "Do what?"

"How can you deliver the work required in a man's job when you have babies and children to take care of?"

"Who said I wanted to have babies? And who said marine biology or anything for that matter is a man's job?"

"Well, my Dad told my sister no one would hire a woman, anyway. Men need the jobs to support their families. A woman without a family shouldn't take work from men with families."

Hard times give some ideas a moral fortitude they don't deserve.

It would have been senseless to debate the topic with Max. "Thank you, Max. I cannot tell you how helpful this conversation has been."

"What can you do with a grad degree in Marine Biology? Will you work for a fishing company that doesn't know where to drop its nets?"

The sarcasm didn't bother her for a second. She was more concerned with preserving sea life, not harvesting it. She left that one alone, too.

***

That night out at the movies had been three weeks ago. Ardis sipped her coffee and refocused on the red wisteria blossoms; they reminded her of her parents in Toronto. She let out a sigh.

"It won't be forever," she had tried to convince them. When she boarded the train to Vancouver, she believed it, too.

"Ardis Avalyn Lowney, you should stay home like other girls."

In stark terms, her father laid bare his opinion about a woman's worth. She wished he were capable of voicing gracious, good charm, saying something like "It's a great way to spread your wings." He didn't, and that did not surprise her. When she applied to the University of Toronto, it was the same. "What do you need so much education for?"

If I were a boy, he would have responded differently.

Ardis excused her father. For his age, his thinking wasn't unusual.

He was a father—mine.

He was head of the house. Such was the structure of society.

It was galling he would not provide financial support, yet he even withheld any speck of encouragement. She understood what men in general thought of women. Women belonged in the home.

How does Mom put up with him?

Ardis loved her mother; she was the diametric opposite of her dad.

When Ardis was still in grade school, her mom cautioned her about people who would expect her to fulfil her duty as a woman by embracing the role of a loving wife and mother. "That might have been appropriate in the past, however, times are changing." Instead, she nudged Ardis gently, directing her toward new ideas and opportunities.

"Ardis, look at this piece on aircraft engineering." She handed her a copy of *Chatelaine* magazine. Elsie McGill is the author. "Remember her? She is the young woman—not much older than you—who graduated from the University of Toronto as an electrical engineer."

Any mention of the local university grabbed Ardis's attention. It was a possible destination for the most fortunate boys, and if her mother had her way, it was possible for Ardis, too. It was more common that women might take liberal arts degrees, and Elsie McGill proved that all areas of engineering were options for women, too.

"Elsie McGill had polio and wrote these articles from her wheelchair." Her mother patted the magazine. "You can study sciences, technology, engineering, and mathematics, too—all areas in which you can really make a difference."

Her mother nurtured her aspirations. "Girls can do whatever boys do, with very few physical exceptions. Girls are better book learners."

Her mother helped cobble together her resources, including gifts and Ardis's savings from babysitting and summer jobs, to fund the undergraduate years. After Ardis left home, she gave her daughter the brunt of the modest annuities she was receiving from a trust fund her parents had left for her. It was enough to set Ardis on her way.

***

After a number of times out at the movies, Pete asked Ardis to join him for a walk from Jericho Beach to see the seals at Point Grey. It was a date, really.

Ardis had put in long days and was tired, but she went anyway, for the fresh air. There was no fuss; it was an informal, afternoon walk at an easy pace. They were learning about each other. For this, Ardis mentally awarded Pete bonus points.

They walked on a forest trail to the university to view the seals, then back along the beach. On returning, they admired the view toward the city and across Burrard Inlet where the city met the mountains.

"It was unfortunate that Max attacked you for supposedly taking work from a man." Pete looked to see her response.

"Yes, a lot of men think exactly that, especially now."

"These are bad times, for sure." They approached a log that had blocked part of the trail. Pete stepped aside to let her pass through first. "They're saying we are in an economic crisis, but I think women are not the cause of a global slowdown. Women are part of the solution."

"I like that idea." Ardis gave him a thoughtful nod. "It's a good time to be in school. Get a good education." In fact, enrolment had surged because young people could not find jobs.

"You said you want to make a movie about marine life."

Pete had listened.

"Yes, a short one, like the newsreels at the movies."

"Oh yes, about the war—those are good. Don't you have to be a filmmaker?"

"I don't know. How hard can it be?" Ardis gestured to a knoll at the top of the sand where a large, weathered log offered a comfortable place to sit and rest.

"Or work for the government?"

"Maybe, I haven't thought of it." She pulled her legs in close, held by her arms. She rested her head on her knees. Her eyes stung. She closed them for a moment.

"You will just go ahead and do it."

She opened one eye. "Sure, why not? Someone has to."

"How do you plan to get on a ship? You need film equipment and know how to use it."

"That's for sure." Her eyes were closed and she was still.

The surf was not even slightly wild. The stories she had told him about this place now seemed exaggerated even to her. Perhaps she had been thinking of the Pacific Ocean at Half Moon Bay on Vancouver Island. What loomed large here was the breadth of Burrard Inlet against the distant mountains.

Their walk and the long days worked their magic on Ardis. She dozed off in the middle of their conversation.

Pete left her for a moment. He walked back down the path.

An object materialized in the surf. Initially, Ardis felt she imagined it. A wave crashed over the carapace and the sea dissembled itself at her feet in a parallax scrolling of foam, rushing forward then backward into the ocean. There on the sand approaching her was a sea turtle the size of a chesterfield.

The turtle lifted its long neck and tilted its craggy head to look directly at her. "What do you. On my beach?"

Her eyes bulged. It was as if she understood its truncated thoughts.

"Mystery of world. Revealed," intoned the turtle, "to you. Who loves. Creatures of sea."

Ardis caught her breath. Her jaw fell open.

"Do not alarm. Why turtles. Not speak?" The turtle laughed. "Turtles. Made language."

This is crazy.

The turtle's smile disappeared. "Human predation. Is crazy. Human pollution. Is crazy. Know you why?"

Ardis nodded.

"When sea and all sea creatures die. Humans die. Yes, for humanity. Sea turtle extinction. Is crazy."

The turtle crawled in a straight line to the top of the beach, picked a spot, and with its flippers, flung sand aside, creating a hole. It laid its eggs. Spread a layer of sand over the eggs. It smoothed over the nest, rocked on it, then turned to Ardis, who was thinking.

How old are you?

"Long. Time."

The ridley returned to the sea.

Pete returned and found Ardis with her arms wrapped around her knees, and her head resting there. He shook her shoulder, but she wasn't asleep. She murmured.

"Are you okay?" His palm cradled her cheek. Her eyes opened.

"I talked with a turtle."

Pete pointed to the tracks in the sand. "You did this to trick me, didn't you?"

"Maybe I wasn't dreaming."

"What do you mean, Ardis?" He pointed to the fresh marks in the sand at the top of the beach near where she sat. "This will take some explaining."

"Did you know turtles can talk?"

He kicked sand at her. "Not a bad job, Ardis. It actually looks authentic."

Ardis couldn't argue. The tracks were fresh.

Pete walked to that spot and flicked some sand aside, almost like the turtle did, and he saw an egg. "Oh my God, it's real."

"So turtles can talk."

"Oh, stop playing." He tousled her hair. "C'mon, there's something you have to see."

She joined him by the water's edge. He pointed to a pod of orcas by the headland.

"Oh, nice," she said.

"So you had a dream."

Pete's calm intensity let her know she would be safe sharing her dream with him.

"I did. Although I closed my eyes I didn't sleep. I sensed the turtle's presence. Then I heard its carapace scratching upon the sand as it slid toward me."

"Exactly, it was a vision." He touched her arm. "The turtle is your spirit guide."

"What does that mean?"

"A spirit guide usually comes in your dreams and gives you messages to help you see your life, understand your challenges, and find purpose. It is up to you to interpret your spirit guide's messages and apply them to your life."

"Oh great, a sea turtle is now my mentor." Ardis laughed. "Is it possible all this marine biology is going to my head?"

"Not at all," Pete responded quickly, "turtles have existed on earth long before any people. They are survivors. Our folklore says that all people and animals live on the shell of a very large turtle."

Ardis nodded. "I've heard of this. North America is Turtle Island."

Since that day, her vision came back to her as she slipped in and out of consciousness just before falling asleep. Dreaming but not dreaming. Asleep but not sleeping. Like a holy oil dripping on water, the dream could not quite blend with reality and stubbornly would not come to life in her sleep as it had that day on the beach with Pete. The images pooled together to hint of truth and tainted every bit of clarity she had ever known before they broke apart and dispersed in the ebb and flow of the river of life, before being carried off in its current.

***

In her usual place at the long table in the library concourse, Ardis was writing her thesis on sea turtle nesting practices. She pushed the wire-frame reading glasses back on her nose as she took stock of her progress. Her paper was coming together nicely. It was the last requirement she needed to graduate with a Master of Science degree at fall convocation.

Focused as she was, she did not see a truck stop in front of the building. A boy jumped out and tossed a bundle of newspapers onto the sidewalk. He cut it open and waved a paper in the air, shouting words Ardis did not hear. Men hurried from the library to see what was going on. A small crowd pressed around the boy, everyone wanting his two-penny copy.

Within moments, a set of footsteps re-entered the reading room. It was Caroline.

"Canada has declared war!"

"What?" Ardis turned to her friend, bewildered.

"That's the headline of the paper. Canada declared war!"

"Oh my God, not now!" Ardis just blurted it out, an instinctual response.

"Yes!"

Ardis recalled what she had learned about the Great War. Tens of millions of soldiers and civilians had died, which had happened in her lifetime. The horrible impacts on families had lingered; the prospect of another war was unimaginable.

Ardis went to the door and looked out on the crowd that had gathered. Caroline had accurately conveyed the crowd's exuberance. The young men welcomed a war. They applauded valour; they were invincible.

"With Germany?" Ardis looked to Caroline.

"Yes, they're saying they'll give the Krauts what they deserve."

The date was September 10, 1939. "Krauts" was a common nickname for German people, owing to their love of sauerkraut piled high on their sausages, a dish that Ardis happened to enjoy.

A week earlier, a German U-boat had sunk the *SS Athenia*. The passenger liner had been carrying students, families, and mostly immigrants. Several ships responded to the distress call. Unfortunately, nineteen members of the crew and ninety-eight passengers, including fifty-four Canadians and twenty-eight Americans died. Canadians saw the attack on civilians as a barbaric first move against England as well as Canada.

It infuriated the students on campus.

"Come, join me." Caroline beckoned. She was always trying to involve Ardis.

"Thank you, Caroline, but I must finish this paper now or my grad will be delayed."

"Good. Then you can graduate with the rest of us." At one time or another, Caroline had included her, covered for her, protected her, and saved her from embarrassing herself.

Ardis shook her head. At this moment, the thought of even more meaningless deaths sickened Ardis. She would be the bland, boring, and unworthy friend; her attention on this paper was what the situation demanded.

Caroline waved to her and joined the men on the mall.

If she wanted, later, Ardis knew where she could find her. The crowd would soon move to a pub on West Broadway, and Caroline would be with it. Ardis did not have a deadline; she had only about an hour of work to do and she was not going to stop now.

***

That fall of 1939 and throughout the spring and summer of 1940, Ardis redoubled her focus on her chosen career path. She went out on the water with study groups, which to her was the best part of school. She quickly gained experience piloting boats and learning the ways of the watery world. Whenever she needed a break, she arranged to join a crew or rent a craft. The greatest benefit was the most obvious one: being on the water meant being outside in the fresh air, rain or shine.

She loved being on the water. She loved the low rumble of the engine as they slowly cruised by the docks. It reminded her of the *Sauble Clipper* with its engines reverberating as they snaked out of the river and beyond the river mouth where its engines opened up and the vibrations quickened.

She took on a volunteer role in the university's education program for British Columbia fishermen, where she gained experience dealing with fish, dolphin, sea turtles, and all kinds of sea mammals. More often than not, the issues she worked with were manmade. Fishing line and netting entangled turtles and seals. Human activities destroyed natural habitats and endangered species. She saw it with her own eyes and she wanted desperately to play a role in saving sea turtles, in particular. She needed to know more about their migrations, habitats, and food sources. Marine biologists needed to do more research of all kinds.

Ardis participated in a research program led by Dean Ellert that focused on an endangered sea turtle, the Kemp's ridley, which populated the waters of the Gulf of Mexico in Florida and Mexico, and along the coastlines of Central America. The location of its nesting grounds had remained a mystery in the marine biology community since Floridian fisherman Richard Kemp discovered the species in 1880.

Did they migrate? Did they have a pedigree across the Atlantic Ocean? Dean Ellert encouraged Ardis to formulate and test her theories.

In her analysis of ocean currents, Ardis identified the west coast of Africa as the most probable location for a Kemp's ridley nesting ground, and the Bahia coast of Brazil as another. Ardis was not aware of any studies in either location. She told the Dean she had to go to Africa and see for herself. To Ardis, finding an answer was more important than teaching.

Caroline told her she was crazy. "Those waters are full of pirates—real-life pirates. You won't get out alive."

Around the same time, the Dean invited Ardis to apply for a new teaching position in the educational program for fishermen, which had been more successful than anticipated. She did, and he offered her a position she could not pass up. She could not believe her luck.

The intense excitement around the declaration of war continued. Only three months earlier, King George VI and Queen Elizabeth had visited Vancouver as part of a Royal visit. When the King called for troops, men eagerly enlisted to fight the Nazis. On campus, male students had to balance their academic priorities with mandatory training in the Canadian Officer Training Corps. Military camps and service buildings transformed the campus.

Women were signing on as well, not to join the ranks of fighting forces, but to serve as field nurses or in various support services in Canada or England. Caroline signed on, and as Ardis expected, Caroline's urgings for Ardis to join became frequent and urgent.

The call of duty seemed to be on everyone's agenda but her own. Ardis loved her country. With her education, service as a field nurse seemed the most appropriate expectation, but with people, she was helpless. Aquatic life did not upset her like that. She felt compelled to help sea life because she could actually make a difference.

***

In the aftermath of her chance meeting with the turtle on the beach, Ardis discovered a surprising gusto in her new life on the west coast. The day before, she had said goodbye to Caroline, who was on her way to

England. Max had already gone over—the day after he and Caroline took the moonlight cruise, that black-tie affair with an orchestra on the Salish Sea.

Pete had gone, too. Before departing, he gave Ardis a silver necklace with an art deco turtle pendant.

"Oh my goodness, it's so cute." Burnished silver outlined the turtle's carapace over a blue opal stone.

"May you live a long, prosperous, and adventurous life." He closed the clasp.

***

Another morning in the garden with her coffee, Ardis welcomed a chance to sit in a patch of sunlight to warm herself. There was no wind; sunbeams were aglow with floating particles. She fell into the moment, and time stood still.

With Pete's departure, Ardis was on her own. All her dearest friends were in service overseas. She wondered whether she would ever see them again.

She pictured herself standing in a makeshift tent at the rear of the front line. Guns in battle boomed sporadically in the distance. Men all around her, wounded and horribly bloodied, clung to life. They moaned throughout the day and night, every day, all the time. She was useless to respond to their cries for help.

Ardis blinked. The beam of sunlight returned to real. She thought of her dream. She knew with all her being what she wanted . . . *a life on water.*

2. The Perfect Cover

Dean Ellert called Ardis into his office. "Ardis Avalyn, this research . . . you couldn't do this in the Pacific Ocean off Central America?"

Other than Dad, he is the only one who calls me Ardis Avalyn.

"No, we do not see this species in the Pacific."

Surely, he knows this.

"This may be difficult . . . with the war going on people won't see the need to do research on sea turtles."

"Then maybe I should enlist too, if that's what everyone wants." She had not planned on playing this card. The sarcasm just slipped out in a moment of impatience.

"No, no. That won't be necessary." The Dean appeared uneasy. She could see he wanted to keep her. "I believe you will make a difference here in our department and in marine biology—war or no war, dammit!"

Her plans were working out better than expected. In all the excitement with the war, her news for the most part went unnoticed. Without fanfare, Ardis had commenced her teaching duties and now she would do some research.

Ardis's parents were not happy that Ardis wanted to go to Africa. "If you go overseas, how will you communicate with us? Maybe you could get a radio," her father wrote.

She humoured her father—a radio was a reasonable idea. She asked the department whether there might be money in the budget for a short-wave radio to communicate home.

Things were falling into place. Yet her good fortune weighed heavily on her. Her friends and colleagues had signed up and put their lives on the line, while she was fulfilling dreams. She could not take both opportunities. She would give up one.

But she could not bring herself to do it.

The Biology department arranged to provide Ardis with a radio. Her project was moving forward nicely.

***

In March, Ellert told her the application for her radio had raised interest; there would be a meeting. In April, Ardis joined Dean Ellert to meet an officer of the Royal Canadian Navy, Captain John Grant.

The Dean introduced her as Professor Lowney.

Captain Grant was a clean-shaven, short-haired, Navy man. He was not quite as old as the Dean. He was direct, with a kind disposition.

They sat in chairs opposite Ellert's desk. Behind the Dean were books, wall-to-wall.

"Professor Lowney, we have an opportunity to work together."

Ardis liked people who made their careers on the water. "Go on."

"Normally, you wouldn't hear from the Navy, but we're in a war—"

Dean Ellert gently cut in. "Captain Grant has briefed me about the situation, Professor Lowney. What you are about to hear should not leave this room."

"Is there a complication that affects my project?"

Ellert cleared his throat. "There is a wrinkle."

"Oh?"

"Your proposal identified your targeted area as the northwest coast of Africa. Today, I want to ask you whether you would consider changing your study area slightly north to concentrate on the waters off the coast of Portugal."

"The preliminary data I have wouldn't support that, sir, in my opinion." Ardis paused. "And what does this have to do with the Navy?"

The Dean lifted a memo. "Professor Lowney, you may recall our university president released a memo to all departments, and I quote:

"From the day of the declaration of war, the University has been prepared to put at the disposal of the Government all possible assistance by way of laboratories, equipment and trained personnel, insofar as such action is consistent with the maintenance of reasonably efficient instructional standards. To do less would be unthinkable."

Dean Ellert set the memo down. "When you are in the field conducting research funded by the university, you will remain on the payroll of the university. As such, it is our understanding that you and your services are at the disposal of the Government but in a limited sense. What Captain Grant asks of you goes well beyond what this memo intended. Go ahead, Captain Grant."

"Thank you, sir." He faced Ardis. "Our interests are mutual."

Ardis nodded. *He wants to offer me naval protection. Perfect.*

"The war is not going well for us. Germany faced no resistance in France worth mentioning. The German army is fortifying its positions. We believe England is the next target. Now, the Canadian war effort is focused on supplying Britain with food to feed her people, and the supplies and weapons it needs to fight a long, difficult war."

Ardis appreciated hearing this information. Although it was very general, it seemed more important than anything anyone could read in a newspaper because it was "Secret."

"We join Britain in battle and we support her in all areas, including gathering intelligence and supporting insurgents in espionage."

Ardis raised her eyebrows as if to say, what has this to do with me?

"Your research of sea turtle nesting grounds will take you primarily to beaches and involve you being on fishing wharfs or in the harbours."

Ardis nodded, impressed that someone paid attention to her research plans, even if Captain Grant had gleaned the information from an application for a radio licence.

"I am here to ask you to consider an idea. We do not want to stop you from your research. We ask that you report any movements and affairs of our enemies that you might encounter in the region."

"I see." She didn't see a thing. She stood and stepped over to the window. "But Portugal is neutral, is it not?" She turned away from the window to look at Captain Grant.

"Indeed, it is. That doesn't mean we cannot go there. We do, and so do the Germans and Italians. We all have representatives in Portugal and we're all watching one another."

"And you want me to go into the middle of that?" Though terrified, she acted as if it were nothing. She paced from the window to the door at the opposite side of the room.

"Yes." Captain Grant followed her with his gaze.

"You want me to report what I see?" She was afraid there was more.

"Yes."

"No one will know that I am reporting to you?" She turned to face

Captain Grant and eyed the door.

"Actually, you would report to a Naval intelligence officer under British command."

I see a torpedo coming right at me.

"My country is at war and I want to help out in any way I can." She was too afraid to say otherwise. "You want me to conduct surveillance of enemy vessels in international waters. How dangerous could it be?" Ardis folded her arms, not looking at Captain Grant or Dean Ellert.

"I'm glad you asked that. If our enemies find evidence that proved you were a spy, your life would be in danger, and if we know of a situation, we would pull you out immediately."

Me, a spy? Nothing scares me more.

"I am a marine biologist. All I want is to follow sea turtles."

"Exactly, it's a perfect cover."

Haha, like what could go wrong?

Her answer was a perfect cover, too. She was in a corner. *What no one can see is how afraid I am to say no.* She responded the only way she could.

"Yes, I will do it," and on impulse, she added, "on one condition."

She was not in a position to set conditions. Naively, she jeopardized her chances of coming out of this meeting with anything.

Captain Grant promised to pass on her request, and Dean Ellert promised to find money in his budget, too, if necessary, but he made it clear to Captain Grant this would be a Navy initiative.

Fulfilling her one condition would not be easy. Sourcing would be an issue, and timing could make it impossible.

***

In July, Dean Ellert released Ardis from her classroom duties.

"Ardis, you will remain on the payroll. Go home and visit your parents. An officer named Garcia will contact you about the radio training. If there is anything you need, let me know."

No problem. She would focus on her research and act as instructed.

She told her parents about the new developments in her research. They were pleased to hear she had switched her focus to Portugal.

"A man came to see you," her mother's eyes shone, "quite a handsome fellow, dear."

"Did he leave a name?"

"Roberto Garcia. He left a number too. Oxford 3-1921."

"That's in the Beach." Her father remembered these kinds of details.

"Garcia, yes. That's for the training to operate the radio you want me to have, Dad."

***

Ardis arrived at Fran's on College. Roberto Garcia stood to greet her. Once she ordered tea and rice pudding, he got down to business.

"I have information for you." His voice was low and hoarse.

"Yes, give it to me. I'll take it home and read it."

"No paper. From now on, nothing is in writing—to protect you."

She leaned in. "May I sip my tea as you teach me how to be a spy?"

"You joke."

"I never imagined doing this, Roberto. That's all."

"Yes, that's the way it is for most of us."

"I see." She sipped her tea. "You are aware of my condition?"

"Yes, actually, I am aware of it. We have to talk. Film-making equipment is a big request."

Ardis sat back. She was afraid they would balk.

"No one enlists with conditions; no officer would sign off on this, ever." He held up his hand. There would be no discussion. "But there is interest here. Not because you want it, but because we do."

The appetite for newsreels is insatiable. Ardis smiled widely.

"What is so funny?"

"One-minute news clips can help win the war; I can do this."

"If we can get our hands on a camera and film in time."

Garcia left. Ardis sipped her tea and savoured the pudding.

That night, Ardis pulled back the covers to crawl into bed and remembered the location of the Farm. *East of Oshawa off Highway 2.*

The feeling of dread returned. "Camp?" It was all she could muster.

Her look of horror made him laugh. "Don't worry, you won't be in a tent. There are barracks. It is a military facility. You will be the only woman in the group. You will be issued a uniform."

Near the lake. "How long?"

"About two months."

"This is much different than expected." She had imagined a half-hour of radio training and maybe ten minutes of trying it out.

He shrugged his shoulders, which in itself was a dismissal. "Yes, there is more to it than I have been able to tell you. You will be an officer in the Canadian Navy. You will operate under the cover of your marine research. One can't operate in the field without proper training."

"No, I suppose not." But me a spy? Preposterous.

What else could she have said? She had no idea what was involved, either in the field or in the training.

I did not sign up for this.

The idea of a training camp did not impress her. Summer camp was the kind of thing she participated in as a girl, although it did open her to possibilities like working outdoors as a marine biologist. But she was just a kid. Now, it was an unnecessary delay.

It might be dangerous.

But the Navy will provide filming equipment. They have taken her engagement seriously. Yes, she would cooperate.

Those eyes. Were they grey or metallic blue?

She would catch that jitney to Oshawa in the morning. She crossed the street to Eaton's and purchased a camisole and stockings.

If she was going to conduct marine research, she had to be a spy.

This will amount to nothing. Right? I will make newsreels.

Her recruitment had been clever on his part. How she came to be a spy was a slick manipulation; on her part, perhaps there had been a little sly manoeuvring as well.

3. The Farm

The only marking by the road was a number on a sign. A few trees provided cover, but otherwise the facility was out in the open in the midst of farmers' fields. The gate to the camp was immediately off the road.

Canadian military authorities established Camp X to train Canadian operatives. It also happened to train some American operatives, but that was hushed. The American military did not have authority to train or equip its operatives because the United States Congress had not declared war.

Officially, Camp X was the Special Training School 103 . . . for the British MI6. The Canadian military referred to it as Project J. And to keep all participants on their toes, the Royal Canadian Mounted Police called it S 25-1-1.

"We call it the Farm." Garcia looked sharp in his Navy uniform.

There were three buildings. The main building was unique in that the windows were seven feet above ground so people could not casually peek in. Ardis saw training rooms. On the second floor, Garcia showed her Hydra's radio room and introduced her to the operators she would interact with when she was in the field. Hydra received and sent all wartime radio communications with the European continent in veiled scripts via Morse code. A large window at the south end of the radio room provided a view of Lake Ontario.

The other two buildings housed the men's barracks, the women's barracks, a gym, showers, a canteen, mess hall, laundry, and equipment rooms.

Ardis lost track of time, meeting many people, including British operatives Ian Bromwell, Kim Philby, and Ian Fleming. By 20:00 hours, she was exhausted from taking in information and standing all day. Slipping between the sheets, she felt glorious. She fell asleep instantly.

***

Awakened by reveille, everyone's day began with running on the road in front of the Farm. Ardis focused her resentment on Major

Brooker, the officer in charge of training, who took pleasure in sharing his experiences from behind the lines in Europe even as he led their runs.

"Keep up the pace, Missy. We're not on vacation."

Immediately following a fifteen-minute shower and change into dry clothes, she attended German language training that was mandatory for all and then Portuguese lessons for her and the British.

Afternoons, Ardis focused on knowledge and skills training, starting with map reading and strategic interests. Garcia briefed her on theatres of war, from land to sea and air. And he peppered his lessons with reports from the field. "One of ours was captured here, yesterday." He pointed to the map. "The Nazis gutted him and hung him in the town square as a warning to anyone who cooperates with us."

Ardis told herself he was pointing to a village in France. *That won't happen in Portugal.*

Another time, the Nazis imprisoned and tortured a handful of villagers of various ages, including "two of ours," Garcia said, for weeks. The Nazis tied them to posts in front of a wall along a heavily used road. "Before we could rescue them, each one got a bullet in the head."

Garcia did not embellish reports. He reported in as straightforward a manner as one could muster. The impact on Ardis was not anything one could see. Images of executions stood out in her memory as if she had been there herself and watched them happen.

Ardis received a handgun. Holding the gun in her hand for the first time, she understood the idea of what it could do, which turned her stomach into a sour pit. Firing it made her instantly aware of the power one gains by wielding a weapon. She learned how to unlock, aim, and fire a gun effectively, quickly, and instinctively.

Ardis was firing on the Nazi officers who executed her comrades. Brooker and Garcia had taught Ardis not only how to kill, but why.

The prospect she might have to kill someone was no longer an abstract idea.

"When we first met, you didn't tell me the truth about what I would be getting into."

"Well, I couldn't very well go around the country promoting a top secret operation to everyone, could I?" His voice was low and smooth.

"Omitting key information is misleading."

"I'm sorry, Ardis. That's war. No one likes the nasty bits."

"Fair enough." She actually respected him for this answer. It was honest. But it didn't address her concern. She was becoming a killer.

That reminded her of "Secret Agent," an Alfred Hitchcock movie about two British agents in the First Great War who had cold feet on an assignment to assassinate a German spy.

Then, of course, when it came to film, Ardis admired Humphrey Bogart above all others. *Bogie is what a spy should be like—a tough-minded, straight shooter.*

***

At first, Ardis found the endurance training unbearable. "You're killing me," she complained to the Major.

"Good," Brooker responded. "Better me than Jerry."

He was right, but she resented him just the same.

Week two was Morse code, including training on short-wave radio operations, the piece that Ardis expected to learn in an hour. It would have been easy to just introduce the Morse code and tell them to learn it. Instead, Ardis learned how short-wave radios worked, how to take apart and reassemble a radio, and how to make one out of an assortment of parts and materials. She learned why radio transmissions were easy to intercept at sea, making coding messages as ordinary text in plain sight an absolute imperative.

Garcia showed her how to create systems of code that could be "hidden-in-plain-sight."

Jerry was another nickname for Germans, similar to Krauts and several more, including Hun, Fritz, Heini, Boche, Schwab, and Squarehead; Garcia warned against using any of them. "They would know." Instead, he advised her to choose a colour and a specific bird to denote the enemy. He set up scenarios using "white" and "albatross" to convey German activities, and ran exercises to make her efficient in coding.

***

Garcia focused on strategic interests. He went through a list of naval movements, such as the direction and frequency of ships of all kinds and the pattern of their movements. He taught her to watch out for a sudden increase in traffic, a buildup of forces, or other patterns that indicate imminent enemy actions.

He briefed her on economic issues the enemy had to contend with, from feeding their armies and civilians to securing the natural resources needed to fight a war.

Major Brooker likewise brought strategic issues into focus. He touched on manufacturing, oil and aluminum refining, and strategic materials such as iron ore, cobalt, copper, manganese, and tungsten.

"Germany was in dire need of wolfram, in particular, to strengthen steel for large-barreled artillery, tanks, and ships. Portugal supplies wolfram to the Nazis. This situation is a delicate diplomatic matter between our leadership and Portugal's Prime Minister. It is also our chief concern," her brows went up, "but not yours," he quickly added. He looked directly at her. "You're on water patrol."

Brooker cleared his throat. "To be clear, disrupting their supply chain is something we have been trying to accomplish for some time and we don't want to mess it up."

What he made clear more than anything was his disdain for her and her mission; she wasn't part of his team of saboteurs.

***

Around the fourth week, a transition in Ardis occurred that was nothing short of miraculous. Her body responded to the training, and the workouts became even more intense. She enjoyed running. Her runs gave her a lift of a kind she had never experienced.

To her surprise, Ardis also enjoyed the focus on self-defence. She was mentally and physically ready to learn moves to escape tight situations. She learned where and how to strike an assailant to weaken them or render them unconscious; how to break arms, legs and necks— that is, how to kill an assailant, if needed—all in the name of self-defence, of course.

Naturally, this led to knife handling.

Ardis received a double-edged knife. She learned how to conceal and use it discreetly. Everything was fine until Major Brooker introduced a skillset for operatives who needed to take an enemy by surprise.

"Silent killing?" Ardis was aghast. "There's been a mistake. I didn't sign on for this."

"It's not that difficult." Brooker mimed the motion of a knife slicing a throat. "A trained hand and a sharp knife make it easier than you might think."

"No, I can't do that. I understood I am to monitor shipping. Provide eyes and ears on the ocean."

"Look, young lady. Here's the way it is." Brooker towered over her, cornering her. "You think you can waltz in here and use this as a free ticket to visit beaches? Oh no. Your life depends on this. The lives of your fellow agents depend on this. Either learn this or go home. No one wants a flake guarding his back."

Ardis recoiled, confused, which only egged him on.

"So why don't you just go home and bake cookies with your mother?" He taunted her.

As if this is just his war. This is my war, too.

She faced him with a hand on her hip and the other in the air. "Why don't you pick on someone who is actually afraid of you?"

Brooker opened his mouth to dish it back—but Garcia cut in. "I'll take care of this, sir." Garcia turned to Ardis. "Come." He pulled her aside to an office where they could talk.

Before he could say a word, she lashed out at him. "Every time we talk, this training becomes more than I signed on for." She was livid. "Enough is enough."

"Let's sit down."

Ardis saw it was a non-threatening approach. She readied herself to repel his argument. She would not be involved with killing anyone. Period.

"Brooker is not the enemy, Ardis. He is trying to save you." He spoke quietly.

"I am not being trained as a regular operative. You said this yourself."

"You will be on your own. Lives—including your own—may be in harm's way."

"No one will bother me."

"You cannot be certain of that." Garcia cleared his raspy throat. "Think of it. Any defensive skills you learn are excellent capabilities to have. You never know when you need them."

Ardis was becoming weary of the stress building inside. "Alright, alright, I get it." She waved her hand and held it up like a stop sign in front of her face.

Both immediately fell quiet. Once again, she had stepped beyond her boundaries.

"This isn't about the war, or Brooker, or you, Roberto. This is about me."

***

Brooker told Garcia that minimum training was nine weeks and individuals typically needed more. Anything less could put that operative and others at risk.

Born in Paris, Major Bill Brooker was a weapons and hand combat expert who trained operatives for MI6 in Scotland.

"The situation in Portugal is considerably different than in France, sir." Garcia laid down the one important fact that was incontrovertible.

Brooker agreed Ardis did not require training to work with partisans and parachuting; he was in favour of more training in explosives and demolition, but he insisted she learn the basics of silent killing.

Garcia proposed a compromise. Ardis would complete the training—including silent killing—and in the field, Garcia could provide further training as needed. "I just need to assure her that she will not be engaged in assassinations."

Brooker agreed with this arrangement. Whether Garcia would be able to hold up his end of the bargain was another matter.

Ardis took the training.

And Brooker made certain she was aware of how bloody messy a killing could be.

"The best way to kill someone silently is to slip up behind them, yank their head back, and slice. Like this." Brooker demonstrated the technique. "Quick, hard pressure with your knife will sever the carotid artery. Your target's blood pressure will send his blood gushing and it might even jet out about a foot, so try to stay out of the way. Your target will pass out in five to fifteen seconds. Beware of what happens in those first five seconds. A counterstrike is not likely but pulling the trigger on a gun could happen; that's what I watch for."

"If you can't get behind them, you need to be fast, from the side like this." Once again, he demonstrated. "Distract your target. Do not project what you are about to do or you could end up in man-to-man combat. Use the element of surprise to your advantage."

Brooker had the trainees practice on each other. He watched each person and gave pointers, except with Ardis.

What's up with that? Is he sulking?

As they were leaving, he finally spoke to her. "That wasn't so bad, was it?"

"A waste of my time," she shot back.

***

Garcia sent her home to spend the weekend with her family, and ordered her to report to the Farm on Tuesday to depart for Lisbon.

"And there is one more thing."

Garcia handed her over to Elizabeth, a non-commissioned officer, for further debriefing, but of a different kind.

Garcia left the room. Elizabeth winked at her. "He's sweet on you."

This irritated Ardis, but she set it aside.

"How are you set for clothes, Ardis?"

"Good, thanks. I have all my usual stuff—sweaters, slacks, windbreaker, and shorts."

"Darling, you need to be prepared for every kind of occasion."

Elizabeth took her into Toronto to shop on Bloor Street. Ardis looked in the windows. "I can't afford to shop here."

"Don't worry, Ardis, this will be taken care of. If your country expects you to risk your life, it had better make you look good."

Elizabeth insisted she get a black dress and a hat, nice shoes and several pairs of stockings. Two more dresses. A jacket, slacks, skirts and blouses, tops, more shoes, scarves and even half-decent jewellery.

"It's the 40s, honey. A woman cannot go anywhere in the evening dressed for adventure in the field. You're going under cover."

Modelling a jacket, Ardis playfully fingered her turtle pendant. Elizabeth frowned, a subtle message to tuck her childish pendant in her pocket.

"In Lisbon, you need to blend with the international crowd. There's the British, who are formal, of course; the Americans, who are casual; plenty of sporty Spanish and suave French, as well as sophisticated Italians and, well, Germans, who prefer to keep fashion sleek, if not uniform—literally. There are even some Russians, I am told, and plenty of European royalty who are escaping the war. You are going to have a grand time. But only if you dress the part."

Ardis did not have a clue how to behave in such settings, and sincerely did not believe she would ever have to.

Elizabeth took the purchases to the Farm, removed the tags, and packed them for Ardis.

Ardis rescued her turtle pendant from her jacket and put it back on where it belonged.

***

Her mother took one look at Ardis and nodded knowingly. "You've been working out." Indeed, Ardis was trim, firm, and fit. Her body was aching from the hard workouts she had completed that morning.

The weekend she spent with her family went by fast, although at times it felt like an eternity. Like so many other young people, she would serve in the war, yet she could not talk about it. She wanted so badly to say "Look Mom, Dad, the truth is—" but she was not allowed to say a word to anyone. In effect, she had to lie to her parents. It made her feel confused and emotional. As she briefed her parents about her research plans and her travel arrangements, she watched them listen and respond to her as if she were seeing them for the first time, when in fact, it could be the last. That night, she said good night to her parents as she had done every night of her childhood. She lay down and her emotions came flooding out. She was letting go.

When she settled down, another feeling arose from somewhere deep within. She felt a buzzing, tingly feeling in her legs, arms, and back. She lay awake trying to understand what this feeling was. There could be only one answer. She was in good shape. She was fit and ready for activity, not sleep. She was wide-awake, anticipating what was ahead of her.

Not so long ago she had been awkward about her role and did not want to contribute to the war effort. She certainly hadn't felt compelled to join. Now, she was going to war. She was confident, emotionally alert, and physically fit, yet unconvinced. What really could she hope to accomplish as a spy?

In two days, she would fly to the Azores. She was bound for Lisbon as a commissioned officer in the Canadian Navy. She wished she could tell Caroline about her training and her assignment, but Caroline was already in England.

To Ardis, Lisbon was an international centre of influence, where men and women were sophisticated and stylish. She was leaving behind her academic life to join a circle of potentially erudite men and women. Life in Lisbon would be fantastic—of this, she was certain.

She played out what she was about to experience in unending simulations, before falling off to sleep with her turtle pendant between her finger and thumb.

4. A Canadian in Lisbon

*U*nbelievable. *The roar of the engines, a ferocious race down a
dead-end straightaway, and a lift-off that made me feel like I
was floating on air. Fantastic. Flew over Toronto and Montreal;
refuelled at Gander.*

It was the first time Ardis travelled on an airplane. She had to
scrounge in her bag for bits of paper to write on.

*I saw planets and stars but the ocean was a void until the moon
appeared and shed light onto the black surface. The engines are a
constant drone. Could not directly see the sunrise but everything
brightened so; peeking through clouds, dazzling on the wing and the
ocean. Which is the greater miracle—flying or the endless sea?*

Not that flying would ever engage her in the way that oceans did. For
her, oceans were a vast reservoir of the infinite wonders of marine life,
whereas flying was a novelty; like most people, she had only travelled by
train or car. And, as can be expected, novelties do wear off. On the final
leg, from the Azores Islands to Lisbon, a plain blue sky put her to sleep.
She awoke as the plane was descending and she had a peek of the city
below. She marveled again at the experience—*the squeal of tires as the
plane bounced then made contact—and the friction of wheels spinning
madly on the tarmac for brief seconds as the plane came to a heavy rest
once again on terra firma.*

Ardis had arrived in Lisbon. She had pictured herself stepping off the
plane at night into shadows and intrigue, as she had seen in Humphrey
Bogart movies. *No such luck, honey.* The morning was bright and hot.
Where the heck was Garcia? There were no suave dreamboats on hand,
either, to deliver cynical ripostes to her wisecracks. *Swell, just swell.* She
surveyed the field; heat waves danced on a single strip of tarmac.
Lisbon's passenger terminal at Portela Airport was mired in construction.
In a café on the terrace, she found a table beneath a life-saving umbrella.
Praise—be—to—God.

Squinting at a hangar across the field, she winced. She fished out her
sunglasses, the ones she wore on the Salish Sea, and put them on. *The
stinging will go away with just a moment's rest. Really anyway, the war*

did not need what little resistance I had crossed an ocean to provide. Cripes, I was fading.

A few men waited on the terrace, their foreign conversation undulating like heat waves, always beyond her grasp. Motors on a road nearby, a plane circling overhead, a man coughing. Her lids quivered with flashes of light as she slumped into a murky realm. Her blonde curls fell forward to frame a face the colour of freshly fallen snow.

A hand touched her shoulder. "Ardis." The husky voice of Lieutenant Garcia was unmistakable. He hovered over her, smiling. Training prevailed over somnolent cravings; she sprang to her feet.

He held out his hand—light and informal.

She followed his cue. "Roberto! So good to see you."

Shoving ringlets from her face, she shook his hand. It wasn't appropriate to salute given that neither was in uniform.

At their first meeting in Toronto, Roberto Garcia was the one who stood to shake her hand. Seven years her senior, he made eye contact with confidence. *No matter how tough a gravelly guy like him may sound, his eyes give away his soul.*

She scrutinized Garcia the way he had done to her. He did not have stubble on his jaw in Toronto. With his thumb, he gestured over his shoulder to a car next to the field. He swung around to glance at it, then back to the men in the café. He offered help with her bags.

"I've got it, thanks." She slung the bag on her shoulder, picked up her suitcase.

The driver stood by the car; he had opened the boot.

"Things may appear quiet." Garcia lifted her suitcase in. "However much it may not look like a war is going on here, believe me, it is. We have our eyes on them and they are not sitting idly by. There is a lot that concerns us, really a lot."

During her training, Ardis had felt comforted knowing Garcia tuned into these critical matters. Now that she was in Portugal, though, the apprehensions he brought to the surface were more real and naturally provoked her. Now, she wanted nothing more than to stare into a deep, clear ocean, which was not only mesmerizing but also calming.

Underway, they motored down the Avenida Almirante Reis toward the city centre. Garcia explained he was late due to the extensive demolition in the Mouraria neighbourhood. Streetcars, motorcars, lorries, and horse-drawn carts of every shape and size choked the road. Workers swarmed the area. So he had the driver take them up to Campo Mártires da Pátria on a hill above the old city.

"The first place of interest on your tour, señhorita."

"Hunh" came out more like a grunt. *His decorum isn't needed.* They drove around a park filled with trees and statues, narrow sidewalks hugging stately buildings, and churches. *What is the big deal?*

"For centuries, wealthy families have lived in these palacetas—small palaces. That one on the right? The German embassy."

"We won't be stopping there, I presume."

"Only long enough to toss a surprise in the front door –" He spoke in a low monotone so that the driver would not be able to hear him.

He grinned smugly. A "surprise" was one of the codenames they learned at the Farm to reference explosive devices. *Was he serious?*

"As much as I'd like to, Lowney. Relax. I'm pulling your leg."

A large swastika adorned the front passage; a soldier stood next to the door ready with both hands on a machine gun.

She laughed, a tad nervously perhaps. His comments were ridiculous bravado, yet they were more in line with the subterfuge she expected, and worked like magic on her. The tension that had been building during her arrival to her first posting slid unnoticed from her neck and shoulders. "Frankly, I am relieved. I thought you were trying to be my tour guide." She tilted her head back and laughed again.

"Not a chance, Lowney. I aim to deliver you back to that little airstrip alive and well in six months."

"That ought to be enough time to complete my research."

"And enjoy the city." He gestured at the sites sliding past the car.

"Do you intend to keep me on dry land?" She spoke with candour.

"Of course not." Within the confines of the car, he turned his palms upwards. "That's not your mission." Again, he spoke quietly; only she could hear him.

She reciprocated his courtesy. "Lisbon *is* quite grand."

If a little awkward, Ardis was sincere. Lisbon was her doorway to

Europe—her first exposure to the continent. The buildings were older, the statues more numerous, the public spaces more plentiful, and the traffic busier than what she was accustomed to in either Toronto or Vancouver. Everywhere she turned, buildings stood poised with determined dignity to hint of Portugal's past splendour.

Well, not everywhere. Ardis saw the stain of disrepair under which the city sagged and, when the car stopped, she heard the melancholy keening of Fado hanging in the air.

"Why?" She wondered aloud. She was not thinking of that sad music. People packed narrow sidewalks. Some carried suitcases or shoulder bags. Most wore long coats for weather that was considerably colder than what they found here.

"Excuse me?"

"Why are there so many people?"

"Ah, that. Yes, they are the tail end of refugees, mostly from France. There had been many more as the Nazis pushed across Europe. They're waiting for passage on ships to the Americas, and for travel visas from Portugal."

"Must be a burden to the country."

"No, they are a gift, actually."

"How so?" She turned to look at him.

He shrugged. "Lisboans are pleased with the extra income."

Eyebrows furrowed, her gaze blurred.

Garcia gestured to the crowded sidewalk. "Shops that sell food, cafés, and bakeries are booming. Lisboans have cash from renting rooms in their homes."

She nodded in his direction. "So the refugees benefit the city."

"Remember, Prime Minister Salazar is an economist. Some refugees are very wealthy. The price of diamonds in Lisbon is at an all-time low. Most carry all the money they have, and their passage uses it up."

"Are they starving?"

"No doubt some are. Some turn to prostitution just to get their families out alive. They are vulnerable to bribery, which is despicable under the circumstances."

"So, delaying them here is little more than a scam."

"Precisely."

They arrived at the Polytechnic School on Rua da Escola Politécnica, where the Faculty of Science was. Ardis took in the columns and the pediment above the entrance. The architecture was classical—anything less would have been out of place. They went up the stone steps between the block pedestals that supported the portico over the grand entrance, and inside.

The Polytechnic School was in Príncipe Real, a neighbourhood west of the Avenida da Liberdade on another hill overlooking the old city.

Compared to the main university campus near Compo Grande, Garcia preferred this location. "All the charm and the action are in the old city. And when you want some peace and quiet, you can step out the back door for a stroll." He showed her the easy access they had from the building into the Jardim Botânico.

He led the way to the office assigned to her, overlooking the inner courtyard. "We put books on the shelves to make it look like a normal researcher's office. We have other more important work to do, starting first thing in the morning."

He did not waste a second.

"Now let's get you settled."

His assistant had booked a room for her at the Pensão Morais off the Avenida da Liberdade. Although the pension was directly below the Jardim Botânico, they needed a cab for the trip around and down the hill. She checked in, dropped her bags in her room, and did not even change. She was so hungry. They walked a few blocks to the Avenida, to a restaurant in the Tivoli Hotel.

The moment they took their seats, a waiter delivered olives and roasted red pepper in olive oil. Garcia ordered a gin martini, looking to her with raised brows.

She shook her head and helped herself to the appetizers.

"I'm having wine with dinner." He opened a menu. "Will you join me?"

"I need to eat or I'll be on the floor."

"What are you hungry for?"

"Roberto —"

"Just call me Robbie." Ardis recalled the first time she met Garcia at Fran's Restaurant in Toronto. The waitress said "Thanks, Robbie."

"That birdie was my buddy's girl," was how he explained it then. He wasn't shy and he liked to have fun—qualities Ardis admired. He was professional when he had to be, yet the way he tossed back a gin martini at their first meeting had revealed he was a bit of a wild card beneath all that propriety he so effortlessly delivered.

Looking at the menu, the unfamiliar swam before her. She closed her eyes, thought of her training in Portuguese but none of that helped her now. "Pick something for me." She smiled, ready to wait for him to pore over the menu.

At once, Garcia recommended the *bacalhau*. Cod was a staple for the seafaring Portuguese.

"Sounds good."

"Right." Garcia nodded toward the far side of the room where black-uniformed Nazis were taking a table. "This is a popular spot." He spoke monotonously without emotion.

Ardis rewarded his sardonic tone with a curt laugh. As much as the training at the Farm had tried to familiarize her, seeing the enemy here in uniform unsettled her. In the dim glow of the restaurant, their black boots and hat brims were obstinately shiny. They were loud, talking in a boastful tone, laughing. The hair on the back of her neck bristled and the frisson of fright flowed through her shoulders and into her arms.

Thanks to briefings by Lieutenant Garcia and Major Brooker, the officer in charge of training, the cruelty of executions was raw in her conscience: firing squads and soldiers torturing helpless civilians. Now, at the table, her repulsion was no less than her initial response to seeing the evidence in grainy pictures. Her imagination filled in the gaps, and she did not feel gentle and kind. She felt violent and vindictive.

Those pretentious bastards.

Yet, she would not let them disrupt her appetite. She looked the other way. She sipped her wine. The cod, potato, and green beans comprised a hearty, home-cooked feast. She ate more slowly and begged off any further activity that evening.

At the pension, she crashed, or at least she tried to. She tossed and turned for twenty minutes then blacked out.

***

Waking in the pension, Ardis felt disoriented. She had slept nearly nine hours.

Cities glowing in the distance; sunlight on the wing—that had been a long day.

Stretching, she did not know what she was feeling more—the effects of a long day of travel, or the training at the Farm before departing.

And now Lisbon. Need coffee, better get moving.

She organized her things. Her eye caught site of the leather sheath of her double-edged knife, poking out from beneath her clothes, and immediately an image from a dream about the restaurant last night took hold of her conscience.

Ardis closed her eyes.

A table full of Nazi officers. Roberto says how many can you shoot before they get you? She started shooting.

Ardis shook the dream from her head.

She pulled out the knife. She adjusted the straps on her sleeve. She practiced pushing it into the palm of her hand and slashing out with it. She was ready.

She needed to clear her mind. What she needed was a run to stretch her legs. But to run outside would have been inappropriate here. Instead, she stepped out for a walk.

She set out along the Avenida da Liberdade. First, she walked to the monument of the Marquês de Pombal, then crossed the wide boulevard and went down the other side. Refugees were out for their strolls, too, and occupied all the park benches. She noted which shops they preferred. The life of a student still engrained in her ways, she nurtured a frugal streak; where they got their coffee, pastries, and sandwiches would be good for her, too.

***

Garcia's assistant, Katya, had assembled a list of apartments for Ardis to consider. Ardis chose a two-bedroom apartment that was on Rua São Marçal, just a ten-minute walk from the Polytechnic School.

At the top of Rua São Marçal she could see the Rio Tejo, a wide river sparkling in the sun. The street descended rapidly into the lower Príncipe Real neighbourhood, situated between the Bairro Alto and Estrella neighbourhoods. Once she became familiar with the city, she told people she lived between the offices of the news journal O Século and the National Assembly on São Bento.

Her preference was to live in a small, seaside community near a beach. For strategic reasons, Garcia advised her to stay in Lisbon.

"When you're not on the water, we need you close by."

There was a downside. The moment she stepped outside, she was self-conscious. She stuck out as a foreigner. Her desire to speak the language would elude her wherever she went. She remained on edge, not knowing when or how foreign operatives might confront her. She did not breathe a word of this feeling to Garcia, of course. It wasn't her style.

Everywhere, these social dynamics hung in the air, invisible, as if they were not even there. But they were. She alone could not change the world. So she went along with the whole ruse as if it were true. As long as she played by the book and didn't challenge the situation directly, she could work around it. Act as if it wasn't there. And it worked.

She was in Portugal. She was twenty-seven. She could end up in the middle of a war zone. Or she could play her part in serving her country, get out on the water to do some research, and go home. Everyone would be happy.

***

Her trunk from Toronto arrived. Katya had it delivered to her apartment. Unpacking, Ardis rediscovered the items she and Elizabeth had purchased on Bloor Street. It was like shopping all over again.

She read the user manual for the movie camera and got a feel for it.

***

Looking out over the Jardim Botânico, Garcia asked her what she wanted to accomplish.

"I want to find and document any sea turtle nesting grounds."

He nodded and said that sounded good.

"And when I see enemy movements, I will report them."

The morning light through the window illuminated one side of his face so she could see the pores of his skin. "Good. Then you are ready for an assignment."

Garcia opened a case. "This is your radio." He paused and looked at her form. "Are you still running?"

"Not so much. The sidewalks are narrow and filled with people."

"Just as I thought. Try along the river where it is flat. Keep an eye out for any suspicious people in and around the port areas—the harbour, the beaches, or on the water for vessels of any kind, especially large ships and U-boats."

Situated on the Tejo River, Lisbon had access to beaches in Estoril to the west and up the Atlantic coast to the north. South of the Tejo, even more beaches could attract nesting sea turtles.

"All this beachcombing is fun, but I need a boat." Ardis wasn't afraid to confront Garcia with her needs.

"I know."

"I need to start looking right away." She gazed across the tops of palm trees.

"I'm working on something for you."

"You didn't tell me."

"There was enough on your mind."

Damn, withholding information vital to the success of my project.

"My people here found a vessel for you, in Setubal. I have a team working on it. They put it in dry dock."

Ardis unfolded her arms and let whatever tension she had been carrying drift away as she pictured the renovated craft on the water.

"It is an old fishing trawler. They scrubbed the hull inside and out, and painted it. Carpenters installed proper stairs to go below, bins amidships to stow gear and bunks for a crew of four plus two extra. They converted the cabin behind the wheelhouse into a galley with a table and chairs."

"Thank you, Roberto. I can't wait to see it."

***

As Garcia directed, Ardis ran along the riverfront, which was less treacherous than the incredibly hilly, narrow, and crowded cobblestone sidewalks in the city. The shipyards were perfect for running. She explored the docks and quays devoted to loading and unloading ships of people, cargo, and fish. She located the boardwalk and connecting walkways, and she became a regular amidst a field of uniformed personnel, refugees, and locals who loved the seaside. She often found herself among a never-ending flow of refugees walking off their drudgery, waiting to escape. In a sense, she belonged.

She took trains to Estoril and Cascais. She explored Sintra. She paid attention to weather conditions and the time she needed to return all the way home. One evening during her walk home from the train, heavy fog rolled in off the river. Finding her way with street lamps buried in a blanket of dark grey terrified her. Judging by the sound of her footsteps on the cobblestone streets in the fog, she was the only person out.

To this point in her assignment, this walk had been her dark and mysterious moment. She was ready for something intriguing to happen. But the city would not reveal any openings for her in which to make a difference.

She turned to the sea, focusing on the beaches north of Lisbon. She worked her way south. Eventually she would check the Alentejo coast, the Algarve, and beyond the mainland to the islands far south and west. She wanted to be on the water soon and remain there throughout the coming months.

I need that boat.

Xisco

5. The Wind Rose

Xisco sat on a boulder, eating a cold potato, and watched the far ridge. For a very brief moment, the horizon shimmered. Sparks, like fireworks, burst amongst trees and rocks. The giant orb rose supremely and glowed magnificently on the ragged red *telha* of rooftops on the hillside below him. Mist clung to the fields in the valley. Roosters crowed. Houses randomly discharged their occupants, who greeted neighbours—some, not all—to no one's surprise, grudges survived generations. Dogs erupted from their compounds, free at last, having barked the whole night long. Xisco giggled seeing Jeronimo harnessing his donkey early—a new strategy to get it moving before its stubborn nature could be realized.

This village was what Xisco knew, having lived in Sonim his entire life. He had walked out of the village in every direction to explore with Archangou and the other boys, and to hunt with his father, typically never far from the gurgling Rio Rabaçal.

At twelve years old, Xisco was a sturdy *garoto*, a young man-in-the-making. Gifted with a cheerful disposition, he and his Papai slept under the stars by the Rabaçal. As long as there was food for all, things were good. The moment Cangou came by, the boys would play out a make-believe adventure. And when alone, Xisco would read the books the teacher had lent him. He dreamed of being with explorers on the decks of their caravels and carracks—the ships on which the Portuguese discovered the world. He would wrap an arm around a forestay. A gentle gust would push a shock of brown hair against the brim of his bleached hat. He would scan the expansive sea to the horizon. All he would see was one line of blue against another, where the ocean met the sky. And when the sun set below the sea, at the very last moment it would explode—just the way it had burst above the horizon that morning.

There was no semblance to reality; all was imaginative and idyllic; and the wind blew. Xisco stood below billowing sails on ships rising and crashing on the waves with seawater washing over his bare feet, sailing headlong beyond the known world into unfamiliar, foreign regions. Like the explorers, he did not know what he might find, how he would survive, or even whether he would return. All was unknown to him now, just as it had been for them.

Rather than taking the lane and following the cobblestone streets through the village, Xisco went in the opposite direction. He sauntered along a terrace of ancient grapevines, the tiny grains of feldspar scrubbing his toes. Since he was old enough to walk, he had learned to respect the vines with their gnarled stems that persisted in the dry granules, sucking the nutrients from below to bear perfect fruit. He did not know how yet, but one day, he was certain, he would have grapevines and make excellent wine, too, just as the men did.

He followed a narrow footpath that led down the steep side of the hill. It veered off to the edge of the hill, where he stopped once again to enjoy what lay before him. This was his life; what would he become? Xisco took in the Señhor's vineyard. The fertile land stretched across the valley to the far line of trees that hid the river from view. On the edge of the field was the Señhor's manor, open on the side that faced the field but walled and gated on the side facing the village.

Like so many villagers, Xisco was a mix of expedient solutions and could adapt like a chameleon to match a situation. He was a warrior—he could be nasty if needed; a laggard, unreliable when not pressed; disloyal, if a different allegiance better suited him; deceptive as needed; and prone to lying, if it served him. He was an artist, of sorts, and a philosopher—always with an eye on the human condition.

In the square, he saw Cangou on his way to Bartolo's Padaria, a bakery, where men huddled around a radio.

Xisco proceeded directly to the school. Above the door of the school, a modest ornamental flourish counterbalanced the large, terracotta script, *Escola Primária*, on the stucco wall facing the square. Otherwise, the one-room school presented a low, unassuming profile. This was as it should be. Located at the highest point overlooking the village, the *capela* had only slightly more elaborate adornments on its holy structure.

In front of the school, children were skipping. The Chinese jump rope had been a gift from the Señhorita's brother in Macau. Two children turned the rope and the others lined up from both ends. They sang a song that started slow then forced the tempo fast and crazy.

> We sail the open sea
> One, two, three
> Now we sail some more
> One, two, three, four!
>
> The sea is getting stormy
> Three, two, one, two, three, two, one
> A stormy, opening sea
> Four, three, two, one—get out!

Xisco joined the nearest line to wait. His turn came. He found himself face-to-face with the girl he secretly crushed on: Cristina, who was one of the few with sandy-blond hair.

She called out to him. "Let's win this one, Xisco." They made eye contact, jumping up and down in unison. Then the tempo increased and she looked down.

"Don't look down! Cristina, look at me!"

She looked at him as the tempo increased. They were skipping together faster than either had ever skipped until the other children screamed "Get out!"

They had done it. They laughed together. Xisco saw this small victory as an opportunity to get closer in a different way, the way he would when he was alone with her, the way his parents were with each other when they thought no one was looking.

Cristina laughed. "I nearly tripped on the way out."

Señhorita Amália rang the bell. The children came running from all directions, crowding through the door and jostling to be first to reach their desks. "Children, I have something special to announce. A job actually."

"A job?" Cristina sat at the other side of the room. "Our fathers need work. Why would there be work for a boy?" Her confident voice expressed surprise.

A hush settled over the class as each child listened to this important news.

"Zé, the foreman at the Montalvão estate, asked me to send over the smartest, strongest boy in the school."

This aroused an immediate debate about who that might be.

Raising her arms, she motioned for calm and quiet. "The boy I have chosen is by no means the biggest, but he is strong and he is among the smartest."

On hearing this, Xisco immediately knew she had chosen Cangou. To Xisco, he was the boy who knew the most about the world. He was the one who wanted to be the leader.

One little child in front was not shy. "Do they want him to work in the fields?"

"No, the foreman needs a *palafreneiro*, a groom, to water and feed the animals and clean out their stalls every day. At the end of our lessons, I will announce whom I have chosen.

"Today, let's talk about the first Portuguese expeditions." Señhorita Amália walked to the side of the room. "Tell me, who was the man chiefly responsible for Portugal's age of exploration?"

Xisco entered this world of adventure and forgot about the teacher's announcement.

There was a moment of silence.

"Nobody? All right then." Amália returned to the chair beside her desk. "It seems you'll need an exercise to learn it properly—"

"I know." Xisco raised his hand and waited to be recognized.

The Señhorita, who was facing the chalkboard, turned around. "Of course you do, Francisco. Stand and tell the school."

"It was Prince Henry, the son of King João the First and Phillippa, his English queen."

"A Queen of Portugal who was English. Tell us more about her."

"Well, she wasn't our only English queen." Xisco recalled that lesson. "The English also had queens who were Portuguese, such as Catherine of Bragança, who introduced tea to the English in 1647."

"Did Queen Phillippa introduce anything?" Cristina's hand shot up. "Yes Cristina."

"Her marriage in 1393 marked the start of the Portuguese-Anglo Treaty, the longest-standing treaty of its kind in the world."

"That is correct! The Portuguese-Anglo Treaty still stands today. Thank you, Cristina." She smiled at the girl briefly before her gaze returned to the boy still standing. "Francisco, you were going to tell us about her son."

"Prince Henry?"

"Yes. Go on."

"He was born in 1394. He captured African lands across from Gibraltar. His father made him governor of Portugal's southernmost province."

"Which was called?"

"The Algarve."

"Yes, good."

"From there, Prince Henry sent several expeditions to the west coast of Africa." Xisco had paid attention.

"Was that so unusual?"

"Yes, everyone believed the waters at the equator were boiling hot, the sun burned human skin black, and huge sea monsters swallowed any ships that went there."

At this, the children squealed. The youngest were truly frightened.

Cangou took advantage of this interruption to steal the attention away from Xisco. "On the radio, they said some people are afraid of terrible monsters in Hell who torment the dead forever." Cangou also destroyed his teacher's efforts to nurture a productive discussion.

"It is the work of the Adamastor and he is coming to get you!" Cangou hammered it up to frighten the children and make Cristina laugh.

Another wave of alarm mixed with the muted whimpers of the youngest ones overwhelmed the calm of the classroom.

"That's enough, Archangou," Señhorita Amália raised her voice over the noise, which brought the room to utter silence. She never raised her voice like that.

"What is the Adamastor, Señhorita?" A child in the front row looked up to her, pleading.

Señhorita Amália glared at Archangou for a moment. Then she responded to the boy.

"The Adamastor is a make-believe monster that was created by one of Portugal's greatest writers, Luis de Camões. Although the monster isn't real, it reminds us of a time before people understood the workings of the natural world and created explanations for them. But don't worry, there are no such things as monsters."

Xisco's mind raced over the images from *Os Lusiadas* that the teacher had shared with them last year. "The grotesque and enormous shape . . . with heavy jowls and an unkempt beard . . . shrunken, hollow eyes . . . its complexion earthy and pale . . . its mouth coal black, teeth yellow with decay."

"Xisco!" The teacher pulled him out of his reverie. "Please continue. What else was important about Prince Henry's expeditions?"

"Well, they did find black people and the explorers came back with their ships filled with gold." Xisco remained standing, ready to respond further.

"That's right," the teacher took over. "Prince Henry never went on any of these expeditions. He relied on the reports of his captains. At the edge of the continent, at Cape St. Vincent near Sagres, Prince Henry built an observatory where he and his assistants could signal to returning ships. Prince Henry and the ship captains studied navigation, astronomy, and cartography—cartography means mapmaking. In the nearby port of Lagos, Portuguese captains equipped nearly all of Prince Henry's expeditions."

The teacher stopped and looked at her students who remained attentive.

"Good, Francisco. You may sit down."

Xisco looked to Cristina for approval, but she would not look his way.

Señhorita Amália stood beside the map. "Henry's expeditions claimed the islands of the Azores, Madeira, and Cape Verde and eventually led the way for a route around Africa." She pointed out the places she named.

"Prince Henry was looking for a river to take him from the Atlantic Ocean to India. He also wanted to find the Kingdom of Prester John."

"According to the legends, Prester John crossed oceans, deserts, and mountains. He established a new kingdom that barbarians had besieged. Desperate for help, Prester John sent messengers back to his Christian homeland in the hope of winning the support they needed to survive. Envoys were dispatched, but they couldn't find Prester John."

The teacher paused. Xisco was afraid she would end her lesson there. His arm shot up.

"If they didn't know where Prester John was, how could they send messengers back and forth? Would Prester John not have written, 'This is where I am'? Then the messengers could have led the armies to Prester John, couldn't they?"

"That is an excellent observation, Francisco." The teacher needed such a spark. "As the stories tell us, explorers set out in search of Prester John. Armies went to Africa. Armadas to Abyssinia. Infantry to India. Adventurers and mercenaries spilled over mountains into Asia. Over centuries, the allure to find Prester John and rescue his kingdom captured the imaginations of the intelligentsia and the wealthy who formed holy unions in their common pursuit . . ."

Xisco pictured columns of worker ants that were organized and methodical, engaged in a frenzy of worker activity.

". . . countless expeditions set out in search of the land of milk and honey and its cities filled with gold where everyone drank freely from the Fountain of Youth." Señhorita Amália quickly scanned the classroom. "An interesting side note, Prester John was the first ever to talk about a Fountain of Youth." She returned her gaze to the students. "Any questions?"

"If I drank from the Fountain of Youth, would I be a child forever?"

"No one knows for sure, how can we?" She deftly turned it back to the children. "But how did explorers decide which way to go?"

"Today, we will learn about the Wind Rose, also known as the Compass Rose." She moved to the centre of the room where a chalkboard and a corkboard dominated the wall. "Our ancient maps usually had a Wind Rose and some even had pictures of the winds that were associated with the rhumb lines of the compass."

She tapped a map pinned to the corkboard with her pointer. There, in the open space of ocean, was a Wind Rose. Then she stood closer so she could point to it with her finger. "I want you to learn the names of the winds by heart. Repeat after me . . ."

She paused to make eye contact with two older boys who were whispering, João and Miguel, until they stopped.

"Levante." Señhorita Amália began the exercise. "Where the sun is born over the Mediterranean Sea."

"Levante." The class repeated.

"Syroco, beyond the Red Sea." Señhorita pointed to Syria. The flowery script of the Wind Rose reminded Xisco of a picture in a history book of a ship with a curvy girl carved on the prow, crashing through the waves.

"Syroco." The classroom replied, mostly in unison.

"Notos." She pointed south to the middle of the massive continent of Africa.

"Notos."

"Africus, the breezes from the barbarian coast." She pointed directly below their tiny country to the imaginary channel of wind rounding the continent and slamming into Portugal.

"Africus."

A familiar pang in his stomach told Xisco the small potato he had eaten before leaving home was no longer there.

"Ponente, where the sun goes to sleep at night."

"Ponente."

Then he was thinking about Tia Beatrice and her *caldo verde*. The idea of the sausage, potatoes, shredded kale, and olive oil caused his stomach to gurgle gently even though he could not smell the onion and garlic. He welcomed the murmuring in his stomach. It was not the ache he felt last winter when things were not so good.

"Maestro, the old man who breathes icicles across the northern seas."

"Maestro." The children knew the lesson as if it were a schoolyard game.

"Tramontana, the wind that spills over the mountains we call home."

"Trás-os-Montes, the mountains we call home." The chorus was so uniform and strong it demonstrated they all knew where their village was located.

"Tramontana." Señhorita Amália repeated with a laugh as Xisco's gaze slid out the window to the hillside bathed in sunlight.

Three small windows along each wall illuminated and ventilated the room. When the teacher left the door open in the afternoon to allow more air to flow through, Xisco had a view of the village square.

"Greco, the breath of our neighbours."

"Espania." The children held their fingers on their noses and nasally giggles rippled across the room.

"Greco." Amália corrected them. "Now tell me what these are. Someone?" Her gaze swung across the room to the aisle closest to the window, and Xisco. His imagination had taken him beyond the village and its little mountain to a ship crashing through waves, its sails filled with Levante as it hurtled westward to the edge of the known world.

"Xisco."

Sitting straight and dropping his hands in his lap, the boy had no idea what the teacher wanted. "I'm sorry, Señhorita, I don't know."

"That surprises me, Francisco." The teacher spoke softly. "You know the rhumbs better than anyone in this school." Her smile indicated it would be different this time. It was a year ago when the same smile faded into a frown. "To the front young man." The Señhorita had been strict with him. "Bend over the chair."

He had known any resistance would be futile, so he lay himself over the chair as he had seen others do before him. She picked up her three-foot sapling that was both supple and strong and lashed him. After the third stroke, she stopped in mid-air and lowered her hand. "You will pay attention to me, Francisco."

That incident taught Xisco the consequences of not paying attention. He learned the hard way that discipline had to be severe. Señhorita Amália was responsible for more than three dozen children in the one-room school.

During the year since that lashing, Xisco excelled under Señhorita Amália's tutelage. His efforts began to show. Knowing the answers. Able to muster more recall. Better details, better grades. His successes also had another effect. He was a peer to Cangou and Cristina, the teacher's favourite students. He had a connection with Cristina.

But this time, 'knowing the answer' was not important anymore. Xisco was surprised when Señhorita Amália let his daydreaming go unpunished.

"Can someone tell me what these names represent?" No one moved. "I just told you."

Once again, she dropped her chin and looked along the aisles of children, sliding past the youngest ones at the front, terrified in stone silence and settling at last on her favourite student who would certainly show all the children how to provide an excellent answer. "Cristina." The teacher sat to hear her response.

Xisco held his breath.

"These are the points of the Wind Rose that guided Portuguese explorers." Cristina smiled at the teacher, then lowered her bright, golden brown eyes.

"How many major rhumb lines are there?" No one dared move a muscle.

Xisco and Cristina locked eyes.

"Eight." Cristina pushed long ringlets from her eyes.

"Pardon me?"

"There are eight major winds, Señhorita."

He exhaled, smiling in approval for Cristina. Of course, she knew the answers.

"Good. The Wind Rose was replaced by–?"

"The mag-ne-tic com-pass." A chorus of voices danced up and down the syllables as if the words cast a magic spell on the children. For Xisco, this moment of levity released an emotional flood as he recalled vividly his tears from the time she used the sapling on him. He was glad everyone had so thoroughly forgotten his shame.

"Please stand and box the compass." Señhorita Amália looked to Xisco.

As Xisco stood, he remembered how he had returned to his seat, and how his skin burned as it rubbed against the seams of his trousers. But now it was different. Of all she could have asked, anything about navigation and rhumb lines delighted him the most.

Today he would not get the same thrashing. Señhorita Amália had walked across the room and now leaned on his desk. His cheeks turned red—she was so close.

"Levante, Syroco, Notos, Africus, Ponente, Maestro, Tramontana, and Greco." He spilled them out in one breath.

"Excellent."

Xisco looked for approval. The Señhorita nodded and he sat, satisfied.

"This afternoon, we will talk about another way to find direction. It is something we all have and we all use to find our way through life. Think about it and see if you can tell me what it is later." Amália paused.

"Oh yes, and before you go, do you want to know who I have chosen to be the *palafreneiro*?"

6. Visit with the Adamastor

All eyes turned to Cangou, who sat straighter in his chair. All the children were waiting for what was obvious.

The teacher paused. "I have chosen Francisco Ribeiro." The sudden noise of everyone talking at once drowned out her words.

"Oh." Taken by surprise, barely a peep escaped Xisco's lips. There must be some mistake. Cangou was the one.

Cangou's response was the opposite. "What?" Immediately angry, vociferous and loud, Cangou commanded attention and this moment was no exception. "You chose Xisco and not me?"

"That's right. I will discuss this with you afterwards, Archangou."

Cangou's eyes bored through Xisco's head as if Xisco had brought disaster on Cangou and his world.

Then silence was in the room.

"Oh, *palafreneiro*?" asked Cristina. "I think you mean *moço de estrebaria*." Cristina was the smartest girl in the school and she was indeed correct. *Moço de estrebaria* was the more commonly used term for stable boy.

Señhorita Amália nodded. "Correct, *um moço de estrebaria*.

"You may go now." The teacher stood to signal it was time for everyone to go.

The cacophony of chairs scraping the floor, and children's chatter erupted as they raced from the room.

Xisco, Cristina, and Cangou remained in their seats, each bewildered by the teacher's choice.

"That job should be mine." Cangou's rage was building.

"I will talk to you later." The teacher looked directly at Cangou, clearly trying to assure him. "Class was dismissed, Archangou."

Cristina left immediately but Cangou appeared to want to stay and argue with the teacher. When she held up her hand, he kicked his chair over and walked in no hurry to the door. He stopped at the door, turned and glared again at Xisco before running to the square.

Xisco was confused. What could he have done? He did not know anything about it. The teacher chose him.

"Xisco?" Señhorita Amália turned her attention to him.

"Señhorita." Xisco remained stunned by the news. His older sister, Julinda, stepped back inside the door. His younger brothers Armando, Vincent, and João peeked in.

"Congratulations, Francisco." The Señhorita walked over to him and stood in front of his desk. "There are six children in your family, Xisco."

"And one more on the way."

"I checked with your parents and they have agreed. This is your last day in school."

"I can't stay in school?" Xisco was confounded. "I know the lessons." School was his favourite part of the day. There was no reason why he would want to leave. "But no more school?"

"No, you will have a job. And you may continue to learn on your own. You can still borrow books. Here, you can take this one." He stood to receive a book about Portuguese fishermen. "Be sure to return it and I will lend you more."

Xisco rubbed his finger on the edge of the well-worn, cloth-covered book. "I am honoured you have chosen me, Señhorita."

"I am happy for you, Francisco, but sad." Her voice became soft. "I will miss you." She wrapped her arms around him and held him closely for a moment then released him. He turned and ran from the room with the book tucked under his arm.

She called out after him. "Tell Zé I sent you."

No sooner had Xisco dashed out the door when he returned.

"Did you forget something, Xisco?"

"Señhorita, you said we would talk about another way to find direction . . . using something we all have and use to find our way through life. Since I won't be here, could you please tell me the answer?"

She leaned over and spoke in a quiet voice only he could hear. "Your heart, Francisco. Listen to your heart. It will tell you where you want to be and what you want to do. You need only listen."

"Hmmm. I see. What about my brain?"

"Yes of course. There are many ways to obtain knowledge. But your heart will tell you what you love to do and if you follow it, you will be passionately engaged."

"I will, Señhorita."

"Above all, read. You are gifted and capable of achieving great things, Francisco."

This compliment made him feel better immediately. She understood his desire to learn. "*Obrigado*, Señhorita."

Xisco had not expected his last day at school to be today. But a job! What an honour to receive. But why not Cangou? Somehow, this did not seem possible. Nor did it feel right. During his two-minute walk to the Señhor's estate, Xisco felt divided on whether this was indeed happening to him, or was it a trick and should he stop it? But he had to go on with it because he owed his parents every bit of help he could muster.

Each step away from the school heightened his awareness this was his last day in school.

He did not approach the front door of the manor, of course. That was reserved for important visitors. He approached at the back next to the street. He went to the gate, which was slightly ajar.

The elaborate gate into the yard bore Señhor Montalvão's coat of arms, carved in wood high above. The date seemed lost, irrelevant, and discordant with the day. 1804 A.D. appeared along with an ornamental flourish carved in bas-relief in the wood. Xisco wrapped his knuckles in as manly a way as possible on the wood. Hearing nothing, he pushed hard against the gate and entered the yard.

The yard was dry and dusty over a base of hard-packed dirt. On the opposite side was the Señhor's manor, a large stuccoed home with two floors and a basement. Near the gate was the stable. There were chickens pecking at the straw on the ground behind the stable. In the shade of the house was a well, encircled by a low wall and covered with a red-tiled roof. There was nothing else in the yard.

Xisco placed the book from the Señhorita on the ground against the stuccoed wall that surrounded the yard.

"Señhor Zé?" He called across the yard. It was quiet but for the constant clamour of the crickets in the trees beyond the yard and the occasional clucking of nervous hens picking in the debris near the back gate. Xisco knew Zé of course. Everyone in the village knew everyone else and their parents, their children, their aunts, their uncles, and even their dogs.

Zé, the foreman, handled the Señhor's business on his estate in Sonim. Before Zé, it was Manuel Paulho. Zé hired workers for spring planting, the harvest, and any processing and transporting of the products. Zé also collected grain taxes from the villagers.

The sun beat down and a donkey in the stable brayed long and senselessly, it seemed, for there was no one there to heed him. For several minutes, Xisco doubted there was even a job for a boy and he would be rebuked for entering the yard.

A door from the manor opened. "There you are." A stocky man with grey hair and a pencil thin moustache looked him over.

"Yes, I'm here."

As Zé looked at him from head to toe, Xisco suspected that Zé compared him to Cangou, who was slightly bigger.

"It's good to see you, Xisco." Zé gave the boy a big smile that put him at ease. "I respect your father, Eugenio. I think you will do well here if you pay attention to your duties."

"I will, Señhor."

"We will feed you, you will sleep in the stable, and I will pay you seven centavos a month."

"I understand, Señhor Zé, *obrigado*."

"The Señhor is here in spring to oversee the planting and in the autumn for the harvest," Zé explained.

The Montalvão family existed behind a veil of privacy, and the villagers caught only glimpses of the family's comings and goings. Everyone in the village felt the family's presence even in its absence.

After dinner, Xisco's Mamãe came to him with a large blanket and climbed into the loft with him to help spread it over the hay as a barrier against bugs. She pinned another heavy blanket to the first one, leaving a flap free for him to slip in and out easily. "Shake these out, Xisco. Keep this space nice for yourself." She put his few clothes in the little trunk in the workroom just inside the door.

The news of Xisco's job rippled through the village. The eldest son of Eugenio and Elena was the stable boy. His future was assured.

About an hour after his mother left, his father appeared at the gate. "I brought you this." He held out a potato for him.

"Thank you, Papai, but I have eaten. Give it to the little ones."

"People are saying 'one less mouth to feed' but soon it will be six again."

"I know. Mamãe told me."

"Another one coming."

Xisco sensed there was something else on his father's mind.

"You were our first son and now first to leave. You will always have a home, Xisco."

"Thanks, Papai. I will make this job work for us, I promise."

Xisco worried what would happen if he could not handle sleeping in the stable alone.

His concern was a fair one. That evening, Xisco delayed going to sleep. He expected there might be another visit, perhaps from Zé or maybe Cangou—that was who he really wanted to see. But no one came. He waited too long and it got dark faster than he expected. It occurred to him he could just go home and sleep in his own bed. It was a sweet temptation. But no, he decided. Everyone would hear about it. He had to stay and show his Papai he could do this.

He did not have a feel for the place. It took forever to climb up into the loft. All was black and he had to do it by feel. He found the blankets in the straw. Although the heat rising off the animals through the floor bore a familiar aura that made him feel comfortable, he was wide-awake. He closed his eyes, drew in a deep breath, and saw himself in his bed at home.

He waited, alert, thinking. He relived every adventure he and Cangou had undertaken—on the hill above the village, in the forests, up and down the valley, and on both sides of the river. Their childhood games had been innocent enough, yet dangerous, for they challenged each other physically to climb trees and cliff-like structures of rock boulders stacked on one another, jumping the rocks to cross the river, though swimming was one area in which Xisco had no abilities. It didn't matter, though. Cangou played with an active imagination, always giving their endeavours historic or mythical contexts that made them feel real. They weren't just kids walking through the forest. They were Templar knights, flanking their enemy—the other kids swimming at the river whom they charged with uproarious effect. In the beginning, their antics attracted a pack of followers that Cangou marshalled until they broke off and formed their own camps. Then they were in a state of war and things became more serious.

Cangou saw the real-life dangers closing in on them and their game. The other boys out-numbered them seriously. He had to be clever, and quick about it, too. First, he put out misinformation about the size and location of their numbers. Using the girls, he started a rumour that the boys from nearby Barreiros, Bouçoães, as well as Aguieiras across the river had joined them. Then, he also led their enemy to think that they were amassing their army on the Barreiros side where they set up a few big, loud boys with sticks behind a makeshift barricade when in fact they were on the Bouçoães side. So when the enemy approached the barricade, Cangou led a rear attack, catching them off guard, and gave chase. It completely unhinged the enemy, who ran from the field never to return.

Thinking of his war games with Cangou, Xisco forgot everything happening in the loft. But he still could not sleep.

He did not anticipate feeling so awake. He had grown up with the rattling of his parents and siblings in their sleep next to him or nearby. Now, there were no soothing sounds. His senses went on high alert. He heard clatters and commotions in the dark he never dreamed possible. Unknown danger surrounded him. No, it was the animals, he told himself. But he did not know exactly what animals were in the stables below him and he could not imagine what creatures expelled such sounds. It forced his mind to consider new suggestions. All the horrible stories he had ever heard about ghosts and evil creatures came to bear on him that night. His mind responded to every stimulant and became productive; a lush and fecund repository where any tormented soul that could not rest in peace could thrive anew. He emptied out the cemetery. He gave life to every dreadful snort and grunt. Every creak, every rustle, every breath expelled, every groan issuing out of the dreams of the animals below caused him to believe he was in the presence of a dark and mysterious power. It was the mighty Adamastor himself. His mind raced over images from *Os Lusíadas* that had come alive. The unkempt beard . . . shrunken, hollow eyes . . . its mouth coal black with teeth that were yellow with decay.

The stench of the stable took on new proportions. He could smell the monster's breath.

In the dead of night, a deep hush fell over the stable and its creatures. Xisco's earlobes prickled from the sounds that issued in the loft around him: a flap of a wing, a crackled stutter of a hen in her sleep, and a board creaking as if a heavy creature were slithering toward him in the straw. Before this night began, Xisco had the heart and mind of an innocent child. By morning, he had visualized death a dozen ways and his innocence was gone.

In the pre-dawn moments before any rooster mounted its barn, Xisco swung down out of the loft and visited with the oxen, pigs, horses, donkeys, and chickens—all calm and quiet—and with the geese that had tormented him throughout the night—now serene. He had been silly for being so afraid. Cangou would have laughed at him. His fear was all for naught. But the experience taught him a lesson: do not be afraid of what wasn't real. Just the same, he would never read Luis de Camões with detachment again.

He found a corner in an empty stall to sit down for a minute and rest. When the rooster crowed, he was in a deep sleep.

***

In the beginning, his father dropped in regularly to see him. He showed Xisco the tack hanging on the walls and explained how to use everything and what he had to do to maintain it. He helped Xisco with the harnesses in the adjacent driving shed and showed him some tricks for working with donkeys, saddling horses, and harnessing the mare to pull a wagon.

At the end of his first month, Zé came into the stable. "You have done a good job." He paid Xisco seven centavos. Zé said he needed Xisco there first thing every morning, plus whenever there were guests, and all day during spring planting and fall harvest, and whenever he needed all hands.

"When your work is done and the tack is rubbed, you are free. Just check with me."

Xisco developed a knack for keeping things in good order and got his work done early so he could spend time with his friends at the fountain or down at the river. On these occasions, Xisco looked for Cangou, but he was nowhere in sight. Was Cangou avoiding him? It was stupid, really, that someone else's decision could affect their friendship like this.

Maybe Cangou wasn't the friend he had believed him to be.

As the *moço de estrebaria*, Xisco mucked out the stables, and fed and watered the animals. He collected and delivered eggs to Tereza. He preferred his role as the *palafreneiro*, the groom, who wiped the tack, and brushed and cleaned the animals. Over time, he learned how to provide specialized care for the animals and how to use the tools and implements to become a farmer himself one day. But was this really what he wanted?

Xisco took the money he earned directly to his mother, proud to contribute to the family's needs. He enjoyed his job although he deeply regretted the end of his schooling. A part of him knew it was unfair. He had no say in the matter. Without school, how would he even know what there was to know? He saw himself fading into the past to a time when there were no books, no history, and no lessons. It would be like having no air to breath. He would suffocate. He felt panic rising in his chest and throat, but resisted it, calming himself, breathing deeply. No, he would find a way. What that way was, he had no idea. He only knew he would die if he let this situation play out for the rest of his life, however short or long that might be.

7. Rocks for Escudos

In his laziest moments when the sun beat down and a thick shroud of heat made his shirt cling to him, Xisco lay motionless, daydreaming, and he noticed the routines of the adults around him.

His father and the men met in the square every morning except Sundays. They walked to the Señhor's stables and into the fields. His mother and sister washed clothes and hung them to dry on vines beneath their window just as all women did.

His mother did not complain; she fondly commented, "It was easier when you were smaller." Which was true. Though not tall, the boys had thickened; their growth marked time.

"When Armando was born."

"When Francisco started school."

Serious difficulties marked time. "When Eugenio was so sick he couldn't get out of bed and was going to die."

Or inconceivable calamity. "When the church one Sunday was so crowded, Padre Fernando took the Mass outdoors and, during Communion, the wind blew the Host out of his fingers." That the Body of Christ plopped on the eye of the frail Señhora Santos was not a good sign for the fading woman who lived the rest of her life in a strict regime of penance and died in fear and misery.

The Good Lord did not stop there. The wind receded, releasing the Host from the eye of Señhora Santos. A fresh gust tossed it into the air. All eyes in the crowd followed its Holy path. Apart from seeing Jesus fly then land on Señhorita Amalia's neck where He promptly slid inside her blouse, nothing happened.

Seasons came and went. One year slipped into the next, all without fanfare. People were hard-pressed to say what year it was. Change? Things remained the same, year after year. There was no expectation things would ever change.

***

Xisco helped his Pai harness his donkey in the cart and load a couple of farm tools they would need. They led the donkey to the road that connected Sonim to neighbouring villages, where they joined other men from the village.

"Is the truck coming?" Eugenio asked Tomás.

"Zé said it is," Tomás grumbled. "Why must we be here so early?"

Gonçalo laughed at Guilherme, the biggest man in the village. "He hasn't had his *mata-bicho*." To kill-the-beast, Guilherme took a shot of *aguardiente* before breakfast. The clear liquor burned all the way down and warmed his stomach.

Dominic, another farmer, chirped in. "His breakfast is *aguardiente*."

Tomás got in his kicks, too. "Guilherme should know. He drinks with the priest." Guilherme was the only one who could keep up with Padre Nando.

In turn, Guilherme would mock each of them every chance he got; bitching with one another was their way to blow off steam.

And so they set out.

The men walked over the crown of the hill above the road onto a plateau where they spread out. Eugenio and Xisco proceeded westward over the uneven, scrubby surface that was pockmarked with stretches of flat rock exposed between wild grasses and brush. Now and then, they stooped and picked up a rock and when they were lucky, they found a large one pushed up by the earth like an angry cyst that they pried out of its socket with a pick and a spade.

They didn't take just any rock. The acceptable rocks were heavier than the rest of the rocks in the field and could be identified by the dull, grey-black streaks of metal—wolframite. They loaded the good ones into their cart, one by one.

"We picked this spot clean last time."

Though they had to walk farther to fill the cart, Xisco was helpful and upbeat with his Pai, and was proud that his Pai depended on him. Xisco would turn eighteen this year.

In the distance, they saw Marco was digging. "I heard him talking." Xisco heaved a good-sized rock onto the cart. "He said there was no end to the vein of rock that was black with wolfram."

Xisco kicked aside a small ordinary rock and there, within years of detritus of dead grass and straw, he caught a faint glint of metal in the dirt. It was a mini candelabrum—blackened from years of baking in the sun and frosting in the cold. He slipped it into his pocket to inspect later, after they finished the work.

Their cart full, Eugenio stopped for the day and turned his donkey back to the road, where they would wait for the truck.

"This is the summer cicadas will sing again." Eugenio spoke absently as if to himself.

Xisco had heard this story many times. "You think this is it?"

"It has been seventeen years."

"A prime number." Xisco knew a little about the subject. "It seems so random."

Eugenio looked at his son. "They trick their predators. If cicadas came out of the ground at the same time every year, the birds and critters would be ready, waiting for them. This way, the cicadas are too many for any predators that happen to be there."

"Allowing more to survive." Xisco added. "Cicadas are clever."

"Any day now." Eugenio picked up a stick, pushed it under a small rock, and leveraged it out of the ground. "They'll return."

He tossed the rock into his cart.

Xisco stuck his hands into his pocket. There, his fingers discovered the piece he had found on the ground. He pulled it out to get a better look at it. The candelabrum had three candles on each side of a tall one in the centre.

The truck arrived and strangers opened the back. They paid cash, escudos, for each cart loaded.

Xisco laughed. Why would anyone pay for rocks?

The strangers were German. They drove their truckloads to the Spanish border where they loaded the stone onto trains.

Hearing Xisco laugh, one of the men on the truck looked at him and saw Xisco looking at the candelabrum in his hand. "Hey Jew, what have you there?"

Xisco didn't understand what the man was saying.

Angered by Xisco's blank look, the man jumped down from the truck. "Are you stupid?"

The man gave Xisco a shove.

Eugenio stepped in. "Don't touch him." He faced down the big man, who grunted and hopped onto the truck. He turned back to Xisco. "Put it away, son. They don't like Jews, and that's ok. We're not Jews, are we?"

"No, we're God-fearing Catholics," Xisco shot back.

On their way home, Xisco asked his Pai what the rocks were for.

"The Germans heat the stone to extract metal. That is all I know."

Xisco helped his Pai haul rock whenever Zé told the men the truck would be at a certain location. The centavos from the strangers were too good to pass up.

Xisco saw his Pai give the money to his Mãe and together they decided what they would do with it. When his Mãe caught sight of him, she shook her head. "Ah, Xisco. Helping your Pai collect rocks was only half a day's work."

Xisco laughed. He knew what she would say next.

"In this family, we work the whole day."

He didn't mind. Zé would be expecting him.

So he set out for *his* stable. Walking past the school, he saw the door was open, as usual. He couldn't resist sticking his head in the door.

Padre Fernando stood at the front of the class. Seeing Xisco, he hurled an epithet at the boy for being late. Xisco wasn't supposed to be there at all. He thought Padre knew this, too.

Xisco played along. He had known Padre Nando all his life. He worked with him in the fields during planting and harvest, and was aware of the Padre's drinking problem. The whole village knew he was a drunk.

The teacher motioned for Xisco to take an empty seat near the door. Señhorita Amália delivered lessons in the areas in which she had been educated, including Portuguese history and literature, and a smattering of philosophy, math, and social sciences. Padre Fernando took it upon himself to deliver the basics: God, the Trinity, and Jesus, and more often than not, he landed on the story of Fatima.

"Twenty-five years ago, Our Lady of Fatima appeared to Jacinta Marto, her brother Fernando Marto, and their cousin, Lúcia dos Santos."

Padre Nando looked pleased with himself. He had strung the correct names together and hadn't forgotten anything, so far, of the story his bishop had instructed him to deliver.

"These appearances of Mary the mother of Jesus occurred far from here in a place called Cova da Iria. It is closer to Lisbon."

Padre Nando wasn't even slurring his words, which was unusual.

"During these appearances, Our Lady told the children three things. She predicted the two younger children would not live long like their cousin. Both the Marto children died during the Spanish Flu in 1918 that wiped out fifty million people. And Lucia became a nun and remains the only living witness to all of Our Lady's predictions."

"Our Lady implored us to pray," Padre Nando continued. "When she appeared in 1917 and 1918, the Great War was coming to an end. The fighting had taken tens of millions of men, women, and children. However, Our Lady's second prediction was that we would have another Great War, which as you know is happening right now. Portugal has been spared thus far, thanks to the wisdom of Prime Minister Salazar."

"The third prediction of Our Lady of Fatima was more like a warning. Our Lady warned us of Russia, where people are poor and hungry because they are Communists. Our Lady warned us that Communism was not good for people."

"Today, we continue to be in great need of Our Lady's comforting words. Do you have any questions for me?" Padre sauntered with confidence to the opposite side of the room.

With the Padre's back to him, Xisco took this opportunity to slip out of the school. He had heard these stories several times. He knew that Padre Nando did his best to make men and women feel guilty about not praying enough for the souls of their children and their elders, much less their own, as a means to coax a potato or two in tribute for his work. He had seven children of his own to feed.

8. Hunt for Wild Boar

As the sun rose over the ridge far across the valley, Eugenio and Xisco set out early once again, this time on foot with their guns slung over their shoulders, on the dirt road toward the river. Beyond the village, the fields soon gave way to savannahs of wild flowers, tall grass, and scrub brush, punctuated by lofty Pyrenean oak. They entered a forest of red pine.

The evening before, Xisco heard his Mãe tell his Pai that she had invited their neighbours and his aunt to join them for dinner, "For the celebration," she said.

"But I don't have a pig," his father responded.

"Don't worry, *marido*, you will bring home some meat."

"But Elena, what if I don't get anything?"

"You always do, *querido*."

His Pai pressed his lips together in a smile and nodded. The customary slaughter and preserving of the pig was a challenge if one didn't have a pig.

Xisco knew his Mãe was right. His Pai knew how to hunt.

"The wild boars are coming back," he said to Xisco.

Xisco nodded. The men in the *padaria* said wild boar had been extinct for a hundred years, but they didn't know the valley like his Pai did.

"Don't believe that story about an extinct white rhinoceros and a chimpanzee," Eugenio added. "For the love of God." He dismissed wild ideas impatiently, but not stories of wild boar.

The Rio Rabaçal flowed from Spain through these forests, west of Bragança. A boar had only to travel a dozen kilometres to reach his Pai's hunting grounds.

If the hunt went well, his Pai would return with a wild boar or possibly even a deer. His Mãe would be happy.

The leaves in the tallest trees flickered in a breeze that did not reach them. The sun was warm and welcome as it removed any chill leftover from the night.

"Let's take a short cut," said Eugenio.

They cut through the holly oak and stone pine between the river and the dirt lane that led past the vineyards and fields to the village.

Eugenio stopped. He placed his forefinger over his lips. "Ssshhhh." A piercing whine filled the space below the canopy of trees.

It was the sound of electricity, if you could hear it. But there were no wires here and no electricity except for the waves of energy that vibrated invisibly in the trees. Eugenio motioned to the general direction of the song of the cicadas, knowing it was impossible to identify the exact source of the sound because it was coming from several directions at once. They stood motionless in a clearing surrounded by pine and listened.

"This is the summer the cicadas sing again." He was excited to hear them. "The cicadas come back all at once, millions and millions at a time. Their predators will consume what they can in a crazy feeding frenzy. The cicadas moult, shedding their larvae skin and emerge as adults with wings. Then there is a mating frenzy."

Xisco knew the story. He was glad to experience this with his Pai.

They continued the hunt; they had to. Before long, they were walking through a stand of broad, ancient timbers in which the trunks of holm oak were widely spaced. They were ducking under the lowest boughs of wax-like leaves that sheltered them from the relentless sun overhead. Tall bracken grew in the rich humus amid the debris of soft brushwood. The scent of the musty earth filled their nostrils.

After ten minutes more, they slowed and stepped carefully, listening. His Pai's instincts as a hunter were usually correct.

Sensing opportunity ahead, Eugenio used subtle hand gestures. With stealth, they approached a clearing. Immediately they saw another hunter was already there. Quietly raising his arm, the hunter—whom Xisco did not recognize—easily made his presence on the other side of the clearing known to them. His Pai acknowledged him. The hunter pointed to a gulch in front of a stand of trees and rock and motioned for them to be still.

His Pai signaled for Xisco to stay back out of the way. Then he raised his gun, pointed at the gulch.

The hunter opposite them commenced the barking call of a roe deer, followed by a low grunting sound. Suddenly, a wild boar burst from the gulch and charged directly at the hunter. Eugenio waited two seconds for the hunter to shoot. Then he fired a single shot. The boar staggered on, its hindquarters dragging, until it fell, inches from the hunter who did not fire a single shot.

"Damn. Good thing you ready, friend." The stranger spoke Portuguese with an east European accent. "You saved my *kiester*." He closed his eyes and shook a moment. He coughed and looked up. "That was close."

"What happened?" Xisco looked to his father. "Why didn't he shoot?"

"His gun didn't fire."

His father and the stranger greeted one another with a nod and a wave.

"That could have ended badly." The stranger was a man of medium build with sun-streaked brown hair and a long beard.

"It was a damp winter." As a hunter, Eugenio was a wise gun handler. "Guns misfire here all the time."

"I was certain it was a roe deer. I didn't get good look, but I heard low grunting noise like roe deer make." The stranger paused before politely changing the conversation. "I am Sam Meyer." He extended his hand to Eugenio.

Sam shook Eugenio's hand. "Eugenio Ribeiro. This is my *filho*, Francisco."

"*Bom dia*, Señhor." Xisco shook hands with him.

"I'm pleased to meet you, Señhor Eugenio."

"You're not from here."

"No, I am Polish. I am mining engineer. I came to Portugal seven years ago."

Eugenio nodded. Sam looked Portuguese; short in height; brown hair and eyes.

"Wow, look at this monster." Xisco used a stick off the ground to lift its snout.

Sam stood over the boar and stretched out his arms to measure. It was longer than Sam could reach. If it were standing, its shoulders would reach up to his thighs. "This is a Eurasian trophy boar. We see in Poland." He stretched out his thumb and baby finger along a tusk. "He would take a chunk from me if you not stop him."

"Then for your sake, I'm glad I did."

"I am glad, too. You have a nice kill, Señhor."

"That isn't right." With eyebrows squeezed in a curl, Eugenio protested. "He is all yours. You cornered him."

"No, no. It was your shot. You killed with one bullet."

Eugenio nodded. "We can share."

"I believed it was a small deer. I have a truck and can help you get it home."

"Alright. Then you're coming to my home to meet my family."

"You are kind, Señhor. I would be honoured."

"This boar is big. He must be at least eighty kilo."

"Easily. More like a hundred."

They carried the boar to his truck, and Xisco carried their guns.

"This calls for a toast." Sam retrieved a bottle of wine from a handy spot behind the seat of his truck along with two thick glasses and a mug. "This wine is from the *cooperativa*. This was a good year." He uncorked and poured the wine into the glasses and the mug that he used for himself.

"*La Chaim*." Sam gave a Jewish toast.

Eugenio paused. Xisco knew his father's puzzled look. "*Saúde*," he replied, the one-syllable toast sounded more like a grunt. He drank deeply.

Sam's truck made the task of bringing the boar home easier for Eugenio. Xisco rode in the middle between Sam and Eugenio. Xisco asked Sam about Poland.

"People there have not been treated well."

Xisco looked at Sam more closely for the first time. It looked as if a chicken had left a trail of criss-crossing hatch-marks in the soft skin around his eyes.

"It is not safe to live in Germany or Poland."

Sam parked in front of the Ribeiro home. Like most houses in Trás-os-Montes, the stable occupied the first floor and their living quarters were on the second floor. The main door was on the top floor at one end of the house, and stairs descended on the outside to land on the hillside where Xisco's mother kept a small garden. Stone stairs went the rest of the way to the road level. Over time, long before Eugenio and Elena raised their family here, little stone walls and walkways in granite and dolomite materials were laid into the ground to create a terrace. Wolframite glinted darkly amidst the accumulation of moss and thatch and wayward vines.

Xisco closed the door to the stable. Although the animals could surely smell the boar and its blood, he did not want to expose them to the sight of the dead boar.

"We will have *prosunto* until spring." Eugenio knew how to salt and age a leg of pork. This would be the same.

Xisco's youngest siblings and his mother came to see. Xisco introduced Sam. They stood around the truck and looked on. The men celebrated the hunt.

"No hungry bellies in the Ribeiro family this winter." Riding his confidence, Xisco touched the tusks and encouraged his brothers to do the same but the fierce face frightened five-year-old Octavio, who still clung to his mother's long skirt.

"I don't like it." Mario, who was seven, turned away from the beast.

Elena took the boys back upstairs and the men set to work dealing with the boar. First, Eugenio supported Xisco to reach up and attach a pulley to a hook on a bracket he had installed long ago, and then Sam passed up a heavy rope to slip through the pulley. Eugenio tied the rope to an anchor on a post and Sam tied the other end around the boar's hind legs. Together, they raised the boar by the hind legs. They placed an oversized bucket beneath it and Eugenio cut the neck wide open, draining the blood into the bucket.

It would take a few minutes for the blood to drain. "Let's have wine." Eugenio took Sam to his cellar at the back of the stable where he kept a cask. He gently turned the wooden spigot and a deep red wine slowly rose in the ochre pitcher he held beneath it. From the pitcher, he poured two glasses of wine.

"That's beautiful wine." Sam put his nose in the glass and gently inhaled the scents. "A wonderful bouquet. Did you make it?"

"No, Zé made this. He is the foreman on the Montalvão estate. I think he makes the best wine. What do you think?"

Sam sipped the wine and nodded. Montalvão had employed Sam on various mining-related projects. Sam knew Zé, as well, but he did not say anything about that now. "My goodness, this wine is smooth. The flavour lasts long in my mouth."

"I like it." That was all Eugenio had to say.

"Better than wine from *cooperativa*. Much better." Sam praised Eugenio's wine.

Eugenio and Sam moved the heavy worktable out of the stable and set it just below the boar, which they lowered onto the table. Eugenio placed another large bucket below the edge of the table, sliced open the boar's gut, and guided the entrails as they slid into the bucket.

Eugenio took the buckets upstairs to Elena to prepare for their dinner.

The moment he set the buckets down, he rested his elbow and forearm gently on her arm because his hands were covered in blood. "Elena, do you remember what I told you about my father? It was a long time ago?"

"No, what do you mean? You told me several things about him."

"That he was a Jew, who practiced his faith in secret."

"Yes, I remember some vague things about that now. Why? Why is this suddenly so important on a day like this when we are so busy?"

From the small window in the centre of the kitchen wall facing the street, they could see Sam talking with Xisco. In that moment, she understood why.

"Oh, I see. You're telling me Sam is Jewish."

"I am."

"Why? Is this a problem?"

"It's just easier if we don't have to tell the children."

"Don't worry, Eugenio. Things have a way of revealing themselves. The children will find out eventually. With him here, it could be easier for you to tell them."

"I don't know. I was hoping to let sleeping dogs lie."

"You have nothing to be ashamed of. We are all good people and don't let anyone tell you anything different. So let's see how it goes, ok, *querido?*"

Eugenio nodded.

"We are running late. Let's make our first meal of boar for dinner."

Normally, the custom was to eat the innards and the blood of the pig in a *sarrabulho*, a stew served with rice, at the noon meal on the day of slaughter. It would be no different with a wild boar.

"So we're having *sarrabulho* for dinner."

Elena, Eugenio, and Sam had plenty of work ahead. They removed the skin then cut off the front legs with the shoulders attached and the hind legs each with the ham quarters attached. Xisco set to work salting the legs that his Pai would hang in the wine cellar. Elena made the *sarrabulho* and also made sausage.

The men butchered the remainder of the boar, salted it, and packed it with more salt in a barrel. Elena came out of the kitchen and popped her head over the railing. "Eugenio, don't forget a roast for Mathilda."

Mathilda was the mother of the school teacher, Señhorita Amália.

"I won't, my darling. I'll do that right away."

Sam cut a good piece of loin for a roast, and Xisco delivered it to the neighbours. He reminded them about dinner, and Amália said she had made a dessert to bring along.

Eugenio took advantage of his time alone with Sam. "You don't eat boar, yet you don't mind butchering it?"

"I'm a hunter." Sam took up the challenge. "To me, it is more important that I help you with this messy job. Plus, you saved me."

Eugenio respected Sam for this.

The older boys, Armando, Vincent, and João, arrived home in time for dinner.

Eugenio sent Armando with another cut of meat to Tia, his aunt. "Remind her about our dinner this evening, *filho.*"

Elena delivered the sausage meat along with the casings cleaned and ready to be stuffed. The time went fast. Eugenio, Sam, and Xisco had to stay focused to get everything done in time. As dinnertime approached, the children gathered in the kitchen, eager to taste the *sarrabulho* that filled the house with a tantalizing aroma. The sun was low in the sky. Elena had the boys fetch chairs from other rooms. She and her eldest, Julinda, prepared the vegetables.

Finally, the men came upstairs, and the guests arrived. Elena joined Eugenio and Sam at the small front window where they were looking at the view below of the fields. "Señhor Sam, Xisco told me you are from Poland."

"Yes, Señhora Elena. I travelled to England. Now I live here in Sonim. Is not so cold here."

But Elena, at the last moment, had turned away to set out three tapered candles on the table. It would grow dark during their dinner.

There were eight adults: Tia Bea, Amália, and her mother Mathilda, Sam Meyer, Eugenio, Elena, plus Julinda, and Xisco. The three youngest boys, Jorgio, Mario, and Octavio, squeezed in between, and the older boys, Armando, Vincent, and João found stools to sit on.

Sam bowed his head in silent prayer.

Seeing this, Eugenio touched his arm. "Sam, pardon –"

"Señhor Eugenio?"

"Can you say your prayer aloud for us? For my family?"

"Of course. My prayer is a song to Yahweh." Seeing only curious looks, he bowed his head and this time placed his hand over his eyes and prayed aloud:

"*Yis'ra'eil Adonai Eloheinu Adonai echad.*" Sam sang in a solemn but sweet chant and he paused.

As if in a trance, Eugenio stammered a reply: "*Barukh sheim k'vod malkhuto l'olam va'ed.*" He chanted softly, not getting all the words correct.

"You know the words."

Eugenio wasn't alone in feeling the tug of traditions. Amália knew them, too.

On his father's face, Xisco saw the look of a child caught with his hand in the cookie jar.

It appeared Eugenio could not believe it, either. Then he exhaled, releasing any former pretense of denial and forgetting. He nodded his head absently and appeared to be accepting. From this moment on, Eugenio accepted the past and stopped pushing it aside. "I learned it as a child."

"*Linda.*" Mathilda loved Eugenio's beautiful voice.

"Eugenio knew the words because his parents were Jews, as were mine." Tia Bea spoke in a matter-of-fact manner.

Xisco, though, did not understand Hebrew. Hearing this prayer for the first time, in a language that ought to have been his birthright, left him feeling cheated of his heritage.

"There are no Jews in Sonim, are there?" Xisco's elder sister, Julinda, defended the myth.

Sam shared his experience. "Years ago, I was in a village near here, Rebordelo, and mentioned I was a Jew. They did not believe me. To prove it, I recited the Shema, the same prayer. They were shocked that I openly admitted I was a Jew. They practiced their faith in secret, a tradition they adopted to stay safe from persecution during the Inquisition."

"They are Marrano Jews." Amália knew they existed because her family were Marranos, and her parents had taught her to keep such information secret.

"Señhor Meyer, can you sing the Shema for us?" Tia Bea once knew it. "This prayer is very common. It is used to greet the morning and to end the day."

Covering his eyes with his hand, Sam Meyer summoned all his training in Hebrew as a young man and sent his gentle, rich voice out into the Sonim night.

> Hear, O Israel, the Lord is our God, the Lord is One;
> Blessed be the name of the glory of His kingdom forever and ever.
> You shall love the Lord your God with all your heart, with all your soul, and with all your might;
> And these words that I command you today shall be upon your heart.
> You shall teach them to your children, and you shall speak of them
> . . . And you shall write them upon the doorposts of your house and upon your gates.

"Amen." Elena was a devout Catholic as were the majority of people in the village. "Thank you, Sam. Now everyone, let's eat before our dinner gets cold."

Mathilda was weeping silently. Even the boys saw it. Amália comforted her mother, taking hold of her hand. Tia Bea was visibly upset, too. Eugenio remained calm and seated at the table. He sat back and listened. In the past, he would have avoided a situation like this entirely or left the table.

They passed the bowls of potatoes, carrots, and cooked cabbage around the table. The *sarrabulho* moved more slowly as each person scooped stew onto his or her plate. They mashed their potatoes to soak up the stew. It was a feast.

The prayer and the food lifted their spirits—Tia Bea's in particular. "You see, Sam, Eugenio's father was Señhor Mario Castro in Valpaços. Mario regularly travelled to Rebordelo and many villages in the area, becoming wealthy in the process but also participating with the Marrano communities. That is how he met Rosa Maria, Eugenio's mother."

"How did they meet?" Eugenio did not know this story either.

"My sister, Rosa Maria, was employed by Mario. The Spanish Flu took Señhora Castro in 1918. But the situation in that household was not favourable to Rosa Maria and her baby. The housekeeper made Rosa Maria feel she was a source of trouble. Rosa Maria was not the type to push her way around. She was trapped in a household with neither status nor rights. Her solution was to go away, but not before making sure that her baby had a home. She brought Eugenio to me and I raised him. He became a brother to my daughters and gave my husband, bless his soul, a boy with whom to fish and hunt."

"Did you ever learn what happened to her?" Elena wanted Tia Bea to share.

"Years later, we learned she lived a modest but happy life in Porto."

"Rosa Maria was your older sister?"

"No, I am the elder. But we were close—Bee e Rosa Maree; my parents rhymed our names, and sometimes Bea e Maria, but never Beatrice and Rosa Maria."

"So Tia, you and my mother were Jewish. I believed you were

Catholic." Eugenio, too, had to adjust his understanding of his aunt and mother.

"Unknown to my husband, we were Marranos. I quietly converted to Catholicism."

"My grandfather was a Marrano Jew." Xisco spoke as if in awe.

"Yes, he was, Xisco. Mario Castro was a good person, as was your grandmother, Maria Rosa Ribeiro. You can be sure of that."

After dinner, Xisco had a moment alone with Sam. "What is this?" Xisco held out the mini candelabrum he had found collecting rocks. "One fellow on the truck saw this and harassed me about it."

With a glance, Sam nodded and smiled. "This is a symbol of the Jewish people, called a menorah. The seven candles represent the branches of knowledge. Notice the one in the centre is higher. It is a symbol of the light of God, which guides all knowledge. Some people say the seven candles symbolize the creation in seven days, with light in the center representing the Sabbath."

***

The Marranos remained a little-known chapter in the history of Trás-os-Montes. They were easily confused with rumours of shadowy ghouls who roamed the forests by the river and on the barren tablelands, the same lands where Xisco and his Pai collected rocks laden with wolfram. Whenever someone found a fragment of a Star of David, a menorah, or other such icon from long ago, a new ambiguity joined the ranks of those already hoarded. The unnamed residents who once carried those icons remained a topic of speculation, the peculiar archetypes of a village myth. No one owned them. Apparently, no one in this village knew any of these people. At least, no one admitted he did.

Families like Eugenio's and Amália's hungered and prospered with the village, season to season. No one was better than the other. They all woke and laboured in the same fog, the same drizzle, the same hot sun. No one touched God.

God remained a distant speck in the firmament.

That night, Xisco lay awake in his bed in the loft, imagining his grandfather, Mario Castro. The Polish mining engineer's story had opened a door to learning about his family heritage as Marrano Jews.

This news slipped quietly into the community.

**

Located away from the village to the north and higher on the hill, Sam's house was made of stone just like all the other houses in Sonim.

Sam invited Xisco to visit. Sam introduced him to Avraham, a man Xisco had not seen before in the village. Avraham immediately excused himself, saying his family needed him upstairs, where he remained out of sight. Sam explained Avraham and his family were on their way to Lisbon, and left it at that.

Sam's house had a different feel to it. Instead of a stable on the lower level, a wood table dominated the space that Sam had cluttered with various tools and supplies he needed for his work in the mines.

Along one wall, a large tarp covered something big. "What is that?" Xisco was quiet, but he was not shy.

Sam pulled the tarp away. Beneath was a motorcycle, a BSA Empire Star, made by the Birmingham Small Arms Company. "I got this when I was in England."

"You went from Poland to England?"

"I worked for a mining company in the north of England, before I came here."

"Can you speak English?"

"Yes, and I will teach you, Xisco."

Xisco chuckled at the idea. "I don't know about that, Sam. I like history and I have a lazy mind. However, I am not lazy. I like to work and make money."

"Then learn English; it is a language for people who make money."

It was a generous offer Xisco gladly accepted. For now, the motorcycle had captured his attention. "Did you come here on that?"

"It took me three weeks—the best trip I ever had."

"I've never seen you drive it." Xisco ran his hand over the saddle.

"Oh, you will." Sam replaced the tarp.

"Can you teach me how to ride it?"

"Yes, I can do that."

Xisco became Sam's helper. Xisco helped Sam with compiling

mining reports on potential properties in the area. For Xisco, this often entailed loading rocks onto donkey carts, but now instead of selling the rocks to the Germans, Xisco was collecting them for Sam to analyse.

The time went quickly by.

Sam taught Xisco how to make fireworks and then they went to nearby villages and towns to set off fireworks displays. Falling asleep riding in the truck with Sam became a new skill in Xisco's repertoire.

Xisco had his brother, Armando, cover for him in the stables.

Xisco enjoyed the regular attention from an adult. One of the nicest things Sam did for Xisco happened soon after their first meeting. Xisco told him that when he went swimming, he didn't have a bathing suit. The next day, Sam gave Xisco his bathing suit. "I've had this for a long time," he explained. "It is not fitting me anymore."

Xisco had his mother take in the waist for him. She said it looked good on him.

As the summer progressed, Sam taught Xisco English words. He ran drills to decline verbs like "have" and "be." Constantly, he tested Xisco's vocabulary, which Xisco took in stride, neither hating nor loving it. To Xisco, speaking English was a game they played to kill the hours together, and he didn't think anything of it.

"But you haven't taught me how to ride your BSA."

Sam went to the motorcycle and pulled off the tarp. "Let's do it."

Carlos

9. Study of Lasting Impacts

The first time Carlos Silva travelled to the north of Portugal, he looked across the dim landscape and said aloud, "*Meu Deus.*" The single-lane macadam road was not unlike hundreds of others on which he had travelled up and down the country. Slow-moving farm wagons and donkey carts impeded his journey and reminded him endlessly of hardship and disappointment, which were the Portuguese way.

Tall for a Portuguese and lean, with black hair and an olive complexion, Carlos was greying at the temples, making him look older than his twenty-seven years. He was aware of his good fortune to be driving an Italian sedan, a 1936 Lancia Augusta that had been brand new the year before when he started these trips. No one else among his community was even mildly interested in the car, except for the ailing blacksmith—one of the brothers who tended to the remaining horses in their service—who taught Carlos how to drive the automobile.

"I am curious, Carlos, what does a priest plan to accomplish by learning to drive an automobile?"

"I want to deliver the truth about Fatima to our people."

"What do you mean?" The old man said with a twinkle in his eye.

"I am not happy that the *Estado Novo* adopted the Fatima story to meet its own ends. Salazar's greatest fear is Communism and that has nothing to do with our faith. Our Lady of Fatima was asking us to be kind and generous with our fellow human beings."

"Your mission will be a great success," the brother declared. "I admire your courage."

The old man placed a well-worn, wooden staff in Carlos's hands. "This was my crozier, handed down to me from a long line of travellers."

A crozier is a long staff carried by a bishop on special occasions. A bishop's crozier has a hook on the end, like a shepherd's staff, for herding sheep. The one Carlos received did not have such a hook. At the top, where there once had been a burl in the wood, was an intricate carving of a *triquetra* or Trinity knot, which was comprised of three triangles intertwined through a circle.

The knotted, hardwood pole was handsome to behold. "I didn't expect a gift, Brother." Carlos ran his hand along the smooth surface.

"My instructions were to pass this on to someone who will take the Word of God to the people. You are brave enough to make such a journey," the blacksmith told him.

Carlos's colleagues believed he was foolish to take on such a project.

The fall and winter before, his project to deliver the messages of Fatima met with sunshine in the Alentejo and the Algarve, where he welcomed the warmth especially during the darkest and coldest nights. As an orphan, he had grown up alone and afraid, especially at night, when he believed evil spirits roamed the earth. In the south, the balmy evenings lifted his spirits and calmed his anxieties.

During the summer, he drove out from Lisbon on weekends and holidays to the countryside nearby. Things went well. He met many people, ate amazing food, and participated at festivals. But on this journey to the north, the skies reached down to the earth and laid a blanket of fog in his path. The dampness got into his clothes and the air turned icy from an air mass blowing in from the North Atlantic.

Miserable, he surveyed Trás-os-Montes and returned to his original feeling about this region—disappointment. The name "Trás-os-Montes" implied a mountainous terrain. Like a Saramago laureate, he had anticipated more and better. But the land failed neither to rise to great peaks nor fall into deep gorges. Trás-os-Montes, behind-the-mountains, was the area beyond the mountains at Gerês, Marão, and Alvão. Sure, there were hills and valleys sloping to the rivers that cut their way to the sea. But they were invisible from where he stood. All he saw was a plateau of endless rock.

Though he was dry in the car, the damp chill was getting the better of him. His thoughts drifted to the weakest fragment of his being, his acceptance of futility. He knew it was wrong to hang onto it. He should have prayed.

When he missed the turn to Mirandela and was too far along to turn back, he felt deflated. He could not help himself. He indulged in his feelings of futility when things were going too well, or now, when they were not going well at all. Finally, in the late afternoon he stopped in Caravelas, a village that looked deserted. There were no children playing in the square. He could not see a Church where he might obtain a room in the house of a local priest. What he found was a bakery café coupled with a general store, the only commercial operation in sight.

A man with an apron behind the counter welcomed Carlos. Before Carlos could say anything, another man, an old man with a thick white beard stood up from a table and offered his hand. "*Bom dia*, Padre," he said to Carlos.

Carlos was glad he had worn his cassock; it opened doors for him. Strangers, like this old man, paid him respect.

The proprietor with the apron provided an introduction.

"This is Padre Pedro. He doesn't wear his collar when he's with us in here."

Pedro gave Carlos a warm welcome. "How can I help you, Padre?"

"I am hoping to find a place to sleep. Would you have a room to spare?

***

Before ordination, every candidate in the Seminário dos Olivais, the Seminary of the Olive Groves, had to complete an academic theology program as well as a pastoral assignment, urban project, or academic thesis. Unique to the Lisbon prefecture, the additional requirement was a brainchild of its Patriarch, the Bishop of Lisbon, Cardinal Manuel Gonçalves Cerejeira, who saw it as a tool to help discover each candidate's strengths and interests. How a candidate performed said a lot about his character, such as his initiative, ingenuity, leadership, and devotion to his vocation. Many candidates did not complete it and there were no apparent repercussions.

Carlos's peers were focusing their efforts on pastoral work, as was their inclination. There was plenty of need for help in parishes across Lisbon. Many priests did not have to move away. They adopted local roles that would assure their position in the order and their continued sheltered existence.

Having grown up in orphanages, Carlos needed to feel he belonged. To him, the Church was the rock upon which he built his life. It was his home. He cared deeply about what had happened to the Church in the past and devoted his life to its future. Yet, however much he embraced the Gospels of the New Testament, Carlos secretly continued to hold onto the emptiness expressed in the Old Testament.

By watching and listening to whatever information he could gather, Carlos learned the Church in Portugal was in trouble. In 1910, following the revolution, the clergy had been condemned for its ties with the nobility, and disparaged for a lack of concern for the material needs of the parishioners. Carlos knew instinctively this criticism was not personal and did not apply to him. How could it? He did not have ties or even interactions with nobility. Besides, he believed in what the Church could do to teach people how to love one another. People had not given up on the Church; they still believed fervently in Jesus, His teachings, and the Saints. To help one another, the Catholic community of Lisbon and Portugal just needed more community participation and spiritual leadership from their clergy, not less.

Carlos wanted to raise activities a notch. Making Church events and special occasions relevant and fantastic was their job.

"Good. We need to draw people in," said Padre Meszaros, Carlos's spiritual director. "Attract them to the excitement of life in the community. Festivals, accompanied by a Catholic service of one sort or another, are perfect."

"I will give them Fatima."

"The apparition of Our Lady?"

"Yes, we are told about evil souls in Hell and Communists in Russia as a means to encourage fear in people to love God and be saved, but I believe the real message is that people need to open their minds and hearts to God."

Carlos saw himself as a disciple taking the messages of the Virgin

Mary to people across the country.

"His evangelical mission is a unique endeavour." Padre Meszaros explained to Cardinal Cerejeira. "He has a vision and wants to make an impact."

Cardinal Cerejeira approved the project and continued to pay attention to the progress of this seminarian. He would use him to share the lessons of Fatima to Catholics in distant towns and villages across Portugal.

Padre Meszaros summoned Carlos. "Your proposal is very good, Carlos. It is what we need. It has been approved."

"Thank you, I appreciate it."

"The Cardinal asks that you disseminate the messages from Fatima. Here are the facts." He handed a list to Carlos. "Learn these and share them every chance you get."

Carlos attended Baptisms, First Communions, Confirmations, Weddings, and Funerals, serving in various roles as needed. At Christmas, Lent, and Easter, he celebrated as an assistant to the clergy in Church rituals. At Holy Festivals, he participated as an assistant and sometimes as an acting clergy; he was, after all, a member of the same community as the ordained. If he filled a need for their services, his participation was acceptable. Whenever he could, Carlos delivered a sermon about the messages of Fatima.

The story of Fatima proved to be popular with the people. Word spread among the seminarians. Carlos shared with them the messages he had received, so they, too, could spread the word to people in Lisbon.

In discussions with Padre Meszaros, they talked about why there was so much interest, especially in the area north of Lisbon.

"They live near Fatima." Padre Meszaros was not afraid to speculate. "As many as 100,000 people were present for the Miracle of the Sun. Many of the older generation were there. They witnessed Fatima or they have family or know someone who did."

**

"Thank you for letting me stay at your house," said Carlos. "It will be just the night; I'm only passing through."

Padre Pedro waved his hand. "It is nothing. I am happy to have a visitor."

He joined Carlos in his car; he pointed the way on the short drive to his home just outside the village.

They ascended stairs at the side of the house to the second floor, entering into the kitchen. An open hearth for cooking dominated the room, and white embers still smoldered there. Pedro put more wood on the fire as he introduced Carlos to his housekeeper, Benedita, who welcomed him. They were glad to have another priest in their home.

"I am not yet a *padre*, Señhora." Carlos broke off, coughing. "I am still a seminarian." He did not yet have a white collar to wear.

Benedita saw his plight and tended to his needs. She cut bread, cheese and a few fresh vegetables for Carlos, who sat at the table near the hearth. Blended with the reek of the hearth, a brume of wet hay and muck from below permeated the room. Pedro sat in the chair beside the only window. Next to him was a small cabinet with rows of books on the shelves and a thick, well-thumbed bible lay open on top.

Both white-haired, deep-wrinkled, stooped, and good-natured, Benedita and Pedro treated Carlos with kindness as one of their own. She told him she had a son and a daughter, who had families of their own now. Between small bites of bread and well-aged cheese, Carlos told them about himself. To wash down the bread, Benedita poured him *aguardiente* with mint in a stubby tumbler of thick glass. When she passed it to him, the lines on her face like smooth-edged carvings curled in a gentle smile; and she poured one for Pedro and one for herself. After another two shots, Carlos was ready for bed where he remained deep asleep until morning.

When he came out, Benedita served him a bowl of broth made from leftover roast, potatoes, tomatoes, cabbage, turnips, carrots, celery, onion, garlic, and salt. Pedro joined him, slurping from his spoon, and slopping soup in his bushy white beard that he cheerfully dabbed with his sleeve.

Pedro poured wine, which he enjoyed even for breakfast. Carlos appreciated the lingering taste of the *terroir* in his mouth as the rich *tinto* slid down his throat as smooth as butter.

That morning, the sky cleared and the air turned warm. Benedita went into the village on her daily errands, and Pedro beckoned Carlos to join him for a walk. At Pedro's careful pace, they worked their way across the yard that backed onto a forest where a trail sloped down into a valley. That was where Pedro collected his wood for the kitchen hearth and hauled it up to his house. Today Pedro remained on high ground and continued beyond the wall of his yard to a lookout a short distance further where he could show Carlos the countryside. It was vast. Low hills lay before them as far as they could see. There was rock everywhere.

"It still amazes me this land supports people." Pedro gazed into the distance. "That people survive on this rock."

"Well, I wouldn't say this land has nothing." Carlos knew from experience that people could accomplish much with the least resources. "Even sand and gravel are needed for construction. Given the right circumstances, any rock can have value to another man. You never know, all it takes is a miracle for the poor Portuguese who live on these barren, rocky lands."

Pedro's white locks gleamed against the blue sky. He pulled out a flask from the breast pocket of his jacket and drank from it. He passed it to Carlos, who also drank, the *aguardiente* burning his throat and warming his stomach. Pedro pointed to a distant jumble of boulders abandoned randomly at the foot of a low range of hills. "Some say that is the work of men in mythic times." Pedro's eyes were black as soft, rich humus. "The work of Sisyphus."

Carlos knew the myth of Sisyphus, the indentured soul who pushed a boulder up a hill only to have it roll back down, then having to push it back up the hill again, endlessly.

"Trás-os-Montes is home to a hardy stock of people. We are survivors."

Carlos could not argue with Pedro's interpretation. Who can say how people endured?

"I've lived here all my life and I know the stories about how people got here. I tell you, I have a theory." Pedro shrugged his shoulders. "I don't have any proof; it is just a theory."

"Sounds interesting. Please, tell me."

"Ok, as anyone can guess, many people here say they are from Spain. I think that is half the story. I think many came from further north.

Have you heard of the Cathar Crusade? Or its other name, the Albigensian Crusade? It took place in Languedoc, in the south of France. This is what I'm talking about."

Carlos had the impression Pedro was telling him something he shared with Benedita, and not many others.

"In the 13th century, the Catholic Church declared the Cathars of Languedoc to be heretics. It formed an alliance with the French king. The king's nobles took the Cathars' towns and cities, lined up their priests, and executed them. Their followers were stripped down to their breeches and sent out into the countryside. They fled into the Pyrenees. French noblemen stole their property and entire towns.

"It was a successful campaign. Over time, the Catholic Church and its allies applied the practices of the French noblemen against any heretics of the Catholic faith, including in Spain. You know of this. It became the Inquisition."

Pedro paused and looked at Carlos. Seeing Carlos was listening, he continued.

"The Cathars and others ran for their lives and I believe they came here, to this God-forsaken land. Here, they found a place to live. And sure enough, the Cathar Crusade did not come to Trás-os-Montes and nor did the Inquisition. When Jews were targeted by the Inquisition, they were persecuted in Lisbon, but not here in the north."

"So, first it was the Cathars." Carlos showed Pedro he understood his theory.

"Yes, the Cathars were Christians who didn't adhere to the Roman Catholic Church, which had become corrupt."

"They were targeted by domestic crusades." Carlos nodded solemnly.

"Yes, the Cathars were vanquished. Everything about them was destroyed—their lives, their musical instruments—they were a very musical people—their books, their histories. I believe a small number of Cathars came into this remote land with nothing. Like Sisyphus, they accepted the terms of their futile condition. They became attached to this barren plateau of rock and made it their home, for good reason—they live free and safe." Pedro searched for a reason. "Anyone not born into this land would surely flee."

No one ever took such conjecture seriously. But for Pedro's sake, Carlos did take it very seriously. "How will I report this to my spiritual director?"

This made Pedro laugh. "Tell him it was my vanity to speak this way."

Carlos recognized the phrase.

"It is all chasing the wind." Carlos recited the lines to Pedro, who tilted his face to the sky and laughed heartily.

These phrases were from *Ecclesiastes*. Pedro had his finger on the pulse of ages-old wisdom that had survived thousands of years. Carlos looked at him with greater appreciation, and showed Pedro he, Carlos, was on track with Pedro's line of reflection. "That is why it is best to work and keep busy. For the wise man and the fool are no different in the end."

Pedro looked in his eyes. "You know the story, Padre."

Carlos did not correct him; Pedro knew what he was saying.

They returned to the house and found Benedita had returned. She stood when Carlos began to take leave. He thanked them and promised to pray for them and their souls.

Benedita whispered in Pedro's ear, and urged him, nodding with her head.

Pedro stepped into a bedroom for a moment and reappeared with a black hat in hand.

"Benedita thinks you might like this." He handed it to Carlos.

"If it fits you, Padre," Benedita said. "Does it fit you?"

Carlos appraised it in a flash. The Iberian horse hat had a flat top and a wide flat brim. He put it on and it was perfect.

"This is amazing, thank you!" He looked even taller now.

Benedita and Pedro were very pleased to see the hat suited Carlos.

"Just as Benedita said it would."

Carlos had always wanted a hat just like it. Feeling yet more grateful to have met them, he departed. Their generosity had been so unexpected; it humbled him.

By the middle of the day, clouds filled the skies and the day turned grey like so many others before, when he was neither joyful nor grievous. His journey had felt this way, so often falling into the in-between times when he calmly observed his short life and saw it for what it truly was: a disappointing exercise in futility. But was it really? He saw Pedro's deep brown eyes and remembered how he released all his cares with a hearty laugh. Did Pedro feel in his bones the emptiness of *Ecclesiastes*: "Smoke, nothing but smoke. There is nothing to anything— it's all smoke. What's there to show for a lifetime of work, a lifetime of working your fingers to the bone?" No, he did not. Pedro had achieved peace with his existence, a fact that Carlos admired. Despite the emptiness, Pedro had chosen meaning in his life.

Following Pedro's example enabled Carlos to shake off his feelings of futility. He no longer was tense inside as he used to be, nor cornered in the land behind the mountains. Alone. Padre Pedro had shown him a path away from futility.

***

That fall, in 1937, Carlos completed his studies in the seminary and accepted his call to the priesthood. He received the white collar. Then he waited to hear where his superiors would post him. Carlos had been to several regions and was familiar with what the needs were. There were many options. It occurred to him that his journeys to the nether regions of the country had qualified him all too well for a posting to such a remote location. He was horrified. He might as well live deep in the Amazonian jungle. He might never come out. He prayed; he did not want to ride on the backs of donkeys between villages for the rest of his life.

He mentally prepared an argument against such a posting to use at his upcoming meeting with Padre Meszaros where he would learn his assignment.

"Carlos, this is from Padre Pedro in Caravelas." Padre Meszaros handed him the letter. "I am so proud of you. Your project proved you understand the needs of Catholics even in the furthest reaches, which was an important factor in determining your placement as a priest."

"It was?"

Sure enough, his concern was coming true; Carlos was too upset to listen further. "Padre, they say that what one does for the first five years after school sets a pattern for what one does for the rest of his life. This is the most important part of my career. I need to make a difference." Carlos had grabbed his spiritual director's attention. He looked Padre Meszaros in the eye. "I cannot do this if I am far away and unseen in some remote village such as Caravelas or even Monsanto, as beautiful as it is. I need to be in the centre."

He looked away, out the window. His future was set.

When Carlos looked at Padre Meszaros, he was stunned to see him smiling broadly. Padre Meszaros even laughed aloud. To his face. Carlos felt crushed that his spiritual director would laugh at him in this predicament. Carlos stood to leave, but Padre Meszaros held onto his sleeve. "Carlos, there is another option I expect you haven't considered."

Carlos could tell by the tone of his voice that Padre Meszaros was being utterly sincere. It was not a trick. It was something important.

"This letter proved that you can be a leader. And it confirmed the impressions of our patron, Cardinal Cerejeira."

Unknown to Carlos, his journeys and his report on the faith of Catholics in Portugal had put in motion an entirely different outcome than the one he had anticipated.

The Cardinal summoned Carlos to an interview. Neither the Rector nor Padre Meszaros knew the details so they refrained from telling him anything. Padre Meszaros did his best to console him. "I think it is good, Carlos. I really do expect you will be pleased."

Carlos went alone into the old city. Within a maze of streets around one of the seven hills on which Lisbon stood, he located Campo Mártires da Pátria, the road that circled a small park at the top of one of the hills. To the west, the streets went down to the Avenida da Liberdade and on the east to the Avenida Almirante Reis, two main thoroughfares that converged in the centre of the city. Squeezed between the three-story buildings that lined the street, he found the Cardinal's *palaceta*.

For this meeting, Carlos wore his cassock and white collar, and definitely not his hat.

The housekeeper led him up a wide flight of stairs to a large room in which the Cardinal worked at an antique desk. Behind the desk, the sunlight streamed in through several windows. The Cardinal looked up immediately from his writing and stood to greet him.

"Padre Silva, welcome." The Cardinal held out his hand, with his knuckles and the large ruby on his ring facing up.

Carlos knelt and kissed his ring as he had seen the Rector do. "Your Eminence."

Cerejeira led him to a pair of chairs in the near corner of the room, sat down, and motioned for Carlos to join him in the other chair.

"I want to congratulate you on your ordination, Padre Silva."

"Thank you, Your Eminence."

"A few days after being appointed Patriarch of Lisbon only five years ago, I went to Rome and was called to serve as Cardinal. Following the ceremony, I was in a private meeting with the Holy Father, that's Pius XI, just as you and I are meeting now, and the Holy Father asked me about my plans for action in the diocese."

Cerejeira paused, looking at him. Carlos expected the Cardinal to ask about his plans. He was prepared to talk about Fatima.

Instead, the Cardinal continued.

"I told him I would begin by establishing a new seminary, the one that you attended, Carlos. The Pope immediately interrupted me. 'Do not hesitate a moment. This is the way,' he said. Pius asked me about the resources I had to deliver this work. I told him 'I will build with Providence.' I had no idea how to pay for it. The Holy Father responded immediately, 'Count on it. Providence will not miss a visit with you.' His words will inspire me forever."

Carlos was thinking, what does this have to do with me?

Cerejeira patted Carlos's hand. "My task was enormous. The years from 1910 to 1930 were difficult for the Church in Portugal. When I became bishop, we had to rebuild. I needed a lot of help and still do. I need men like you, Padre Silva, to lead and to build the Catholic faith in our beloved Portugal. We base our vocations on our spiritual and theological formation, Padre, but now we must turn our attention to our world and take relevant action if our Church is to survive and prosper once again. This is why I want you to go to Rome. I have nominated you, Padre Silva, to study Canon Law in the Pontiff's seminary, and they have accepted you."

Carlos stared at the Cardinal, speechless. This was not what he had expected.

Carlos returned to Moscavide in a daze.

It took a moment for Carlos to comprehend exactly what the Cardinal offered him. The details were confusing, exciting, and terribly unbelievable, all at the same time. His fellow seminarians, Padre Meszaros, and the priests who taught at the seminary were uniformly thrilled with the surprise announcement and were happy for him.

When the excitement of his news settled down, Carlos exalted in his good luck. He would see the Vatican from the inside. Be a part of it. He held his ambitions in check and adopted a pious and studious demeanour as laid out in the teachings of St. Augustine. He prayed, and every day, he brushed up on his Italian. He would learn Vatican law and fulfil the role required of him in Portugal, whatever that might be.

10. Anagni, Italy

In the spring of 1938, Carlos Silva arrived at the Pontificio Collegio Leoniano, the Pope's Collegio, where Carlos would attend the bulk of his courses. Located seventy kilometres south of Rome in Anagni, the Collegio itself was a long, four-storey structure with stone cladding that dominated a ridge overlooking valleys in front and behind.

The first event on the agenda was a congregation of the school's new participants, who gathered in a hallway beneath a glorious staircase where the din of their voices echoed up into the great expanse above them. When it was time, doors swung open to the main salon and the men streamed through the doors. The orderly fashion in which they entered and took their seats suggested some had military backgrounds. All were ordained priests, garbed in floor-length cassocks, and had filed down the aisles of churches around the world for at least a decade, including Carlos Silva.

The salon featured an exceptionally high ceiling, a row of tall windows with classical frames in white, and walls of sunny yellow. At the front, a massive portrait of the college's founder, Pope Leo XIII, dwarfed the speaker, who on this occasion was the Rector of the Collegio, Padre Ottorino Sivio Piccardi.

"Fathers, look around you. As attendees of this *Collegio*, you represent the next generation of leaders. Henceforth, you will assume duties as assistants to bishops and cardinals as program coordinators and as leaders of innovative initiatives. As you progress, your superiors will turn to you to manage change, to troubleshoot, and to fix whatever has broken. Over time, your schedules will become busier as you lead review panels and studies. To no one's surprise, promotions to formal positions will follow. As I said and I will say it again, look around you. Among you are future Rectors, Monsignors, Bishops, and a select few will become Cardinals. Who knows, maybe even one among you will become Pope."

The speaker acknowledged sparse laughter with a smile, and met the gaze of the priests seated in rows before him.

"As I welcome you, I also wish to give you guidance. None of this will come easy. You have an enormous workload ahead of you. To become expert in Canon Law, you will learn precedent-setting cases that span centuries on key issues affecting Catholics across the world. To advise your superiors and to lead, you will also become expert in Business Law in your respective jurisdictions. Our Church has become a large, complex organization that operates in virtually every domain in the world. It will be up to you to manage these assets. Nothing you do, will be done by you alone, nor for you alone. Everything you do, will be done in conjunction with your colleagues, who are on the same team, Fathers. All that we do is for the common cause of the Holy Mother Church."

"And this is how we share in God's glory here on earth."

***

On Saturdays, Carlos and a new colleague, Paulo, an Italian priest, explored Anagni on bicycles and rode into the surrounding countryside. They seemed an odd pair. Next to Carlos, Paulo was short. The priests called him *il piccolo*, the little one, and sometimes *il Re*, the King, after their sovereign, Victor Emmanuel III, who was five feet in height.

The village and countryside oozed mediaeval charm. Carlos was enamoured with the ambiance of the churches, stone palaces, courtyards, gardens, and country manors. "The scenery is utterly gorgeous." Carlos pictured generations of prosperous families.

Paulo did not see the fuss. "What? Don't you have courtyards and fields in Portugal?"

"Yes, of course we do. It's just different." Carlos compared what he was seeing to the view in Trás-os-Montes that he had shared with Padre Pedro, who helped him rise above the futility in the world to find meaning. Here in Anagni, that understanding seemed especially relevant; *Ecclesiastes* itself no longer seemed important.

"This scenery is just so much more hopeful."

Carlos changed living in Italy. The emptiness of futility fit better with his former world that seemed always filled with sorrow. In Anagni, he experienced laughter and sunshine. He was doing well in the Collegio. He felt more assured with himself, more self-satisfied.

With newfound confidence, he discussed his life with Paulo.

They often sat on the hillside behind the college where they had a great view of the valley and the hills on the east side. One day, Carlos told him about Padre Pedro.

"It was as if Pedro were laughing in the face of God." Carlos shook his head, fondly remembering Pedro. "I admired him for seeing beauty in such a desolate, depressing place. He made *Ecclesiastes* come to life."

Paulo was thoughtful. "There are treasures throughout the Bible, certainly. Don't forget they are just literature. They present a view of life from another time."

"Views which remain relevant." Contrary to his brightening outlook in Anagni, a darkness permeated his inner life. "*Ecclesiastes* is one of the great books of wisdom."

"It's outdated. You need to purge the old worldview from your mind. The world has come a long way. Existence really is a beautiful thing." Paulo was adamant. The proof was in the beautiful scenery all around him.

Perhaps Paulo was right. Carlos was not convinced. "We'll see, Paulo, we'll see."

For a time, Carlos flushed out the Old and embraced the New. He continued to flourish in his studies and in life. He was not about to admit anything to Paulo, though. The change gave him a new face to wear in the world.

***

Every night, the lamp on his bedside table cast a pool of light over his books and papers well into the very early morning hours just after midnight when most people were asleep. Carlos would often wake up at his desk or on top of his bed with a book on his chest.

As the Rector had cautioned, the workload was intense. Carlos's curriculum focused on Canon Law and always touched on history, philosophy, theology, civil law, and property law. His skills in Italian and Latin improved with constant use. Cardinal Cerejeira required Carlos to also study financial services, including banking, insurance, real estate, and equities, where he made contacts with experts who kindly assisted him whenever he had questions.

Prior to his studies, Carlos was not even aware of any commercial ventures on behalf of the Church, but it did not surprise him. In Anagni, he learned that his involvement in commerce would be inevitable. He would need to manage money and properties, roles he had not envisioned for himself.

Paulo told him he should take better notes about how to preserve wealth. "You need to build a base of power. That's how bishops and cardinals gain influence in the Church. Typically, popes came from wealthy Italian families. One son would be a financier, one would be in the military, and another would be in the Church. Some, like Cardinal Boetto, the Jesuit in Genoa, have come from poverty and built steadfast careers in the Church. But he is the exception."

"What is your situation, Paulo?"

Paulo laughed. "I am second son. My family is rich enough to make me sick."

"And I am poor as a church mouse—what a pair we make! Should I be grateful to know you or afraid you might step on me?"

"No, but my younger brother might. He is a Black Shirt."

"You're kidding."

"I wish I were. He is headed for the military. Fortunately, my father believed in the rule of primogeniture and my eldest brother inherited the family estate, which he wisely maintains. He is a reasonable man, and powerful."

***

Carlos and Paulo transferred temporarily to the seminary's main location in Rome, where they would undertake a light schedule for two terms. The main campus of the Pontifical seminary was on the grounds of the Basilica of St. John Lateran, located five kilometres from Vatican City in Rome.

With their spare time on Saturdays, they explored the city.

It was a Saturday. Carlos and Paulo wandered around St. Peter's, immersed in the altars, statuary, and tombs. The Pietà, a sculpture by Michelangelo depicting the Virgin Mother Mary cradling Jesus across her lap, engrossed Carlos. In one moment, his eyes were sliding across the statue, in the next, he was fixated on her arm that braced the lifeless Jesus, and in that same moment, he realized what the love of a mother truly meant and all that he had missed as a child. As a boy, Carlos felt ashamed that he had caused his mother's death, or worse, that he was not wanted. Either way, a terrible disappointment had permeated his life.

Carlos had stopped and gazed upon this statue several times over recent months. This time, the great joy that accompanied his personal revelation transformed him, and then he felt overcome by grief as if death had torn his mother's breast from him.

Paulo wanted to leave in the afternoon because it was not safe to walk in the dark. Carlos forgot Paulo's wishes as he consumed himself with experiencing the love of a mother for the first time in his life. Carlos could not leave. Turning his back on The Pietà would have been an apostasy of love for a man who had ached to feel this comfort of a mother's love.

When Vespers began, the chanting drew him back into the grand nave of St. Peter's and lifted him into the clouds beyond the ceiling. He prayed; he thanked God for giving him this day as the setting sun illuminated the stained glass high above him.

Within minutes of setting out for the Basilica of St. John Lateran, the moonless night turned black as clouds rolled in. They walked quickly through the pools of light under the street lamps and the shadows in between. They passed an old man in an alley. People hurried to their homes. Cars rumbled and tires squealed on the cobblestones. The chiseled face and raised chin of Il Duce greeted them eerily on posters in the lamplight of every open square they passed on the hour-long walk between Vatican City and St. John Lateran.

Their route took them past the Altare Della Patria and the Colosseum, which Carlos had seen so many times now he did not even glance at them.

On a corner not far from the seminary, they came upon a group of Black Shirts. The ones they usually saw chanted slogans such as "*Credere, obbedire, combattere!*" and "*Fascismo è libertà!*" But this lot was hanging about under a street lamp. They didn't appear to be the type to believe or obey anyone, but fight, yes.

It was too late to turn another way. Carlos and Paulo continued to walk toward them. A big fellow eyed them, spotting easy prey.

It was no secret the Black Shirts terrorized members of the clergy and anyone soft on helping the poor and disadvantaged. The situation had improved with The Lateran Accords, Mussolini's treaties with Pope Pius XI in 1929 that recognized the Vatican City State and its properties outside the walls of Vatican City while the Church recognized Mussolini's state. Also, Mussolini recognized Roman Catholicism as the official religion of the nation. The mood changed considerably when in March of 1937, Pius XI issued a letter for priests to read in all German Catholic Churches. The letter protested racism against Jews and subtly attacked Hitler without naming him. The goodwill toward the clergy evaporated, even in Italy.

His eyes down, Paulo attempted to walk past without trouble.

The fellow stepped in front of him. "I don't like people who hide Jews."

"Excuse me?" Paulo was polite even when threatened.

The man grabbed Paulo by the shoulder, punched him in the face, and quickly kicked him in the gut. The Black Shirt intended his kick to be lower but Paulo was so short he took it full in the stomach.

Paulo crumpled to the ground with gasps for air. Carlos leaned over Paulo, comforting him. "Paulo, you'll be fine, take some air, you'll be fine, I'll take care of you, you'll be fine." The sight of blood pouring from Paulo's nose angered Carlos.

The one who attacked Paulo stood over them. He nudged Carlos with his foot. "I'm not done with him yet. Leave him alone or you'll be next."

"Yes, you are done with him." Carlos spoke firmly, standing in front of Paulo, his arms at his sides. "Leave us alone. We haven't done anything to hurt you."

"Hey boys, we have a saint here." The Black Shirt hated the clergy.

"Leave 'em alone, Leo." One of them didn't want to beat up a priest.

"Naw, and spoil my fun?"

Carlos was annoyed this guy thought nothing of hurting a vulnerable person like Paulo. "Why don't you just turn around and go home? Then nobody else gets hurt." Carlos made the suggestion in a firm, solid voice.

The Black Shirt swung hard. Carlos dodged it, and as he did, he jabbed up into the ribs of his attacker.

Paulo's eyes widened. Instead of receiving an extremely hard blow, Carlos had struck back at his attacker.

The surprise on the Black Shirt's face gave Carlos a twinge of pride. Having grown up in an orphanage, Carlos learned how to fight boys bigger them himself. He knew how to get in a jab here and there, and how to tire out an opponent.

The guy now came at Carlos swinging even harder.

Carlos stepped back as the man's fists swished the air in front of his face once and then twice. Carlos threw a fake and Leo's hand came up to block it as Carlos caught him with a left jab, knocking him backwards, stunned. Carlos followed it with a right to the eye and then a left to his solar plexus. For good measure, he gave the bully another right to break his nose and laid him flat on his back.

"That's enough! You proved your point." A Black Shirt stuck up for his downed buddy. "Now get out of here."

"Thank you." Carlos replied calmly, catching his breath.

Carlos assisted Paulo to his feet. "Are these friends of your brother?" He whispered to Paulo. "I am so sorry this has happened to you. I should have anticipated it."

Paulo limped away with one hand rubbing his stomach and the other holding the side of his face. "We aren't supposed to hit people, Carlos. We're priests."

Carlos felt stung by Paulo's anger—an admonishment when he expected gratitude.

***

When their appetites for antiquity had been satiated, their Saturdays became opportunities to take long walks.

On Via Carlo Emanuele, a side street near the Basilica of St. John Lateran, Carlos discovered an orphanage run by nuns. He had the idea he would like to experience orphanage life anew, and give back what he had received. He wanted to offer his time. He asked Paulo to accompany him.

A nun answered his knock on the heavy, front door.

Carlos introduced himself and Paulo. They were priests attending the seminary, and offered to assist with the children. She smiled. "Bless your hearts, Fathers. Please come in."

She wore a starched headpiece featuring a pair of white wings. She was a member of the Daughters of Charity, an order of nuns with which Carlos and Paulo were already familiar—they operated the kitchens that served the seminary community.

She showed them the main floor of the facility, where activities involving various groups of children were underway. She introduced the visiting priests to the nuns on staff that day. She suggested Carlos and Paulo might help with the older boys. Would they like to join activities?

"It would be a perfect fit for him." Paulo, who had been quiet to this point, reached up to pat Carlos on the shoulder. "Carlos can teach the boys how to resolve their differences."

Although Carlos heard praise on the surface, he felt the dig.

***

Carlos preferred the tranquility before sunrise to pray. As day broke, he was often at Lauds in the Basilica where the sunlight streamed through the stained glass windows—the perfect imagery of Christ's resurrection and the perfect accompaniment to the many voices resonating in unity through the Basilica to hail a new day and praise God in all His glory. He was emotional as chanting flowed into his being, reminding him of his fortuitous vocation.

Every day, Carlos played games in the courtyard with the boys. He supervised, he coached, and he helped them deal with boys' issues. He knew what they might experience and he approached his role with an open, nonjudgmental attitude. The boys loved him.

During his first week at the orphanage, he noticed one of the sisters observing him. She looked familiar but he could not place where he had seen her. So he introduced himself. Her name was Sister Laurenza; he immediately noticed her green eyes.

"You are in my theology class," she looked directly at him.

When Sister Laurenza spoke, he noticed she had a crooked eyetooth on one side and her smile was the whitest he had ever seen.

Carlos beheld her peaceful radiance.

"I sit at the back of the class. I don't want my wings to obstruct other students' views."

As a member of the Daughters of Charity, she, too, wore a headpiece with starched white wings that pledged to carry her off into the blue with the slightest breeze.

The next day in class, she was there at the back. She kept to herself, focused on taking notes. Carlos may not have noticed her if he had not met her at the orphanage. But he should have. Sister Laurenza was about four years his junior. She was nearly his height. Smooth brown skin, which would be soft to the touch. Freckles across her nose and cheeks. Her green eyes were bright. She was vibrant.

How could he have missed her?

***

Outside the classroom, Sister Laurenza was relaxed. Friendly. Carlos felt drawn to her. His interest in her began innocently enough watching her interact with the children. Sister Laurenza demonstrated unconditional love.

The orphanage on Via Carlo Emanuele was in a two-story house that had once been a handsome villa with a walled yard. The dormitories were on the second floor. There was one for all children under six years old, and two for older children divided by gender.

Carlos no longer spent most of his time in the yard, weather permitting, the common room, and the dining room. He joined Sister Laurenza in the preschool room where she spent most of her time. When he arrived today, he found her in the corridor.

"Come here, darling." The three-year-old was in tears. "What has got you so upset?" She picked up the little boy and looked in his eyes. The boy's frown dissolved and in seconds, she had him smiling and laughing.

"You would make an excellent mother." Carlos blurted out his compliment without considering whether this comment was appropriate, given her vocation.

He could see his comment flustered her. She turned red; she looked angry. Before he could apologize, she left the room with the child in her arms.

Carlos had killed their friendship right there. He just knew it.

The next time he saw her, he addressed her formally. "Sister Laurenza, I want to apologize for my comment the last time we spoke. It was inapppro—"

"There is no need to apologize. I wasn't offended."

"I embarrassed you."

"Not at all. You made me admit something I have been pondering, so I thank you."

She appeared truly pleased. He saw her white teeth as she smiled and felt her green eyes on him. She was not looking down or away, but right at him.

In the dining room for dinner the next day, she asked him about his life in Portugal before he joined the seminary. Was he happy there?

He enjoyed the attention.

He lived within a sphere of his own making within which he told himself who he could trust, rely on, and turn to. If someone were to love him, he would be able to share in such a mutual trust. He could let her in.

In a short time working together, they formed a relationship. When he was away from her, he would think of things he would ask her or tell her. Their relationship became a little bowl into which they poured their respective experiences and nourished each other. He soon forgot who said what and when. It was as if everything had originated in him, yet he could clearly remember her telling him specific stories.

Carlos continued to help at the orphanage, and they grew closer together. He felt as if he had known her forever and would continue to know her forever. They had entered a state of relationship that was foreign to him. When she looked at him, she was imploring him to act, to do something, anything. It was awkward, yet he kept going back to her and feeling the thrill of her company.

One day, there was a hint of her hair falling out from under her white cornette. She stood and turned away from him. He watched as she took off the starched headpiece and her auburn hair fell down to her shoulders. Her hair gleamed in the sunlight streaming in the room. She smoothed out her illuminated hair and deftly twisted it into a knot that she locked in place with a clasp. She replaced her cornette and turned around to face him with a smile.

"There, all better."

When he looked into her eyes, he felt warmth and a familiarity within himself that he found exciting. She had shown her hair, which would have been natural had she not been a nun. Her actions roused a desire far greater than he had been feeling.

He shocked himself with his response to her. It undermined everything he stood for. Why had she shown her hair? What had he done? Had he encouraged her? It was one thing to have doubts about one's own vocation, but to play a role in undermining the vocation of a member of another religious order was scandalous. Then he remembered her imploring look. Was his response to her positive enough? He did not want to lose the special connection they shared. He became a jumble of nerves and worries.

***

The term ended and the seminarians from Collegio Leoniano returned to Anagni to resume their regular courses there. Generally, the seminarians were glad to get out of Rome for the summer and return to the countryside, though not Carlos. He was beside himself. For the first week back in Anagni, he lived day-to-day in a quiet panic, afraid that his days at the orphanage were over.

Gradually, the summer sun and the relaxing country breezes had a positive effect on Carlos. As the days came and went, he began to see himself the way he had been before he went to Rome at the end of last summer. His level of anxiety subsided. He had to become accustomed to not seeing Laurenza. He lowered his expectations.

He prayed for Sister Laurenza and for the orphans. He prayed he would see her again.

In the third week, his superiors asked him to drive other seminarians to Rome. He made the trip between Anagni and Rome frequently. He returned to the orphanage to be with her. God had answered his prayers.

***

One day, Sister Laurenza told Carlos she could like a man like him. Suddenly, the unspoken boundary between them was shattered. He was flattered to think she actually felt this way about him. The experience exposed him to a completely new world of sensitivities, for no one had ever loved him like this. Whenever Sister Laurenza was not in the room or the building, he anticipated the next time he would see her.

He told her he had never experienced what he was feeling for her. He corrected himself. "I never expected this for me."

"Why not?"

"I didn't think it was possible."

"It is, if we want it to be." She spoke softly, looking him in the eye.

"What about you? Are you willing to give up what you have now with your order?"

She told him she was alone in the world and being a nun did not change that. She wanted a partner with whom she could share her life. "You helped me realize I want recognition on a personal level. I want to feel something real that connects me with another person, not a group, or a religion. A real human being."

"I'm afraid I was not very helpful to you in the long run, in your vocation as a nun, I mean." He could have been talking about himself, about his own vocation as a priest.

"Of course, you're not."

Carlos detected anger.

"I think you're having trouble hearing me, Carlos." Her tone was patient. "I am having doubts about what to do with my life."

Neither of them spoke and the silence between them was unnatural. To ease the tension, she told him the Daughters of Charity made their oaths on an annual basis. It was normal for women to join one year, leave the next, and even return.

The annual oaths were a flexible approach that Carlos could not help but admire. If he had to get a job, he would have to improvise quickly. He did not know how to support a family, but nor did anyone else. If he could leave for a spell, he could test his ability to get a job, make money, and support a family. The most directly applicable topics of his studies would have been the financial services courses. He could get a job in a bank. He could buy and sell equities.

But family? The idea shocked him. He remembered Padre Pedro, who lived with Benedita, his housekeeper, like a married man who just so happened to be a priest. Or the dozen or so other priests he had encountered in Portugal while he worked on his project for two summers. "It could work in Portugal, where the priests in remote villages have wives and children."

Suddenly, a posting in a remote village was not such a bad idea.

He knew what he was doing. In the same way he had tempted fate by entertaining his weakness for the absurd, he was testing his oath of celibacy. He expected he had done this privately, to himself and for himself. He had not acted in an immoral way if he only imagined it. He had worried whether it was possible to sin in thought only. Was it a sin if he harmed no one? He had asked this of himself and he had searched his conscience. God would surely know whether he had sinned.

He told Sister Laurenza he did not know if he could do it.

She understood. It was a big decision. She pointed out they considered these very large matters when they hadn't even held hands, ever.

That evening, the children were in bed and the house was quiet. They went into the kitchen for a snack before he went home, as was their routine. As he was saying goodbye, he took her hand and looked into her eyes. She stepped closer and before he knew it, they were embracing.

Her firm body pressed tightly against his. He nearly brushed his face against hers; though they breathed the same air, there was no kissing. They just held each other.

Out of the corner of his eye, he saw movement. Was somebody there? The house had a solid limestone floor. Anyone could move up and down the corridor unheard.

Someone unknown to them had interrupted their quiet moment. That someone was likely another nun, but it did not matter to him.

"That was nice." Her words were silvery in his ear.

"You are lovely." His reply was breathy.

Then he left.

That was how they started.

***

He helped to put the kids to bed, and then they met in the kitchen for a glass of water before he would return to the Seminary.

Carlos expected a hug like the first one. A minute, perhaps. He held her in his arms and squeezed. She expelled a breath and reached around his shoulders. She leaned away.

He was not going to let her get away so soon. He placed his hands on her waist, pulled her in, and held her tightly.

They stumbled sideways into the pantry. He lifted her onto the table so their eyes and mouths were level. They kissed tentatively, then tenuously, tantalizingly, and totally—aroused by their closeness.

Not taking anything off, they explored each other with their hands. He pulled her legs open with insistent hands and pushed their clothing aside. She reached for him.

The green in her eyes was dark and her lips were soft.

Their first time was intense, yet they knew what to do. They could have controlled their feelings for one another; they did not restrain anything. It was wrong, and they knew it.

There was no giving, only taking. Carlos and Laurenza stole each other's heart. Nothing that was wrong about it mattered anymore. It just felt like the best and right thing to do. They could worry about the consequences later, tomorrow, whatever they may be. For now, they were in love.

11. Clerical Conceptions

The months went quickly by. Their studies demanded their attention, and playing games in the orphanage with the children diverted them. They fell into a lighthearted connection. The children naturally occupied much of their conversation, as did their schoolwork. They told each other how they came to be there. Carlos's experiences travelling in Portugal proved to be especially interesting to Laurenza, who hadn't gone anywhere before she came to Rome. And they rarely spoke of making a break from their vocations.

The tranquillity they had come to expect during that period of blissful denial changed when air raid alerts began to broadcast fear. British bombing now extended beyond the factories in the north of Italy, and no bombs had fallen on Rome, at least not yet.

That winter, the Sisters of the Daughters of Charity doubted the villa on Via Carlo Emanuele could safeguard the children. The Sisters of Maria Bambina, who lived in a separate wing of the Lateran seminary and operated the kitchen, invited the Daughters of Charity and the sixty orphans they cared for, to join them in their wing, starting in April.

And Carlos received a letter.

***

By Christmas 1940, Carlos and Laurenza were completing end-of-term papers and studying for exams. Each was facing a crush of schoolwork. He didn't ask her about her work, yet he was quick to tell her about his schedule that was especially difficult. He said it required his intense focus, and he enjoyed the challenge.

"I want to finish here. I worked hard and I won't throw it away."

Once the stress of school was out of the way, he would be ready to go away with Laurenza, if that was what they would decide. But they hadn't decided anything. He hadn't even discussed it with her. Such a conversation about the future did not seem important at the time. Their hands were already full.

He had received his plane ticket home, and with everything going on, he didn't know how to tell her.

Laurenza expressed frustration with moving the orphanage; it overwhelmed. Her task was to pack up and oversee the move of the kitchen, including the pantry where she and Carlos had spent precious moments together.

"I am looking forward to getting this done. There are only a few weeks before we finish school, and then we'll be free of this." The idea of their imminent emancipation cheered her.

"I have my plane ticket." Carlos blurted it without any prelude.

"Oh." Laurenza became quiet.

"The Cardinal didn't even ask me. He just sent it."

"When are you leaving?"

"Next week."

***

On the day of the move, Carlos took a break from his studies to help. With the men hired to do the moving, he assumed a hearty, hail-fellow-well-met joviality that pervaded his day. He cajoled the older children into doing their part. The little children engaged Sister Laurenza in one kerfuffle after another as they acted out their crankiness. He did notice that his cheeriness had no effect on her; if anything, it had an effect opposite to what he intended.

Finally, they had a moment alone. Taking pause, Carlos regarded Laurenza, who looked bloated and ready to collapse. "You look exhausted." He felt her tetchy mood; he dared not say anything more.

"What would you expect?" It was blunt.

"Here, sit down," he offered a chair.

"Now?"

Men carrying a table entered the room under the direction of a nun, who paid no heed to Sister Laurenza. There would be neither rest nor privacy that day.

"Perhaps we could go for a walk."

"Do you think I can take a break from this?" Green eyes flashed.

He attributed her irritation to stress, yet there was a sadness in her. The move had disturbed the fecund environment in which their relationship had flourished.

The closeness they shared in the old villa on Via Carlo Emanuele ended on that day. It did not just fizzle out. Something snapped. The next day, Carlos could not find Sister Laurenza anywhere and no one could tell him anything about her whereabouts. She was gone.

Carlos spoke to Paulo about it. "I haven't seen Sister Laurenza today. Nobody will tell me where she is. She wasn't well; I'm worried."

***

The letter Carlos received contained news. The Holy See had appreciated his initiative as a seminarian in gathering and reporting the mood of congregations across Portugal. In particular, Carlos's theme of the "lingering effects of the Fatima miracle" had met with approval.

The letter was from Cardinal Cerejeira, himself.

"The new Holy Father encouraged me to build a ministry to continue this work. I need you to take charge of it. Besides, there's a war on and Rome is not a good place to be," wrote Cerejeira. "I need you back home, Father Carlos."

The Cardinal had anticipated Carlos's completion of the program in April and advised him of arrangements for his return travel to Lisbon. His airplane ticket would arrive in early March. He instructed Carlos to wrap up his papers, say his goodbyes, and return to Lisbon on that plane.

***

Everything was happening in slow motion. Carlos had put off talking about his departure. He didn't know how he and Laurenza would manage next steps. Now she was gone. There would be no discussion.

Her disappearance left him reeling. He enquired with the sisters. Their policy required them to protect the privacy of their members at all times. "Did anything happen to Sister Laurenza? Was she okay?" They would not confirm anything. There were too many unknowns.

All he had to go on was speculation. So Carlos made assumptions. Either she was sick, or she was upset and disappointed with him, and she fled. She didn't die.

Carlos told Paulo that he hadn't seen Laurenza since moving day. He did not let on about the extent of his relationship with her, which was a private matter between himself and Laurenza and no one else. Nor did he say anything about leaving the priesthood after graduation.

"My Superior in Lisbon made travel arrangements, and my departure is in two days. Paulo, I must go."

"Yes, I remember you telling me, but it got lost in the commotion. I'm sorry." Paulo appeared upset with Carlos's news. "How can I help?"

"If you could, keep an eye out for Laurenza. I think she needs help."

***

That night, Carlos lay awake, going over the events of moving day at the orphanage. Laurenza was upset and angry. Was she angry with him? He paced his small room. Why had she left without saying goodbye? Why hadn't she said anything? He collapsed on the bed and slept fitfully. He woke with burning eyes.

Carlos had an intense longing for Laurenza.

He proceeded with morning prayers. He asked God to forgive him and his sins of the flesh. He held his life together; yet, he had mixed feelings about everything he had known and ever done with Laurenza.

If she did not want anything to do with him, fine.

He would dwell only on appropriate and respectful images. Whenever he thought of Laurenza, he would substitute her image with a more appropriate one, such as Mary, the Mother of Jesus.

This was his last day. There was still so much to do. A list of wishes flashed across his eyes, an overwhelming choice. He panicked. His thoughts turned to Laurenza. In keeping with his yet fresh resolve, he substituted an image of Mary.

He would not let Laurenza remain a temptation for him. Like Padre Pedro, he lifted his face to the sun and laughed. He let his stress go. He laughed deeply at himself and his world. He accepted this peace with his life. He recommitted himself to his patron, the Cardinal.

***

Once in Lisbon, he reported directly to Cardinal Cerejeira.

Looking up over his reading glasses and seeing Carlos, Cerejeira stood to greet him. "Welcome back, Carlos." He shook his hand.

Carlos noted there was no kissing the ring this time. "Thank you, your Eminence. It's good to be back."

"I was concerned . . . your mentor had recommended pulling you out before anything could happen."

"What do you mean, your Grace, before anything could happen?"

Cerejeira looked over his glasses. "He didn't want to lose you to an orphanage."

"Excuse me?"

Mention of the orphanage in Italy caught Carlos off guard. He didn't expect this now, among the first words from his patron.

"I am surprised you knew about the orphanage." Carlos mused in a non-threatening manner. He hoped the Cardinal did not know about Sister Laurenza.

"Padre Meszaros was diligent with his reports."

"Reports, your Grace?"

Carlos never spoke of the orphanage to his superiors.

"In any case, I'm glad to see you made it out safely."

Carlos looked at him, puzzled.

"With Italy entering the war, you were potentially in a war zone."

"The air raid sirens did sound but otherwise, there was no indication the war would reach us in Rome, your Grace."

"Wars have a way of progressing in unpredictable ways."

"That is true. The Black Shirts were nasty with the clergy, sir."

"Your time in Rome has served you well, Monseñhor. Now I expect your knowledge of Canon law and the ways of Rome will serve us well."

Carlos was comfortable with this quid pro quo exchange: his education in Rome, for a lifetime of legal services in Portugal. "They will, my Patron."

This was more in line with what he had expected.

***

How did the Cardinal know about the orphanage? The first time Carlos had embraced Laurenza, he had seen a shadow. Was someone watching him in the orphanage even then?

Such thoughts annoyed Carlos after Laurenza went missing.

There were few channels of information, and if they did not go directly to the Cardinal, which was unlikely, they had to have gone through the Seminary.

Padre Meszaros, his spiritual mentor.

So Carlos paid Padre Meszaros a visit.

Padre Meszaros was happy to see him. "We got you out just in time. Italy is under attack." He spoke to Carlos as if he was an old friend.

Carlos was not in the mood to make small talk or pretend he wasn't upset. "I understand you were aware of my friend, Sister Laurenza." He looked Padre Meszaros in the eye, showing he wasn't cowering in fear.

"Sister Laurenza may not have been so lucky."

Carlos envisioned Sister Laurenza; she was vibrant, adorable. "I had the feeling she fled to her home town."

Padre Meszaros sighed. "I can only wish it were so. In any case, her involvement with you was unacceptable."

Irked that his mentor would judge him, Carlos challenged him. "You told me you had girlfriends, even after entering the seminary."

"Ah, yes, that's true. I had girlfriends. I wouldn't have been concerned if you had girlfriends, too." He placed emphasis on the plural.

Carlos frowned. Suddenly, he didn't know the man.

"It's when you have only one is the time to worry."

Carlos dismissed this explanation. "It was a personal matter! Your intervention prevented me from resolving the situation on my own." In anger, Carlos paced.

"What happened to Sister Laurenza was tragic," his mentor offered.

"Tragic? What do you mean?"

"My contact reported that she disappeared," said Padre Meszaros. "They believed she either fled the city or was killed."

Laurenza was dead. The room suddenly lacked air. Carlos sat, his eyes cast into the recesses of memories from his last hectic days in Rome. Why was she unable to meet him? Was she under orders to stay away? Or was she really killed?

"How did she die? An air raid? Where?" Carlos had to know.

Padre Meszaros wouldn't respond.

Still Carlos peppered him with questions. "Where did it happen? On the street near the seminary?" He was thinking of the Black Shirt that picked on Paulo—Leo, the bully, with whom he had fought.

"I don't know, they couldn't say."

"Who? How do you know this?" Carlos pressured him.

"My usual contacts," Padre Meszaros admitted.

"If Sister Laurenza is, in fact, dead, which I don't believe, then her superiors are responsible for putting her into danger. And you! You meddled in our lives."

"You blame your superiors? Consider your own hand in this."

A steely calm had fallen over Carlos. If Laurenza was dead, then nothing mattered. He would not debate this. He needed to get away. Without another word, he left the room.

"We saved you from disgrace and ruin." Padre Meszaros shouted to him as he walked down the corridor.

***

A week later, the Cardinal promoted Carlos to Episcopal Vicar.

Carlos had not expected this. In a flash, he expressed his concern. "But I haven't done anything, Your Grace."

"Carlos, you were the first Portuguese to complete the program for leadership at the Pope's college. I have plans for you to take charge of a few things, Monseñhor. I want our people to know that when you are talking to them it will be as if they were speaking with me."

The Cardinal was the first to use the new title that would become official in a ceremony in Cerejeira's cathedral in Lisbon.

***

The Bishop of Lisbon normally did not celebrate the appointment of an Episcopal Vicar. For Carlos Silva, Cerejeira made an exception. He gathered his senior clergy for a grand ceremony in Santa Maria Maior, the Patriarch's cathedral known as the Sé. They packed the ancient cathedral with the fortress-type towers.

In the vestibule before the procession commenced, the thurifer lit the charcoal. On the Cardinal's signal, he spooned frankincense and myrrh into the thurible, replaced the cover, and managed the long chains to swing it gently and disperse the incense as he walked.

The cathedral erupted in song—a canticle like the ones Carlos heard in Rome at St. Peter's. The procession began. After the cross bearer, the thurifer led the line of celebrants to scent their path down the side aisle, around the back, and up the centre aisle through the congregation.

Carlos was thrilled, yet alarmed. He recognized some priests from his travels along with the Rector of the Seminário dos Olivais, and his mentor, Padre Meszaros. It was daunting to see so many elderly faces, while he, the Episcopal-Vicar-to-be was so comparatively young. How did they feel about his appointment?

What made him so worthy?

He allayed his concerns by focusing on the proceedings as if he were attending like everyone else. He paid attention to the Cardinal who addressed the attendees directly.

"If this historic cathedral is the heart of the Catholic Church in Portugal, then you are its soul," the Cardinal told them. He praised the clergy for their continued "veneration" and "dedication" to their Holy tasks.

"I have learned that our Concordat with the Estado Novo is more important to our mission than I understood was possible," Cerejeira said.

The Concordat was the agreement Cerejeira had made with his long-time friend, António de Oliveira Salazar, Prime Minister of the Estado Novo, the New State, as they called the fascist government that replaced the short-lived democratic republic that had ended centuries of monarchial rule. On their pulpits, priests had been challenging and undermining the authority of ministers in Salazar's government. The parties bickered, back and forth, in public.

"When Prime Minister Salazar agreed to fund our schools, I knew it would be good for us because the education of children is necessary if we are to save their souls from the temptations of Satan.

"We do not preach politics. We do not take sides. We do not quarrel with the state. Our job is to attend to the spiritual needs of families.

"We administer the rites of Baptism, Holy Communion, Confession, Confirmation, Marriage, the Last Rites of Extreme Unction, Death, and Burial. We bring people into the light and love of our Lord and Saviour, Jesus Christ.

"Our role is clear. We fulfil the spiritual needs of families. Which brings me to my second topic—Fatima.

"The Holy Father, Pope Pius XII, encourages us to share with our parishioners the miracles and messages of Our Lady of Fatima to the children. We do this daily.

"Let us rally around the words of the Bishop of Leiria, Dom José Alves Correia da Silva," Cerejeira nodded respectfully to the bishop seated with his peers at the front of the congregation. "Bishop Silva proclaimed that the visions of Our Lady of Fatima were true. I quote, 'the visions of the children in the Cova da Iria are worthy of belief.'

"In this spirit, I encourage you to share the messages of Our Lady of Fatima with families across Portugal. Show them God's love, in the name of the Father, the Son, and the Holy Spirit." Cerejeira traced the sign of the cross in the air, conveying his blessing on his clergy.

The sweet voices of choir boys responded, soaring high above the rumblings of the "Amen" that echoed among the massive pillars, up to the plain, unadorned barrel vaulting high above the nave. Sweet sopranos cried out, clear across the city. And the depth of the male congregation joined in, every rank, every sonorous depth, and every resonant note lifted their conjoined spirit above the aisles, the ambulatory, and the upper triforium. All members of this congregation experienced this psalm, and on this occasion, they chanted the *Magnificat* like a force majeure to overcome all evil in the world. The cathedral burst with canticle after canticle and what the basilica could not hold spilled out onto the adjoining hillside.

The Cardinal shifted focus to his new Episcopal Vicar. The Cardinal moved into the centre of the sanctuary and his bishops flanked him. Each gripped his crozier and looked resplendent in his vestments and his tall, pointed mitre upon his head.

Carlos was humbled when the bishops encircled him for the blessing of his vestments. With each piece, the bishops took turns to say the prayer associated with that vestment. They replaced his black cassock with a purple one. They added a white cotton amice over his shoulders and a long, cotton alb over the purple cassock. Around his waist, they tied a purple cincture. Then each bishop anointed a part of him with oil, from his neck and hands to his feet. The Cardinal anointed him last, smearing the fragrant oil on his forehead and cheeks.

Cerejeira placed around Carlos's neck a long, red stole that fell the length of his torso in the front. Then the Cardinal hefted a red chasuble over his head.

Reacting to the bulk of the vestments, Carlos straightened his shoulders, causing Cerejeira to smile. "Yes, it is a heavy burden." Cerejeira spoke in a low tone that only Carlos could hear. "Over time, you will become accustomed to your role, but don't let it weigh you down and don't ever dismiss it lightly."

"Obrigado, your Eminence."

One last time, Cerejeira spooned frankincense and myrrh into the thurible, replaced the cover, and then swung it in the air as he walked around Carlos, stopping to wave the burning incense to the congregation on both sides of the cathedral. Then, Cerejeira handed off the thurible to an acolyte.

The Cardinal had succeeded in his objective. He had placed great and holy expectations upon the shoulders of Monseñhor Carlos. Cerejeira signalled to his co-celebrants to gather.

The cathedral again erupted in song. The recession retraced its steps down the centre aisle through the congregation, around the back, and up the side aisle into the vestibule.

The celebration was over, yet the choir sang several more psalms as the congregants poured out onto the narrow sidewalks of the Alfama.

Carlos advanced with a rock-solid bearing of dignity.

12. Monseñhor on a Mission

It was already eight o'clock in the evening when one of the Cardinal's drivers knocked on the Monseñhor's door, Number 22, of the Nova Pensão Camões, a boarding house that fronted onto Praça Luis de Camões.

"Ah, it's you." Carlos was surprised to see Maria João this late.

"The Cardinal asked me to bring you in."

"Sounds urgent." Carlos had wondered when the Cardinal would engage him in something important. For months, his role had been pastoral, saying Mass in the Sé, visiting local parishes, and assisting the Cardinal with his ceremonial duties by standing in his place. They were roles any priest could have filled. Certainly, he loved performing such duties. But the Cardinal was not utilizing his expertise in Ecumenical law or any law for that matter.

"He asks you to bring what you need for about four days. I do not know what for, Monseñhor. He told me to pack a bag, too."

"Looks like we are going for a car ride." He was in need of such an adventure.

"We are, Padre."

In ten minutes, Carlos emerged. Maria João put his suitcase in the back seat. Carlos handed over his wooden staff, the beautiful and unusual one given to him by the elder Brother who taught him how to drive. Maria João put it in the back with its length jutting between the two front seats. Carlos tossed his hat from Benedita and Pedro on the back seat.

It would be a short drive to the Cardinal's palaceta.

Maria João gave Carlos the kind of ride he enjoyed. He pressed down on the gas pedal and kept it there as long as he could. They sped north on Misericórdia to Jardim Príncipe Real where they turned right and zigzagged down the hill and crossed the Avenida da Liberdade at Rua das Pretas. Carlos had to grab onto the handle above the side window, the "Holy Shit" handle, as he called it. On the other side of the wide Avenida, Maria João wended back up that hill on side streets and barreled up to the park where he turned right again and was at the

Cardinal's palaceta on Campo Mártires de Patria.

"Thirteen minutes, Monseñhor."

"You're good, Maria João."

"It's this car." It was a 1939 Alfa Romeo Berlinetta. "So fast."

Carlos entered and the housekeeper nodded to indicate he should go in. Cardinal Cerejeira greeted him with a nod of his pen.

"Take a seat." He motioned to the chair in front of his desk.

These people were tired. They had been working all day and no longer had the energy to put into niceties.

Cardinal Cerejeira looked at Carlos. "Are you ready to conduct some business for me?" This was not a question, but an introduction. "With the war, wolfram has become a precious commodity. The Nazis need it to strengthen steel. As you know, Portugal has significant reserves."

"No, your Grace. I wasn't aware of wolfram."

"Alright then, we have some work to do."

Carlos straightened his back in the chair. This was what he had been waiting for, his call-to-arms. Whatever Cerejeira said, he would deliver.

"For now, let me say a few things," Cerejeira began, as if he were writing it down, collecting his ideas. "One. As we know, wolfram is a natural resource that Portugal is blessed to possess in considerable magnitude." Cerejeira gave Carlos a moment to let that sink in.

"Two. This is an opportunity for us to capitalize on Portuguese resources, for the benefit of the Church and Portuguese people. It makes sense."

This was true.

The opportunity was there for anyone to capitalize on, but the war had distracted everyone and few were even aware of it as Cerejeira was. His friend, Salazar, who controlled the trading of wolfram at the highest level, had commented on it. "The smart money would stake a position now," Salazar had said. "The demand is there."

"Three. You must learn the business issues around wolfram. Once we have mines, how are you going to get them producing and how are you going to sell their output? Think about these next steps. Watch for ways and opportunities."

Cerejeira told Carlos he could hire consultants to recommend strategies and oversee projects; the consultants will hire the managers; and the managers will hire the labour. Let them each take an appropriate share of the earnings, he said.

"These are the main items you need to know. Over time, you can fill in the gaps. Get information. Do what you can. Ask people for help. Let's work together."

That alone was a great incentive. The Cardinal was smart and connected. Carlos could learn a lot from him.

"There is some interest from Rome. I need you to initiate and lead a project, and take it to fulfilment. Can you do this, Monseñhor?"

"Yes, your Grace."

The Cardinal delegated all the details to him. Carlos would have to learn fast to make this happen.

"Good, let's start with the first step in your assignment. Carlos, do you think you could find some wolfram mines we might purchase?" Again, it was not a question.

"In the north, your Grace?"

"Yes."

"I would need to do some research, your Grace." Carlos didn't know how he would find wolfram mines, but he would find a way.

"My cousin's husband in Trás-os-Montes would be a good person to start with. He will know someone who owns a wolfram mine." Cerejeira wrote down the contact information. "Go there and meet him. I'll let him know you're coming."

"Yes, your Grace."

"But don't tell him what you want. Find a way to make it sound as if this is for someone you know in Lisbon."

"But what shall I tell him my business is for going there?"

"You will think of something—give them more Fatima."

The Cardinal had sprung this on him at the last minute but Carlos was confident he could manage the challenge. The Cardinal's decision to invest in wolfram was not a typical religious activity, which in the beginning didn't bother Carlos. He expected some commercial activities. Nor did the politics of war and commerce pose any issues to Carlos. He was more concerned about his own performance, not the value of the decisions taken by his superior.

So Carlos accepted his assignment graciously, believing it was the kind of work a young lawyer-priest trained in the Vatican ought to perform on behalf of the Holy Mother Church.

The Cardinal talked about the benefit his work would bring the Church. It would take great sacrifice, including time away from home.

"My source confirmed an opportunity exists and timing is critical. This is why you must go now. A car and a driver are here for you, waiting outside. Listen, about the car—my friend tells me this Berlinetta projects the wrong image for a Cardinal. Perhaps it would be more appropriate in your employ; so let's think of it as yours now."

At the start of the day, the idea of owning a car was the furthest thing from his mind. He had no interest in owning things. Yet the automobile appealed to him. He had enjoyed his driving experiences during his studies in the seminary in Lisbon. He looked forward to driving the Berlinetta himself, which he would do soon enough.

Carlos left the Cardinal's palaceta. Maria João opened the passenger door of the Berlinetta and Carlos slipped into the back. This was going to be an overnight journey and he needed to rest as much as possible.

The headlights of the Berlinetta threw tall shadows on the buildings along the narrow streets as the car sped out of the old city.

With admiration, Maria João called this vehicle a real Italian beauty. For Carlos, the term conjured another image: Laurenza. He saw the freckles on her face, the whiteness of her teeth, and the striations of green that made her eyes so remarkable.

Sprawled in the back seat of the long, black Berlinetta—his Berlinetta—Carlos was on his way to the village of Sonim that was little more than twenty-five kilometres from the northern border with Spain and about four hundred and sixty kilometres from Lisbon. It was late October, the season when a trip to the north of Portugal would have been a delightful parade of colours in a golden light if the sky had not been overcast and he had been travelling in the day. But he wasn't. It was a dark night and there was nothing to see.

It was just as well. He needed a rest. The unplanned, late evening meeting with the Cardinal had confirmed his thinking. The Cardinal needed him, a belief that reassured any concerns he had about being useful and serving the Cardinal well. He had never envisaged himself in such a role. What did he know about mining? Absolutely nothing.

Carlos remained dressed in the long, black cassock he wore for the meeting. He should have changed. As he had learned on his previous travels across Portugal, a bulky cassock was not the sort of garment you want to wear on a long journey in the car. But at least it was keeping him warm. With the steady hum of the engine and the noise of the tires on the road, Lisbon fell farther and farther behind. Carlos drifted off to sleep after Coimbra, which wasn't even half-way. Finally, he fell asleep.

In his dreams, his Italian beauty delivered him smoothly all the way past Vila Real before he awoke with a start.

"Where are we?"

"Valpaços, Monseñhor."

Carlos knew exactly where they were. Valpaços was the last town before heading northeast to Sonim, his destination.

He had slept longer than he thought he would.

Carlos returned to resting his head back and released a sigh of acceptance. The nature of his work and the challenges he faced were new territories for him. He never thought he'd be undertaking any task relating to mining apart from blessing the miners, their children's marriages, baptizing their babies, and burying their dead. On the surface, it might seem odd for the Church to be in this business. However, it made sense to him. The Church could not take in enough money from the collection plate to pay for its needs, was the way Cardinal Cerejeira expressed it to him. If there was money to earn in a profitable venture, why shouldn't they get in on it too?

***

Cardinal Cerejeira closed the door behind Carlos and returned to the sitting room in his inner chamber. "Let's see how that turns out for us."

Waiting for him was his friend, António Salazar, the prime minister.

"Your choice of candidates is excellent." António sat in a big, stuffed chair. Next to him on the side table was a tall vase full of long-stemmed roses. Pole lamps at each end of an ornate, striped chaise directed reading light onto the lap of anyone who sat there. "If an issue were to arise from this venture, his connection to the Vatican will distract everyone sufficiently and minimize any damage to Lisbon."

António and Manuel had been close friends since their days as students at the University of Coimbra.

"Things have gone well for us, António. We have our agreement."

Manuel was referring to their Concordat in which they had agreed the state would support Catholic education, and the Church would stay out of local politics. It was necessary to end the constant bickering that had paralyzed the Church.

"It was pure pragmatism on your part and I agree it is working."

Manuel rightfully gave António credit for the solution. For Manuel, the Concordat protected the clergy from further persecution. Plus, in exchange for funding primary education, António had obtained a gag order on the clergy.

"Yes, we do, and there are no inappropriate skeletons in our cellars," said António. "In fact, there are none at all."

The Bishop of Lisbon laughed. This was their own private joke about the cathedral, which locals called the Sé. The initials S.E. stood for *Sedes Episcopalis*, which means the seat of the bishop.

While every other cathedral in Christendom had a sarcophagus in the basement, the Lisbon Cathedral didn't have any basement at all. Christian Crusaders built the cathedral in the 12th century on the site of a mosque they had destroyed.

"Manuel, you are concerned about the remodelling of your Cathedral but, you know, our concerns here are cerebral. Your architectural vision is not a threat to the new cultural order. It is a wonderful example of the Catholic revival—the regeneration of the Catholic faith through the miracle of Fatima, which I'm sure you love to remind your faithful, occurred only 22 years ago."

"Yes, yes, we do have our Fatima, Prime Minister—a stroke of genius on your part."

"To both our benefits, Cardinal. I cannot tell you how useful it is to have God on our side against the Bolsheviks. I also have the agreement with Spain, so there should be no more fighting or bickering on the Iberian Peninsula as long as I live."

The Iberian Pact, signed by Portugal and Spain only a few days before the end of the Spanish war the previous March, helped to strengthen Salazar's friendship with Franco, the Spanish Head of State. Salazar provided General Franco and his fascist Nationalists with access to a seaport during the early part of his war when they were landlocked. Just as important, their pact had thus far kept Hitler out of the Iberian Peninsula.

"Then you should be happy, António. You gave Franco the courage to say no to Hitler."

"I am, Manuel, I am very happy. Now I must convince Churchill our neutrality is necessary."

"Why? Our affairs have typically aligned with the British."

"I have no intention of changing that. I just don't want to declare it."

"Would that not strengthen our position and bolster our security?"

Manuel already knew the answer from previous discussions. He asked because he enjoyed giving his friend an opportunity to discuss the ideas that he could not share with anyone else.

"Maybe so, but it could compel Hitler to attack immediately. He needs our wolfram. It would open another front for our allies in London who have their hands full enough already."

As Prime Minister, António was in direct discussions with Churchill. Their senior staff communicated regularly.

Manuel pieced together this logic. "So you go on letting Hitler's operatives buy our wolfram. We get Hitler's gold and Churchill can bomb Hitler's factories—to hell, I would add."

António nodded. "It seems the best option for us."

"Our affairs here in Lisbon are incomprehensible to anyone but ourselves." Manuel was fond of repeating ideas António had often expressed. It was one of the standing tenets of their dialogue.

***

Midmorning, the Berlinetta rounded the fountain in the square at the centre of Sonim and proceeded straight to the manor where it stopped under the portico. Carlos spotted a wild-looking, barefoot boy in breeches and a well-worn blouse that was common for men in these parts. The boy looked like a rough kid, not unlike the bullies he had encountered in the orphanage. He disembarked, stretched, and disappeared into the manor where Inez, the housekeeper, greeted him by name and introduced herself. Before she could lead him into the Señhor's study, the Baron emerged to greet the Monseñhor.

"Monseñhor, welcome. Your visit is most welcome. You give us a great honour."

Montalvão was short with straight, slicked-back white hair with streaks of black that stubbornly held on to their youthful hue. At forty-seven, he was over-large in the middle and moved ponderously to preserve his breath. There were bags under his eyes.

"Señhor Baron de Montalvão." Carlos addressed his host with the same level of formality and respect. "Your cousin, the Cardinal, sends his greetings and I thank you for having me as your guest."

The men shook hands amiably and after an appropriate exchange of small talk, Montalvão rang for Inez to show the Monseñhor to his room.

The Señhor gestured with his open palm to the inner hallway.

Inez led the Monseñhor down a short corridor, turned right and another quick right, then up a flight of stairs and along another hallway. She opened the first door on the left and stepped aside for him to enter. "If you need anything, please let me know."

"Yes, may I bother you for some coffee?"

"Yes, of course, Monseñhor." She closed the door behind her.

He removed his shoes and looked around. From his second-floor room, he looked out over the fields. Far in the distance, he could see the edge of the forests.

He lay on the bed and stared at the midmorning light streaming in. "I will rest for a few minutes." He dozed off in seconds.

**

An hour later, Carlos emerged from his room wearing a plain black suit and shirt, with his white collar neatly visible. The light from the overcast sky played tricks on him. He felt he had slept through the night.

"I made fresh coffee for you, Monseñhor. I'll bring it with us."

Inez poured him a cup then led him through a wide salon and outside to a patio where the Baron sat in the shade of an enormous fig tree, reading a newspaper.

She placed his coffee in front of the Monseñhor.

"Many thanks, Inez."

"Your driver shared this." Montalvão showed Carlos the *Diário de Notícias*, a newspaper from Lisbon. "We don't get regular news here."

Carlos recognized the Arc de Triumph and the column of Nazi soldiers and tanks. The photo was from the previous year. "France remains on everyone's minds. The talk is all about who will be invaded next," said Carlos. He drank his espresso in one draft.

"Ah not to worry. Thanks to our Prime Minister, we are neutral." The Baron poured the Monseñhor a glass of red wine from a clay pitcher. The wine had been ready on the table, breathing. "And we have our neighbour's support." He referenced the Iberian Pact with Spain.

"We have." Carlos nodded. "Salazar's foreign policy works well."

Montalvão was interested in this topic. He had been waiting politely until the Monseñhor joined him. Then he began drinking the wine without him. He was now at the stage where he wanted to drink more than just a few sips. He immediately picked up his glass of wine, signalling his desire to toast. "To your health, Monseñhor."

"And to yours, Baron."

Carlos took a mouthful of wine so the flavour could saturate his taste buds. "Is this your own wine? It's excellent."

"Yes, it is, thank you. My foreman is good with the grapes." Montalvão swirled his glass as he spoke. "This one is seven years old."

Upon the completion of the toast, Tereza, the cook, came onto the terrace with a pot of hot soup. "Boa tarde, Señhors," Good afternoon, gentlemen. "I made for you a bean and cabbage soup."

"Thank you, Tereza." He returned his attention to his guest. "But you didn't come here to talk about the war in France." Montalvão smoothly picked up the thread of the conversation that interested him most.

"In part, I did, I suppose. You see, I have an acquaintance in Lisbon who believes the war will increase demand for wolfram."

"Your friend knows a lot about this business, Monseñhor."

"I am sure what he knows pales in comparison to your knowledge of the matter, Baron." The cultivated land stretching out beyond the manor implied a degree of wealth and influence Carlos had anticipated.

"Sometimes it doesn't seem possible Trás-os-Montes is at the centre of anything, but we are indeed at the centre of the wolfram universe." He paused to sip his wine. "My villagers collect rocks with wolfram to sell to Germans. They collect what is visible on the surface."

"Oh, interesting."

"Yes, there seems to be as much rock here on the surface as anywhere around the region and they say it is just the tip of the iceberg." Montalvão paused again. "Why, are you interested?"

"The fellow I mentioned is willing to pay well for information leading to the establishment of a wolfram mine."

"There are a number of mines already. Within thirty minutes away."

"Oh, good. My friend wants to buy one—more than one, if he can."

"You came here to do this?"

"No, no. I came for another reason." A white pallor hung on his words. "In mentioning this I am only doing my acquaintance a favour –"

"He is willing to pay well, you say?"

"I assure you, Baron, yes. But the real reason I came here is to feature your village in a newspaper article about Fatima." Carlos surprised himself by suggesting the idea, which he previously thought of but dismissed because it seemed far-fetched.

"You do?"

"Yes. The Cardinal suggested your village might be a good candidate and I wanted to see it for myself. If it's okay, I'll come back with a journalist who can write about it and take some pictures."

"Why would you want to do that?"

"There is great interest across Portugal and beyond in how the Fatima miracles can impact our people. Even the Pope wants more."

Montalvão's eyebrows scrunched together and his head tilted.

"What with Fatima, the wind storm off the Atlantic last winter and the Fatima Storm two years before that—did you see that?"

Carlos was referring to the unusually vivid Aurora Borealis that had appeared two years earlier. Solar energy disrupted communications around the globe. Catholics saw it as a sign that God was about to punish the world, as predicted by the Virgin Mary to the children at Fatima. Last year, war erupted and engulfed Western Europe, proving a second prediction.

"Women and men were crying in the streets," the Baron contributed. "They didn't know whether to be happy or sad. It was a confusing time."

"Perfect. I will include these miraculous events for your village." Carlos sat back in the chair and laughed, a modest belly laugh, and smiled at Montalvão. "We will create some excitement in this village that people will remember, no?"

"I suppose." The Baron was not the sort who welcomed excitement in his village.

"When would be a good time to do this?"

"The Festival of Nosso Señhor do Bonfim would be a good time."

Tereza served them flank steaks smothered in onions with a tomato and rice pilaff on the side.

"Tell me more about your friend," Montalvão spoke between mouthfuls, "the one who wants wolfram. What does he want exactly?"

The planted seed had taken hold and Montalvão wouldn't let it go.

"Oh, him. He will pay handsomely is all I know."

"For what exactly?"

Carlos picked up his glass of wine. "He will pay for information about which mines to buy and who owns them."

"That's all?"

"We will need a report with estimates of how much wolfram is in the ground and a recommendation of how much to pay for the mines."

"A package, then."

"Yes, a proposal. My friend needs to know the right people who can make a deal. You are a businessman, Baron. You understand how important it is to get good information before making a decision or else you wouldn't be making money off your land."

"You are right about that, Monseñhor. Here in Sonim, I have grapes and wheat, and I have other properties further south with olives and cork. They keep me busy."

Carlos knew little about the cork industry. As a boy, he saw workers strip the bark off trees. The cork industry was a good fit with the nation's wine industry. "And now you want to get into mining?"

"Monseñhor, I already have an interest in a mining property."

Montalvão wiped the corners of his mouth with a serviette.

"You own a share in a mine. I am impressed."

"About your friend, I think I can help him. I know a mining engineer who can provide a report such as you described."

The Baron knew Trás-os-Montes very well, along with all the people who mattered.

"Can he start on it now? Then my friend can expect a report."

"It should not be a problem."

"Good. Please keep this between you and me. I don't want my name connected to a business transaction in any way."

"I understand. You have my word." Having this new business opportunity fall into his lap was good for the Baron. He made a mental note to thank his cousin, the Cardinal.

Montalvão and Carlos shook hands to seal their arrangement.

The house was cool when Carlos stepped inside from the terrace. Inez greeted him. "The village priest heard you were here."

Carlos smiled and nodded, "That would be perfect. Thank you."

Inez led him through the salon to the front foyer. Off to one side opposite the Señhor's study, the salon was ideal for receiving guests.

"Good afternoon, Padre." Carlos held out his hand.

"I am Fernando, at your service." Padre Fernando tried to kiss the Monseñhor's hand.

Carlos stopped that nonsense and shook his hand. "Padre Fernando, good to meet you. Thank you for seeking me out."

"I would like to give you a tour of the village. The people would be happy to meet you."

Carlos had a full understanding of what this would entail—an afternoon of exchanging pleasantries. "Padre, I would be delighted if you would show me the village today."

Carlos took a minute to change back into his black cassock. He added a purple sash around his waist and a pectoral cross and chain around his neck. With his Iberian horse hat, Carlos presented villagers with an image of a notable cleric. At the school, children froze in awe of this important priest. He paused at the village fountain and the café in front of Bartolo's Padaria before walking the hill to the capela. Word of a visitor from the Vatican had spread. Many people wanted his blessing, which he gave willingly and with a congenial spirit. It made him feel important.

The people, in turn, were impressed. The Monseñhor had come from the Vatican, and worked with the Cardinal in Lisbon. The Pope himself asked him to come to Trás-os-Montes.

In late afternoon, Carlos excused himself from the square. Inez arranged for him to have a light dinner in the dining room off the kitchen, where he chatted with Maria João and the staff as each one dropped in for their dinner. Carlos met the foreman, Zé; he had already met Tereza and Inez who had served him, and Xisco, the young ruffian he had seen earlier.

First thing in the morning, he bid goodbye to Montalvão and his staff. His car was waiting. Maria João was sitting in the shade and the stable boy was polishing the headlamps.

"Monseñhor, you have a splendid automobile." The boy spoke with him politely. "It is the sign of an accomplished man." Xisco looked ruefully at the long curve of the fenders over the wheels.

"Xisco, I didn't catch your last name."

"Ribeiro, Monseñhor. I am Francisco Ribeiro."

"I look forward to seeing you again, soon, Francisco Ribeiro." Carlos got in the car. He waved to Xisco as they pulled away.

***

Montalvão summoned Zé. "Bring me the Polish mining engineer."

Part Two, 1942

Lisbon

13. Tartarugas, Santa Cruz

As they approached the coast, Carlos rolled open his window so he could savour the seaside air. At the town square, Maria João pulled over. Carlos took off his shoes and socks and placed them on the floor behind his seat. Fortunately, he wasn't wearing his cassock, just his white collar under a black shirt. He took out his walking staff, his jacket, and his hat, glad for the chinstrap; it was breezy.

Carlos waved goodbye and walked down the path that zigzagged across the steep slope to the beach. He loved to see the cliffs that rose above the beach in a magnificent corrugation of ochre, sand, and putty-coloured rock as if God made the layers of sediment to stand upright like pillars to mark this site in a glorious way; and life had wrinkled them.

He walked barefoot, allowing the sea to splash his rolled pants. He carried his crozier from the old blacksmith. It was November, and chillier than usual. His feet were freezing. He did not care. He felt a presence there and he did not feel alone. He liked to believe his parents died at sea, somewhere beyond these cliffs and beaches.

The wind bounced off the water and battered his ears, threatening to throw his hat off into the rocks, but Carlos pulled the cord tighter and pushed on, his head tilted into the wind.

Carlos would purchase properties and conduct confidential business activities that a commercial or corporate lawyer would do.

The wind tossed the salty spray in his face, stinging his eyes. He licked his lips and smiled with the pleasure of these familiar sensations.

His job was to take advantage of the situation for the benefit of the Holy Mother Church. Cardinal Cerejeira had been clear about this.

Above the sand, the surf, and the thunderous booming of water against the rocks, the great cliff stood like a bastion of hope against the incessant Atlantic—an image he had invented in his youth. He concocted himself as the mountain. The ocean, the surf and the wind—in every kind of nasty weather configuration—was God. What God threw at the mountain was a test of his character, his faith, and his ambition.

Now, issues of propriety dogged him along with challenges to his vocation that were greater than he had expected to encounter throughout his lifetime. His sense of what was good and right to do had become less clear. As a youth, he saw black and white. Now, there was a lot of grey where he had smudged the lines.

The life he left behind in Rome was one such challenge. He drifted willfully into his memories of Laurenza that he had sealed off like a treasure trove for moments exactly like this, when he needed a mental lift. He wanted to feel them, relive them. He dwelled on the imaginary life he might have had with Laurenza, if she had not fled. He didn't have any reason to suspect there had been any foul play or that she had been killed. Maybe she had just run away from the situation.

He focused his attention on the surges that washed his feet, refreshed his conscience, and swept the temporary presence of his footsteps away before rushing back into the sea. He walked on in this thoughtful ruckus, mindful of nothing but the brevity of his own existence.

A woman equally engaged in the soapy signals the surf was sending to her, trudged—like Carlos with her head down—in his direction. As their paths met, they nearly bumped into each other. Each looked up startled in the same instant, disoriented. Something passed between them. It was a mutual, instant recognition. Of the two, he was the one more intensely distracted and reserved. She, on the other hand, appeared to be more forward and outgoing. She saw his collar under his windbreaker and at once, she engaged him.

"Padre, bom dia."

Her accent was foreign and jagged when it ought to have flowed like the foamy sea over the almond sand. "É uma dia gloriosa." Then he switched to English. "I love this beach in every weather."

The woman looked immediately relieved. The burden to speak the language had obviously stressed her. "It appears we both love a windy beach, eh?" She hollered over the blustery noise of the beach.

Carlos appreciated her friendliness. "I am praying for this wind to stop." The spray soaked his upturned face as he motioned at the sky. He meant it as a joke.

"I will pray, Padre, for sailors seeking shelter in a storm." Again, she projected her voice over the din of waves and wind.

He retracted his impressions; she was a serious individual. "God will hear your concern for others and will surely grant you an Intercession." He hollered back at her.

An Intercession was a prayer for assistance on behalf of others.

The woman thanked him. "Obrigada, Padre."

Carlos experienced a Eureka moment. Meeting this woman was a signal from God that enabled him to see what was right in front of him. He had to pursue his ambition as an official of the Church, which was a path his mentor in the seminary had cultivated in him and encouraged him to choose; or he could honour God through his service to people, which was the vision he held when he had started out. It was a stark choice that identified the politics he had not wanted to articulate.

The honesty of this woman's face caused a sudden clarity to burst from his conscience. It was a moment that enabled him to identify the crux of the matter he had to face. The pressure of not knowing evaporated. He relaxed.

"Would you care for a hot tea?" He made the offer impulsively.

"Yes, I would love that." Her willingness to talk suggested she had spent much time on her own lately and no doubt appreciated this kind offer from a priest.

"Great!" He pointed to the path up from the beach where he had started. "There's a restaurant at the top."

They plodded through the sand a short distance and started the stairs in somewhat awkward but necessary silence as they concentrated on the strenuous climb.

She was either English or American, he expected.

On a landing, the woman paused. "My name is Ardis, by the way." She offered her hand.

That was an unusual name; he was certain Ardis wasn't a common name. "It's a pleasure to meet you, Ardis." He felt the warmth of her hand as he held it firmly in his own for a moment. "Call me Carlos."

They carried on. The fact they were strangers who met on the beach dissipated with each step so that by the time they reached the top, having tea together was the most appropriate thing they could do. They took in the spectacular view of beaches to the north and south then went into a restaurant that dominated a small square.

She took off her gabardine windbreaker and handed it over. "That was a good way to build an appetite."

He could have walked much farther, but he was pleased with this change in circumstances. He hung their jackets still wet with spray.

At the front, Ardis took a quick look at the menu. "I am ready for a glass of wine. Will you join me?"

Before they sat down, they ordered wine.

The place was empty and they took a table in the back by a window where they had an excellent view of the ocean and the strand below. "I'm starving." She pushed back her windblown hair.

"You are obviously not Portuguese."

"That I am not. I am Canadian." She nodded and proudly smiled.

"Ah, Canadian! What brings you to this part of the world?"

The wine arrived. Carlos picked up the terracotta clay pitcher and filled their tumblers.

"I am searching beaches for evidence of sea turtle nesting grounds."

"That's interesting. Here's to finding tartarugas!"

Drinking wine in glass tumblers was the Portuguese way.

"I learned another Portuguese word for sea turtle—cágado—but I

definitely like tartaruga better. It is the best word in the entire language."
Ardis did not shy away from expressing her enthusiasm for sea turtles.

The waiter returned with a platter of almonds, grapes, cheese, olives,
and bread for them to nibble on.

"Mmm. I detect a bias."

"Definitely. I want to save sea turtles, particularly the Kemp's
ridley—a species whose nesting grounds are unknown. If I can learn
where they are, perhaps along the coast of Portugal or more likely West
Africa, I can help protect them."

"Protect them from what?" Carlos liked to show he was listening.

"Well, for centuries sea turtles were predators in coastal waters, and
now sharks are winning." She sipped her wine. "Fishing trawlers are
taking more fish than ever. We are learning about impacts of pollution on
marine life. If we destroy their habitat, how can they survive?"

"This is quite an unusual past-time you have."

"It's my job. I teach in the University of British Columbia, in
Canada, and I am here to research turtle nesting grounds in the Algarve.
It's probably crazy that I'm here today—"

"In this weather, you mean?" Carlos wondered why anyone else
would be out.

"There is no evidence sea turtles nest this far north. They prefer
sunnier climates."

The waiter served a salad of lettuce and tomatoes with balsamic
vinegar and virgin olive oil. They started into their salads right away.

"At least this is what we know about sea turtles and I'm thinking,
yeah, that's because turtles leave their tracks in the sand on a hot, sunny
day. But what if they were to come up on a beach like this one today?"

"The tracks would be washed away in the surf and the rain?"

"Exactly. Unless someone is on the beach at the time to see them, no
one would know they had been there. So I am just testing a theory. It
helps that I love exploring beaches, which I do all the time. It all began
when I saw this turtle. There it was on the beach. This monster sea turtle
like I've never seen."

"What, today?" Carlos sat up. "You saw one today?"

"No, this was in Canada." She took an olive and sipped her wine.

Carlos sensed her distraction. She seemed to withdraw. "I love your passion, Señhorita."

"I can't help myself—I'm obsessed, I confess. But the conditions were different, and it got me thinking. And that's why I was on the beach today."

The waiter served steaming pasta with a pesto of pine nuts and cilantro.

"I see. So you observe and take notes."

"Oh yes, and when I find nesting, I aim to shoot some film."

"You make movies?" Carlos pictured large and heavy equipment.

She nodded. "I'm learning how."

His own plan to have a journalist take a picture and write an article about his Fatima sermon in Sonim was outlandish, but this woman's plan was utterly alien.

"I hope to make a film about sea turtles in Portugal," said Ardis.

"I'd like to see that." He had seen documentaries about how the Portuguese loved and respected Salazar, especially for keeping Portugal out of the war. Maybe her idea to make a documentary was not so crazy.

"Oh, you'll have to come to the Algarve then."

"Ahh –" Carlos had not been specific enough. He didn't want to go to the Algarve to see the sea turtles. He just wanted to see her film.

"I will be in the Algarve soon. I will be in Lisbon 'til then."

"Good, then join me for dinner." Carlos was obliged to offer the visitor some hospitality.

14. At Rossio Square

Going out for dinner did not happen right away. The next time Ardis saw Carlos, he gave her a tour of Santa Maria Maior, the Sé, where the Cardinal anointed him as Episcopal Vicar.

"This is where I work when I am in the city."

On their way out of the Sé, he retrieved his hat from a hiding place near the door and put it on as they stepped into the sunlight.

"It gives you a macho look."

He took off his hat, and showed her. "It isn't flimsy like the *Cappello Romano* that vicars and bishops wear." He staked his reputation on substance. He tapped it.

"It makes you look Spanish."

"You have a point, Señhorita. Not only do Portuguese and Spaniards share the Iberian Peninsula, we share certain elements of culture; a certain style."

"Maybe so, but the Spanish have Flamenco."

"We have Fado."

"They have Barcelona and Gaudi, and –"

"And we don't."

She laughed with him, appraising him.

Down the street, they stood on a corner dominated by yet more churches. Ardis leaned back to look at the towers. "I love this; so majestic yet sad."

"The wealth you see, Señhorita, is from centuries ago when we had power but what do we have now?"

"You have decent wine."

"Ah, the Douro. And don't forget our Port; the British love our Port."

"You have the Algarve, where I hope to find sea turtles."

"And great beaches."

"Your coast is the best part of the country."

"I hear they make a tasty *tartaruga* soup in the Algarve."

Ardis swung her bag at him. "How can you say that?"

***

Upon receiving the mining report from Montalvão, Carlos submitted it with a recommendation to Cardinal Cerejeira. He worked closely with the Cardinal during the purchases, representing him at meetings with other lawyers, agents, and vendors.

The Vatican purchased the Adoria mine near Cerva, advancing the funds through Banco Ambrosiano. Through Banco Nationale Portuguesa, the Church of Lisbon purchased a mine at Vale Das Gatas just east of Vila Real. A private company, arranged through the Cardinal, purchased a third mine located near Panasqueira, located east of Coimbra. Mining managers and staff were retained in all three and production continued without pause.

Following the purchases, Cerejeira summoned Carlos. They had anticipated this moment. The focus had turned to selling the output of the mines. They had discussed who the interested parties would be—either the Germans or the British. As there was no commodities exchange, he needed to talk with each interested party to see which would pay the best price. They speculated that his contacts on both sides would be mid-level consular officials. Carlos had collected names. His driver, Maria João, helped him to identify key individuals in the consular offices, and pointed them out to Carlos.

That his driver was on top of this information was not a stretch. The wartime atmosphere of Lisbon made such subterfuge the stock-in-trade of individuals like Maria João.

"Keep your relationships private," Cerejeira advised. "We don't want any attention and nor do they. Everyone wants to keep things moving quietly."

Cerejeira explained that the Germans did not want to draw attention to their supply chain. The British did not want to enflame public opinion, particularly in America, which remained a bystander in the war. Likewise, the Church did not want its association to be public knowledge. It was best to operate under the radar.

This made perfect sense. Carlos admired Cerejeira for his knowledge. He imagined the Cardinal had read many history textbooks and papers until Cerejeira let it slip who his closest friend was: Salazar. Of course! Cerejeira's analysis had to have come straight from the Prime

Minister.

In any case, Carlos could not just walk into the German Embassy, which was only two doors from the Cardinal's palaceta on Campo Mártires da Pátria. From Maria João, he learned that consular officials from all sides were frequenting the hotels and salons in the city. Each side had its favoured location, but that did not keep the others away. It was a party atmosphere, where everybody was watching everybody else.

Carlos summed it up for Cerejeira: "The city doesn't sleep at night."

"Then nor should you."

***

As usual, skies were blue, and for February, the sun was hot.

No matter how pleasant the weather was, Ardis wore a jacket. Unseen, afternoon breezes off the ocean could chill quite suddenly.

The work on the boat was still underway.

During the early weeks of Ardis's time in Lisbon, her exploration of the local beaches was probably the best thing for her. It gave her a chance to settle in, and at the same time, got her out. But now she found herself becoming restless.

She monitored the waterfront, the only official assignment she carried out regularly. It motivated her to keep up her runs.

She took out her movie camera equipment and shot film of Lisbon public squares. She focused on the refugees, who crowded narrow sidewalks and spilled onto the streets. Waiting. Cars and trucks honked at them to get out of the way. With good luck, she also captured several shots of Nazi SS taking coffee in an outdoor café.

Her challenges were all part of living during a difficult time and she learned to cope with them. The greatest test was dealing with the unknown. As events unfolded, people did not know what was happening, or what to expect. Propaganda was common. Leaflets were handed out.

Ardis wrote a text for the voiceovers and enlisted a graduate student to contact the Prime Minister's office to ask who developed their film. The student used the same company and learned how to edit the film and record voiceovers. They also managed to create a professional cover screen with the title, "Refugees and Nazis Crowd Lisbon."

Many German officials carried on regular lives and duties even in the area where she lived. She did her best to learn what she could about their activities. What she saw and did not report were innocuous movements that had more to do with the personal needs of the individuals in the uniforms than with the affairs of state or their navies and armies.

She did her duty gamely. To keep her mind alert, she created "what if" scenarios and their possible strategies, tactics and outcomes.

I need to think like a spy.

The idea made her laugh aloud. It seemed so preposterous, still.

***

Carlos left the Cardinal's palaceta and Maria João drove him the short distance to the Avenida da Liberdade to the Tivoli Hotel, one of the popular hotels where consular staff from both sides often gathered.

Maria João parked the car on a side street. Carlos walked in a side door and found his way to the bar. He wore a plain black shirt, a jacket, and slacks so that his clothing was not shouting out he was a priest. He stood at the crowded bar and ordered beer.

Establishing the initial contact seemed to be the most difficult step. The rest would fall into place if only he could just get started. He should do it properly from the beginning, and he needed to be patient.

He tasted his beer as he left coins for the bartender. He drank deeply then turned and surveyed the room, spotting a key contact, Manfred Wiesentrauser, a German diplomat whom Maria João had pointed out just the other day. He was standing by a table, talking to his colleagues. He was dressed smartly in a diplomat's uniform: a double-breasted, light navy tunic; a sheathed dagger on a belt; and black trousers with thin stripes down the outside seam.

Wiesentrauser left his comrades and came along the bar towards Carlos. He looked an amiable fellow with a medium build and fair hair and not the least intimidating.

Impulsively, Carlos reached out as Wiesentrauser came near him. Wiesentrauser stopped. He looked at Carlos, alarmed.

"You don't actually use that, do you?" Carlos nodded at the dagger.

Manfred laughed politely. "Nein, it is for ceremony."

Carlos offered his hand. "I'm Carlos Silva." He made eye contact. "Have a minute?"

"Ja, how can I help you?"

"Come." Carlos turned toward the bar. "Let me buy you a beer."

"I drink Riesling." Manfred stepped to the bar. They were shoulder to shoulder.

Carlos ordered Riesling for him and a refill for himself.

Carlos introduced himself. He needed to establish a business partner and he was confident from Maria João's informal report that Manfred had the same need. It was all about wolfram. He also adhered to the protocol of confidentiality Cerejeira had described: professional, discreet, and helpful in delivering much needed wolfram.

"I understand you are in a position to buy wolfram, and I have lots of it to sell."

"*Wunderbar*. Then we are going to be good friends." Manfred spoke in hushed tone that only Carlos would hear.

The straightforward approach was effective. Manfred responded tactfully, as an intelligent man would, without artifice or ploys. His response demonstrated he would respect Carlos's need for confidentiality as well.

Manfred laid out what he knew about the supply of wolfram and the prices. Upon learning the production total from the four mines that Carlos represented, he smiled. "This makes my life a lot easier, I tell you." Manfred revealed it would represent at least five per cent of total supply, maybe as high as ten per cent, an exaggeration no doubt.

"Padre, I have to go. So I will be brief. I can offer six hundred ounces of gold for every ton of wolfram."

"Gold?"

"Ja, all the payments have to be in gold because there had been an issue with forged currency. I want our transactions to be efficient so I offer to pay in gold."

Carlos did a quick calculation. The price of gold was about £8.75 per ounce, so he rounded it up to nine pounds. Six hundred ounces would be just under £5,400 per ton of wolfram, which was well within the range of what he expected.

"Where should we ship it?" Carlos wanted all the details.

"Nowhere. We will pick it up. Trucks. No other way in this damn country."

They were lucky to have the trucks. Last June, the Nazis invaded the Soviet Union, a massive undertaking that bled their resources across Europe. The fact he had trucks at all was a testament to the fact his mission to deliver a supply of wolfram was a priority.

There was a brief pause. Carlos was debating whether he should accept this without even having an offer from the other side.

"We will give you a bonus of two hundred ounces for each mine." Manfred negotiated with confidence. "Ja, it's a lot of gold. I must ship it to you."

Carlos focused on the gold up front. "Oh, okay. I need it divided into three portions. Can you put it in three smaller chests?"

"Chests—like a pirate's chest?" Manfred laughed at his own joke.

Realizing how silly his request sounded, Carlos rephrased it. "I don't mean the chests must look old and worn as if they were buried for centuries. I am thinking of small wooden boxes. Do you know what I mean?"

"I'm sure we can arrange that."

"Good. Deliver them to this address in Vila Real." Carlos quickly jotted down a name and an address on a slip of paper and handed it to him.

His initial concerns about his assignment faded away. Carlos had assumed he would be shuttling between hotels for several nights in a row, working the smoky salons, haggling with operatives. Things had gone smoothly. This would be easier than he thought.

***

At his next meeting with Cardinal Cerejeira, Carlos briefed him on how he had maintained his relationships with his new contacts, selling production in three-month intervals.

"You have impressed me with the speed in which you delivered results." Cerejeira commended Carlos.

"Thank you, your Grace."

The Cardinal let him know that a layperson would support him, which made him happy. He did not feel it was God's work.

"I have a new mission for you, Carlos. I want you to follow up on your report of the lingering effects of the Fatima miracle on the people of Portugal."

"Yes, your Grace. I have already arranged to deliver a sermon to the village during a festival coming up this summer."

"Yes, I heard." The Cardinal nodded approvingly as he turned away, signalling the end of their meeting.

***

Ardis entered Praça do Rossio and advanced along the edge of the broad square. She spotted Padre Carlos on the other side, sitting in the sun, reading a newspaper.

What a nice surprise; wanted to see him.

No cassock, white collar, or hat. Plain black shirt, jacket. Trying to blend with the pigeons? Haha. Surrounding him. Soon they'll land on his head and soil him. Hahaha.

Go over, say hello, have a chat.

She changed course to cross the square and join him.

A cloud of pigeons erupted and a Nazi officer appeared to walk through it to join Carlos. Ardis stopped dead.

The officer sat beside Carlos on the bench.

They know each other. How about that? This can't be good.

Her mouth ran dry.

A planned meeting. Hold on, is Carlos an informant?

Carlos brandished his rolled newspaper in his hand, an expressive wave that just happened to be in her direction.

He's telling that Nazi everything he knows about me. That is all I need—a Nazi hunting me down to kill me when I am alone with no one to help me.

Cripes Alcadie, I feel ridiculous even thinking it.

Abruptly, she spun around and went back the way she had come.

The Major said locals are friendly to both sides, providing information for cash. But Carlos? That takes the biscuit. He seems a decent person. He's a priest for pity's sake, and priests don't do that sort of thing. Or do they?

15. Commissioning the *Water Dog*

Ardis climbed Rua São Marçal to meet Garcia in a bakery café across the street from the Polytechnic School.

The bakery was crowded with men leaning on the counter, dinking their espressos.

I will get in, get out, as the Major said.

Ardis took a moment to decipher a handwritten menu. All the options were variations of espresso, which she did not like. Asking for an ordinary coffee was not possible.

Now, to say this properly . . .

Her efforts to understand any barista had proved futile. Discussion typically ended in confusion, and attracted attention.

"*Eu quero um galão.*"

She had ordered an espresso served in a tall glass filled with steamed milk. It was the closest thing she could find to a coffee she would have back home.

". . . *e um bolo, por favor.*" She pointed to a pastry.

She took a table in the back, spent a moment to savour her pastry, and lingered over her coffee, well, most of it, before Roberto arrived.

"*Bom dia.*" This had become their usual greeting—either that or a casual "*Oi.*"

Ardis went right to her news. "You remember I went to Santa Cruz to check out the beaches, right?"

"Yes. How was it?" He put a spoon of sugar into his double espresso and stirred.

"The coast is lined with cliffs so the scenery is amazing. The beach was beautiful."

"Yes. So what? Why are you telling me this?"

"I met a priest on the beach."

"Oh. Okay." He took half his espresso.

"We had lunch. We met in the city. He gave me a tour of the Sé."

"No kidding." He took a large bite of his almond croissant.

She nodded; he chewed.

"You're seeing a priest?"

"Not like that, Roberto. We're just friends."

"Weird."

"Yesterday, I saw him meet with a Nazi officer whom I believe is a diplomat."

"Really. Where?"

She glanced over her shoulder. Two women were ogling Garcia and giggling.

If Caroline were here, she would be egging her on, saying things like 'He's too hot for you.' So would Mom, in a less provocative way, of course.

"Rossio Square."

"Why do you think the Nazi was a diplomat?"

"His uniform. More like a formal business suit; so much better than the SS uniforms."

"Yeah, their diplomats come to the bar from time to time."

"I'm meeting the priest for dinner at the Tivoli this Saturday."

"Well done, Ardis. What's his name?"

"Carlos Silva. He's a Monseñhor."

"Good work. I'll be there."

Ardis visualized Garcia at her table with Carlos.

"I have news for you." Garcia redirected their conversation. "The boat is ready."

"Finally! Let's see it today."

"Can't. But tomorrow morning works. It will take the full day."

So tomorrow it would be. Ardis retreated to her apartment and focused on the menial tasks of organizing the clutter of equipment cases, film canisters, and papers.

She packed a duffle bag for her clothes to take on the boat for an undetermined time.

***

Garcia loaded her gear into his car. On the ferry across the Rio Tejo, he handed her a communiqué from Dean Ellert marked "personal."

"Oh what's this? From the Dean? How nice."

"Read it."

"Dear Professor Lowney, it has been brought to my attention you were close to your classmates Caroline Drago, Max Dietrich, and Peter Nahalano. It is my sad duty to give you this report.

"Your classmates were posted in separate units in the south of England. We understand they each took leave from their respective duties to meet up in London. That evening, a bombing raid killed all three. This is all we know. Please accept my condolences. We honour the ultimate sacrifice they made so others might live in freedom."

"Here at UBC, we will always remember them. Ardis Avalyn, I am especially proud of you and your research. Come home as soon as you can. We need you here. Sincerely, Dean Ellert."

Her wrist with letter in hand came to rest on her knee. She turned to the railing to grieve at the passing seascape of the Rio Tejo.

Garcia gave her time. "They tried to include you, too, but were unable to locate you."

"Oh, I see." She looked down for a moment then raised her eyes to meet his. "If I had been there, I would have died with them."

"That is conjecture, and not an actual fact."

Ardis recalled their going away, saying goodbye. No one expected this. She held an image of Caroline, Max, and Pete on the wide lawn in front of the library, listening to their chatter about the people in their class and on campus. Walking along the Mall on campus. Caroline looking resplendent in the ball gown Max had insisted on getting for her . . . to wear on their cruise on the Salish Sea, where they danced to "Moonlight Serenade" played by the orchestra on the ship. Those times they had shared now felt like an eternity ago. The spark in Caroline's eyes when Max said Ardis ought to have fins, and Pete wanted to see her gills.

Those guys.

Her warm memories became a furnace of molten anger. A fierce, hot hate for the Nazis gripped her. For the first time, she valued the Major's insistence that she learn silent killing. Now she had good reason.

***

"There it is." Roberto found the trawler in a slip near the end of a wharf.

The tide was low. Her eyes travelled across the top rigging.

She looks tight.

The name of its home port, Setubal, appeared in block letters across the stern. Garcia pointed out there was no name on the bow.

"As first skipper, Ardis, you might want to give her a name; and I will have it added."

"Thanks. I will."

The dockside ladder was old and thick, smoothed by salty spray. Ardis climbed down to the deck and Garcia used an old boom with rope netting to lower her gear and a cooler to her on the deck. They stowed the gear and inspected the trawler.

In the wheelhouse cabin, Ardis ran her fingers over the new wood. "I love the smell of freshly cut cedar."

"It needs a coat of lacquer."

"It is gorgeous as it is."

"We painted the exterior surfaces and below decks," he said. "I expected it would help to get rid of the stench of fish."

The aura of the sea permeated the well-worn wood.

"I don't mind. I see a weather-worn trawler I can count on." Ardis rubbed her hand over the framework. "When things get rough out there, she will be seaworthy."

Garcia presented Ardis with a flag and pennants from their college that the students who refitted the boat had made. She raised the Portuguese ensign on the stern mast and he hoisted the college burgees on the spreader near the top of the forward mast.

"It's all yours, Captain." Garcia gave charge of the trawler to Ardis.

"Aye-aye, sir." Ardis looked at him with a grin. "Did you just promote me?"

Garcia laughed. "It was a figure of speech."

"Do I even have a military rank?

"No, but your pay grade is comparable to mine."

"No way," she said, her face scrunched up like a half-chewed caramel. "Ha, ha." She frowned. "That's unlikely, and you know it."

"Well, almost."

Ardis took off her shoes and settled in for a sunny day on deck. She approved of the solid grumble of the engine as she steered the trawler out of the harbour. She spotted four dogs playing in the water among the fishing boats. "They seem to be right at home."

"The Portuguese Water Dog—Cão de Água—is popular among fishermen," he said.

Clearing the river mouth, Ardis pointed the bow to the far horizon and opened up the engine. Without hesitation, the propeller churned up a mighty force and had them cutting through the water smoothly. Ardis throttled down and set the engine to idle in neutral; it did not sputter out. Then she engaged the propeller at a modest speed and steered the trawler in a weaving pattern through the calm waters as if she were going through an obstacle course. The water was like glass and she was cutting the surface like a skater on ice, making the first ripples. "It responds well. This trawler is excellent, Roberto. It definitely meets our needs."

"Great, then you are all set to proceed on your assignment."

Ardis nodded. Deep down, the vibrations of the vessel comforted her.

"You know, Lieutenant Garcia, it's great, thank you. The burgees are a nice touch."

She felt awkward expressing herself and a little choked up. She watched him break into a big smile. In the sunlight, the grey in his eyes had become lighter and the blue bolder.

They continued cruising directly west for another fifteen minutes.

No land, no boats, and nothing on horizon. Good time for lunch.

Ardis cut the engine. As the boat coasted to a standstill, she got out the cooler.

They took their sandwiches to the bench at the stern.

Sea is calm. Sun is warm. All is good.

Yet, the news from home clouded her conscience. For her, the war had brought adventure, not death. Until now, that is.

Caroline and the boys suffered a terrible ending.

The war became intense. The Nazis were attacking England. Like most people, Ardis feared the Nazis were winning.

I could be next to die.

Although it was highly unlikely it would happen at that moment, she was aware death could happen any day when least expecting it. But the odds of her death happening in the near term had risen dramatically.

The boat rocked suddenly and a subsequent wave splashed over the gunwales, spraying the deck. Ardis hung on and Garcia was knocked onto his side on the deck.

The sea had definitely changed.

Ardis was about to laugh, but instead she erupted with a shudder. She held back; she didn't want to break down in front of Roberto.

"Everything will be okay, Ardis." Roberto demonstrated an empathy she did not expect.

That was all it took. She broke.

It was as if she sagged into the bench seat with her legs crossed and tucked beneath her—a casual Lotus position.

"I'm sorry about your friends, Ardis."

Her tension, her fears, her trained response to danger, her paranoia, her difficulties with the language, her sudden longing to be home in Canada . . . she held her face in her hands. She settled down, though too late; she became self-conscious, which led to her feeling embarrassed for displaying such weakness.

"I think I'll stay here on the boat for a couple of weeks."

Garcia returned to Lisbon and Ardis remained in Setubal. As he departed, she told him the name she wanted for the boat.

"Cão de Água."

***

People say they love being by the water, on the water, or in the water. For many, it is an idyllic dream they pursue only when they go on vacation or maybe when they retire. Few people actually make their careers and spend their whole lives on the water.

Ardis was one of those people. Being on the water was exactly where she needed to be, to think things through, beginning with what had happened to her friends.

Yet, she had many regrets she wished she could do over, too.

With Caroline, her loyal friend, Ardis would relax from her studies and spend more time with her. All Caroline wanted from her was her friendship. She would listen more closely to Max, and give him an audience that he deserved. And Pete, poor, lovely Pete, she would love him with all her might, for he deserved it.

On the water, Ardis became adept with coding and using the radio. Her sightings of German and Italian naval movements were not rare events. Their ships made port in Lisbon, as did the Allies. For her safety, her notes contained no references to the enemy shipping she had identified. What she recorded was the marine life she encountered.

She swam every day, with a rope tethering her to the boat.

Every four days or so, she stayed overnight at a pension in the centre of Setubal near the market. It was a convenient way for her to access facilities and to replenish her supplies from nearby shops. People were friendly. She kept a low profile at the slip where she docked overnight. No one bothered her and she got on well on her own.

It was time for her to cruise south to the Algarve. The fact remained she needed support. She could hire a ship hand out of Setubal. A better idea was to hire one or two of the students that Garcia had had working on the boat. To do this, she had to return to Lisbon.

Ardis returned to her apartment on Rua São Marçal. Life in Lisbon carried on as before, except for one thing. At Camp X, the mantra had been "Trust no one." She was considering now whether this applied to her friend the priest, who apparently had meetings with the enemy. It did not sound like Church business. So what was Carlos up to?

16. Dinner at the Tivoli

Carlos was first to arrive in the spacious lobby. He chose a cushioned armchair in a setting among tropical plants, wicker chairs, settees, old steamer trunks, side tables with hurricane lamps, and a view of the two entrances Ardis was most likely to come through.

Since meeting Ardis on the beach at Santa Cruz, Carlos had met up with her twice and enjoyed her company. She did not wear the burden of oppression that so many people around him seemed to model. She was new-world fresh, passionate about her career, and enthusiastic about learning anything to do with Portugal. He never knew what to expect from her. His only concern was he might like her a little too much. He did not intend to fall into another situation like the one he'd left behind in Italy.

This evening, they would have the dinner he proposed when they met in Santa Cruz.

The other unfinished piece of business was less clear-cut. She had suggested he could join her to look for turtles on beaches in the Algarve. That was a much larger commitment that he had no intention of following up on. If he did not know her and appreciate her keenness for her work, the suggestion itself would have been improper. From her, though, it felt natural. There would be no strings; he could count on that.

As a Monseñhor who obtained his education in the Vatican, he was obliged to ensure his actions upheld the highest, moral standards. His superior would censure him if he joined a woman on a boat to a destination like the Algarve.

The Cardinal could even frown upon his meeting with Ardis here, in a fashionable hotel. But, he reasoned, meeting Ardis for dinner nicely dovetailed with his assignment; it was his job to be here. It was vital for him to fit in with this crowd.

A steady flow of men and women were going into the dining room now. Even the adjoining bar was filling up. If Ardis did not arrive soon, they would not get a table.

His concern was short-lived. Ardis came through the lobby in a whirl, waving to him from across the room. He returned the wave with more emotion than may have been appropriate. Suddenly, he was self-conscious. He lowered his arm, cleared his throat, and stood to greet her.

"It's so good to see you, Carlos."

"We may be too late. I am sorry, Ardis. We may have to find another place."

"Oh no, please, let's stay. I've been looking forward to the band."

She wore a conservative skirt and a jacket, and carried a small purse.

"You look beautiful, Señhorita." His compliment was sincere.

"Did you expect to see me in my windcheater?" She smoothly deflected his compliment.

"Actually, I did. I hadn't pictured you in a setting like this."

"That was how I felt when we met on the steps of the cathedral." That day, she had just stepped off the number twenty-eight streetcar when he came out of the cathedral to meet her. "You were wearing your cassock."

They went directly into the restaurant. There were no tables left, so they took seats in the adjoining bar. As they entered the room, the band started playing Mack the Knife.

Ardis loved the music and the crowded bar. She leaned in and raised her voice. "This is really something!"

Yet, returning to the Tivoli, Ardis was anxious to see the Germans, all in uniform, now occupying the middle of the room directly in front of the band. Much laughter emanated from their tables, and the sight of Nazi SS sent a chill down her neck. She scanned the room, looking for the exits in case she needed to get out of there quickly.

At the bar, Ardis recognized Ian Bromwell. He was with his colleagues, Kim Philby and Ian Fleming, all of whom she had met at Camp X. The Brits mingled with the Americans, and crowded around the bar where she also spotted Garcia. She did not let on she saw them.

Though the band was not as large as the volume of the music suggested, it played belligerently into the night and the music echoed down the corridors of the hotel and out the open windows into the wide Avenida da Liberdade.

Couples danced in the crowded space in front of the band. This was a young, well-heeled crowd. Like Ardis and Carlos, most were in their twenties and thirties. The energy in the room was palpable as they responded to songs, singing along, dancing, and clapping to show their approval. Adding to Ardis's apprehension, the women wore swanky dresses, whereas her skirt and jacket were decidedly cautious. Her scarf was a modest attempt to add colour, though it did lend her some security.

Ardis recognized the song, "La Vie en Rose." It took her back to her garden, where she heard it on the radio.

Across the room, Ardis spotted the German officer whom Carlos met at Rossio Square. He looked at her. She immediately looked away.

When she looked again, he was coming her way and the first thing she did was look for the exits. Too late. He reached her table and stopped.

"Monseñhor Carlos!"

Carlos stood and shook his hand. "Manfred, how are you? We just arrived for dinner but there were no tables."

"Ja, Lisbon is full." He gestured with an arm to the crowded room. "The rest of Europe is in a blackout and this city is a big party." The diplomat was showing off his clean accent. In fact, he was a trained linguist.

Unlike the SS, Manfred appeared friendly and approachable. His fair hair and the sophisticated cut of his jacket made him look gentler somehow, which irritated her because he was the enemy. *He wasn't supposed to look decent and respectable.*

Carlos invited him to join them. She watched in disbelief as Manfred pulled up a chair and sat down. Everything she learned about protecting her cover came rushing back to her. *Try not to fraternize with the enemy. It only increases the risk of you blowing your cover.*

She glanced at Roberto by the bar and frowned. He was not even looking her way; he was talking with an attractive, well-dressed woman.

The diplomat turned to Ardis and smiled. Ardis was cornered. "The Monseñhor continues to surprise me." The diplomat looked at Carlos, tilting his head and nodding ever so slightly toward the fraulein, indicating he required an introduction.

"Yes, of course." Carlos assumed his formal voice. "Señhorita Ardis

Lowney, I present to you O Señhor, Herr Manfred Wiesentrauser, *Oberinspektor* at the German Embassy."

"Please, call me Manfred." His eyes travelled immediately to her turtle pendant.

"Thank you." Ardis politely held her hands on her lap; clenched. She was afraid he would want to shake hands with her, or worse, kiss her hand. She focused on his badges.

Manfred regarded her in a non-challenging way. "You are noticing my insignia."

She had never seen any real Nazi insignia or the people who wore them, up close, with her own eyes. *He is so close he could reach out and grab me by the throat.* She could not let her guard down for a second.

She nodded, looking at his face. "As a graphic, it's quite good, actually."

So is that face. He would do well in the movies, opposite Bogart.

There had been a presentation on ranks and badges at Camp X. Ardis remembered that an Oberinspektor was a senior level.

"It is industrial art deco." He was proud to show off his knowledge of design.

It depicted an eagle with its wings outstretched along a flat line at the top. A silver-wire embroidery of a round oak wreath encircled the patch. In the centre, in the clutch of the eagle's claws, was a small swastika, also encircled.

"Ja, it makes me think of Tamara de Lempicka. Know this artist?"

His blue eyes looked into hers. Ardis looked away, tongue-tied.

"I saw her work in Paris about ten years ago. I love her work."

Tamara de Lempicka was a Polish painter of art deco studio art in the 1920s best known for her stylized nudes of over-sized figures.

A server cleared and set their table, providing menus. Carlos ordered a bottle of Riesling, Manfred's favourite.

The band launched into a German song.

"Do you know this song?"

She shook her head.

"*Bei Mir Bist Du Schein.*" He looked into her eyes when he said To

Me You Are Beautiful, then closed them in a dreamy gesture. "How I loved to go to the jazz clubs in Berlin. It was a *moment incroyable* in my life. Before the war, of course. Then things changed and will never be the same again." He opened his eyes and gazed fully upon Ardis. "*Mademoiselle*, you look German."

"Some German, French, and Italian."

"If I may say, *vous êtes très belle*."

Ardis fought hard not to blush, acknowledging his compliment with a smile and a nod, but turning her thoughts away from him.

I should give Carlos attention but . . .

She couldn't miss this opportunity to learn about Manfred. "I didn't realize diplomats wore uniforms," she directed the focus back on him. "Is that a German tradition?"

"The uniforms? *Non*, they were introduced before the war. The idea, they said, was to make the Foreign Service fit into the Reich's idea of *Einheit* . . . that everyone is an integrated part of the whole. We are political soldiers now. My superior officer told us it was a message to career diplomats to get in line with the new regime."

"Mmm." Ardis was intrigued. "I would imagine the older ones didn't like the uniforms, especially if they didn't wear them in the past."

"It is true. They were afraid they would look like *porteurs d'hôtel*."

The image made Ardis laugh.

The waiter returned with the wine. Carlos suggested they order their dinner. Having already eaten, Manfred declined. Carlos and Ardis ordered the special. *Bacalhau*, which she had had here on her first day with Garcia.

"Unfortunately, I must depart."

Carlos wanted to talk with him alone but it would have to wait for another time.

"Before I go, I want to say, *Mademoiselle*, you know about me, but I don't anything about you. What do you do?"

Tell him your cover story. Keep it simple.

Ardis avoided eye contact, but that did not deter Manfred. "Are you American?"

Ardis lowered her eyes in a gesture that could be interpreted as a polite, affirmative nod. In fact, facing an enemy officer for the first time caused a moment of panic.

Don't trust his charm and friendliness, kiddo. He is onto me.

"I am Canadian." She looked into his eyes, watching for a sign.

His eyes are clear and deep like water.

"Ah, Canadian, *wunderbar*. I have relatives there."

He did not even flinch.

"Ardis teaches Marine Biology at the University of British Columbia in Vancouver, Canada. She is doing research at the Technical University of Lisbon."

"Ahh, Marine Biology," said Manfred, gesturing to her pendant. "Sea turtles are a passion of yours, I see."

Ardis smiled, tucking her pendant under her scarf. Ardis shifted the conversation to Manfred. "Relatives in Canada? Whereabouts?"

"North of Kitchener, in a village called Mildmay."

"I know it well!" Hearing the names of familiar places dear to her childhood excited Ardis. "My parents took me to Sauble Beach on Lake Huron. We would stop at Leo Weber's butcher shop in Mildmay for the sausage. They called it bologna but it was the best summer sausage."

"I understand there are many Germans in the area."

"Yes, Kitchener was called Berlin before the Great War."

"My relatives spoke of it." He smiled at her.

Manfred had found an opening into her life and had taken it.

The waiter returned to serve their dinner and refilled their glasses.

Ardis placed her napkin on her lap. "Where is your family from?" Now she was genuinely interested in Manfred.

"I grew up in Ribeauvillé, a village in Alsace." Manfred spoke wistfully. "We are south of Strasbourg and north of Basel, Switzerland."

"It sounds French."

"Yes, it is. My family is French and we lived in a town with a French name."

"Wasn't Alsace given to France after the Great War?"

"Yes, it was. Whenever there was a war between Germany and France, Alsace went to the winner. For the past year, it has been back in the hands of Germany."

Ardis folded the napkin and placed it next to the utensils on the table. "And now you are in the German diplomatic corps? How did that happen?"

"I studied Spanish and Portuguese in Strasbourg. Then I studied German in Mannheim and I was recruited by the German Foreign Ministry." Manfred looked around to see who might be watching. "As a rule, Germans don't trust Alsatians to fight the French. They sent my fellow Alsatians to the Eastern Front to fight Russians. The Foreign Service wanted my language skills or I would be on the Eastern Front, too. The Spanish War created a need for administrators, and then they posted me here. Now I handle various matters of trade and some diplomacy, not so much the intelligence side. The SS and the Gestapo are in charge of secret, high-profile matters and I'm okay with that."

"So you're not a spy." Ardis was emboldened by his friendliness.

Manfred laughed. "No Fraulein, you are more likely to be a spy." He and Carlos thought that was funny.

Ardis laughed with them.

"Fraulein Ardis, if there is anything I can do to assist you, please let me know. I would be happy to help." Manfred gave her his card for the German embassy with his phone number.

"Thank you, Manfred. Now, if you'll excuse me."

Manfred jumped to his feet to help with her chair, as she left for the Ladies room.

His eyes follow her as she walked away. "Here is a woman who diligently conceals her features when so many others are exposing theirs—to everyone's disappointment. Wouldn't you agree, Monseñhor?"

Carlos laughed. "I never saw her like that, but you nailed it on the head, Manfred."

Draped though she was in excessive material, which was her style, she possessed a slender hourglass figure even Carlos could not miss. He recalled she wore a clutch of scarves the last time, too.

Manfred flashed him a conspiratorial smile.

"I am enchanted by her happy-go-lucky charm." Carlos did not mind confessing his feelings about Ardis to Manfred.

Reluctant to depart from his new friends, Manfred held the back of his chair in his fingers. "Please give my apologies to the Fraulein for leaving without saying good night. There is a reception this evening at the Parque in Estoril. A command performance, you might say."

The Parque Hotel was a favourite gathering place for the German community.

"There will be so many Nazi uniforms one may think he was in France." Manfred shook his head with aversion to his evening's prospects, and waved to Carlos on his way out.

Carlos scanned the thinning crowd. Few Germans remained. Their numbers dwindled as others departed for Estoril. The crowd remained thick around the bar. He recognized a few from the British counsel. He didn't know the Americans. Compared to the Brits, they tended to be less formal in their dress code as well as their demeanour.

***

Alone in the washroom, Ardis let herself laugh but the urge quickly dissipated.

What has gotten into me? It must be the stress.

She dabbed the edges of her eyes with cold water on the corner of her dainty handkerchief.

Something is going on between those two. They are likely talking about it right now.

She smoothed her blouse and skirt in the mirror.

When Ardis stepped out of the washroom, she saw Roberto at the end of the corridor. He walked toward her and as he passed by her said, "Meet me in the lobby."

Ardis shrugged, languorously scanning the corridor. No one had seen them. She turned and followed him at an easy pace.

Garcia waited behind a screen of bushy palm trees in clay pots. She sat beside him.

"Damn you're good, Ardis. We've been trying to figure out Manfred for months."

"That's what I told you. Carlos has dealings with Manfred. Could be wolfram."

"I just needed to confirm it. Bromwell said he's the one." Garcia leaned in closer. "I need you to follow the priest. Go wherever he goes."

She nodded.

"We need to know where he gets the wolfram, how much, which mines, and when. We cannot have you out on the water 'til this is resolved."

"You just changed my orders. What happened to surveillance of shipping?"

"Turtles can wait," he whispered. "Ardis, this is your military objective."

She nodded and turned back to the restaurant.

Now I'm facilitating the saboteurs? I will do this mission inland if I must, and then get out on the water. I won't abandon my research for Brooker.

***

Ardis spoke the moment she returned to the table. "Carlos, you didn't mention you were a Monseñhor." She had to speak over the music.

"I didn't?"

"No, I think it means you are unaccustomed to talking about yourself. Or that I occupied our conversation talking about sea turtles and didn't even ask you about your work."

"Oh no, it just didn't come up."

"Well, you'll have to tell me about what you do."

"I can do that."

"Carlos, by the way, when you go to the festival in the north, would you like to have movie pictures of your sermon?"

"Never considered it, why?"

"It might be more effective than a newspaper article. Catch more attention, you know?

The Miracles of Fatima will make an interesting newsreel, too.

"That's an idea. Why do you ask?"

"Before I go out on the water to film sea turtles, I'm practicing my filmmaking. I could make a movie for you."

***

As the days dropped away, Carlos finished preparing his sermon. Once he confirmed the arrangements with Ardis, he informed Cardinal Cerejeira he had found a Canadian with film equipment to film his sermon in Sonim. He did not even try to explain that.

Now he had an amazing opportunity to show his superiors what he was capable of doing. Ardis would capture it on film. He felt lighter. Though he didn't show it. He tried to be nonchalant about it.

What Carlos did not factor into the equation was the fact his Berlinetta was unsuitable for more than two people. Carlos sent Maria João home.

***

It occurred to Ardis that maybe Carlos was not a priest at all. Maybe he was undercover, too. Was she in more danger? Is he going to take her to an inconspicuous spot and kill her?

She kicked herself for not confirming his vocation. She had seen him coming out of the cathedral but that did not mean he was in fact a priest.

***

The Berlinetta was a game changer. The other cars he had driven were oversized and underpowered vehicles that he had to coax and cajole only slightly less than horse-drawn wagons. The Berlinetta was a muscular vehicle in which changing gears, cornering and downshifting were pleasures. Stepping on the gas lifted him free of his burdens as he flew up and down the cobble stone streets to her door.

He pulled up to Ardis's building and tooted the horn.

She stuck her head out the second-floor window and waved for him to come up. She handled last minute matters and he carried her things to the car, making several trips down the stairs. The Berlinetta provided little trunk space. He carefully fit Ardis's gear into the back seat—a small suitcase, a duffle bag, a toolbox, a bulky camera, a large tripod, and two reels of film in canisters.

"How long are we going for?" He wasn't above chiding her.

"Yes, that camera is bulky, isn't it?" She reminded him she was doing this for him.

Heading north out of Lisbon, he drove at a more leisurely pace. His experience as a driver in Anagni and Rome had taught him to let his passengers grow comfortable with his driving.

Ardis did not display the slightest trepidation.

"Carlos, I've been thinking about this festival that celebrates The Lord of the Good End. It is interesting that the Portuguese regard dying on a cross as a Good End. It strikes me as being slightly euphemistic, don't you think?"

"Euphemistic? You mean a nice way to say what makes people uncomfortable?"

"Yes, that's right."

"In the seminary, we studied Latin, of course, as well as Greek. Yes, the Good End is a euphemism and it's also a metaphor, which is another Greek word."

"I didn't know these words came from Greek."

One glance at her told him what he suspected. Her eyes were glazing over. She was going to fall asleep.

"The Good End is a metaphor for salvation. It celebrates Jesus dying on the cross as a sacrifice to obtain forgiveness for the sins of humankind. I am not so sure salvation is what is in store for us, however. There will be parades. People will dress in their best suits and traditional costumes. Someone carries a cross and leads a procession but they do not re-enact the Way of the Cross, thank goodness."

"Mmmm. I am looking forward to this experience."

He could tell she would prefer even more to sleep.

Many of the towns and villages they passed through were preparing for festivals of their own. He glanced at her. Her head was bobbing down, unconsciously fighting sleep. She would have a sore neck if he left her. He took the pillow from her hand, tucked it between her head and the window, and persuaded her head back to rest on it.

He was vulnerable to her.

Carlos settled into the rhythm of the road. He shifted gears easily and the scenarios that bothered him trailed away. His mind wandered with the moving countryside.

What bothered him could not be his involvement in buying the mines or selling wolfram. These thorny issues had pierced his conscience but not his sleep. They were necessary tasks and his participation would not last forever.

He considered his current assignment. He was on a mission to tell people stories about the miracles of Fatima.

He paused there. These miracles increasingly bothered him. The more he told the stories, the more implausible they seemed. They gnawed at his vocation. How could he hope to help others feel God's love if he could not believe it himself? He had achieved enough self-awareness to know that feeling bothered by his conscience was a sure sign he was doing something he should not be doing.

At the same time, he was skirting the edges of propriety with Ardis in his car. But Ardis was a friend. She was not the temptation; his ideas about her were the temptation. Some would say this was the work of the Devil, but Carlos did not buy into that nonsense. He was committed to God.

Still, he had not done anything wrong . . . he had not hurt anyone or created any conflict. He had not crossed any forbidden lines of behaviour, or so he thought. Crossing forbidden lines of behaviour was exactly what he had done with Laurenza.

He imagined Laurenza waking each day in her Italian village. Did she hope that he would seek her? What if with every sunset her heart was beating with love for him as she faced each night alone? He did not have to let this happen; she could be in a remote Portuguese village with him. They could live a happy life in peace. They would not be doing anything wrong.

The practice of priests taking partners was common enough not to be an issue. But the Cardinal had supported his education and training in Rome. If Carlos did that now, it would be a fiasco. Or, what if she wasn't waiting for him at all? Then he ached for her as one who has lost his love forever. He was teary and resisted the feeling.

He shook his head as if to rid the idea from his mind. Another woman was asleep beside him in the car. He was attracted to her as well. Perhaps it was time he admitted this to himself.

Carlos questioned himself—was he a man of conscience? He intuitively knew right from wrong. These women were the forbidden fruit. Everything he believed in, everything that had always guided him in his life of piety and chastity, he had chosen a long time ago.

Things were happening fast and he could not change a thing. He took solace in the fact it would not be long now before he could settle everything.

He thought of Laurenza. He would never want anyone else, if he were with her. Or did he love this woman who slept beside him in his car? It was a ludicrous idea that made him want to laugh like Pedro.

Trás-os-Montes

17. Festival of Nosso Señhor do Bonfim

In Sonim, the Berlinetta descended into the village illuminated by a full moon. Ardis pressed her forehead against the glass to see narrow cobblestone roads lined with fieldstone walls and stone houses.

Like ancient villages in a fairy tale.

She saw inhabitants completing their end-of-day duties. Men in coveralls slung farm implements on their shoulders; women with scarves on their heads and long, plain dresses herded barefoot children in well-worn breeches.

Like stepping back centuries.

Carlos brought the Berlinetta to a stop in front of the home of their host. Ardis stretched her arms and legs as Carlos stepped out and surveyed the manor.

Within moments, Señhor Montalvão came out. "Welcome Padre, welcome Señhorita Ardis." The Baron gave each one a toothy smile as he shook their hands. Zé helped bring in their luggage; Inez showed Ardis to her room.

Ardis went back down immediately. She had to remove film canisters from the car, or the morning sun would destroy them.

Zé went inside to locate dry storage while she moved the car to a cellar door in the yard by the stable. Left to it, Ardis commenced unloading the canisters and her equipment.

From the stable, Xisco saw this strange woman moving equipment, and came out to investigate.

"*Boa noite.*" Xisco joined in to help her. "What are the tins for?"

"They have film, to make a movie."

"You make movies?" He had seen documentaries about Portuguese agriculture and another about how Prime Minister Salazar helped Portugal avoid financial disaster. He saw them once in school and once when everyone in the village crowded into Bartolo's Padaria to see the films projected onto a big screen.

How can a boy in this village know any English?

"Yes, I'm learning how to make a movie," she replied.

"Too fast, please, thank you to slow down."

"I am a marine biologist."

"What does a marine biologist?"

"What do I do? I study life in the ocean. My specialty is sea turtles."

"There are no sea turtles in Sonim, Señhorita." He grinned at her.

"You're funny," she said.

"What does *uma bióloga marinha* want with movie camera far from sea?"

She laughed. "What's your name young man?"

"Francisco."

"It is a pleasure to meet you, Francisco." She shook his hand. "My name is Ardis. I teach in a university. In Canada."

Visitors to the manor did not engage the *moço de estrebaria* in conversation. Xisco looked more closely at the woman who talked with him and told him about herself. She talks like a teacher. Only his mother expressed herself like this, and his teacher.

"What is your job, Francisco?" She took an interest in him.

"I care for animals in my stable. I feed them. I clean their stalls and put down fresh straw for their beds." He spoke tenuously, fearing a trap.

"Oh, *você é o cavalariço.*" Ardis was trying out her Portuguese.

Xisco looked at her with apprehension. *Este chame não é uma palavra.* He did not have the heart to tell her this "cavalarico" is not a word. As Cristina had said to the teacher, *palafreneiro* is the formal term for a groom, and *moço de estrebaria* is the common term for stable boy. Though it sounded good, this other one—*cavalarico*—is not even a word.

Wishing to please her, Xisco nodded in agreement. "I am the *cavalarico*." He paused, forming a question. "What is special about sea turtles?"

"Well, for one, turtles have lived on this planet far longer than humankind. They are survivors, although they face a new danger now."

"From what? Why?"

"From humans. Fishermen take them with their nets, and construction destroys their nesting grounds. They deserve to live here— they were here first! We need to protect nesting grounds and help sea turtles survive.

"Our roles are alike."

Though extreme, she saw the link. "Do you think I am a *cavalarico* of the sea?"

His eyes opened wide. "And I am a *cavalarico* of land."

"Have you ever seen a turtle?" It was Ardis's turn to engage the boy.

"I have not seen, Señhorita."

"Have you seen the ocean, Francisco?"

"Only in books, Señhorita. In my imagination, I sail ships on the ocean."

"You strike me as a well-travelled young man."

"I am, Señhorita. I want to be an explorer."

"Oh, I see. What will you explore?"

"I want to look for a place no one has found—the Kingdom of Prester John. Have you heard of this place, Señhorita?"

She shook her head.

"It is a legendary place where milk and honey flow over streets of gold and everyone drinks from the Fountain of Youth."

"Wow," she responded.

"But they are just myths. People needed stories to give them hope."

"Oh, so you don't really want to find this place."

"I am looking for hope, Señhorita."

It was an innocent comment that set off questions. Ardis paused.

Xisco took advantage of the moment. "Are you going to the

Candlelight Parade? Want to come with me?"

She had not heard of it. "That sounds interesting. Yes, let me get a sweater."

Inside the manor, she found Monseñhor Carlos and brought him along.

"This is Francisco." Ardis introduced him.

"Good evening, Monseñhor."

"Xisco shined my car." Carlos had changed into his cassock and white collar, and he wore his wide-brimmed Bolero hat.

"That's me—you remember!" Xisco smiled then looked down to hide his frown. He didn't trust the clergy, at least not their local priest, Padre Fernando.

"Of course! What is new with you?"

Xisco considered what would be important to a man of religion. "I learned my grandfather was a Jew—a surprise to us all."

"That would be a surprise." Carlos looked at Xisco more intently.

"But we are Catholic." Xisco assured him, as if he were saying, isn't it obvious? Xisco had been raised as a Catholic like everyone else.

It was steps to the square. The fountain was gurgling in the moonlight.

"Did you know, Xisco, our culture is rich with beautiful stories that are common to both Catholic and Jewish religions? Muslim, as well, actually."

"I've heard of a holy book called the Qur'an—is that for all of them?"

"The Qur'an is for people who practice Islam," Carlos said.

"Just as the Bible is for Catholics?"

"That's correct. And just as the Torah is for those who practice Judaism. Did you know the same cultural traditions 2,000 years ago were the basis for the Qur'an, Bible, and Torah? These holy books share some of the same stories."

"I did not know they were related."

"Most people don't." Carlos rinsed his hands in the fountain. "If you read the Torah, you can read about Adam and Eve, Abraham, Isaac, and

Moses."

They resumed their walk.

"In school, our teacher said Jesus was born Jewish," said Xisco. "More than half the class decided that he must have become Catholic when he died. But some of us believed Jesus was born Jewish, lived, and died Jewish."

"I think so, too," said Carlos. "The Catholic Church developed later."

"So these religions present the same approaches to living?"

"Definitely. Despite anything you may hear about any people on this planet, all religions show deep respect for people. As a species, human beings value life."

"I agree," Ardis contributed.

They climbed cobblestone streets through the village and admired the decorations for the festival. Crosses decorated stone walls, buildings, and doors. The praying hands, Jesus on the cross, the Virgin Mary. There were little altars on street corners adorned with flowers and candles, all of it prepared in the hope of marking their streets and bringing favour to their homes and families.

"Xisco, there are many ways to find God," Carlos declared. "However, the Catholic Church teaches that only the sacraments offer salvation."

"What?" Ardis showed her surprise. "Do you mean that outside the Catholic Church there can be no salvation?"

Carlos nodded. "Jesus himself was clear on this. He said, 'The only way to the Father is through me.'"

"That can't be right," said Ardis.

They had arrived at the top of the hill. A racket of music, chanting, and prayers filled the square in front of the capela. Torches lit the scene. Everyone held a candle. Xisco guided them into the thick gathering, parting the way for them.

A woman thrust candles into the Monseñhor's hands; he passed them to Ardis and Xisco, and they lit them from the candles of others. As farmers, the villagers were chanting prayers to the Virgin Mary to grant them good health and bountiful harvests. Another group in purple tunics was chanting a different prayer as they performed a ceremony of public penitence and reconciliation. With everyone in the crowd either chanting, praying, or just talking and laughing, the noise level in the square was nothing less than raucous.

Ardis hung back, engrossed with watching everything going on.

Carlos saw this, and returned to her side. "These rites have been passed down since the 16th century," he explained. "The farmers believe these prayers must be performed or a dire consequence could afflict the village."

"And you know all the words."

"They are chanting Vespers, the prayers to mark the end of day."

The band was not the usual village band. There were string instruments, a cymbalist, a drummer, acoustic guitars, and a clutch of women who sang sad ballads. In the next song, a rhythm with a strong drumbeat emerged and the procession began. They moved down the Avenida Señhor Bonfim, led by the lay brothers of the Church. With the scent of beeswax in the air, the brothers walked barefoot and wreaths covered their heads. All the participants in their colourful traditional costumes formed in front of the *capela* and followed the candlelight parade as it snaked its way down the hill.

Xisco disappeared into the crowd. Ardis and the Monseñhor joined the parade. She leaned closer to him, and whispered. "So if I'm not Catholic, I'm going to Hell?"

He shook his head. His frown was nearly imperceptible.

"That is what the Church teaches, yes." He whispered equally quietly in her ear.

"Do you believe it?"

He shook his head. "No, it's old dogma and I'm not concerned. The Church is like a huge ship. It takes a long time to turn around."

When they reached the square, the procession reordered itself as the participants mixed with each other based now on who was dancing with whom. Many people stood off to the side or sat wherever they could.

Ardis and Carlos stood on the high ground at the west side of the square where they could see it all. "I wish I could film this. It's so beautiful."

Old women came around the square and shooed all the bystanders, including Ardis and Carlos, into the space where the dancing was taking place.

All around, people joined hands and arms, and danced.

"I don't know how to dance like this!"

"That's okay, just put your hands up here on my shoulders." He lifted her hands in place. "And lean back. Go backwards. Trust me, I'll lead you."

Then he showed her the step. "It's easy, just do this." He showed her the steps and counted them off. "One, two, three . . . one, two, three . . . one, two, three . . . one, two, three." She followed his instructions and stepped backwards, which made her feel vulnerable but she trusted him.

"Is this what they taught you in the seminary?" She spoke in his ear, unable to resist taking a fun jab.

"One never knows when a priest is called upon to dance . . . with the Cardinal." He spoke the last words so only she could hear them.

"Or the Pope!" She giggled and watched him throw his head back and laugh.

He spun her to avoid a very young couple who plowed pass them out of control.

"I think you passed the course, Padre."

When the song ended, they stopped moving. Their arms fell to their sides as they waited for another song, and it came immediately.

It was a traditional reel and it drew everyone onto their feet and into the middle, except the old men and women who couldn't dance anymore.

Strong, athletic-looking couples took the middle and danced in circles in one direction, and Ardis, Carlos, and everyone else joined hands and circled around the outside in the opposite direction.

The dancers in the middle spun swiftly in a tighter, maddening circle as Ardis, Carlos, and everyone around the outside tightened the circle around them.

Fireworks exploded directly above the dancers, and lighted the frenzied scene below in sudden brightness that receded quickly to an eerie glow as the dance reached its final pitch. Once again, fireworks exploded above their heads. The dancers collapsed together in a heap of giddy laughter. Ardis lost her balance, too. Strings of firecrackers around the perimeter of the crowd signaled the end of the dance.

Ardis saw couples embracing, kissing. He helped her up.

"Where did you learn to dance like that? And don't tell me it was in the seminary."

"At the orphanage. One of the women who helped made it her mission to teach us how to dance. Then we went to events like this one and we had so much fun."

***

A cock crowed far above in the village. Xisco rose from his blankets in the hayloft, swung through the opening in the floor, splashed water in his eyes and was out in the yard in a minute.

The morning air carried a whiff of petrichor, the musky odour of dry grass and wet earth—not unlike the nose on a quality pinot noir—that arose when a small amount of rain moistened the dry earth. Xisco believed he had detected the familiar aroma of the stable. He breathed it all in deeply. To him, they were the same.

He surveyed the azure sky. The village will welcome the early morning drizzle. The weather had been dry, and today was beautifully hot and dry, and as such, quite remarkable for this time of year.

After completing his work in the stable, Xisco helped Ardis carry her equipment up the hill. Together, they found a couple of locations in the shade from which they could obtain good views of the procession and the sermon.

Xisco said hello to passers-by. His brother Armando stopped by with his tuba. Ardis asked the brothers to stand together for a photo.

Ardis was filming as the main procession started, once again, at the capela at the top of the hill on Avenida Señhor Bonfim. Well ahead of the main procession, costumed villagers carried a statue of Jesus on a litter, and stopped occasionally to perform mini plays. An acolyte carrying a cross on a high staff led the procession, including the Monseñhor, Padre Fernando, the local acolytes, lay brothers and finally the band in a parade down the road to a clearing on the side of the hill.

Today, the deafening boom of the bass drums, Armando's tuba, and the various horns and wind instruments of the slow-footed band compelled the giant snake-like procession to inch forward in a dead march. The "Nimrod," a variation from Sir Edward Elgar's *Enigma Variations*, was a heavy piece. Its drawn-out pace made it difficult for Carlos and everyone in the procession to move gracefully.

Finally, they reached their destination. The Monseñhor led the party into position and assumed his place on a dais of earth surrounded by pots of red mums. The band discovered an appropriate rhythm with newfound confidence. The procession of villagers filed into place. The Church servants were behind Carlos, the band was at the front on the near side. The villagers occupied a wide arc on the grassy hillside facing the Monseñhor. It was a natural amphitheatre.

Monseñhor Carlos held up his hand to signal the band to stop. But their leader had whipped up the band that played even louder now that it had taken its position and were no longer distracted by marching. The band had reached the climax of the song and the conductor did not intend to stop just yet.

An old woman turned to her companion. "They do this every year."

She spoke to a boy beside her. "Pass me a few stones, *menino.*"

"Here." She passed her friend two stones. The women flicked the stones at the conductor.

Off to the side of the women, Xisco watched as Ardis caught it all on film. He was embarrassed for his village.

"*Pare! Pare!*" Stop, the old women insisted. All but the trumpet player halted. He carried on loudly until the trombonist nudged him.

"Way to blow it, Enrico." A pocket of giggles burst out at the front of the crowd among the people who saw what was going on.

Miffed, the conductor glared at Carlos a moment then took his seat. Monseñhor Carlos cleared his throat once again and looked over the crowd as it finally fell silent.

"Today, we are expressing our love for Nosso Señhor do Bonfim." The Monseñhor paused in between sentences for effect. "The lesson of Jesus who died on the cross for our sins is the heart of our holy values here in Portugal."

Xisco looked at Ardis and shrugged his shoulders.

"My friends, what is the Good End? This festival celebrates how our

Lord chose to die on the cross as a sacrifice to obtain forgiveness for our sins. It does not mean we must die as he did. It means loving and forgiving one another.

"God has chosen Portugal to be an example, a catalyst, for the entire world to see. We know this from the miracles of Fatima.

"I am sure you all know what happened at Fatima. I'm not going to go over that again with you. We all know that Our Lady of Fatima predicted the death of two of the children. She predicted the Spanish Flu that wiped out fifty million people. And she warned us of Russia."

Standing with Ardis, Xisco had a good view over the crowd and could see how everyone reacted. Many did not pay attention to the Monseñhor.

"This happened only twenty-five years ago . . . In 1917, the Great War was ending . . . the war took tens of millions of men, women, and children.

"We needed Our Lady's comforting words," the Monseñhor continued. "People needed hope. For several months, Lúcia, the eldest surviving child, promised that the Lady would perform a miracle on a specific day, 'so that all may believe.'

"And as you know, on October 13, 1917, a massive crowd gathered . . . some say it was as many as a hundred thousand people.

"They witnessed the Miracle of the Sun. The sun appeared to change colours and to rotate like a fire wheel that spun off multi-coloured light across the landscape.

"Witnesses said the sun appeared to plunge towards the earth, which frightened many into believing it was the end of the world. Or that they were seeing the effects of an alien ship from outer space."

The Monseñhor's audience in Sonim erupted in chatter, but he carried on.

"Others suggested they witnessed an eclipse. In the Lisbon newspaper *O Século*, a reporter named Avelino de Almeida wrote that the sun "danced."

"What that massive crowd saw was the sun dancing in circles before their eyes. It was a miracle of faith that was given to them by the Lord thy God Himself."

Xisco saw the surprise in Ardis's eyes.

"Remember, this Miracle of the Sun was predicted by Our Lady of Fatima. Another prediction of Our Lady came true only four years ago on January 25, 1938."

Xisco leaned closer, eager to hear this.

"Many of us here today witnessed this great miracle of light over Portugal and indeed over Europe and around the globe.

"Here in Sonim, this miracle of light is known as the *Coroa de Señhor do Bonfim.*"

Ardis didn't understand; she looked to Xisco.

"He's talking about the Crown of the Good Lord. I saw that with my Pai."

The Monseñhor continued. "It meant that God was about to punish the world with war, famine, and persecutions against the Church and the Holy Father.

"As you know, the year after the Corona, another Great War started. Once again, soldiers are dying in Europe. The destruction, the atrocities, and the killing of innocent people continue to occur across Europe to this day with no end in sight.

"But not in Portugal. Does Our Lady of Fatima protect Portugal? Yes, she does. Portugal remains neutral and the war has not touched us."

This topic gripped the entire audience.

"However, there is another kind of war going on in Portugal. Our war is the daily struggle to find food to feed our families so we may all live healthy and happy and honour her Son, Jesus Christ.

"Beware the war in Europe and across the globe is a profound struggle between the forces of good and evil; of freedom and tyranny. This war is a struggle that pits the free world against dictators— Germany's Hitler, Italy's Mussolini, and Japan's Emperor Hirohito, who wages a cruel war against China.

"Thanks to our Prime Minister, António Salazar, Portugal has remained outside these awful conflicts."

There was a smattering of applause throughout the audience.

"We owe gratitude and devotion to Our Lady of Fatima for protecting Portugal. Please kneel and receive the blessing of Our Lady of

Fatima, the mother of our Lord and Saviour Jesus Christ, Nosso Señhor do Bonfim.

"In the name of the Father, the Son, and the Holy Spirit."

"Amen." The crowd gave a large, enthusiastic response.

The band played again. Monseñhor Carlos led the procession away from the side of the hill. The band and all the people followed him. Carlos looked over his shoulder to Padre Fernando for guidance. "Where do we go from here?"

"To the square."

***

When they reached the square, a party was underway. The men had brought out tables and chairs from the café; a fire for cooking was ready. Xisco and Ardis watched women stir large kettles of *guisado*, a stew that was thick with vegetables and a little beef, over the fire.

Xisco and Ardis relaxed on the stone ledge of the fountain and caught their breath. It had been a busy day. Xisco narrated the shenanigans going on in the square, where a light-hearted spirit had taken over the men, who brought out small casks of wine for the wine tasting. Xisco pointed out how the men presented the women with tastings, and asked them which wine was their favourite. In the muddle of boasting and joking around that followed, there were no clear winners. The differences in the wine were marginal. Their methods and their grapes were all pretty much the same and overall the quality was excellent. Xisco translated their comments to one another for her and explained what was going on.

Carlos arrived in the square. He wore dark brown pants, a plain shirt, and a sequined vest, decorated in the style of Portuguese tiles known as *azulejos*.

"Look at you." Ardis clearly admired his garb. "You look ready for a party."

"We are genuine Portuguese." Xisco also wore such a vest—his with a red rooster in beads and sequins on his back.

The men converged on the Monseñhor with their wine. They offered high praise for his sermon. Eugenio produced three cups and poured each of them a taste. Carlos, Ardis, and Xisco toasted the men, tasted the wine, and emptied their cups. Another man stepped forward with his cask under his arm and poured a round.

Then the vintners waited to hear which wine each person chose.

They repeated the tasting several times. The women offered bread that went well with the wine and helped clear their pallets.

Xisco complimented the Monseñhor on his sermon. "I found the Miracle of the Sun interesting but I'm not sure I can believe it."

"It is difficult to imagine a dancing sun, spinning like a pinwheel," the Monseñhor responded.

"That wasn't possible, was it?"

"Perhaps not."

To Xisco, the concept was implausible. "Some people say the dancing of the sun is what happens when anyone stares at the sun too long. They also say that among those who attended were evangelists, who truly feared that the sun would incinerate them all if they did not fall on their knees and pray. That fear spread from one person to the next all across the hillside and whipped the crowd into a frenzy. Everyone, including the organizers, feared for their children's safety."

Ardis nodded to show her support for Xisco. "I heard that the phenomenon was a natural event caused by light hitting particles of sand in the atmosphere from a sand storm off the Sahara Desert in Africa."

The idea she expressed was well known. Southern Europe occasionally experienced a variety of impacts from their neighbours across the Mediterranean Sea. They called it The Saharan Effect.

"Yes, arguments deny the claim," the Monseñhor acknowledged.

"Or it was caused by a meteorological event like the Aurora Borealis that took place four years ago." Ardis had learned this in school.

"Yes, the Fatima Storm," confirmed the Monseñhor. "God works in mysterious ways. It doesn't matter what explanation there is for the motions of the sun."

"But why not, Monseñhor?" Xisco wanted a better explanation. "If it can be explained, how can it be a miracle?"

The Monseñhor was at his wit's end. "Okay, let's say either an aurora or a sandstorm or both were necessary to enhance the effects of staring at the sun. It does not matter what explanation science can provide. What matters is that it happened *where* it was predicted to happen and *when* it was predicted to happen . . . and it was witnessed by a massive crowd of people."

Xisco and Ardis stared at the Monseñhor, absorbing the idea.

The Monseñhor had given them the official Church dogma on the topic. "This proves it was indeed a miracle." It was everything he had.

"A miracle?" Like a hawk with a sharp eye on his prey, Sam stood off to the side and waited for the right moment to strike. "So this is what it takes to save souls?" His challenge hung in the air.

"Oh-oh." Xisco knew Sam and his views very well. Sam did not speak up unless he felt morally obligated to confront an injustice.

"A miracle grabs hold of a person's imagination. It strangles the life out of intelligent thinking. It suffocates logic. It commands belief," said Sam.

He looked at the others for support or objections, but saw none. So he continued. "People who witness a miracle have no choice but to believe. A miracle demands obedience and it robs us of our free will. There is no faith."

In the dimming light, Ardis and Xisco watched Sam warily, and kept an eye on the Monseñhor for his response. The Monseñhor did not rise to Sam's challenge nor seek to defend the view he had expressed.

Ardis frowned.

Xisco caught her eye and shrugged as if to say, "What's up with Carlos?"

Carlos had nodded to each of Sam's statements. It was as if he processed the ideas and wanted to agree but could not or he would have contradicted himself and everything he believed in.

Sam shook his head and turned away. He had no interest in watching a priest struggle to face the truth. That was a private problem.

Xisco signalled to Sam that it was time. They slipped away.

With the sun sinking below the far ridge, dusk had fallen quickly on the square. Men lit torches and over the next few moments, word rippled through the crowd that the Señhor had invited everyone to a performance featuring the village orchestra. The men led the crowd out of the square, past the school, past the Señhor's manor, and into the adjoining field where they huddled on the benches that had been set up for them beside the orchestra.

Within moments, the white-haired Señhor stood on an empty crate and raised his arms for attention.

"I am so happy to welcome you to our harvest party." The Señhor had become tipsy from drinking with his men, who rallied around him now. "This evening, we are adding something new to the occasion."

Xisco looked up and saw stars were out. The timing would be perfect.

He heard laughter and clapping. He saw the Señhor nod to Zé to begin the show. The men doused the torches.

Xisco could feel anticipation grip the crowd. The people who had all been talking, laughing, and carrying on, quieted down as their eyes adjusted to the darkness. With lowered voices, the fun continued with outbursts followed by shushing. Xisco wished he could be with them. His parents and all his siblings were there. Tia Bea, the Señhorita, and her mother, Matilda. He looked for his old classmate Cristina.

A thunderous boom ruptured the air above their heads, bounced off the mountain behind them and echoed off the buildings in the square. People in the crowd recoiled in fright, and then released a collective gasp. With impeccable timing, a guy fell over, pretending he had been shot. The people in the comedian's immediate vicinity broke up with laughter, a child cried and everyone in the audience started talking at once. The show had begun.

Immediately following the opening canon, the orchestra members caught their communal breath and commenced an abridged version of Tchaikovsky's 1812 Overture, a dramatic piece in which all the strings, horns and percussion instruments in their small band could play with unguarded enthusiasm.

People in the crowd giggled nervously, not sure of what to expect next. Could the rockets shoot at them? Explode in their ears? Give everyone burns? No one could say decisively one way or another whether they would be safe because few of them had actually ever seen a fireworks display.

Then they lit a series of three Roman candles, starting with the farthest away and ending close to the audience.

The band made great cuts in the score to complete the piece in the time allotted, exerting their greatest efforts when the fireworks were bursting in the sky. In the intervals of darkness when there was no great display above their heads, the band lowered its volume and allowed suspense to build between the bursts of colour.

A series of rockets shot upward and exploded. The first one presented an umbrella pattern as a necklace brocade that melted slowly in ripples of small stars, inciting "oohs" and "ahhs" from the crowd. In the next one, coloured stars exploded high above in trails of a flower, alive with sparks.

Another rocket rose in the sky, creating the appearance of a curved tree trunk before it burst into six large trailing stars that presented the fronds of a palm tree.

The pause between each rocket was only moments, which the crowd did not even notice as people talked and carried on more and more loudly with their party. The band played resolutely with a restrained vigour, trying to match the drama of the explosions of light overhead with greater flourish.

The fireworks continued. One was falling leaves and twinkling stars that fluttered down to the ground. In another, coloured stars flashed on and off. Then a small, rotating tourbillon—a pinwheel—threw out sparks and rotated wildly in spastic, spiral flight paths.

One rocket emitted a burst of eight stars that travelled up and out in artful trajectories before burning out.

The grand finale came with an intense bang followed by a bright shower of flashing and popping light. It ended as smoke and ash descended on the Square. Then another intense bang signaled the end of the show. The crowd erupted in applause, cheering and whistling raucously into the smoke-filled darkness just as Sam emerged from the cloud to take a bow.

The men picked up torches and led the way back to the square. The men placed the torches around the perimeter, lending a dramatic atmosphere to the festival.

The women ladled the guisado from the kettles. Candles appeared on the tables and men returned with their casks to serve wine to accompany the dinner.

The band played a different style of music than what they played the evening before at the Candlelight Parade. Others came forward as well, to play an accordion or a guitar, or to sing. People were moving to the rhythm, and getting on their feet and dancing. A traditional song by the band drew many into the middle to dance.

Eugenio and Elena joined the dancing. Señhor Montalvão strolled around the perimeter with Zé. The Señhor joined the Monseñhor and Ardis. Sam, who had done work for the Señhor, also joined the group. The men returned with their casks and the wine tasting began anew. Cristina, along with Amália and Martim, joined the party. Xisco watched for Cangou and sure enough, he appeared shortly after, too.

Everybody danced. Even Sam got up, starting with an easy Yemenite step that he livened up with a hop and a clap. Xisco clapped for Sam and cheered him. As the music sped up, Sam swung in a circle with his right foot over the left and then back behind the left, a basic *Mayim* step. Sam pulled Xisco in and others joined him copying his steps until there was a line of dancers that eventually joined and formed a circle. Sam led them through the dance, adding a hop and a kick that the young people did until they ended with a big cheer.

The young men in the dance clapped Sam on the back. Then they reached for their wine jugs.

"There is nothing better under the sun or moon, than to eat, drink, and be merry," Sam declared.

The band played a Portuguese reel. Xisco asked Cristina for a dance.

They imitated the others, hopping and spinning around the terrazzo with relatively decent success despite, or because of, Xisco's gently inebriated state. Tradition required them to step on each other's toes at least once before the song ended, which they did.

The next song was a ballad and they remained on their feet, ready to dance. The singer was Umdina whose serenade was sweet and strong.

"I knew you would be studying," Xisco said. With a red flush on his face, he threw back his head and laughed. "Cristina, the night is young and so are we. This is our time to sing." He pulled her closer.

She recognized his allusion to the French tale they had learned at school. She pulled back from him to look him in the eye. "You are like cicadas singing from the trees. All summer long you sang while I worked like an ant and stored food for the winter."

"I am a Mighty Cicada and I will eat your food!" Xisco was light-headed.

They both laughed.

But then she turned serious. "I will study hard, earn my certificate, and have a career." Her mood had turned suddenly dour. "What will you have?"

Xisco stated what he had known forever and what he had lived for. "I will have my garden. Like my parents, I will have a family. I will make wine and I will dance."

"I don't think that will be enough for you, Xisco. You will want more." Immediately, she added, "I know I do."

18. A Brutal Thieving

The spring of 1942 marked a new beginning for Señhor Montalvão, the Baron of Sonim. He was the wealthiest man in Sonim and neighbouring villages, yet his income disappointed his wife, who openly rebuked him, "In Lisbon, you will never amount to anything."

After his visit with Monseñhor Carlos, Montalvão received a telegram. A shipment had arrived in Vila Real. That would be his reward for identifying three wolfram mines for the Monseñhor's people in Lisbon. Three *pequeno* chests.

Montalvão was not stupid. His weakness, he realized, was his reliance on his mining engineer, Sam Meyer. Sam had located the properties, written the report, and set the groundwork for three quick sales to the Monseñhor's contacts.

More importantly, Sam managed Montalvão's wolfram mine that was turning out to be his most valuable asset. Montalvão needed a mining engineer now more than ever. If he wanted to keep Sam, Montalvão had to reward him.

***

Having arrived early for a business meeting with the Señhor, Sam dropped in to see Xisco, with whom he enjoyed spending time. He sauntered around the stable, beginning in the area of Xisco's hayloft, inspecting the tack, making remarks casually in English.

"It is nice out today," Sam began. Sam had already shown the boy how he estimated the mining potential of a piece of land and how he made fireworks—topics that didn't spark any real interest in the boy.

"I heard there was a storm," Xisco replied.

Reassessing the boy's skills and his prospects for the future, Sam saw that Xisco would do well in the world if he were to learn some English. "Where?" He quizzed him like this, every chance he got.

Xisco was at an age when he could learn and retain a new language easily. "In the north, on the ocean," he replied.

"Near the ocean." Sam made the correction in the least controlling manner possible. "I heard they receive snow there."

"Sometimes, we see snow here, too," Xisco offered in return.

"Ahhh." Sam slipped further into the stable to see the animals. He talked with the chickens. He scolded the goats. He gave wide berth to the pigs. Petted the cows and thanked them. Met with old friends, the horses. Scoffed at the donkeys.

Xisco followed along and played Sam's game.

"Do you believe in one God?" Xisco asked the donkey, which made Sam laugh.

His query carried the weight of an overdue notice. It had been several months since Sam had promised Xisco he would teach him about Judaism. But the English lessons had taken precedence.

Sam had no choice but to engage. "Yes, I do," said Sam. Xisco had posited the matter squarely in front of him.

"Then what is this about duality?"

Again, Sam laughed. "Ah, duality," he responded. "That has to do with people. We believe every person and thing in creation contains both good and bad, a spiritual side and a physical side. This duality divides us, and when we are split, we are not whole with God. Our purpose in life is to get rid of any challenge to God's unity."

"How do we do this?"

"Each day on waking, we wash our hands and thank God for another day. Throughout the day, washing my hands reminds me of my mission in life."

"It helps to keep you focused."

"Yes."

"You are selective about your food."

Sam stepped out of the barn and back into Xisco's area with the hayloft. And he spoke in a low voice, not wanting animals to hear.

"We avoid pork and shellfish, which are forbidden. We don't combine meat and dairy. We eat only meat that has been ritually slaughtered and salted to remove all traces of blood and is certified kosher."

"That seems like a lot of trouble."

"Not really. That's the butcher's job. I say my prayers."

"At bedtime?"

"In the morning, at noon, and in the evening."

"That is a lot of praying."

Sam looked to the hayloft and nodded, thoughtfully. "I suppose. Each of our patriarchs instituted a prayer: Abraham, the prayer for the morning; Isaac, the afternoon; and Jacob, the evening. Throughout my day, prayers are my touchstones that guide me in my mission to rid my life of material distractions."

"You are very devoted."

"I aim to live a humble life. Such is our way. I function very well in isolation or in small groups. Privacy is important."

"That doesn't sound so inspirational to me."

"We will see about that." Sam laughed. "There is a transcendental aspect of our teachings that remains as revolutionary now as it was a thousand years ago. The theory is plain and its practices are effective in exposing a person to possibilities that are not visible to the eye but only to the anointed and only over time."

"Why is this so different?"

"We experience forces that we otherwise couldn't understand. Long ago, these forces were called angels."

"Angels exist in Catholic teachings, too."

"Yes, but in our story, angels are not celestial beings. They are bits of unspoken information, thoughts, and feelings that we exchange. We share energy at a personal level; our communications travel on the existing connections between God and His creation. The experience is mystical."

"Wow. That is interesting."

"I am walking to your father's house. Would you like to join me?" Sam forgot all about talking with the Señhor.

"Sure. I just have to tell Zé I go." Xisco left Sam in the stable. "I come back."

Zé was busy with the Señhor, so Xisco told Inez he was walking with Sam to his father's.

Learning that a secret state of being and communication were possible was exhilarating. The possibilities swirled before Xisco. Whatever it was, it was his. He had a right, if not a responsibility, to gain some knowledge and insight. And he was curious. In some ways, he became intense though such tension did not have a chance with him. Xisco absorbed what he could and the rest of it just slid off his back like water off a duck.

***

That morning, Ardis and the Monseñhor also went for a walk up to the road above the village. They returned via the capela and passed by Eugenio's. On seeing them, Eugenio waved. They started talking and of course Eugenio invited them to share a glass of wine.

With Ardis's movie camera on his shoulder, Xisco was filming. Ardis wanted to tell him to put it away, but did not want to embarrass him in front of everyone.

Eugenio beckoned them to follow him through the stable into the back where he stored his wine. Joints of salted boar hung from the ceiling. He filled a clay pitcher with wine from the barrel and set out three glass tumblers on the workbench, which he filled from the pitcher.

"Saúde," said Carlos, raising his glass to Eugenio.

"Saúde," Eugenio and Ardis responded.

They sipped the wine. When his guests nodded approvingly, Eugenio smiled broadly. "*Bom*," he said and excused himself. He went out and up the stairs to call Elena to join their guests. She returned with him and accepted a glass of wine, too. The party repeated their toasts and Eugenio refilled their glasses.

Sam arrived. Once again, Eugenio filled glasses and everyone toasted Sam.

By the time Zé pulled up in his truck, Eugenio's and Elena's guests were very relaxed and enjoying the day.

"Good afternoon, everyone. Nice to see you all." Zé accepted a glass of wine, though he had more work to do that day. He looked to Sam, who was talking with Xisco. "I have something for you, Sam." Together, they unloaded a small chest with a hinged lid.

With the camera on a tripod, Xisco rolled the film.

A swastika stamped on the crate could imply the crate was part of the signing bonus Carlos had arranged with Manfred. If Carlos made this connection, he did not show it.

"We better open this inside," said Zé.

In the stable, Zé handed Sam a key. "This is yours."

Sam unlocked the latch and lifted the lid.

Sam stepped back. A look of confusion replaced the smile on his face. "What?" The colour drained from his cheeks.

Xisco reached in to scoop a handful of gold rings and other trinkets but Sam's arm shot out and grabbed his hand. "I would not touch it if I were you."

"I wasn't going to take anything."

"No, it's not that. You just don't want to touch it at all."

"Is that a pair of glasses?" Xisco pointed to a frame sticking out of the small mountain of rings, earrings, chains, broaches and—

Carlos peeked in. "What is this?"

"This is payment from Germans for services, Monseñhor." Sam spoke with cold indignation. He looked at Zé. "But do you know what this is?"

"They made a collection from citizens," said Zé, "to help pay for the war effort." Zé was comfortable with an explanation Montalvão had given him.

Sam shook his head. "I wish it were so. Nazis took everything from my people."

"The Jews?" Carlos hadn't heard about this.

"Yes. The situation in Poland worsened every year. First, they gave armbands. They marked their shops and businesses. There was looting. Then to protect Jews, or so they claimed, they herded Jews into ghettos and locked them in. The Nazis said the enclosures protected the people, but they are prisons. They lost all their possessions. I think this is what we see here."

"Oh?" Carlos looked at the bits and pieces of sordid evidence. What they hinted of, he could only guess. He had no knowledge of the armbands, curfews, the closing of Jewish shops, and the segregation of Jews into ghettos. If Sam said such things occurred, he had to take his word, and the horrible images would seep slowly into his consciousness.

"Look, there are teeth," said Xisco.

"These are from the Jews." Sam sat down on a stool.

The Monseñhor stepped back, confronted by terrible visions of men, women, old people, children, whole families cruelly stripped of their possessions. Having their gold teeth ripped from their mouths was a brutal thieving of dignity—with no limitations on abuse.

Carlos had authorized the bonus payments of gold. But he did not do this. Even if the stories were true, how could he be responsible? He was not involved. He did not support Nazi crimes.

He imagined how many hundred wedding bands were in that chest, and how many marriages and families the Nazis had ripped apart.

For a moment, no one did anything. No one knew what to do.

Xisco stepped forward to comfort Sam as his parents, Zé, Ardis, and Carlos watched on.

Yet, Carlos didn't dare think of how many people had had their teeth ripped from their mouths because they contained gold fillings. He ignored the long line of people, all of whom had lost their dignity. He held onto one belief and held onto it firmly.

He didn't do it.

"How could God let such a thing happen?" Carlos whispered, testing an idea.

Sam frowned and shook his head. "No God of yours or mine wanted this to happen, Monseñhor. This was the work of evil people. The sick perpetrators of these crimes are far away. They control nations and armies and are beyond touch—unless they are defeated in war. We allow them to win when we take their money."

Carlos stood. He flung aside the contents of his wineglass. He paced.

Eugenio tried to recoup the moment. There had been enough stress and confrontation. He busied himself with pouring more wine for his guests.

Ardis was thoughtful. "This is the most terrible thing I've heard coming out of Germany. It means money is scarce to pay for the resources needed for the war effort."

Sam concurred. "I heard all resources were scarce in Germany.

Scarcity of fuel and even food hits everyone very hard."

Xisco had filmed the chest of Jewish gold. Ardis had him stop and put the camera away. She returned her attention to the conversation.

"Señhor Sam, can I ask you something?" Ardis was trying to understand the situation.

Sam nodded.

"Why did you help in the first place? Didn't you know who the buyers were?"

Sam shook his head. "I expected the mines were purchased by new money in Lisbon—either British or American. The Monseñhor was involved, so I assumed it had to be so. But my thinking was only partly accurate. The customers were German."

Hearing his name put Carlos further on edge. He stopped pacing.

"Isn't that so, Monseñhor?" Sam looked to Carlos for confirmation. "Look, you are upset about this gold as I am. I think you are one who did this."

Only Montalvão was supposed to know about his involvement. "Me?" Carlos feigned ignorance.

"You did this, with Señhor Montalvão. I know because I was the mining engineer, who prepared the report, including recommendations about which properties to buy."

Carlos recognized the name Sam Meyer from the report.

"Funds came from Banco Ambrosiano, the Vatican bank," Sam continued. "That was the clue that tipped me off, and then pieces fell into place—such as the timing of your visits to Sonim. Only you could be the contact the Baron refused to name."

Carlos could not deny it. "I helped. The gold is from the Germans."

"I expected it so."

"So we're both to blame."

Sam was the recipient of gold stolen from his own people.

"I am so sorry this happened to your people." Ardis stepped up.

"Our past will haunt us forever if we don't stand up to these people and say no, you cannot do this to us any longer. But thank you, Ardis. I appreciate your kind thoughts."

"This crime is unforgivable—even during an all-out war."

"I agree. To avenge this, I must become a killer, too."

"If that is what it takes to end such madness, then so be it." Ardis shrugged her shoulders as if to say there could be no other way. "I'd rather be guilty of stopping a killer, than standing by and watching it happen repeatedly."

Sam nodded. "We pay a frightful price to live in terrible times. I will be happy when I stop the next shipment of wolfram."

***

Ardis, Xisco, and Carlos walked in the dark back to the Baron's estate. Carlos walked ahead with his long stride, wrapped in thought, forgetting his companions.

Ardis took things into hand. "Xisco, how do they get the wolfram out of Portugal?"

"They use trucks. They take back roads to Spain. It is very close."

The walk was short back to the Montalvão manor. The Baron greeted them on arrival. Ardis asked the Baron whether she might use the telephone later if it was convenient. Then Ardis made sure that Carlos found his way upstairs into his room. When she returned, the Baron politely vacated his study for her to make a phone call.

She dialled Garcia. At the start of the conversation, she spoke with Garcia at a normal volume. As the conversation progressed, she lowered her voice. "Can you pass on information to my family? I am deeply concerned that my Uncle Walter cannot pay his debt to my cousin Dan. I think he stole Judy's gold jewellery—Judy, that's his daughter," she explained. "I am sure that my Uncle Walt is flat broke. Give my regards to all for me, okay? Thanks, Garcia."

Uncle Walter was Germany. Dan was code for Portugal. Uncle Walter's daughter Judy? They might miss that one. Judy was not in the code. But it would have to do.

"Dan has been working so hard and is quite productive," she continued. "He will begin sending his cookies next week." Ardis hoped that Garcia would understand she had just told him a wolfram order was ready and would begin shipping next week.

"We may go for a drive to see the countryside just north of here.

They say the view of Spain is a good place to take pictures." With Xisco's help, she even provided targets.

***

Major Brooker was in Porto when he received word from Garcia. Brooker quickly assembled his team for an operation that destroyed a train track, a bridge, a key road and a convoy of trucks.

***

Sam left the chest with Eugenio, who tucked it away in a corner of his stable.

That evening, Sam went to see Montalvão. It was late when he arrived, but Montalvão received him. Sam was visibly upset, agitated. Montalvão had Inez bring in the candelabra from the dining room and he made small talk, expecting Zé to return and give him some support.

Sam told him he believed the buyers of the wolfram were Germans, not Portuguese, or Italians as they had guessed, and the payment was stolen gold. This put Montalvão on the defensive. He told Sam citizens committed to the war effort donated the gold. Sam insisted the Nazis stole the gold from Jews. Montalvão argued, suggesting Jews willingly contributed to the war effort. Seeing the situation was hopeless made Sam so angry he was afraid he would take his anger out on Montalvão. He left immediately before he did anything he would regret later.

Montalvão reconsidered the situation. Did the German people not donate their gold rings and jewellery to pay for a cause in which they as a nation believed? This was what he and Zé had believed. They had been naïve. He was stunned to realize the Nazis stole the gold items from Jews in a ghetto. It upset Montalvão to learn how the Nazi fascists operated.

Montalvão was ashamed and angry. The fatigue from too many late nights sitting at his desk, poring over his ledgers, had caught up to him. "How could they do this?" He slammed his ledger on the desk in anger and paced his study in quiet resentment. His understanding had been much different from the truth described by Sam. He did not doubt Sam, who had proven himself a straightforward, honest man. Montalvão accepted his word as truth. He shook his head. "It makes sense. It could happen."

Apparently, it did happen. The truth was so brutal it did not seem plausible. It revealed a cruel and inhuman treatment of innocent people.

Montalvão turned white like his hair; he rubbed his stomach. He looked as if he had seen the faces of all those people in a ghetto looking at him. He looked as if the eyes of their ghosts were watching him and nodding in understanding. They were all saying he, Montalvão, was the one who did this to them. But he was not! He did not know. How could he? "I will give it all back; I will send it to these people in the ghettos. I will give their gold back to them, all of it."

Montalvão stopped where he stood, stooped over his desk. He wished he could undo what the Nazis did. Montalvão understood their lives, the peace they once knew, could never be returned, or replaced. The crimes against all those people were all on him. He gripped his stomach, which had constricted in a tight knot. His hands went to his head where the veins felt like they were pounding out of his skull. He rubbed his arm—his left arm where a shooting pain brought on a terrible ache. He crossed his arms over his torso as if his whole body ached. The raging, throbbing in his chest and brain burst.

He dropped to one knee. Then he rolled over and onto his back, a move that looked as if he planned it. Alone in his study, he heard the crickets in the still evening. Detached now forever, he and the tension slipped away. The tapers in the candelabra fluttered as an unexpected draft passed through them.

His heart was still. The lenses that once beheld his world now adorned his slackened face like coal-black, unblinking obsidians.

19. Penchant for the Ride

At the first light of day, Sam departed Sonim. He could no longer stand on the sidelines and do nothing.

He stowed his motorcycle in the back of his truck under the large tarp, and left the village. He went first to the By The Way Café and asked Harratt to store his truck out back for him, and then he pulled off the tarp and hit the road on his motorcycle.

Sam traveled without drawing attention to himself. He carried few possessions, dressed as if he was poor, and had a way of counting out his coins as if they were his last. He blended into a crowd, with one exception. He had a penchant for riding his BSA Empire Star on the open road. It was his *Fahrvergnügen*, his pleasure for driving.

It made for an odd site with his long, curly beard plastered by the wind onto his shoulder and his dark bushy eyebrows sticking above his goggles.

Sam went to Lisbon. On the way, he stopped at cafés for basic sustenance. He talked with people, told them his mind. "The Nazis pay for your wolfram with gold stolen from the Jews." The table of men he was speaking to did not want to listen.

In Lisbon, Sam went directly to the British embassy on the west side of the old city, on Rua São Francisco Borja in the Lapa, an area of small palaces. He found the embassy easily enough. He identified it by the line of refugees queued up in front. Sam bypassed the line, as he was not there on that kind of business. Embassy staff tried to shoo him away, to dismiss him. So he made a loud racket in reception. Normally, he was the type of person who did not cause disturbances of any kind. He was pleased that a senior officer of the embassy came out to see what the fuss was all about and took Sam aside where they could talk in private. Sam told him his story, beginning with the fact that Portugal was supplying Germany with wolfram. "Tell us something we don't know." According to this officer, it was a well-known fact. "But we don't promote it to the public." Sam was stunned.

Sam told him about the payment in stolen Jewish gold. He believed this would move him and the embassy into action. It was the type of information, he was certain, the British could not have known. But indeed, it was. The officer acknowledged it was "a twist" and told Sam outright that his government could not allow such news to spread to the British people or to the Portuguese and Americans. "It would force our hand. We would have to take drastic action and it would disrupt our relations with our citizens and our allies in this war."

The fellow seemed to know a lot for a bureaucratic officer, Sam surmised, not pleased with the response he received. He had expected the British would fully share his view. He had lived in England. He knew that democracy and liberty were important to the British because they took up arms against tyranny, except when it did not suit them, apparently.

As a conscientious person, Sam was motivated to object to the injustice against Jews in Germany. He continued to poke as many hornets' nests as he could find.

The American Embassy was only six or seven city blocks away within the Lapa neighbourhood, on Rua Sacramento à Lapa. But no one at the American embassy was available to speak with him. So he got back on his motorcycle and rode past the Basilica Estrella and down past the Assembleia Nationale and up to the Bairro Alto.

He stopped at the office of O Século, the newspaper. Within minutes, he was talking with a reporter who covered national politics. Sam gave the reporter a story of national interest. The newspaper could tell the world about Portuguese support for the German war machine.

The reporter did not ask for more information. He nodded his head politely and thanked him for sharing his story. "I imagine this is difficult for you –"

Sam cut him short. "My situation is not the issue. Will you print my story?"

"No, Señhor Meyer, we cannot. The Policia de Vigilância e Defesa do Estado . . . you know, the PVDE could make our lives very difficult. They would shut us down in a second. I'm sorry."

The Portuguese Secret Police operated an extensive network of informants. One could never be too careful.

"Oh, so the PVDE is censoring you?" Sam's accusation may have seemed like an innocent one, but the volume of his voice drew attention.

The PVDE were involved in everything from censorship and eavesdropping to oppression of political activists. Salazar's Portugal was conservative and Catholic, and it was especially sensitive to any opposition related to communism, socialism, liberalism, and anti-colonialism.

That evening, the PVDE picked up Sam Meyer and detained him in a cell for a week. The PVDE's purpose with Sam was the same as it was with everyone—to sow terror and fear. To intimidate. To motivate silent compliance. To control and suppress the dissidents, especially Communists.

Each day, they took Sam into a room and asked him the same things again, without any response. "You may not spread such information to the public. There is a war going on."

Sam rubbed his brow and expelled his breath. He closed his eyes to rest them.

On the eighth day, they released him.

"If you talk, you will not go into a cell."

Sam, bless his heart, did not heed their warning. He was not concerned for himself. He had a newsletter to print.

20. No Absolution for the Downtrodden

No one can see change coming. To make such a claim, a person would have to compress time as we know it, and dance in the stratosphere. That is where change can be seen drifting in from the Bay of Biscay and across Galicia before clouds condense, and Saharan air blows across the Iberian Peninsula to imbue the sunsets red and gold.

In Trás-os-Montes, a storm comes suddenly and shocks all animals with torrential downpours and gale force winds. Knocks men down. Washes away dust that has gathered for years. Steals lives and slips away. Life returns to normal as if nothing happened. In this land beyond mountains and rivers, seasons pass, people die, and stone remains stone. *Antes de mil anos todos seremos brancos.* It will all be white in a thousand years.

There is no point in worrying about anything. What has been will be again; what has been done will be done again; there is nothing new under the sun.

***

At the gate to the cemetery, Monseñhor Carlos turned to face Señhor Montalvão's young adult children, Olympio and Gloria, and a small group of mourners comprised of staff from the manor and men who worked the fields, including Zé, Eugenio, Xisco and all the men they worked with. "Gather in, gather in." The pallbearers set the casket down in front of the gates. Monseñhor Carlos pointed to the stone plaque set in the arch above the entrance.

"MISEREMINI MEI, SALTEM VOS AMICI MEI." Carlos read loudly for all to hear. "This is from the *Book of Job*, Chapter 19." He provided the Latin text from memory: "MISEREMINI MEI, MISEREMINI MEI, SALTEM VOS AMICI MEI QUIA MANUS DOMINI TETIGIT ME."

He scanned his audience, looking for interest. "It means . . . Have pity on me, have pity on me, at least you my friends, for the hand of God has touched me.

"The *Book of Job* tells us that God allowed Satan to strike Job down.

Satan afflicted Job with disease and injury and took all his material things. But why would God allow this to happen to a good man like Job?

"It was a wager between God and Satan. Satan wanted to prove that Job only loves God because he has everything. And God wanted to show Satan that though he loses everything important to him, Job would remain faithful to God.

"During Job's ordeals, his wife told him to curse God, but Job remained faithful. His friends blamed Job's sufferings on his own actions, saying that Job must have sinned.

"In the end, God restored Job, who acknowledged that humans do not know everything. God then blessed Job with twice as much as he had before his trials began.

"The *Book of Job* is one of the oldest stories in the Bible. It presents a conundrum that still bothers us today: why bad things can happen to good people.

"But unlike the view that Job and his peers had that God was above and outside the human experience, existing in another world of eternal life, our view today is that God is more immanent within our world. He permeates our world. He is omnipresent.

"God is close with us in our world. He is a part of our lives. He lives and breathes in us. If the dead could talk, they would tell us to let God into our hearts so that we may all love and care for one another as God intends us to do.

"Now let us go into the cemetery and commit the soul of Señhor Montalvão into the hands of God."

After the last rites, the family went into its manor, as was the custom. The Monseñhor returned to the *capela* along with the others who needed to return their vestments to the sacristy. Xisco helped Ardis return her equipment to the Montalvão manor.

The people who participated in the funeral did not return to work as they normally would have done. They returned to the village at a pace slower than even the funeral procession, as if there was a reluctance to depart. Xisco watched faces he had known his entire life. The unspoken emotion that he saw in their eyes moved him. "People are sad."

Ardis did not give it any thought. "There was a funeral. Isn't this the way funerals work?"

"No, there was a need for more to be said."

"What do you mean?"

Xisco could not put his finger on it. Perhaps it was because the funeral for the Baron lacked any real sorrow. No one cried, not even his children. He wanted to savour the mood. He sensed a longing to linger a moment in conversation.

"We were there to grieve for the Baron, but we did not grieve, not really. Nobody had a chance to grieve for our loved ones, or for ourselves, either."

Some people gathered in the main square, some in courtyards, and others who did not attend came out and joined those who did. The sky was *azul*, a clear blue; the air was warm. It was a nice day to drink wine.

***

After the funeral, Xisco returned to his parents' house where others also gathered. He invited Ardis and Carlos to join them.

What was on his mind was his dream to support a family here in Sonim. He had seen how challenging it was for his parents to feed, shelter, and clothe their family. He knew children had to protect every scrap of food they received, especially during the cold, damp winters when all they could do was huddle under heavy blankets in their beds. At least in their beds they enjoyed any warmth that rose through the floorboards from the pigs in their stalls directly below. To feel warm, men and women drank shots of *aguardiente*. Even children warmed their bellies with the foul fuel. Were they the downtrodden?

Upstairs, Elena entertained the women. She served mint juleps made of *aguardiente* and lime juice. The women cut bread into small pieces and put olives and almonds on a tray to send to the men.

Eugenio handed Carlos a glass of red wine. "It's good for the soul, Padre."

Carlos drank a few glasses of wine too quickly. "Here, drink some water." Eugenio slowed him down, hoping to prevent a crisis. Eugenio carved thin slices of *prosunto* and Elena brought the tray of *salgados simples*, savouries to go with the wine.

Carlos was unengaged and apart from the men who were talking loudly in a festive mode, the wine having taken effect quickly on their collective mood. Xisco lingered nearby, always interested in what was happening with these older friends of his.

"Carlos, are you okay?" Ardis nudged him.

Carlos nodded. "Just thinking, perhaps I will walk *El Camino* in penance." His back was straight and the cloud of worry was gone. "Or is it time we visit sea turtles?"

"Are you up for that, Carlos?"

Carlos looked into her eyes. "Yes, Ardis, I think I am."

"You are?" His answer surprised her. "Good. I do need a crew."

"Yes, let's take a long voyage . . . to the Azores," he added.

"The Azores?" Xisco looked up, surprised. "You are going to the Azores?"

"Actually, that might be too far," Ardis cautioned. "Why don't we start with the Algarve?"

"That would be fine," said Carlos. "I haven't been there for so long."

Xisco didn't hesitate. "I've never been there. Take me, too."

But Ardis focused on Carlos. He would be the kind of travel companion with whom she would feel safe.

Xisco persisted. "It may be my only chance ever to go there."

This made Carlos smile. "It's probably a good idea to have him along. Then it would look better to the Cardinal."

"I can work on your boat," Xisco appealed to Ardis. "I can clean, run errands. You name it. I'll do it."

Ardis turned to Xisco. "Maybe. Don't get your hopes up."

"I will not, Señhorita."

That evening, the three of them walked through the village. As Xisco predicted, it was a beautiful night with lots of stars. The moon rose, a welcome distraction from the darkness they encountered that day.

"I want to see the stars from the middle of the ocean," said Xisco.

"We're only talking." Ardis looked him in the eyes. "Understand?"

Carlos grinned. "I can't wait, either." His worries had receded.

Approaching the Montalvão manor, he saw the moonlight reflect off his Berlinetta. "You did a great job shining my car."

Carlos laughed loud with a crazy sparkle in his eyes.

***

Ardis took a telephone call in the Baron's study.

"Ardis. Are you there?"

No mistaking that husky voice. "How are you, Garcia?"

"I'm fine. I'm more concerned about you." The inflection was worry, tinged with urgency. Like Mom and Dad, although Dad could be pretty cool. Mr. Grace-under-pressure, he was king. He could lead armies under siege. Yet, Garcia had a purpose for his call. "Ardis, I need you to return to Lisbon. Immediately. We have a situation."

An awkward silence gripped the air.

"I trust this means I will be going out on the water soon." She served it up plain as day so there would be no mistaking what she wanted. It was an old strategy to get what she wanted from her parents.

It put Garcia on the defensive. "That is our target," he conceded. "First, I need you to keep an eye on Sam Meyer, will you?"

It was his tone, his desire to please. It was because he also needed eyes on the waters, which was her original mission.

"It is time for you to come home—I mean, return to Lisbon." He spoke in a softer tone. "You have been there long enough."

***

To locate Sam Meyer, Ardis looked for Xisco. He would know where Sam is. She checked the stable and spoke with Zé, who had not heard from Xisco.

"It is unusual for him to leave without letting me know."

She thanked him and went to see Eugenio. He hadn't seen Xisco or Sam, either.

In the square, she met Xisco coming out of Bartolo's Padaria.

"I have been looking all over for you." Ardis did not hide her frustration.

"I am here, Señhorita."

"Sam is in danger and needs our help."

"I think you are right about that. He can be a crazy man."

"Leaving us was the worst thing he could do. He needs to be smart about who he talks to."

"Then what do you propose?"

"Do you know where he is? We need to find him."

"I've been looking for him, too. He could be anywhere in Trás-os-Montes, Lisbon, or Spain."

"Then it's time to go to Lisbon."

Xisco was ready and had been for weeks. He told Zé, who asked him to send Armando, his brother, to take his place. It did not occur to him to ask his parents; he told them. His Papai didn't say no; he asked Xisco if he was sure. His mother fussed, suddenly unprepared to release him. "You're still a boy." She pushed a lock of hair out of his eyes.

"You didn't say that when I went to work in the stables."

"That was just around the corner, Xisco. This is different."

Fortunately, Xisco would join a Canadian professor of marine biology and the Monseñhor. What better companions could Xisco have on his first big venture from home?

His Pai raised an eyebrow. "Where will you go after your voyage with the Señhorita and the Monseñhor?"

"Maybe Brazil or somewhere that's not as poor as Portugal."

"Oh yes, *filho*, we are poor, but this is our home." To his Pai, it was better to have a home and be poor, than to have wealth but no home.

Xisco understood his point. He had tried to make a life there but things didn't turn out as he had hoped. Now, he wanted *conhecimento*, knowledge. He wanted experiences.

Early in the morning, Xisco and his Pai walked down the street.

"Xisco, a boy must leave his parents if he is to become the man he is destined to be." Eugenio shook his son's hand and gave him a hug.

Xisco waved goodbye.

As of this moment, he was on his own. Xisco left his family and Sonim behind.

On the way to Lisbon, Xisco had Carlos and Ardis stop at the By The Way Café, where he had gone with Sam during the times they did fireworks in nearby villages and towns. Harratt welcomed Xisco by name and told him Sam left his truck for him. Harratt handed him a note.

Xisco, the wrongs we have seen are
unforgivable. Someone needs to stand up and
say it is not right. This time, that person needs
to be me.

Work hard and make us all proud, Xisco.

Samuel Meyer

p.s. Please see Benjamin Pedra de Campo in
Vila Real and tell him you are there to help me
take care of a few things.

***

The road to Lisbon meandered along stone fences through the
countryside and the middle of every town and village.

"Portugal is big. So many towns, so many Sonims." Xisco was
seeing his country for the first time.

Watching villages drift past reminded him of how he loved to watch
clouds float by in the sky. His mind wandered and allowed him to think
through his big ideas. He knew one profound fact. He had seized an
opening and he would pursue it possibly for the rest of his life.

Lisbon

21. Demands of Diplomacy

Manfred walked at a steady clip from his apartment in the Baixa to his workplace at the German Embassy on Campo Mártires da Pátria.

Something was up. There was a great need for rubber and materials to build *Kübelsitzwagens*. They needed trucks. Some said to invade Russia.

Manfred's job was to supply wolfram. He knew they would need more.

His route took him through Praça do Rossio where the temptation to relax in a café would stall anyone of lesser character. Beyond Rossio, the climb on the steep cobblestone streets left his back dripping with sweat, especially during the hot summer months.

Manfred preferred the cool fall weather. He longed for the sunny yet crispy cool autumn days of his youth when Alsace celebrated the grape harvest. His thoughts jumped to the cool evening when he first met Ardis Lowney with Monseñhor Carlos at the Tivoli Hotel. After meeting Carlos, Manfred increased the supply of wolfram. Things were going well.

***

"There! You can see the river!" Carlos pointed. In the waning light, the Berlinetta motored around the monument of the Marquês de Pombal. Ardis and Xisco looked quickly before they swung onto the broad

Avenida da Liberdade. For a moment, they saw the river through a gap between the hills, but the view was quickly lost behind young trees that lined the wide boulevard separating the lanes of opposing traffic.

"Such a grand avenue." The bustle of people and cars, elegant shops and restaurants, and five-storey buildings that rose unnaturally high along the avenue astonished Xisco.

At Restauradores Square, the boulevard became an open plaza parading ornate renaissance architecture. At the bottom of Restauradores, the avenue cut across a small connecting plaza and into Rossio Square— another large, wide-open plaza.

Next to Rossio was yet another plaza, Praça da Figueira, which was home to a popular *mercado*, a market where farmers and artisans sold their goods.

At the bottom of Rossio, Rua Augusta and several other parallel avenues ran through the Baixa neighbourhood to Praça do Comércio, the grandest of Lisbon's public spaces by the river where pageantry greeted ships returning full of goods and treasures from around the world.

In the Baixa, street lighting came on. "Everything looks so cheerful." Xisco was charmed. "And so many people are out at night."

They went along Rua Augusta as far as the gated entrance of the Praça do Comércio before turning. They arrived in the Chiado at Rua Garrett, where Ardis saw Alemanha / Deutschland displayed in the windows of a shop on the corner. German propaganda sought to convince Lisboetas of their common interests, which was not a difficult sell. Along with Prime Minister Salazar, a chunk of the population feared Communists. Hitler was a natural ally.

Passing through Praça Luis de Camões, Carlos pointed out the boarding house where he lived. They skirted the southern edge of the Bairro Alto and turned onto Rua de O Século to reach Ardis's apartment on Rua São Marçal in lower Príncipe Real.

Carlos and Xisco unloaded the Berlinetta and carried everything up to her flat on the second floor. The windows on the west side drew Xisco. He discovered he had a partial view of the *Assembleia Nationale* and the Rio Tejo in the distance.

His travelling companions were tired. Carlos would call in the morning. He gave Xisco the number for his phone in the boarding house at Nova Pensão Camões in case he needed anything. It had been a long drive for Carlos; he bid Xisco good night and left at once. And Ardis went to sleep early as well. Xisco remained awake, looking out the window of his bedroom at a restaurant's neon sign that illuminated the cobblestone street below. He watched people jumping into taxis. After twenty minutes, he too was asleep.

***

A week earlier, Monseñhor Carlos had called Manfred. Carlos expressed outrage about the gold that the Germans delivered to their client, and demanded it never happen again. The Monseñhor had never sounded so irritated.

Apparently, there was a shortage of gold at the time of the shipment to Monseñhor Carlos. Manfred could not resolve Carlos's complaint. Manfred wished only that the pesky Sam Meyer would go away.

Another bit of news unsettled Manfred. Carlos said he would go out on the Atlantic Ocean with Ardis, and spend time with her in the Algarve.

Since meeting Ardis at the Tivoli, Manfred had had her on his mind and wanted to learn what he could about her, but he didn't get a chance. Manfred had been busy, and then Carlos was in the north, with Ardis.

Manfred felt attracted to Ardis, yet he found good reasons to feel very uneasy about her. People did things for others or spent time with them only if it served their own interests. What were Ardis's interests with Carlos?

The last thing he wanted was a woman undermining his supply of wolfram, especially now that he had orders to increase production so drastically.

Manfred made inquiries at the university and confirmed his suspicions. Ardis Lowney had no classroom teaching duties. She came and went as she pleased. She carried camera equipment. She had a grant from her home university to study sea turtles. Really? That did not sound like a strategic investment of resources during wartime. Or was it?

Manfred feared she photographed more than just sea turtles. Wolfram mines across the north of Portugal served his needs. Was she conducting reconnaissance? The Allies were unable to prevent him from purchasing wolfram, but that did not mean they would let him deliver it to *Deutschland.* Was it her mission to undermine all his accomplishments?

Manfred kept his suspicions about Ardis to himself, for now. He liked her, wanted to get to know her, and did not want to see her in any trouble on his account. If his superiors questioned him, he needed an excuse. If her cover was valid and she was not an operative, disrupting her would disrupt Carlos, which would disrupt his wolfram supplies.

He sensed she was authentic and true. Only a marine biologist would wear a childish turtle pendant like that over her dress.

It would not be wise for him to be wrong or look foolish. He decided to confirm what he knew about her quietly.

***

The next morning, Ardis woke early and found Xisco already up. He was reading her copy of the Tourist Guide to Lisbon. She pointed out a few "must-see" sights, and gave him some money for lunch. "I will be home around six o'clock. Meet you here?"

"May I walk along with you?"

They walked up Rua São Marçal to the Polytechnic School. Ardis pointed out the Jardim Botânico, and went inside to work. Xisco strolled into the park, and found a secluded spot to sit on a bench for a spell.

On arriving, Ardis learned that two visitors were on their way to see her and Garcia.

Her visitors turned out to be Kim Philby and Ian Bromwell, whom she first met at Camp X.

"Good to see you again, gentlemen."

"Haven't seen you since the Tivoli," said Bromwell.

"Let's get started," said Philby, the senior officer. "Where's Garcia?"

A flood of students crowded into the corridor in front of the office, making a racket.

"He will arrive in about forty minutes."

"We can't wait."

"Is there something I can I do for you?" Ardis spoke louder above the noise.

"Let's go outside." Philby led the others along a corridor, down a flight of stairs, and out to the Jardim Botânico. They found a bench in a corner in the shade.

Behind them, hidden by the foliage, Xisco lay on a bench and listened.

***

At Campo Mártires da Pátria, Manfred marched through the shaded lawns and cobbled pathways of the park and into the German Embassy. The Ambassador's assistant met him inside. "The Baron would like to see you right away, please." Her reconnaissance of his exact arrival left no doubt he was to go now.

The office of Baron Philipp von Heschen-Guther was at the midpoint of the long hallway.

Manfred put on his hat, buttoned his tunic, and tightened his tie, keeping an eye on the trim, hourglass figure of the Baron's girl Friday the entire way to his door where she paused a moment for him to catch up, then led him in. She exited, closing the door.

Manfred mustered the mandatory salute, „Heil Hitler," the signal of his subservience that he dared never forego.

Dusting a bookcase off to the side was a cleaner, whom the Ambassador ignored. Manfred thought she was unusually pretty. She winked at him, which took him completely by surprise. She smiled openly, out of view of the Ambassador.

Manfred blushed from her attention.

"At ease, *Oberleutnant*. Have a seat, *bitte*." The Ambassador gestured to the leather chairs in front of the bookcases. The Ambassador was a handsome, fine-featured, impeccably dressed gentleman who had a reputation as a clever manager of issues and events within his purview.

„*Guten morgan, Freiherr*." Manfred removed his hat and sat in the far chair, knowing the Ambassador preferred the nearer one.

Before sitting, the Ambassador pulled another chair into the group. Manfred expected they would wait for another person. Then the cleaner slid into the chair.

Startled, Manfred readjusted his impression of this housekeeper.

Again, she smiled broadly at him, clearly enjoying the moment. She had bright blue eyes and long brunette hair twisted inconspicuously in a knot out of the way.

"Marguerite, this is Manfred."

Marguerite shook his hand. „*Oberleutnant.*"

Manfred smiled, not knowing how to address her.

"Marguerite is a member of the Abwehr."

Manfred stood a little straighter. The Abwehr was Military Intelligence.

"I asked the Baron for this meeting because a change is coming and I want you to be aware of it." She glanced at the Baron and he nodded approval. She continued.

"As you know, Salazar has imposed strict limits on the amount of wolfram we may take. However, our orders are to increase our wolfram exports by whatever means we can, short of declaring war. The *Fuhrer* does not want a war here."

"How can we do this if we are at our limit?" Manfred spoke with respect.

"That's up to you and how much your suppliers can be motivated by gold." She leaned in closer to him. "The mines are close to Spain, use your imagination. Create false shipping labels. Hide it in containers. One of your colleagues runs ghost trains at night."

"We truck it out." Manfred wanted her to be aware of his limitations.

"Good, your quota has been increased by fifty per cent."

"How can I meet that?" His voice betrayed his alarm.

"Smuggle it on the backs of donkeys, if you have to. It's up to you."

"This is not a debate," said the Baron. "The Gestapo is taking our trucks."

For an uncomfortable moment, they sat in silence as the implications sprayed havoc like a volley of machine gun fire.

"The Abwehr is not concerned with the details," Marguerite said.

The Baron broke the impasse. "To win this war, we pursue an aggressive industrial program. A vital ingredient is the wolfram."

To this point in the war, Manfred had been safe. „*Ja, mein Freiherr.*"

"Each of us is entangled by this order," Marguerite said. "The Fatherland, the Abwehr, this entire Portuguese mission—all of this is on the line. If one of us fails, we all fail. If we work together, we all win. And if for any reason you cannot meet your target, let us know so we may fix things."

The weight of her words hung in the air.

"Although none of us chose this path, it is our fate to be part of this. We shall live or die by how we choose to respond, and I say we choose to live."

"Spoken like a true Abwehr agent—one of the many skills I love about you, Marguerite."

The Baron and Marguerite knew each other better than Manfred had expected.

Marguerite stood. She would depart back through the servant's entrance as she had come. As an afterthought, she stopped and added, "*Ach ja*, my commander has heard about a Jew named Sam Meyer." She looked into Manfred's eyes. "This dissident cannot continue. Your orders are to file an official complaint."

"That would be a démarche." The Baron knew very well that Manfred was familiar with such official diplomatic complaints. He explained it as a courtesy to Marguerite. "Send the démarche to Sampaio. He can give it to Salazar."

Luís Teixeira de Sampaio was Secretary General of the Foreign Affairs Ministry.

"Marguerite, a moment. Then he turned to Manfred. "That will be all. Return with your draft in one hour. *Danke schön*."

Manfred wrote a quick draft of the démarche; then returned to the Ambassador. On the way, he saw Marguerite exit from the servant's entrance. Fixing her hair, she passed through the corridor to a rear door. It was a quirk of the layout that he should see her at all.

Manfred had not expected this pressure. He believed he was in a backwater and would be safe in this war. Now he was a critical cog in the wheels of the Nazi war machine.

***

"That diplomat, Wiesentrauser, has people asking about you." The students had annoyed Philby and now he took out his frustrations on Ardis.

His voice roused Xisco from his daydreaming.

"That really rankles," she responded. "I haven't done anything, really."

Xisco lay still, disoriented, and focused on the voices. That was Ardis.

"You went to Trás-os-Montes with the Monseñhor. That put you on his turf."

"That's what you came here to tell me?"

Xisco moved closer to hear them better.

"We are here to convey an order. You need to silence Sam Meyer."

Ardis well understood silencing meant killing. "That doesn't make sense. Sam Meyer is a good man. The community respects him. He was merely objecting to an injustice."

"When there's an order, whatever it is, we must execute it promptly." Philby was not open to discussion. "That's how war works."

So it wasn't going to be easy, after all. "Kill?"

Xisco's eyes widened.

"That's correct. Do whatever is necessary."

"Why me?"

"You know everyone."

"I understand." Ardis wanted to protect Sam or someone else would kill him. Rather than leave it to another person who would do it for sure, she accepted. "Alright, I'll take care of it."

Philby was watching her closely. "Look, the order is to silence him. If you can find another way to make him be quiet, that would be fine with me."

"I get it."

Philby hesitated. "You sure you don't want help?"

"I can handle it. This is what we're trained for, right?"

***

Returning from the Ambassador's office, Manfred found two Gestapo agents waiting in his office, sitting at his desk and the guest chair, the only chairs available in his small space.

"Got anything to drink?" The one at his desk seemed to be the one in command. Manfred recognized him. Reimer. He had a nasty reputation, even among his comrades.

"In the drawer, bottom left." Manfred had no choice but to comply.

"Oh, I didn't see it." Reimer had rifled through his desk.

He found the bottle of *schnapps* that Manfred liked to nip on now and then.

"I have glasses." Only two. Reimer filled each to its brim and gave one to his accomplice.

"We want the Jew, Samuel Meyer. Where can we find him?"

"I don't have contact with him, other than through my contact in the north."

"He's no longer in the north." Reimer's voice revealed a pleading tone.

"Then I can't help you." Beneath that gruff exterior, Manfred saw that Reimer had a boyish look to him.

"He was warned, but he hasn't stopped." Reimer was indifferent to any reasons that anyone might have to live and breathe. "No more warnings."

Manfred shrugged. He honestly had no direct contact with him.

"We are bringing him in." The other Gestapo agent advised Manfred.

"We will deal with him ourselves." Reimer spoke to his associate. He raised his glass of *schnapps* and said, „*Deutschland über alles*," then downed his *schnapps* and left without even a sideways glance at Manfred.

***

In the Jardim Botânico, Xisco watched Philby and Bromwell leave the garden. He heard them get in their car and drive away. He must stop Ardis. He came out from behind the shrubs and was surprised to see she was still sitting on the bench in the shade.

"You can't do this, Ardis. Sam was only speaking up for what is right."

"I know, I know, don't you think I know that?" Ardis displayed a flash of anger that, like her role as a spy, she had hidden.

She had upset Xisco. She let out a deep breath. "I'm sorry, I've alarmed you."

"You are *um espião*. You're not a marine biologist at all, are you?"

"Yes, I am. I'm just helping out because my country is at war."

"And now you're going to kill Sam?"

"I have no intention to do that. I agree with you; he should not die. But that's up to him, now, isn't it? If he doesn't stay quiet, they will send someone to kill him. You heard him; there is a war going on. Sam cannot undermine our efforts to fight the Nazis. Period."

"No, not here. Portugal is not in this war."

"Oh, yes, it is. Many people think your country is helping the wrong side."

"We're neutral!"

"Portugal is selling wolfram to the Nazis, who need Portugal if they want to win this war."

"But Sam hasn't hurt anyone. I will not let him die."

"I agree. Let's talk to him. It will be up to him to decide. Let's go find him."

"Ardis, your secret is safe with me."

Ardis went inside to get her jacket, which gave her roughly one minute to think this through before she went back to face Xisco again. How much could she tell him? Did he only say, "Your secret is safe with me" to protect himself from her? It embarrassed her to think that she had frightened him into thinking she would kill him, too. What had she become?

In the worst-case scenario, after talking with Sam he could still refuse to stop what he was doing. Then she would have no choice. She would have to do it. Could she really kill Sam? No! Of course not. But, not killing Sam would mean disobeying an order. What would they do with her then? Do they bring spies home to be court-martialed? Discharged in disgrace? Or left for the enemy to finish off?

Why cross this bridge before she got there? She could not delay.

Whether or not she would follow the order, she needed to take her knife with her. She shuddered with the concept of using it on anyone's throat. It was so sharp it would slice through in a second. As she slid it into the hidden pocket in her sleeve, her hand shook so much she was afraid she was going to cut her wrist open.

When she returned to the garden, Xisco was gone. She didn't know where to begin to find Sam without his help. One person could help her—Carlos.

Ardis took stock of her situation. Xisco knew she was a spy, and he knew her orders.

Garcia would learn of it, he always did. She didn't have much time. If she could not resolve this quickly, Garcia would pull her out right away and she didn't want that. She wanted to get out on the ocean and do her research.

Will Xisco not tell anyone, really? She was falling. There was no floor. There would be no soft landing.

22. A Chasing of the Wind

The housekeeper welcomed Carlos when he arrived at the Cardinal's *palaceta*. "There was a call for you. A woman named Laurenza."

Laurenza was alive! Positive, happy images of Laurenza and the children in the orphanage flooded his senses. And she was in Lisbon. A sense of relief swept through him; his prospects brightened.

For now, though, Carlos had to focus on his meeting with the Cardinal.

Carlos updated the Cardinal on the physical and mental state of the young Baron, Olympio. Which took Carlos back to the death of Montalvão. The gold jewellery. The disappearance of Sam Meyer. Carlos briefed Cerejeira about the mining engineer who had advised Montalvão. He reported it all.

When leaving, he remembered to report his expedition with Ardis, but it was too late. The Cardinal had already closed his journal and was leaving the room, moving on to the next item on his list.

No matter. Carlos had enough on his plate.

He watched all day without seeing any sign of Laurenza. He doubted the message. Perhaps there was a misunderstanding. He would ask the housekeeper about her. Language differences could create confusion.

Groggy with sleep, he hurried to Lauds at Santo António across from the Sé. At the tiny Jardim Augusto Rosa, he saw her sitting on a bench, reading a book in the first light of day. She lifted her eyes off the page, and they made eye contact. Her face lit up. She stood, walked briskly toward him, and then broke into a run. They collided and held onto each other tightly with no care in the world but for each other.

"I believed you were dead." His eyes and smile expressed his happiness to see her alive and well in front of him.

"I was afraid you might think that." The Daughters of Charity strictly protected every member's personal information.

"Either that or not wanting to see me." Self-doubt was endemic to orphans.

"Oh Carlos, I'm so sorry."

"Where did you go?"

"Another house in Rome."

She didn't tell him that she had a baby. His son.

"How did you find me?"

"Padre Paulo told me where and how to look for you."

Carlos smiled on hearing of his old friend. "Padre Paulo?"

"Yes. First, he said, confirm that you were indeed in Lisbon. The last Paulo heard, you had been assigned to the Seat of the Bishop. They gave me a phone number. Oh! I'm so happy I found you, Carlos."

"Where are your things? Do you have a bag?"

"Yes, I have a room at a convent near here."

Carlos raised his eyebrows.

She obtained attendant care with the nuns for Paulo, who was eighteen months old and she had no intention to tell Carlos about their son, whom she named Paulo, after Carlos's colleague.

"Just a bit further past the Sé.

"Ah, São Vicente de Fora."

"Yes, that's it. I asked which of the churches nearby offered Lauds. They all would of course, so I asked which one was the favourite of the local clergy."

"You are clever." He pulled on her hand, trying to pull her back to him.

She put herself squarely in front of him. "Have you thought about us?" It seemed an innocent question.

Since Rome, Carlos had held Laurenza in his mind like an invisible friend with whom he shared his thoughts and feelings. Certainly, whenever he was engaged in a new task. She was his escape and his diversion. If he were with her, he would not have to deal with the undesirable and unwanted aspects of his life.

"You have been my constant companion."

"I bet you didn't think I'd ever just show up like this."

"That is so true." The vision he held of her was no longer neatly packaged and stowed away for when he needed it. She was standing right in front of him.

"Are you hungry? Would you like to eat?" They went into the Baixa to find a restaurant. He told her about his recent experiences in Trás-os-Montes, repeating the story about the chest of items stolen from Jews.

"That's terrible!"

Laurenza was kind and empathetic. He saw that telling her this was not appropriate after being apart. They had so much else to talk about.

"Have you considered how we might make a life together?" It was his turn to put the question to her.

"That is why I'm here."

"Yes, and what do you see us doing?"

"Have a family, Carlos, as we talked about in Rome."

Rome seemed so far away. Carlos had forgotten those conversations. He didn't have time for such long talks. How could he make time for a family?

"There's so much I want to share with you, Carlos."

"I know, me too."

"I want to be sure you are ready." She looked at him expectantly.

Carlos felt confused. He no longer had the capacity to respond to the "real" her. Not that he didn't care for her and appreciate her for coming to find him, he did. But his emotions were wound up with recent events.

"I'm sorry. I have much on my plate."

"You are in a rough place now, aren't you Carlos?"

He appreciated that she saw this and understood him. He was not in any mental shape to assume any responsibility. "I am very much immersed in my work."

"My presence here is overwhelming then."

"Yes, it could be. I have responsibilities. The Cardinal says I am a business advisor, but I know I'm little more than his stand-in. I cover some of his workload."

"That's good, isn't it? That is what you want?"

"I suppose. I'm just not sure it is right for us to be involved in some of the businesses we are in . . . to make money for the Church . . . to pay for work being done on his cathedral."

"The Church does need money and has to get it from somewhere."

"Yes, I know. But it may be wrong, all wrong."

"What do you mean?"

"I can't talk about it—it's upsetting. I'm committed to go to the Algarve. I thought I'd take a break. Think things through."

He told her about Ardis and her marine biology research.

"When are you going?"

"In a couple of days."

"Before you go, can you show me Lisbon, Carlos?"

They walked back the way they had come, and stopped at the Santa Luzia *miradouro*, where they looked over red rooftops of part of the Alfama and the Rio Tejo in the distance.

There was little time before he had to leave Lisbon. So they made a plan to meet again the next day and when he returned as well.

Laurenza's arrival in Lisbon forced Carlos to revisit his vocation. That evening, sleep eluded him. He stared at the ceiling and imagined a new life with Laurenza. Her smile was shining brightly, directly in his line of vision, and all he needed to do was take it. It would be all too easy to have her in his arms. He would be a fool not to.

23. The Aljube

S am Meyer was working quietly on a typewriter when the PVDE and Gestapo burst in. They smashed things up, hauled him away, and threw him in the Aljube.

To the prison guards, Sam appeared unafraid, perhaps only curious of what might be in store for him. He appeared indifferent, unengaged.

"You will fit in here," the guard said, looking down on Sam's diminutive frame. "Others of your kind were here long before you."

During the Inquisition, the Aljube imprisoned Jews. The guards brandished that part of their history proudly.

His cell was an arm's length wide. There was no space to move. No daylight; it was a dungeon. The guards distributed food and water sporadically and grudgingly in tiny portions.

They tagged Sam for removal to *Campo da Morte Lenta*, a prison camp on Tarrafal, an island three thousand kilometres away at Cape Verde off the coast of West Africa. This Camp of the Slow Death was for the most disruptive dissidents.

***

Xisco waited; he watched whatever was happening on the street below. When the telephone rang, he jumped out of his skull. He picked up the earpiece carefully. The voice was Carlos. Carlos said he would pick up Xisco in ten minutes for a tour of the Sé.

The Sé was humongous compared to the *capela* in Sonim. Across the street from the Sé, was another church, down the street was another, and there were several beyond the Sé. "There are not enough people in this city to fill all these churches."

Carlos took Xisco shopping in the Baixa. "You need new clothing."

It wasn't as if Xisco's clothing was out of place. They were hand-me-downs from another family or handmade by his Mamãe. When Carlos left, Xisco laid his new clothes out on his bed to show Ardis when she got home.

He put on the new pants and shoes and went out to explore the old neighbourhood around Ardis's apartment. He played make-believe of what it would be like to live there in the middle of a city so full of energy. He stopped for coffee, watched people, and listened. He went to a market for lunch. Could he make a life here?

***

The Aljube interrogated its prisoners to obtain the names of friends and colleagues in the prisoner's political network. The guards punctuated each interrogation with a beating.

When asked about his relationships with friends and family, Sam Meyer looked at his interlocutors blankly. What crossed Sam's mind was how this information could be relevant; for it was clear, his captors were not interested in making anyone's life better.

Sam didn't belong to a political network and wasn't part of a team. He didn't have any colleagues. The interrogations, and the beatings, continued. He clammed up and never uttered a word. Nor did he wail or howl as other men did.

The walls resonated with screams as they had centuries ago, though now the squeal of streetcars just outside the Aljube's walls helped to drown out the screeching and wailing inside.

***

Sam had two houses. The one in Sonim was a safe house for Jewish refugees who arrived in Portugal through Bragança. The other one, operated by a refugee named Céphise, was in the Alfama, the old Jewish quarter in Lisbon.

The Alfama was a warren of tightly arranged flats and houses on narrow roads and passageways that opened up into little courtyards. The Jews built their homes on the sides of hills; so many houses had upper and lower doors. The 1755 earthquake, fire, and tsunami did not destroy them. Alfama was one of the few neighborhoods in the central old city that survived, and made an ideal place for refugees to blend in and effectively disappear.

Following the directions from Sam, Xisco found the house all right. Rua Casa da Achada, the street of the house of the found, was one of those little enclaves below the castle walls.

The housekeeper asked if he was Xisco. She let him know that Sam wanted him to take over his room. Her name was Diana.

Sam's calculation that he would not return shocked Xisco, presenting an implication that Xisco tolerated only because he had no evidence to refute it. "I expect to return with Sam. May I look in to see whether he left me any messages or clues of his whereabouts?"

Sam's room was on the third floor, on the east side of the building against the stone cliff below the castle. It had a back door that accessed a dank and empty terrace. The room was modest; it suited Sam's personality. He was absent most of the time anyway.

In a chest of drawers, he found an envelope addressed to Xisco Ribeiro. It contained cash. He didn't look at the money nor count it. He tossed it back into the drawer where he found it. He went back down the stairs.

Diana's eyes were full of sadness.

Believing he only missed a meeting with his friend, Xisco hadn't felt so bad. But now there was mounting evidence things were different. Sam had not been back in days.

Sam would have communicated with him or he would still be here looking for him. And he certainly would not have left his things like that. Something was wrong. Then Xisco remembered the note from Sam that he received from Harratt. "Someone needs to stand up and say this isn't right. This time, that person needs to be me," Sam had written.

Xisco checked in with Carlos. "I did not find Sam where he said he would be."

Carlos suggested he could check with Ardis, too. He would show up, Carlos assured him.

That evening, Xisco talked with Ardis. She would do it first thing in the morning.

"Xisco, I can use my connections to help you find information about Sam." She spoke in a soft, low voice. "I need you to remain absolutely quiet about my role. This is between you and me only. Carlos cannot know. No one can know. It is a matter of life and death. For both of us." She looked him in the eye until he nodded, an important affirmation she counted on.

***

A guard pushed Sam to the narrow stairs and gave him a shove. Tied behind his back, his hands were of little use to him. Dazed, he hit the wall and staggered. Somehow, he managed to not fall into the black hole that gaped like the hungry mouth of a monster that never gave up a meal. A harder shove and his feet would not have touched the steps, though his face surely would have. He slumped against the wall and in so doing, grounded the projectile that his body would have become. Instead, the guard grabbed his shackled arms by the chain that joined them, twisting his arms unnaturally back, and dragged him down, an alternate method that was more destructive to Sam who was passing in and out of consciousness due to pain and only vaguely aware of the hell hole he was in.

***

On her walk to the Polytechnic School in the morning, Ardis reflected on Sam's disappearance. Ardis liked Sam. She appreciated how Xisco looked up to him like a student to his mentor. Ardis promised she would help find Sam, and she would.

She hoped this investigation would not delay her research. But if it did, so be it. She would help Xisco no matter what.

In the corridor, she said hello to Katya who wanted to know whether she liked the apartment. They chatted for a minute. Ardis told her she was in a rush and needed to see Garcia as soon as possible. Katya waved her in.

Garcia welcomed her back and Ardis told him she was unable to locate Sam Meyer in Sonim. All she knew was that Sam left Sonim in his truck and arrived in Lisbon on a motorcycle. However, she had lost track of him.

Garcia nodded. "Have a seat. I think we can help you with this."

First, he let her know the PVDE (Portuguese secret police) allows the German secret police, the Gestapo, to operate with impunity in Portugal.

Garcia did not know Sam's current location. He said they could only guess. The British agents had been quick, though, to recognize Sam's motorcycle, an Empire Star made in England.

He pulled out the dossier on Sam. It did not contain much, but what was there was damning. It held a few copies of Sam's flyer.

"Picture this—Sam flying through traffic on his motorcycle, passing these out by the handful. We have learned he delivered them to Communists, liberals and other groups. How he connected with these groups so fast is a mystery. We think he's a quick study."

Ardis picked up the flyer. The headlines blared protest: "Fatima is Estado Novo Lie. A Big Hoax. Salazar Sells-out Allies. Let's All Get Drunk."

"The flyers were quickly passed around. Many fluttered in the wind on the streets. People recognized the incendiary nature of the writing and didn't want to be caught with it in their possession. Sam moved fast on his motorcycle. He was efficient. Until he got picked up."

"By the PVDE?"

"By the Gestapo. One of our guys saw it happen. He heard them speaking German. They pulled Sam out of a print shop in the Baixa. They were in such a hurry they left his BSA on the street, so our guy brought it in."

Garcia gave Ardis a few minutes to read the flyer. She didn't know how she missed the header on her first glance: "God in Heaven and Salazar on Earth."

Fatima is Estado Novo Lie

During the 1930s, the Estado Novo changed the facts of 1917 and 1918 events. The Virgin Mary did not tell Sister Lucia that Russia was a threat. Salazar did, through his friend Cardinal Cerejeira.

Together, these two old school chums, Salazar and Cerejeira, rewrote what happened at the appearance of the Virgin Mary at Fatima and the Miracle of the Sun that they claim is a miracle.

A Big Hoax

Old school chums Salazar and Cerejeira, who are now the leaders of Portugal's Church and

State, have given us a big hoax.

The Cardinal got a miracle that enables him to fill his churches across the land.

Fascist Salazar got God on his side to fight Communists—his greatest worry. His lies manipulate us, keep us in fear, and forever enslave us in his fascist State.

Salazar Sells Out Allies

Prime Minister Salazar and the Estado Novo have abrogated Portugal's 1393 treaty with England by selling wolfram to the Germans, which, as you know, is at war with England.

When the Nazis paid for Portuguese wolfram, they paid with gold stolen from Jews. What the Nazis are doing is criminal, and any leader who supports the Nazis is a criminal. Salazar ignored the terrible stories coming out of Germany. Salazar is a criminal.

Let's All Get Drunk!

Most Portuguese are illiterate. When asked about his policy on education, Salazar replied, "Who needs education to work in the fields?"

This comes from the same man who said, *"Beber vinho é dar de comer a um milhão de portugueses."* Drinking wine feeds a million Portuguese.

Salazar wants the poor in Portugal to remain poor. He wants women to stay at home and have more babies. He won't build schools, roads, or universities. Instead, he gives us Fatima and wine.

At the bottom of the page was a line of text that resembled the header. "We all have our God in Heaven, but is Salazar the one you want to lead us on Earth?"

Garcia shook his head in disagreement. "I think what Salazar meant was that the wine industry provides income to a million Portuguese families," Garcia said. "Sam missed the metaphor, which is understandable because everyone drinks like a fish."

Ardis set the flyer down, and sat back. "These are strong objections. It is really too well done, for Sam's sake."

"I'm afraid so." Garcia nodded. "To the average person on the street, things do not appear so sinister. Salazar saved this country from financial ruin in the '30s and now he is keeping the country out of a devastating war. He is a national hero. Salazar is revered for his intelligence and leadership."

"Except by an agitator like Sam."

"It's all political. Sam believes the Fatima miracles are Salazar's way of counteracting Communism. Salazar does come down hard on dissidents."

"But my friend is close to Sam and wants to find him."

"That's the boy." Garcia looked at her. "Xisco."

"Yes, Xisco. How can we get his friend out of jail?"

"Know anyone close to Salazar? Because that is what it would take—no one else can do anything about this.

"I do know someone actually. Carlos works for Cardinal Cerejeira."

"Oh, of course. But you can't ask him or you would blow your cover with him, too."

"Look, I'm sorry. Maybe it's time I just tell him –"

"No, absolutely not. But that doesn't mean we can't use Bromwell."

"Bromwell?"

"Yes, Bromwell and Carlos already know each other from their wolfram dealing. Carlos would appreciate Bromwell may have "other" duties as an employee of the British consulate. He can tell Carlos that he is aware of Sam's connection with the boy, Xisco. He doesn't even have to mention you."

"Oh, I like it."

"I will set it up. Ardis, this means you have to remain quiet. Let it come from Carlos."

An hour later, Carlos contacted Ardis at her apartment. He had information about Sam to give to Xisco. "Listen, we need to act fast." He wanted Ardis to have Xisco ready at her apartment where he would join them.

"Xisco is here. We will wait for you."

He arrived in ten minutes. "Sam was put in jail," Carlos announced as he entered. "Sam was far deeper involved than any of us could have anticipated." Carlos waved a flyer in the air.

Xisco scanned the flyer and understood it for what it was. Political protest.

"Where is the jail?" Ardis had been listening closely.

"The Aljube," Carlos replied. "No one, save Prime Minister Salazar, can help him. I asked Cardinal Cerejeira to talk with Salazar. He agreed."

Xisco brightened. "So there is a chance?"

"He will call us the minute he has an answer."

They waited there, by the phone. "If the Cardinal can get through to the Prime Minister, it will be quick, maybe twenty minutes. If not, he will let me know."

Carlos had known about the Aljube for a long time, but did not know it was still in use.

Cerejeira called. Carlos grew very still during this conversation. At one point, Ardis and Xisco could hear the Cardinal because he was speaking so loudly. Carlos reddened.

"Yes, Your Excellency. Thank you, Your Excellency." Carlos set the phone down. "The Cardinal claimed asylum for Samuel Meyer. That made Salazar angry because the Cardinal had that right and by invoking it, the Cardinal took the situation out of Salazar's hands. The Prime Minister was angry with him for involving him in this. According to the Cardinal, Salazar had never conceded, ever, even to the strongest of nations. In the end, he said fine, you have asylum for this man—this one time."

Carlos wiped his hand across his face and jaw. "We must go there now. The guards will turn him over to you."

The street in front of the Aljube was busy with streetcars that rattled and squealed as they ferried their loads of passengers. Across the street, a walled compound surrounded the rear of the cathedral. A hundred years ago, the Aljube had been an Ecclesiastical jail where the Catholic Church punished those that broke Canon Law.

Carlos parked his car on the sidewalk and the three of them darted across the street in between the traffic and streetcars.

The entrance to the Aljube was a tall set of black doors with a flat iron grate in front. Carlos reached through the grid and banged a heavy metal knocker on the door. A small aperture in the door opened and a face peered into the darkness. "What do you want?"

"We are here for Samuel Meyer."

The heavy door swung inward slowly and a strong man with keys unlocked the gate. He swung the grid outward.

"*Entschuldigen Sie.*" Three men shoved passed them, knocking Xisco to the ground. The Germans jumped into a car. The passenger in the front seat stared at Ardis as they pulled away. It was Reimer, the Gestapo.

Sam staggered out a step and collapsed onto Xisco and Carlos. His face was swollen, bloodied, and bruised. He did not speak. Blood was crusted in his hair.

Xisco and Carlos laid him on the sidewalk away from the steady flow of people, some of whom stopped to watch.

Sam could not keep his eyes open. His breathing was shallow. His eyelids were too puffed up to flutter. They twitched.

"Sam! We have you Sam; we'll take care of you."

Sam did not respond. His swollen jaw was slack. He lay still.

"No, no, Sam." Xisco was trying to stop the inevitable. "Stay with me, Sam. Don't leave me, Sam."

Xisco looked at Carlos and Ardis—a demanding look. Do something, his eyes pleaded. Neither Ardis nor Carlos could say anything. Ardis's eyes were welling up with tears. Carlos's chin quivered, his lips pressed tightly against his teeth. He shook his head.

"No, he's okay." Xisco denied what was happening. "We just need to get a doctor. He'll be okay, help me."

"It's too late, Xisco." Carlos spoke gently. "He's gone."

"Sam, don't leave me." Xisco pleaded with Sam.

Xisco was not ready to accept what had just happened. Sam should be talking with him now. Xisco's eyes filled with tears. He took hold of Sam's hand and he sensed the broken bones there, so he held his hand gently. "I'm so sorry, Sam. "I'm so sorry." Tremors gripped and released Xisco. He pulled his legs in tight and sat cross-legged beside Sam. He leaned over Sam and wept without any care for himself or the world.

The scene on the sidewalk had created a spectacle. Carlos saw police coming through the crowd. He went to move Xisco, but Ardis stopped him. "Let him have this."

Carlos intercepted the police and explained what just happened.

The police accepted his explanation, there on the doorsteps of the Aljube. They had seen this sort of thing before, where another police force had brutalized a citizen, and they knew there was nothing they could do about it. Filling out a report would only complicate everyone's life unnecessarily. Instead, they did the right thing. They took charge of crowd control and called for someone to pick up the body.

Ian Bromwell appeared at Ardis's side. He did not say anything. His presence surprised her, yet assured her. Her sadness, her fears, and her instincts were all jumbled up.

"He's dead." She whispered.

"I will go with the body and get a report." Bromwell assured her. "Carlos knows me."

Finished with the police, Carlos returned his attention to Xisco. He asked him if he would like to say a prayer for Sam.

Xisco gave him a confused look. "Would Sam be okay with a Christian prayer?"

"We pray the best we know how."

Xisco nodded consent.

Carlos knelt beside Xisco. "In the name of the Father, the Son, and the Holy Spirit." He reverently crossed over Sam's heart. "Our Father, who art in Heaven, hallowed be thy name . . ."

Xisco joined Carlos in saying the Lord's Prayer followed by a Hail Mary. The prayers made him feel better immediately. It centred him.

Carlos blessed Sam's body and made the sign of the cross over him again. He stood up.

Ardis huddled briefly with Carlos. There was a man with her.

"Carlos, this is Ian Bromwell. He's from the British consulate and he knows you."

Carlos recognized him. "Bromwell." Carlos nodded to him.

"Ian has offered to help. He knows what to do. But you have to stay with Ian and assert authority over the body." She looked at him for agreement. "Can you do this, Carlos?"

Carlos nodded. It made sense to have outside help.

"Carlos, you could call a rabbi. Get help with the service and burial." Ardis was thinking ahead. "I will take care of Xisco."

Xisco remained beside Sam.

An ambulance from the city pulled up to the sidewalk and two attendants came over. Carlos intervened before they got to Xisco. Within moments, Carlos had explained the situation and arranged for himself and Bromwell to accompany the body.

The attendants approached the body with a stretcher.

With a mix of hesitation and assurance, Xisco stepped back from Sam's side on the ground beside the Aljube. He was reluctant to leave him. He didn't want to see Sam in this condition anymore. He wanted to remember the Sam he knew. Already, he was having trouble blotting out the image of his bloodied and swollen face. He understood there was nothing further he could do for Sam, and if anything, he would only obstruct these men from doing what needed to be done.

Ardis took hold of Xisco's hand and held it as they moved Sam into the ambulance.

Carlos handed Ardis his car key. "Use my car." Carlos followed Bromwell into the back of the ambulance and it pulled away. The spectacle was over. The crowd dispersed.

"Just like that." Xisco looked to Ardis. "He's gone."

The air seemed warmer, the noises on the street louder. It was as if time had stopped.

***

Carlos arranged for Sam's funeral and burial with a rabbi who was an old friend of Sam's.

He washed his body, dried and dressed him in a white muslin fabric, a *yarmulke* or skullcap, and a prayer shawl.

"Sam sacrificed his life to show us there are bad people in the world," he sighed. "Thank you, Sam. We already knew this."

He put Sam in a pine box along with his bloodied clothes because the blood of a person was as holy as his life and deserved proper burial.

The rabbi told Xisco the most important thing he could do for Sam was to help him find his final resting place.

Members of the Jewish community gathered around and joined in prayers. "God has given, God has taken away. Blessed be the name of God." The rabbi read from the *Book of Job*. He tore a black ribbon and handed it to Xisco to pin on his shirt.

Afterwards, they shook Xisco's hand and conveyed their condolences. Xisco was not surprised to learn the Lisbon community loved Sam, too.

The memories of his times with Sam in Sonim brought tears.

Ardis put her arm around his shoulders and hugged him.

Carlos was less sympathetic. "Death is a fact of life we all face."

***

Ardis took Xisco to the university to see Ian Bromwell.

"It's my fault," Xisco blurted once he was in the car. "I should have been there for him. I could have saved him."

"There's nothing you could have done. None of that was up to you. Sam was a very smart man and he knew exactly what he was doing and what the risks were."

Xisco felt all jammed up inside. "I hate Salazar and his PVDE."

"The most important thing is, Sam was thinking of you."

"What can be accomplished from dying?"

"He believed it was important to tell others and stand up for what he believed in.

"People like me?"

"No, if he wanted you to do anything he would have asked you." Ardis spoke gently, plainly. "Sam denounced what wasn't right. It cost him his life."

They were silent as Ardis maneuvered the car into a spot.

"I guess you're relieved you didn't have to do it," Xisco said. "I heard them give you the order, in the Jardim Botânico."

She turned off the car and turned to him.

"Xisco, I didn't kill Sam. That Gestapo—Reimer—killed him. Can you think of any reason why I would accept that order to kill Sam?"

"No, I can't."

"To protect him! If I didn't accept the order it would have been given to another person."

"Ah, I see."

"And you know I was working with you to find him. To warn him."

"Ah, ok. Ardis, I believe you."

"Thank you. This is important to us as friends."

They went in.

Xisco recognized Bromwell from the Jardim Botânico.

"Xisco, I'm sorry about what happened to your friend," said Bromwell. "I hope this brutal repression doesn't hurt you."

"What do you mean?"

"It is easy to get angry and die for a cause, yet so unnecessary. This war will end eventually. Portugal will be free of the Gestapo and PVDE. You don't have to do what Sam did."

"Oh, good," Xisco said.

Bromwell led Xisco to the place where he stored Sam's BSA, which his colleagues brought in after the Gestapo picked up Sam.

"You know how to ride this thing?"

"Yeah, Sam taught me."

"Alright then," Bromwell flipped him the keys. "I believe these belong to you, Rocker."

Xisco looked at him, puzzled.

"That means biker."

Xisco liked that. "Yeah, I'm a Rocker. Like Sam."

24. House of the Found

In the morning, Xisco went out for some fresh air. He headed west, walking up and down then up again—such were the hills of Lisbon on his aimless route. The skies darkened and winds picked up, forcing people to take shelter. Xisco walked on in the gathering gale, the rhythmic pattern of his steps working like magic on his heart, pumping blood to his arms and legs, and feeding his brain. He dabbled in sacred memories, celebrating conversations with Sam and their lives in Sonim.

"Saúde, Xisco."

"Saúde."

The toast to good health was barely a grunt yet it communicated hope and an expectation of what life ought to provide.

Xisco's disappointment hung in his throat.

In the Jardim da Estrela, Sam's face, bloodied and inflamed, haunted Xisco.

The Gestapo had tortured Sam, a horror that consumed the air Xisco breathed. Even with wind racing down the park full into his face, Xisco's cheeks emitted a hot flush; he bled tears. The fury of the tempest entangled him in Sam's misery as if it were his own.

Standing before the great cathedral, where families with their little girls in dresses carrying little purses, scurried into the church, the winds died down but the bruises on Sam's swollen hands bothered him. Xisco felt an intensity in his own hands. His fists throbbed and his fingers tingled with anger at that church and everything its beautiful family stood for.

The clouds burst, drenching the park in much-needed rain. Xisco stood under the black sky and invited the chaos to take him. Thunder boomed as lightning lit the giant trees and walkways. Watching the rain calmed him. He took deep breaths and expelled them as he watched rivulets of water in the gutters rush along walkways throughout the park.

Alone in the park, he slumped onto a bench and let the wind and the rain have him. His body shook with waves of tremors as he wailed and railed against his God who had let it all happen.

"Por que?"

He asked only "why."

The way back home reaffirmed his feelings. There was no one looking out for Sam, for him, or for anyone. He felt sorry for those little girls. One day when they learn that bad things happen to good people no matter what they do—there wasn't anything one could do to avoid evil in the world—they will be disappointed, too.

This life was not what he had expected. It had become one big, wet, disappointment.

He returned from his walk, soaked. He changed into dry clothes then joined Ardis in the living room. He picked up a book.

He felt Ardis watch him. Thankfully, she left him alone.

When Ardis pulled the curtain wide to look out the window, he could see the skies had cleared. The sun was shining.

"Why don't you collect Sam's belongings?"

So he did.

***

The steep hill on Rua São Marçal would make anyone feel winded, including Ardis, who was in reasonably good shape. She mounted the steps below the columns and the pediment at the entrance to the Polytechnic School.

Who am I trying to kid? A sense of dread pervaded her steps. Garcia will send me home to Canada.

She said hello to Katya, but Ardis didn't stop to talk.

Katya nodded to go in.

Garcia was looking over the Jardim Botânico. She stood beside him for a moment and took in the view, too, the same as she had the day she arrived. She had come full circle.

Garcia gave her an expectant look. "Yes?"

She shrugged her shoulders.

Her tour of undercover duty was now coming up to nine months—three months beyond what it was supposed to be.

"The Gestapo likely have you in their sights."

The murder of Sam Meyer made her shudder. What would they do to her? The implications exhausted her. There was no way around it. Her presence was no longer defensible. She had to leave Portugal.

***

Xisco returned through the narrow passageway to Rua Casa da Achada. He parked the BSA in front of Sam's house. He would take care of Sam's things.

Diana welcomed him solemnly. "Xisco, Sam asked me to welcome you here. I have a room ready for you. Will you stay?"

"Yes, for a few days, Diana, before I go away for several weeks."

Sam had known exactly what he was doing. Xisco reread the scrap of paper from Sam. Sam had asked him to talk with his lawyer, Benjamin Pedra de Campo in Vila Real. And he had told him Céphise coordinated the refugees coming to this house on Rua Casa da Achada.

"I haven't met Céphise yet. Is she here, can I meet her?"

"She is at the Leitaria Moderna on Rua de São Cristóvão."

He walked. The Leitaria Moderna was a tiny place below the passageway. The waitress squinted her eyes. "Xisco?"

He nodded.

"When you drove past; I knew it had to be you. I am Céphise."

He sat at the only seat by the front window. At the back, an old woman sat on a stool, watching him in a friendly manner. She got up and put a *pastel de nata* on a plate. She nodded toward Xisco and handed the plate to Céphise.

Céphise came out from behind the glass counter with the *pastel de nata*. "You look hungry. Eat this." Céphise was petite with a narrow face, gold-brown eyes with flecks of green, and shoulder-length brown hair streaked from the sun. She was his age, if not a few years older.

The egg custard tart was delicious and he told her so.

Customers came in for their *café da manhã*; the Señhora served them to let the young people have this time.

"We are all sorry to lose Sam. He was well-loved here."

"You didn't attend the funeral."

"Sam told us not to. He said it could bring trouble."

"But I could bring trouble, too."

"That is true. Sam said you are necessary."

"Oh?"

"He said you are a son in every way."

Xisco smiled. Sam had been kind and good to him.

"Sam said you help with the refugees."

She nodded to a middle-aged couple who said good morning as they exited. "They are from Saint-Nazaire. They went to work one morning and Allied bombs destroyed their house. They lost four children."

Another woman ambled up the street. "Her husband was killed in the war." She looked onto the street. "Those children playing there? They were orphaned." Céphise looked down in her lap. "I lost my parents, too, and all my brothers were either killed or taken away."

Nothing in his life could compare with her loss. "You are very brave," he said. He pictured his parents and his siblings in the village.

"Sam didn't have to die." A few tears spilled down her cheeks.

Xisco comforted her. "I'm sorry." Their mutual loss gave them an opening. He gently put his hand on hers, though only for a moment.

Xisco remembered that Ardis expected him to return that evening to her apartment on the other side of the old city. He needed to let her know he would not be there.

He used the phone in a tiny alcove near the front door. He told Ardis he still wanted to go to the Algarve. He gave his address on Rua Casa da Achada and the phone number for Diana.

"I have Sam's room."

"Thank you for telling me," Ardis said. "We leave in two days."

Sam's house in the Alfama contained several small apartments for Jewish families to live in as they waited for passage to the new world. Xisco saw them coming and going. Diana told him Sam charged only those who could afford it. She maintained the house and served dinners to welcome new visitors and say goodbye to those leaving.

Céphise came to see him. He had nothing to show for himself. She looked at him from head to foot and back.

"O mon Dieu," she said. "Let's go."

"Where?"

"I want a ride on your Empire Star." She was direct. "I have always wanted a ride on Sam's motorcycle."

Sam had installed a rack on the back to carry his gear. Xisco strapped a cushion to it and invited her to climb on. He showed her where to put her feet. "Hang on to me."

Céphise guided him through the maze of streets around the castle to the north side of the hill. They went down the hill and back up another to the miradouro Esplanada do Lago da Graca, a scenic lookout, where they admired the view over old Lisbon.

"Sam lived a life of adventure," said Xisco. "He grew up in Poland, travelled to Macau, worked in England, and rode his BSA from England through France and Spain to get here."

"I didn't know he was in Macau." Self-composed, her gaze went beyond the rooftops to distant views of the city.

Xisco was absorbed in watching Céphise.

She broke the spell. "Come on, let's go."

Her accent was different. He could not place it.

They got back on the BSA and rode across the city, under a huge aqueduct, and up to the top of a forested hill to the west of the old city. They stopped to look at the view of the Rio Tejo and the Atlantic Ocean.

"I've never heard the name Céphise; it is very pretty." Xisco felt comfortable with her.

"Merci, Xisco. My *grandmère* and my great *grandmère* were both named Céphise. I was the only girl in a family of six boys, all older, and my parents were going to call me *Septième*, the seventh. But when I was born on the birthday of my *grandmère*, April 24, my *grandpère* was thrilled and naturally assumed my name would be Céphise. So they called me Céphise *Septième*. The seventh brings luck, they said. When I got into trouble, they called me *Chanceuse d'être Heureux*."

Xisco tried to imagine her family but could only think of his own little brothers and his sister. "Lucky to be Happy—that's funny, I have always thought of myself as lucky."

He saw her wipe an eye. She looked happy.

"You are French and you are a Jew?"

"*Oui*. I come from Bordeaux. I grew up in a family that practiced orthodox beliefs," Céphise explained. "We believed our lives were a test. In each of us, good and evil battled it out every day."

"Orthodox Jews wear black and follow strict rules. But you don't."

"Sam said to blend in, so I adopted typical Portuguese clothing."

"Céphise, do you still practice the orthodox faith?"

"Not really. But I maintain many small gestures."

"How did you learn to speak Portuguese so well?"

"Since I was fifteen, I worked in the Portuguese consul in Bordeaux."

"Why did you come here?"

Standing at the edge of the *miradouro*, Céphise leaned her forearms on the wall as she straightened her back. "I helped Portuguese consul-general Dr. Aristides de Sousa Ribeiro to produce travel visas for Jews to escape the Nazis. After what happened to my family, he helped me get out. He arranged for me to meet Sam, in Sonim. I was in your village for a few days before coming here."

Sitting atop the hill looking out to the Atlantic, Xisco came to see Céphise with fresh eyes. She had encountered much sorrow, yet she was happy and at peace with herself.

They returned to the city and rode down the Avenida da Liberdade. As usual, the refugees were everywhere—in the gardens of the Avenida, the cafés of the Baixa, and at Terreiro do Paço on the Rio Tejo. They formed lines and waited on the esplanade by the river, in the travel agencies and shipping companies, and at the consulates and embassies.

Céphise worked with refugees, helping them navigate their way in the city. "They need travel visas from Portugal. They need passage on a steamer. They need money from relatives."

Xisco envisaged what it would be like for refugees when they received their news, their visas, their tickets for passage, and finally when their dates of departure arrived. Their sad joy would be felt by everyone around them who remained suspended in the limbo that Lisbon had become. He looked past the refugees to the beautiful but run-down images of a city and a nation he once loved.

Her apartment, like Xisco's, was on the top floor. She was on the other side of a central stairwell, away from the stone cliff. On the west wall of her living room, a door—flanked by a bank of small windows—opened onto a large terrace, a rarity in a city of Juliette balconies.

She held the door open for him to step onto the rooftop terrace, which presented an unusually spectacular view of the old city. Such a terrace would normally be empty and unwelcoming; but this was an attractive living space. Céphise pointed out the improvements Sam had made, especially the bamboo screen suspended over the centre of the terrace to make the space livable in the hot summer months. Around the perimeter, he had placed large pots of young palms that provided a natural dimension to the outdoor terrace. Céphise said she added the acacia table and chairs, and watered the potted garden. Taking care of her terrace was a commitment and a joy that centred her in her home.

Xisco inspected the pulley system Sam had created to open and close the bamboo panels. It was so like Sam—minimal and effective.

"The apartment is large for one person but Sam insisted I take it. He said one day I would need the space."

"He wanted you to have a family."

"I thought he did it for himself and I was the caretaker. I always expected him to return."

Sam had given up all of this. The terrace had been an inventive creation of his imagination and yet it had been only a small piece of Sam's life before Xisco met him in Sonim.

Dusk had slowly crept up around them. The streetlights came on in the city and homes below them. The sultry evening gave way to the kind of balmy evening no one wants to leave.

***

When Garcia entered her office, he found Ardis looking out the window, day dreaming.

"What'ya thinking?" He didn't expect an answer.

"Yesterday, I was crossing the Praça do Comércio and I spotted Carlos with a tall woman with brown hair. I believe this was Laurenza, whom he met in Italy. Even from far, I could read the body language. Her arms seemed to be imploring him to do something. Laurenza was leaning in and pressing him with words. Carlos was back on his heels."

"Who is this Laurenza?"

"She was a nun; they had fallen in love. Anyway, the scene would be obvious to anyone. Laurenza was making demands. Carlos was confused and disengaging. It was a lover's quarrel."

Ardis turned to look at Garcia.

"I can't go home now, Roberto. I came here to do research."

Ardis had a valid point. She had completed her reconnaissance with Carlos in the north. The boat was ready. She even had a crew.

"People will be suspicious if I *don't* spend time on the ocean."

This time, Garcia did not challenge her. Her mission was important to him as well. Naval interests in coastal waters remained keen.

***

Xisco found the black ribbon among his things. He didn't need the reminder; he still thought of Sam every waking minute.

Staying miserable hadn't been in his nature, but he couldn't shake it. He was unable to concentrate or to lift a finger to do anything. When he wasn't restless, he was tired, and when he wasn't tired, he was sleepy.

"I'm thinking I won't go with Ardis and Carlos to the Algarve," Xisco mused. "Maybe I will go home to Sonim."

But Céphise did not agree. Over the course of an afternoon, she provided ample argument. "This is a big opportunity." "Not one you want to miss." "It won't come again." "You will regret not going." "Sam wouldn't want you passing up adventure because you're sad about him dying. He would not approve and you know it."

"Though I will miss you, Xisco, you must go to Algarve."

In the morning, she led him out. Diana followed.

"Goodbye, my friend." Céphise kissed him on both cheeks. "I'll see you when you return."

He scooped her into his arms and hugged her. She held him.

Diana hugged him, too.

He strapped his satchel onto the BSA, kick-started it, and departed down the passage.

The Alentejo

25. In Waters off the Coast of Portugal

A rdis led Carlos and Xisco to a berth near the top of the pier. "It's a converted fishing trawler. It's seaworthy and will get us where we're going."

They saw "RV *Cão de Água*" decorated in script on the bow. On the stern below the name of the boat, plain block letters said "Setubal."

"Welcome to the Research Vessel *Water Dog*." She translated the boat's name literally. "The name pays tribute to the *HMS Beagle*, the ship on which Charles Darwin sailed to the Galapagos Islands and wrote much of the *Origin of Species*."

Naming ships after dogs was a British Navy tradition. Adopting this tradition, Ardis chose the name of a much-loved breed of dog that swims well and was popular with fishermen: the Portuguese Water Dog.

"The *Water Dog*. I love it," exclaimed Xisco.

They put their food on board, Ardis's film, then their duffle bags and Ardis's camera equipment. They stowed it all away. Ardis wrapped her camera, all her equipment, and film in towels and an old sheet to protect them from the salty air.

Xisco unstrapped his duffle bag from the back of the motorcycle and passed it down to Carlos, who moved it to the top of the stairs and passed it down to Ardis. She stowed it on the bunk she had assigned to him. Then, using a boom on the pier, Xisco and Carlos loaded the BSA Empire Star and secured it under a tarp beneath the dinghy in front of the wheelhouse.

That night, they slept on the boat dockside. The hold that formerly stored the catch was converted to a low cabin amidships with bunks in the bulkheads. The aura of the sea permeated the well-worn wood. They settled in, each snug in a bunk, listening to water lapping on the side of the hull as the trawler gently rocked in its moorings.

***

They woke early and cast off as the rising sun erased the sphere of stars above their heads. Like the coastlines of the Rio Tejo and the Algarve, the Arrábida shore between Setubal and Sesimbra runs in an east-west direction. After leaving the river, Ardis kept as close to the north shore as possible so they could scan the beaches for sea turtle activity.

"Xisco, can you please read to me the names of the beaches as we pass by?"

"I will read, Señhorita. This one is Praia da Figueirinha." His florid Portuguese showed he was proud he could read.

"Praia dos Galapinhos."

In the dawn light, Ardis scanned the beaches, looking for signs of sea turtles. Monseñhor Carlos took the wheel. Between the beaches, he accelerated the boat.

"Praia do Portinho da Arrábida."

Past Sesimbra, they slowed for a last, small beach. "This one looks promising."

"Praia do Ribeira do Cavalo."

"Here's something." Ardis inspected it. "Possible turtle tracks in the sand."

Carlos put the boat in neutral and took a turn to look through the binoculars. The tracks weren't much to look at in the dawn shadows, but there they were.

Their search ended as they passed the headland at *Cabo Espichel* and the coastline turned north. Ardis set a course towards a planet, hovering above the horizon in the deep purple of straggling darkness in the west. Behind them, the mauve wash above the land, now a silhouette, was slowly transforming the sky. A magnificent watercolour emerged from the scarlet flourish of the rising sun. Far in the distance, they saw whales breaching, one after another. "Those are humpbacks!" Ardis knew her sea mammals. "They put on a good show."

They headed west south-west in a wide arc until they could no longer see the shore, passing freighters in the shipping lanes on their way into Lisbon. Ardis surveyed the shipping with binoculars, scanning the surface in all directions.

She sighted an object on the surface, thinking it was a whale. Perhaps. It was too large to be a turtle. But it was well above the surface. A conning tower? It submerged before she could observe it better and properly identify it. But she saw it. When she had a chance, she would report seeing a submarine.

"What's that?" Xisco pointed over the starboard side, to the west, at two o'clock.

Ardis examined it with the binoculars. "Congratulations, Xisco. Your first sighting is a pod of orcas." She looked toward Carlos. "Xisco is taking to marine biology quickly. He won't want to be a *cavalarico* anymore."

Carlos turned to Xisco with a smile. "*Isso é mesmo uma palavra?*" Is that even a word?

"*Não, ela acha que isso significa moço de estrebaria.*" She thinks it means stable boy.

They shared a knowing look, a rare moment of consensus between them, as Ardis continued to explain that killer whales were the largest of the dolphins.

For hours, they cruised in a southerly direction, gradually heading back to shore. They adjusted to the ever-constant sun, getting out their hats and sunglasses. Carlos put on his Iberian horse hat.

Xisco remarked on the many different kinds of sea birds they had seen. Ardis provided him with names that came at him too fast and numerous to remember: storm petrels, shearwaters, Northern gannets, Arctic skua, cormorants, and puffin. Seagulls were plentiful. "Look at the size of that seagull!" Xisco pointed to an all-white bird that was exceptionally large with a wingspan of more than two metres.

"That's an albatross."

***

On the open sea, Xisco quickly discovered an unexpected inner calm. His favourite place was on the bow where he could be on the lookout for sea creatures. Being in this space never bored him. It was time to explore, to create, to be. The events of recent weeks all dropped away as he contemplated the vastness of the ocean and his small place within it.

Xisco lowered the binoculars, letting them hang from the strap around his neck like a loose anchor to bump against his ribs. The brown of his eyes was indiscernible as he squinted in the sunlight. He put on his sunglasses, also tethered on a cord. It was a two-step operation he was learning to execute without tangling the straps. His hat had a chin strap, too, a necessity on the water he gladly accepted to save it from being blown away.

Xisco preferred gentler breezes that coaxed the sweet odour of fish from the well-worn deck and misted a hint of salt on his lips.

He looked back to the wheelhouse. Carlos was at the wheel. Xisco instinctively didn't trust any clergy; historically, they were complicit with the aristocracy. Ardis was in the seat opposite, persistently scanning the surface in all directions. Ardis seemed to enjoy his company, always engaging in animated conversation. How could she? Especially after learning Carlos helped the Nazis.

Nazis killed Sam.

Xisco sat cross-legged at the bow. He wondered how Céphise was doing and whether her house was full of guests.

His concerns were normally with his own situation, his quest to find his way in the world. Now he was drawn to the long view, as far as he could see. He stared across the water, his hat pulled down for shade from the sun.

Life was difficult. It constantly challenged. It never got easier. He must make his own way and make his success positive and appealing to himself so that he was happy, not to please anyone else. Just himself.

"But what will I do?"

Although Xisco had finagled his way along by offering to do anything to help, as it turned out, life on the water was easy and relaxed;

they all shared in the tasks. He gladly kept an eye out for sea life, which was all that was asked of him and the least he could do.

The trawler plowed steadily through the smooth, gently rolling ocean. The rhythm of the engine, the erratic splashing of water on the hull and the sun roasting on the deck pulled him below the surface into a labyrinth of memories where his future choices summoned him. But when he blinked, all he could see was the surface of the water. He continued to stare as the sun bounced off each crest and ripple, and outlined the form of her face, her sparkling eyes.

"Xisco, I will never forget you." She had released him and set him free.

Now his sense of the outcome was different, perhaps more honest. He had lost her. Would he ever see her again? He was turning nineteen next week and when he returned from this adventure life would go on. Or would it? Perhaps he wouldn't stay in Portugal at all, not even Sonim. But where then? Brazil? Or make his life on the sea? He laughed at himself, thinking of himself as an explorer. How silly. How juvenile. The laugh felt good. He tried it out again. This adventure was a fun excursion. There was nothing to be afraid of, except when it was over. He would survive, as long as—again he laughed—as long as he didn't fall in. There were sharks in these waters!

His mind turned to the certain handholds on the deck he could grip onto, including the heavy cables that stabilized the two masts. The forestay secured the forward mast to the bow. Side stays secured each mast to the gunwales on both sides and two backstays secured the aft mast to the transom at the stern. He needed to hold on less and less. Soon, with more practice, he would let go of them and walk freely without handholds. He giggled at the idea. It was easy to do now as they were cruising in smooth waters. But what would happen when he encountered rough seas? There was no safety net.

How different these handholds were from the ones he left behind. Sonim was a way of life that was everything a young adventurer like Xisco needed. At the crest of their little mountain was the *capela*. The cobblestone streets. The fountain in the square at the centre of the village below the mountain. The Señhor's manse and walled-in yard. The fields everywhere below, the fenced-in cemetery beyond the vegetable gardens on the dirt road to the Rio Rabaçal. The wild savannah and the verdant forests. His school. The books he had read. The names of every person and family and all their dogs. His aunt, his siblings, his father and his mother. These he held onto tightly. Every path, lane, and cobbled wall throughout his village. He knew them all and could move through the village as fast as anyone could. He had been on a path and was happy. He ached to be there again.

The incident in front of the Aljube in Lisbon came rushing back.

He needed a handhold then at that very moment more than ever. An idea left him reeling. "What kind of God would allow that to happen to a decent man?" There was no answer. He had done everything he could not to think about what happened for it took over his mind and consumed him. Nothing could quell his shaken world. There was nothing to stop his mind from revisiting the scene but wilful abstinence. He learned to shut it out, turn it off, and not let it happen again. He did not want to be pulled down into that vortex to the deep black bottom of creation.

He abandoned the daze in which he found himself and looked back to the wheelhouse. Ardis was at the controls and Carlos was in the seat opposite.

The Monseñhor waved to him.

"Hunh." Xisco muttered his contempt.

***

"I envy the ease he displays—such composure." Carlos nodded toward Xisco. "He seems to have great fortitude." Carlos sat on the opposite side of the wheelhouse.

Next to him at the ship's wheel, Ardis sat in the Captain's chair as her feet dangled above the floor—the only detrimental feature of the boat's retrofit that she had yet to address. She wore government-issued aviator sunglasses that reduced the glare, and her blonde curls fell on her shoulders.

"He is dealing with a gross injustice perpetrated by his mother country." Ardis was keeping the *Water Dog* on a course that required some attention though there was nothing in their path as far as the eye could see. "He misses a new friend." She was trying to piece together an explanation. "And don't forget, he's away from home for the first time."

"Home? He's a teenager and teenagers love adventure." Carlos responded quickly to the easy part. After a brief pause, he continued in his thick accent. "Life is full of sorrow and without purpose. God's way is a mystery."

Ardis pushed the loose curls from her face. She could see he was trying to do the same as she was—find an explanation and give things an order they could live with—but life was without purpose? This idea, coming from a man whom she believed would have a more positive view of the world, confused her.

"He will find his calling and he will accept that death comes to us all. As for the girl, it's not as if they were together for a long time."

"I'm surprised, Carlos. You don't seem to have much empathy." Ardis was looking now with binoculars. *How could a priest believe that life has no purpose?* She would bring that up later. For now, she wanted to learn more about Carlos and knew her best approach was nonchalance so that he would remain open. "For a priest, I mean."

Carlos looked down. "You are right, Ardis. I am sorry. I have been insensitive." His tone was serious and formal while his khaki shorts and a light cotton shirt were casual and relaxed.

"I cannot imagine how I would feel if I lost a dear friend." She looked him in the eye. "As for the girl, think back to how you felt at his age when you fell in love."

She wanted to hear him talk about his own life.

The man with the olive complexion didn't even flinch. "What makes you think I fell in love when I was his age? Or ever for that matter?" The white pallor on his words didn't show against his olive complexion.

"It's never too late, Carlos." She teased him. "Oh, I forgot. You are a priest." She was embarrassed for him.

Carlos remained serious as usual. "I admit I am human."

"Just think, if you were Protestant, you could get married. You are intelligent and attractive, Carlos. Women would fall for you."

"Well, I can't. It wouldn't be right. I am not allowed."

It was a firm rebuke and she got the point. "How old are you, if you don't mind me asking?" She could be direct when wanting information.

"I have thirty-two years. And you?"

"I am twenty-eight. If being a priest is what you want, so be it. Put your collar back on. Live your life with conviction."

"It is what I want."

"But if it's not what you want—and I say this with respect—open up and you may discover new possibilities you may never have even considered. You might even have fun."

He breathed deeply, looking tense again. "The choice isn't that black and white, Ardis. There are more than two options. I can have a fun-filled life as a priest who embraces life and all it has to offer. Just because I choose not to have intimate, sexual relations doesn't mean I can't have meaningful relationships."

"Carlos, I saw you last week, in Lisbon. With a young woman. Long brown hair, tall –"

"Yes, that was Laurenza."

"She was very pretty."

Carlos smiled.

"You looked close. I mean, when you stood together. It looked as if you knew each other—you know—very well."

"When I met Laurenza in Rome, she was a nun."

"What happened?"

"Oh my God, what didn't happen?" He was buying time, putting his thoughts together. "It was around the time I was pulled out of Italy. War had been declared and the Cardinal wanted me back in Portugal. There was a lot going on and we were separated. I believed she fled to get away from me. We were in love. It was a terrible time."

"It looked as if you were quarreling."

"She wants me to leave the priesthood."

Ardis frowned. "You have a lot going on."

"Too much."

"What are your plans now?" She studied the ocean over his shoulder, looking for any sign of life in the water.

"I want to fulfil my orders and get back to my mission as a servant of God and His Church. I have done things I'm not proud of. I'm trying to make amends for what happened with the gold stolen from the Jews."

She studied him; the sunlight illuminated his brown eyes revealing streaks of grey.

"Why must you believe you're responsible for everyone's mistakes?"

"Because I'm a priest. My role is to be a guide and I failed."

"The entire situation was truly shocking, Carlos. I was surprised, too."

"I should have handled it differently." On impulse, he reached out for the binoculars. "My turn, Ardis." He set his mind on the ocean.

"Actually, I was surprised you were involved at all."

"I was wilfully blind to what was happening and I have only myself to blame." He searched the vast surface of sparkling reflections.

She considered what would help him most right now. "Perhaps this time away will give you a chance to sort it all out, as you said, and make amends."

"I hope so." He passed the binoculars back to her. "If I were not here, I would be walking at Praia das Amoeiras."

"We will find a beach for you in the Algarve."

"And what will we do for him?" He motioned to Xisco at the bow of the boat.

Neither of them mentioned the real source of Xisco's heartache. They had backed away from a topic that was taboo.

26. Time in its Wholeness

Xisco and Carlos were sitting on the bench along the stern of the boat when Ardis came back up on deck. The three of them opened their beers and toasted. "To sea turtles."

Ardis handed Xisco a bag of bread crusts she had collected to feed the seagulls.

Standing in the centre of the deck, Ardis surveyed the empty horizon, rocking slightly in sync with the boat. The sun was relentless. There was no wind. Everything was still and quiet, except for the constant lapping of the water against the hull and the occasional gust that flipped the burgees near the top of the front mast.

Xisco tossed a few pieces of bread crust into the water and watched them sink. "Where are the fish?" Xisco expected to see dozens of fish strike the bread.

Suddenly, three large fish zoomed in and the bread was gone. It all happened in the fraction of a second. "See that? See that?"

"They were huge." Carlos confirmed his sighting.

"Here they come, here they come." Ardis was pointing.

In the distance, they saw a school of dolphin seemingly flying through the air, approaching from the southwest.

On the other side of the boat, a school of small fish was breaking the surface. The boat attracted sea life.

"This is a perfect time for a swim." Carlos said over his shoulder on his way to change. "Come on Xisco. Put on your bathing suit, let's go."

"I never swam in deep water before. It's the ocean."

"There's nothing to worry about."

Xisco tossed him a snorkel and a mask. "I will keep an eye out for sharks."

Carlos didn't venture beyond the area near the stern.

Xisco and Ardis watched the dolphins as they streaked underneath and surfaced only feet away. "They're having fun." He was surprised to recognize their animal intelligence.

Then he watched Carlos in the water as the dolphins passed by him. One swam next to him an arm's length away. When it sped off, he surfaced and released the snorkel from his mouth. "Did you see that?"

"That dolphin was watching you, Carlos." Xisco lay on his stomach across the wide, flat gunwale at the stern and stared into the water. He dropped bread crumbs to attract more fish. A school of silver-coloured fish came up to take some and darted away. Carlos dropped under the surface to see them.

"Señhorita, I try not to think about Sam, but I cannot help myself. I go over everything that happened before –"

"There's no rush, Xisco. Take it easy on yourself." She scanned to the east where the shoreline would appear when they were near enough.

"What is your dream, Señhorita?"

"My dream? Ahh. My dream is to find the nesting grounds of the Kemp's ridley, a sea turtle whose nesting grounds are a mystery."

"And if you find these nesting grounds you will be happy?"

"I will try to help preserve them so they may survive."

"Don't you want to find a husband and have a family?"

"Maybe. That is a different kind of goal, and I will deal with that later. Finding the nesting grounds is a professional goal."

"I don't have a professional goal." Xisco scanned the area around the boat for sharks.

"Once you have decided on a career for yourself, your goals will come to you. If there was one thing you want to do or discover or invent, what would it be?"

"That's not so easy."

"When you are ready, you will know. Keep learning and experiencing new things."

Thanks to his Papai, Xisco learned how to hunt and fish, too, but he would never be as good as his Pai.

The puzzle of what to do with his life rested front of mind. There was time.

***

Xisco's probing had stirred considerations about her own situation that she had set aside for some time now. Ardis didn't have that part of her life sorted out yet. Her field research was not delivering the results she was hoping for. It was becoming clear that significant nesting would occur in the warm Mediterranean Sea or further south along the coast of Africa.

The truth of her situation was beginning to sink in. The needs of the war had redirected her research. Despite the war, she still hoped to succeed. This expedition would count as a marker in time. From an academic perspective, the outcome remained neutral.

She set up the movie camera on its tripod in the wheelhouse to have it ready in case she wanted to get some shots.

Caroline would have laughed if she knew Ardis was on a boat with a stable boy and a priest. She lingered there in the open ocean, where the guys were deeply engrossed in being boys. This was her chance to play, too. Lord knows she needed a break.

***

Xisco was on the foredeck, warming in the sun when Carlos sat down beside him. With half a hope to chase him away, Xisco immediately shared his thoughts. "What I love about being on the ocean, is that it shows me just how small we are. When I think of how vast the universe is, I feel smaller yet."

Carlos jumped in. "Which helps me appreciate the all-powerful nature of our Creator."

"I believe in God, but I don't." Xisco didn't care what Carlos thought.

"That is contradictory." Carlos challenged him.

"Yes, I feel ambiguous."

"That strikes me as a lazy or convenient answer." Again, Carlos challenged.

"I do think about God and religion—often."

"Many people don't these days."

"I don't fault anybody for their beliefs." Xisco looked at him. "People have their own cultures. No religion is better than another. It's just what people know."

"Some are more primitive, so I agree."

Xisco did not agree. "Plato, the Greek philosopher, described the shadows of flames dancing on the walls of a cave as the images of human understanding. This insight remains valid today. Each religion and culture is like a fire that shines its own light. And what do people see on the walls of their caves? Images. Only images."

"Of what though?" Carlos was engaged.

"Of God. The images of God that are all around us. God is everywhere."

"But that doesn't tell us who God is or anything about Him." Carlos reverted to what the Church taught.

"Exactly. I believe any images of God cannot be anywhere near accurate. Our images reflect only our wishes of what God might be, but we can never really know."

"Do you think God is kind or merciful?"

"If God exists, He must be a mystery. This is all we are capable of knowing."

Carlos shrugged. "Then why believe in God at all?"

"If we don't have a God, then who put the ocean here and not on Mars?" Xisco held his hands in the air, miming the vastness between his outstretched arms and hands.

Carlos countered him flatly. "God did."

"One day, science will explain what we don't yet know. There is no need always to assign what you don't know to the existence of a deity." It was a put-down he had harboured for such a time as this. A put-down for weak people.

Carlos stood. "I will leave you to your errant wanderings."

Xisco smiled, satisfied.

***

In the wheelhouse, Ardis put her arms in the air in a shrug, a question mark. The noise coming off the engine was too loud to allow normal conversation. Xisco knew she was asking, "Well, see anything?"

He too shrugged an expression in reply that said, "I'm sorry Señhorita but I did not see a thing." In fact, he hadn't been looking. She could tell. He returned to the wheelhouse. "All that water and sky are so big. They make me feel so *pequeno*."

Carlos pointed beyond the port bow. Xisco looked in that direction. "Was that a turtle?"

She pulled the throttle back. The noise level dropped off and after the engine was purring smoothly again, she cut it. The boat glided quietly through the water until it appeared still in the long, smooth swells from the north.

Ardis was in the wheelhouse on the starboard side; she had to go out on the deck to the other side of the boat to see what he was talking about.

"It certainly is!" She grabbed the binoculars to observe the turtle. "It's a loggerhead. The carapace, which is its shell, is a reddish brown and the underbelly, if you could see it, would be a pale yellow." She looked up. The turtle was no longer there; it had submerged.

"Let's have a break," she sighed. "The turtle may surface again in this area and we might get a better look at it."

There were no white caps on this water. The swells were barely noticeable. Perfect time for a break. After all, one didn't enjoy nature in a forest by blasting through on a motorcycle. Why do it in a boat on the ocean?

Over the gunwale, Xisco saw fish come up to check them out. The water lapped against the hull. Occasionally, the green and red of the Portuguese ensign at the stern flapped in the balmy breeze, and the pennants on spreaders on each side of the mast behind the wheelhouse flipped over and snapped in a gust, and fell again.

"It's a nice day." Ardis shrugged her shoulders. "Let's enjoy it."

Ardis loved to be on the water and she wanted Xisco and Carlos to share the joy she experienced. These times without an agenda were exactly what they needed to relax.

"Let's have some more of that beer. Give me a hand, Xisco?"

They went into the cabin behind the wheelhouse. The galley was just wide enough for one person to work. In the rear of the cabin was a table.

Ardis lifted the heavy lid of the cooler built into the galley cabinet. She passed out sandwiches. She pulled beer out from deep in the bottom of the cooler and passed them to Xisco to take out to the deck. They had more sandwiches and enough other food to last two days on the water. They would replenish their supply as they went so it was fresh.

Xisco dropped a few crumbs of bread in the water. Carlos joined him to see the fish that came to the side of the boat.

Ardis used the distraction to take care of a routine task. Quickly, she tapped out a brief communication in Morse code to her colleagues at the Technical University of Lisbon.

ROUTINE STATUS. HEADING S TO ALENTEJO. SPOTTED WHITE ALBATROSS. MADE MY DAY. REGARDS, A.

She had coded her message using the "Hidden-in-Plain-Sight" guidelines Garcia had established to deter enemy vessels that could intercept it. The "white" refers to the U-boat and her salutation indicated there was no urgency. This would appear to be a routine message providing notice of her location.

A relay station in the Azores would pick up the message and forward it to Camp X in Oshawa, Ontario, where they would decode and log the message.

Feels awkward. Mildly devious. As if I'm play-acting being a spy. That's it, play-acting. Nothing will come of it.

"Touch wood." She tapped her knuckle on the wood railing for good measure.

Xisco happened to be looking in the right direction when a humpback whale breached off the starboard bow. He saw it all, from the moment its nose broke the surface to the moment it came crashing down, drenching the trawler in a fountain of splash and spray. A second and a third display by other members of the pod of humpbacks that crossed paths with the *Water Dog* followed. One swam next to the boat, lifted its head out of the water, and waved its massive flipper at them. Xisco saw his eye and the bumpy barnacles all over the mottled grey mass.

Before diving, the whales raised their tails. "See how they lift their flukes before a deep dive?" Xisco was startled to find Ardis and Carlos right behind him. "Each whale has a distinct pattern on the underside of the tail." Ardis explained how marine biologists identified the individuals.

The humpbacks disappeared. Carlos and Ardis resumed their routine in the wheelhouse and Xisco cast an eye over the water in the direction the pod of humpbacks had taken. He assumed a lookout position at the stern for a change.

Well past Sines and Porto Covo, they saw a school of Bluefin tuna race under the boat, an immense spectacle. Then a commotion erupted on the surface in the near distance. Ardis idled the *Water Dog* and went out to explain what was happening as she pulled the movie camera on its tripod onto the deck.

She filmed the tuna herding sardines and anchovy into a tight circle. Above the water, a variety of sea birds noisily called out before they dove to snatch some prey.

"It's a feeding frenzy."

She pointed out the second dorsal fins and the sickle-shaped tail forks of the speeding tuna as they herded sardines, anchovy, and mackerel into a frothy, splashing ball in the centre. Dolphins joined in the fray.

"I am amazed every time I get to see something like this." Ardis recorded the event in her research journal.

In Vila Nova de Milfontes, they explored the village with white stucco houses, red tiled roofs, and narrow streets. They went to a restaurant, which was so small they sat outside on the terrace adjoining the square.

It had been a long, beautiful day in the sun and they were exhausted. They returned to the *Water Dog* as the constellations reclaimed the sky. Xisco and Carlos collapsed into their bunks. Both fell asleep within minutes.

Ardis stared at a patch of moonlight on the opposite wall at the bottom of the stairs. Her thoughts drifting, Ardis somehow landed on Manfred. *He is a decent person.* She could almost have forgotten he was a member of the German diplomatic corps. *It does not matter, though.* The idea that he had any power to make her like him made her feel very uncomfortable.

It is very likely he is a spy in some capacity or other. He is my enemy. Full stop. Still. Does he even know what wrongs his country is committing as it aggressively invades its neighbours and steals their wealth and resources to fuel its war machine?

What justifications for the war do Germans receive? What does he believe? Does he actually believe the Nazis are in the right? Or is he tricked and bullied along with the entire nation?

Ardis doubted he could know and still follow orders. She pitied him. She would not allow herself to become accustomed to Manfred. She would deny herself from following that tendency. The truth did not apply to spies. She wanted to remain accustomed to the mores of decent men like Roberto.

The rhythm of the water rocked her gently in her bunk. She turned her mind to bigger issues and certainties that soothed her mind and never failed to put her to sleep. Her favourite: "The one thing we know for sure is that change is constant." This made her think of a flowing river that caused her to lose track of awareness and drift to sleep countless times.

Another good one was, "Who knows what the world will look like in 100 years?" Until she met the sea turtle at Burrard Inlet that day with Pete, she tended to dismiss the idea that humankind would destroy itself with war. She also wanted to believe that humankind would not destroy the natural environment through pollution. But what the turtle said rang true. She wondered why religions did not have sea turtles in their firmament, as indigenous cultures did, which she learned about during her time in Vancouver. She believed the differences between religions would eventually disappear.

She still wasn't asleep. She arrived at an idea that perplexed her deeply. "All that you hold dear may no longer be present. We just do not know. Change always happens." This was a return to the first question. It was an endless loop.

Lapping endlessly against the hull, the ocean rocked her gently to sleep in her bunk, where she remained throughout a rotation of the firmament.

***

In his office, Manfred considered the directive to send any unneeded trucks back to the Fatherland. As a favour to Xisco and indirectly to Ardis, Manfred did not seize Sam's truck. He knew the Polish mining engineer had a French truck; Sam got it from them in the first place. After what happened to Sam, Manfred did not have the heart to steal the truck from Xisco.

Then he put his mind to Carlos and Ardis. Why, really, did they go to the Algarve?

He needed information. He could request surveillance, but he ruled that out because it would draw attention from the Gestapo and the SS. He had one correct course of action.

He fantasized how nice it would be for a change to focus all his energy on winning the love and affection of a beautiful mademoiselle like Ardis. But alas, that was not to be. It would be wolfram, wolfram, wolfram, all the time.

He wished he could be back home in the Alsace. Would this war ever be over? Nothing meaningful had happened to improve his life on a personal level. What he wanted more than anything was to find a partner. Would all his old friends be gone? Would all the best women be married?

A knock on the door breaks him out of his daydream. "The Baron wants to see you."

Once again, Marguerite, the Abwehr agent, was in the room.

Without formalities, the Baron addressed Manfred. What are the wolfram numbers?

"Unofficially, double, Baron."

"How did you manage that?"

"I did as you directed, *Freiherr*. I paid top prices even when they quadrupled. I paid in gold and I added incentives for a speedy response."

"And your suppliers know not to report any increase in the numbers?"

"Everyone wants more gold."

„*Vielen dank, Oberleutnant.*"

Manfred took this opportunity to report that his principal contact, Monseñhor Carlos, had gone to the Algarve. The Baron said he was aware—the Monseñhor reported to the Patriarch of Lisbon who is a close friend of Prime Minister Salazar.

Manfred had already reported there was a woman involved. Today, he updated that, saying he was afraid she might distract Carlos.

"Yes," confirmed the Baron. "I will leave that to Marguerite. Now, if you will excuse me, I have another meeting."

In fact, the Baron didn't have another meeting. He just didn't want to be party to the discussion that was to come.

Marguerite took charge. "Plans have changed. I need you to do something else for us."

"I need you to trail Ardis Lowney. We believe she is a spy who reports your wolfram dealings. We also believe her contact with the Monseñhor and Sam Meyer was not a coincidence. She is getting in the way. I want you to find her and report back."

"I'm a diplomat, not a spy."

"Are you a German? Your accent doesn't say so."

"Of course, I am."

"This is war. We must win or die."

Manfred nodded.

"Ja, Fraulein, I do not know how to find them. They are on a boat."

"Then I'll put you on a U-boat. It can take you right to them."

***

The *Water Dog* continued south. The seemingly endless beaches along the Alentejo coast were soft sand—a treasure trove environment in Ardis's quest for signs of sea turtle life. They counted more than a dozen turtle trails on various beaches.

"These results are so appropriate." Ardis recorded every sighting, noting there was definitely a trend. "Remote beaches on the edge of tropical zones may occasionally serve as rookeries, but it is less common." Yet, she was agitated. "The results are positive; but they aren't overwhelming, not even slightly."

For two long, beautiful days, they witnessed fascinating scenes of bountiful marine life, and captured much on film. Xisco developed expertise in handling the movie camera so she let him operate it all the time.

The days had been a perfect, unbroken calm. Too perfect. As they continued south, the string of soft beaches along the Alentejo coast had fallen away.

27. Breath of the Adamastor

The shore was dark and foreboding, an unassailable wall of rock and jagged cliffs. Above the trawler, a bedlam of black and grey clouds choked off what daylight remained. *Cabo de São Vicente* was the southwestern-most tip of Europe.

Growing swells prevented the *Water Dog* from passing close enough to the shore for Ardis to see anything. Xisco felt the swells in his stomach, up and down, and the occasional lurch made him hold on tighter.

Xisco remained perched at the bow. The sea swelled, frothy. The air had cooled. The spray off the sea became a spitting rain tossed in his face by gusts of wind. He clung to the mainstay, fascinated by the crash over each crest and the hull slamming spray into the air. He looked crazed with excitement.

Ardis stuck her head out the door. "Xisco!" She raised her voice over the din. "It's not safe out there; come on in."

Xisco reclaimed his handholds as he crossed to the wheelhouse; the wind slammed the door behind him. On her feet behind the wheel, Ardis dominated the wheelhouse. On her starboard, Carlos frowned and shook his head as Xisco took his place port side.

"It's wild out there." Xisco clearly enjoyed this.

Ardis didn't share his excitement—she felt a suffocating dread. Though seaworthy, the trawler was too light and should have been off the water in such seas. Ardis steered the trawler with fresh insistence, urging the *Water Dog* forward. "We must get to Sagres." Given the wind and waves, the ten kilometres to Sagres felt like a hundred.

For the love of God, girl. You will get us all killed.

Xisco looked where the Adamastor was bellowing into the wind. The sea monster's breathe expanded outward, creating a crack in the harmony of all things and initiated a chain that caused the sun to erupt and hurl a gargantuan blast at the earth. When the Adamastor breathed, an aurora danced in the night at the North Pole, an ocean warmed, a glacier melted, a cloud formed, and one thing was certain: a wind blew. In the vacuum, another wind rushed in to fill the void, creating a chain of voided spaces, of winds rushing in and winds rushing away.

Carlos pointed.

Dolphins appeared to lead the *Water Dog*—an unnatural event in such stormy seas—and sped ahead below the surface, coming up regularly in their signature move to breathe in air. It was as if they were saying, "Come this way! Come this way!"

"Let's try to get the dolphins on film," Ardis said to Xisco. "Whatever you do, keep the camera dry in the wheelhouse."

Wind laden with rain hit the windshield with a splat.

The sky and sea had transformed into a turbulent entity that showed God in heaven above was angry. An obvious and unusual change in the dolphins' behaviour marked his presence. The main pod of dolphins continued onward ahead of the *Water Dog*, and a small group breached on the port side, drawing attention to the area beyond the stern.

There, a hundred metres behind the *Water Dog*, a periscope broke the surface.

The pod had split, which captured Ardis's attention. It was in their nature to behave with intelligence and purpose. So, why split up?

Through the camera, Xisco saw a Leviathan crash through a wave as it emerged from the deep. Xisco had captured it on film. He pointed to the alien silhouette against the western sky. "Ardis, Ardis, look!"

Xisco filmed the elongated mass as water rushed off its sides. The monster hissed in the rolling water as its valves opened to exchange air.

Carlos winced in disbelief. "A submarine?" His praying hands shook as he tampered with the crucifix on his chest.

They peered through the rain. There were no markings on the broad side of the conning tower. With one glance, Ardis saw the pointed bow of a shark's snout. The conning tower was rounded at the front and two guns protruded from the flat deck, a large canon aft of the tower and a small canon in front. The battleship grey was another telltale sign. "A U-boat." Saying it aloud confirmed what she did not wish to fathom—a U-boat had tracked them to that very spot in the vast, open ocean. Ardis expelled her breath.

Xisco understood what this meant. Ardis feared capture. If she waited for them to board the *Water Dog*, the outcome would be a disaster. The Nazis would shoot her. They would shoot all of them.

She pushed the engine to full throttle and the trawler caught a swell that heaved them forward. She looked back over her shoulder. Through the rear window of the wheelhouse, Ardis saw the U-boat slice through another swell. An officer on the conning tower with binoculars was looking right at her.

Ardis altered course, trying to break away; make a run for it. The officer's arm came out and his fingers urged the sailor on the tower to do something, quickly.

Ardis swung the wheel in the opposite direction. Carlos hung on and prayed. But the sudden change threw Xisco in the wheelhouse. He held onto the camera, landing on the table in the centre of the galley.

She changed course after each swell. Xisco filmed from a porthole, and Carlos crushed against Ardis. All hung on as they zigzagged away.

Carlos mouthed a prayer.

The U-boat fired a canon.

The ocean erupted like a fountain that crashed on the wheelhouse.

"Any dolphins hit?" This was her first concern.

Carlos stepped out of the wheelhouse and scanned beyond the stern. He searched for any sign of blood and dolphins. Fortunately, they had disappeared.

The wind and waves muffled the crack of a lone gun firing.

Xisco filmed through the cabin window toward the U-boat.

A thump on the deck seized his attention. Xisco's jaw fell open as he drew in a breath. Ardis's fingers were white as she gripped the wheel. A worst-case scenario had unravelled beyond her control.

Carlos lay supine on the deck.

Though he continued filming, the fear on Xisco's face fell away; he was angry. Carlos reclined on an elbow, and then lay back, a rush of adrenalin pumping in his blood.

"Oh my God, Carlos!" Ardis was terror-stricken. She trimmed the engine and went to him.

Ardis felt the terror perhaps more than he did. In the past when she had encountered marine life that had been injured, she was choked with anguish as if she were the one strangling in a fishing net or slashed from neck to toe by an Orca.

"Oh, my God." Ardis repeated it like a mantra; she was in shock.

"God didn't do this." Carlos tried to be funny. He had blood on his face and neck, which drew their attention.

Xisco had set the camera on the floor of the galley. He frantically searched the blood on Carlos's neck. "Where is the wound? Where is—"

"My leg. Here." Carlos was clutching his right thigh, which was soaked in blood.

Neither Ardis nor Xisco noticed the wound, nor for that matter the rain skittering across the deck. Carlos was getting soaked.

"Let's move him in." Xisco grabbed his arm and started pulling him.

Ardis grabbed the other and they slid him into the wheelhouse. From below, Xisco brought a mattress, some blankets, and a pillow. Ardis checked the boat. Swells were carrying them to shore. There were breakers.

The attack ended. In the commotion, the U-boat slipped away unannounced, as it had arrived.

Ardis started the engine and pointed the *Water Dog* out to sea. She called Xisco to the wheel, pointed east. "Take us that way."

Ardis retrieved a First Aid kit in the galley. She removed a wad of dressing and pressed it on the wound. Carlos howled. "*Fácil, fácil.*"

Ardis felt the sting; except for her, the hurt was more acute. Her distress flowed down on him as if she were a mother tending to a mortally wounded child.

She applied firm, even pressure to stop the flow of blood. She took off her belt and wrapped it like strapping around his leg above the wound to reduce his blood loss, like the bandage. Then she propped up his leg over a coil of rope. Carlos started shaking and she tucked an extra blanket around him.

Xisco created space; then crouched close. "Can I get you anything?"

"Whiskey?"

"You make jokes at a time that is not funny, Monseñhor."

Ardis dug into the First Aid kit. She found morphine.

"This ought to work." Ardis filled the barrel, removed the air in the syringe, and jabbed the needle into his leg.

Xisco was impressed. "Where did you learn to do that?"

"Basic training." He didn't ask further and she didn't say it was at Camp X.

Ardis watched Carlos as the drug took hold of him. She could see his tension fall away. "Oh Carlos." She hugged him. She just held him. The fear of losing him bounced 'round and 'round her brain. She couldn't lose him.

***

Through the blur of shock and morphine, Carlos could feel the pressure of her arms on his shoulders and the closeness of her holding him. It was the nicest gesture she could have done for him and he would not forget it ever.

***

Ardis straightened up, wiped the rain from his face, and looked into his eyes. "I'm so sorry this has happened to you, Carlos."

Carlos needed medical attention now. Ardis confirmed Xisco was on course to Sagres. She went below and quickly tapped out a message.

EMERGENCY. ATTACKED BY SNIPER ON GERMAN U-BOAT. ONE WOUNDED. NEED A DOCTOR IN SAGRES. ARDIS.

The time for coding messages was over. She didn't care if the Germans could read her message. She wanted them to read it. She wanted the whole world to read it.

***

At a desk, the lieutenant on duty focused on completing a report. The knock on the door was an unwelcome distraction.

He was about to say yes, enter, when the duty officer walked right in. She handed him the recent communications.

"Ardis was reporting her movements out of Setubal and on the Alentejo coast of Portugal. But they are in trouble now, and the details are not clear, sir."

"Thank you. I will take care of this. Meantime, send the British envoy in Lisbon this message." He wrote quickly, "Need medical assistance in Sagres Harbour." He handed it to her. "Let me know the moment you hear anything further."

The lieutenant took the papers directly into Lieutenant-Colonel Cuthbert Skilbeck who had assumed command of Camp X only weeks ago. "We have an agent in distress, sir."

The lieutenant handed over the brief. His commander read it quickly.

"First, forward this to Mediterranean Command. There may be a vessel in the area that can get that U-boat. Then find out whether medical resources are available at Sagres."

"We are on it, sir, through the British consulate in Lisbon."

"Good. See what they can do and keep me informed. This is Ardis Lowney. Her wolfram reports about the German lack of resources to pay were interesting. Those communiques went to the top. She is a valuable set of eyes in the field."

***

Xisco held the *Water Dog* on an eastward course. Intuitively, Xisco understood the need to face the waves straight on, rather than let them roll the trawler over. One wave in particular, nearly got the better of him. The boat rocked and the mast leaned way over and back. Ardis looked into the wheelhouse. "Everything ok in there?"

He waved her off. "Ya, I got it. I pierce the waves." He wasn't sailing. He was riding the waves and the blustering breath of the Adamastor. He was good at it.

The wind and rain battered the wheelhouse. The monster that lived in the sea was aroused. It hurled a storm of the most ferocious waves it could muster to drive Xisco back to Trás-os-Montes. Xisco laughed aloud at the image of the Adamastor he had conjured. His drama elevated him above the scene and calmed him with a vision of what he needed to do. Like a veteran fisherman, he piloted the *Water Dog*, hurtling fearlessly down the troughs and confidently crashing through the swells. He took advantage of the forces; he didn't work against them as novices were inclined to do. In so doing, he mastered them.

Fierce but short-lived, the storm subsided; the Adamastor could claim this round, but where might the devil be now? Xisco knew the myth in which seamen invested their souls. When the storm receded, the devil advanced, looking for a new opening to ravage.

28. Sagres

The town of Sagres straddled a high shelf of land perched on rocky ligaments and tendons that clutched the sea and embedded its craggy claws in sandy beaches. On the east side of the claw, a long, manmade breakwater protected a harbour. Next to the jetty were the docks, and next to them was the east harbour beach. In the middle of the bay were sections of claw that had broken away ages ago.

At the helm of the *Water Dog*, Xisco approached the passage into the harbour with caution. At the bow, Ardis scanned the water for signs of underwater shoals. Something amidst the rocky islands caught her attention. Xisco followed her eyes. There, nestled in amongst rocks was a different danger.

It was the U-boat.

It sat low in the water with only its conning tower above the surface. He grabbed the movie camera and filmed it there in the shadows. Amidst the wind and rain in the waning light of day, the grey tower blended well with the rock, hulking together in an inhospitable group. It was waiting like a sly wolf to pounce on them and kill them all, certainly, this time.

The U-boat didn't move.

Xisco piloted the *Water Dog* into the harbour, nice and easy. Then Ardis traded places with him to take the trawler all the way to the top of the wharf and squeeze into a space opposite another trawler where some loading appeared to be underway. Xisco dropped the fenders and leapt up onto the dock. He tied in the bow then went to the stern and Ardis threw him the line. He pulled the boat in and fastened it to the wharf.

In the shadows on the other trawler, Xisco heard fishermen talking.

A uniformed harbour officer came out of the marina office waving his arms at the *Water Dog*. "You can't stay there. You're in the way."

"We have a wounded man on board, Señhor."

"In that case, bring him in." The marine officer signalled with his arm to Xisco, to get the transfer of the wounded man moving, then turned abruptly, and held his hand up to stop a truck that was approaching the dock. The men in the truck got out to investigate.

Xisco called to the officer. *"Por favor, Señhor.* We need a doctor."

The officer went in to call the doctor.

Xisco listened to the fishermen and it hit him. They reminded him of the men who collected the rock in the truck on the road in Sonim and paid his father escudos.

They were Germans.

Xisco stayed with the boat. He listened, staying close without being caught.

***

When the rumble of the engine stopped, an entire band of turmoil across Carlos's brain ceased. An idea took shape. The shooting was an act of God. It was just retribution.

The *Water Dog* rocked and bobbed against its bumpers, and Carlos slid into unconsciousness as if trapped in a rip tide. His sense of time and place, and even his identity, his beleaguered self, sank with worriless ease, joining a watery world of muted light and sound, and spiritual fluidity. Incandescent memories paraded against a pale and indifferent circumstance; then broke the surface whole only to descend again. He drifted this way in and out of consciousness.

***

Ardis had radioed ahead for assistance and now they had to wait?

She sat with Carlos, looking at his face that was surprisingly still. When she pulled the blanket higher on his chest, he opened his eyes. Seeing her, he smiled.

"Ardis." Carlos's voice was cracking.

"It's okay." She stroked his face, wiping tears she had spattered on him. She wanted to tell him what happened but she was afraid the truth would be unwelcomed. "Carlos, this shooting—it was my fault." She wanted to say she cared for him but her guilt entangled her.

"Are you taking responsibility for all humanity?" He repeated the allusion she had made to him at the start of their voyage.

She recognized his little dig. "But in this case, I am the guilty one."

"You cannot be held responsible for the actions of others."

She leaned in. "How are you doing? Hang in there, Carlos. A doctor will be here soon."

He nodded with his eyes. "You are great, Ardis. Obrigado."

"The marine officer is calling for help." She rested her hand on his arm. "I will be back soon." She patted his hand.

His eyes closed and he went to sleep.

It was just as well. She checked in with Xisco on the dock.

"They're German," he whispered.

The fishermen continued to talk . . . "Setubal . . . get work on a trawler . . . fish the Grand Banks off Newfoundland."

On hearing him mention Newfoundland, Ardis felt the hair on the back of her head and neck stand up. The prickly chill of frisson lasted only seconds but reinforced her instincts. *What are German fishermen doing on Portuguese trawlers on the Grand Banks?*

The seaman was wary of his friend's proposal. "They shoot spies, you know."

"Better than sitting in a tin can with depth charges exploding all around you."

A German officer came out of the marina office. Wide-eyed in the dark, Ardis recognized Wiesentrauser. His presence was out of context, away from Lisbon where she met him only months ago. "That's Herr Wiesentrauser." She spoke in a quiet voice so as not to wake Carlos.

Xisco was puzzled. "How do you know a German officer?"

"Through Carlos. He's a diplomat in the German embassy."

"I didn't know the Monseñhor knew such people."

"It was a surprise to me, too."

Wiesentrauser walked past them to the boat in the slip opposite to them. The fishermen did not salute Wiesentrauser. "*Oberleutnant*, we have enough diesel now. Are you coming back with us to Cádiz?"

"No, I will get a car. I will drive back to Lisbon."

Ardis's German wasn't good enough for her to hear that Manfred didn't arrive by car. Nor did he say he had been on that U-boat.

Wiesentrauser went into the marina office.

Ardis grabbed Xisco's elbow. "The U-boat is going to Cádiz." Her instructors at Camp X told her to look for this kind of information.

Wiesentrauser returned to the other trawler. He said *auf wiedersehen* as the sailors pushed off and headed out into the dark.

Ardis kept her eyes on Wiesentrauser, who watched the vessel trail away into darkness at the end of the jetty.

"Good evening, Fraulein."

"Herr Wiesentrauser."

"I'm glad I found you. The Monseñhor told me you were travelling this way. Is the Monseñhor available?"

"A sniper on a U-boat shot Carlos."

"Nein, nein. That cannot be."

"Why did you shoot at us?"

"I didn't shoot at you. It was a trigger-happy idiot under orders of a damn fool."

"Carlos was wounded."

"They told me they didn't hit anyone."

"They were wrong."

"Thank God he is alive. Is he okay?"

"See for yourself." Xisco interjected, pointing to the galley.

Wiesentrauser returned his attention to Ardis. "May I?" He asked permission before stepping on deck.

She nodded.

Wiesentrauser stepped onto the boat. In the galley, he crouched beside his friend and touched his arm.

They watched Carlos open his eyes. He patted Wiesentrauser's hand then covered it with his for a moment before letting his hand rest across his prone torso. This upset his visitor.

"Carlos, I'm so sorry, I didn't know. They told me no one was hit."

Carlos smiled, humbled at once by his friend's sincerity.

"I feel so ashamed." Wiesentrauser confessed. "This is terrible."

"Why are you here?" Xisco stood next to Ardis.

"Why? My colleagues needed assistance." He turned to Xisco. "I'm sorry, young man, I do not know you."

"Xisco, Señhor."

"Hello, Xisco. My name is Manfred."

"I don't understand how you knew we would be here."

"The Monseñhor told me he would be here with Fraulein Ardis, so I radioed ahead and asked the kapitan on the U-boat to look out for her."

Ardis blurted, "You're joking." *Was there no need to panic?*

"I wanted to locate you."

If he's not lying, the shooting was my fault.

"I am glad to find you." Wiesentrauser explained why. "I've never visited the Algarve."

Now he's a tourist. Bogart wouldn't let this go down without a fight.

"Let's get this straight," Ardis replied. "We ran from your comrades because we were afraid they were going to kill us."

As a diplomat, he knows his Ambassador will have to explain why a German U-boat attacked a research vessel flying a Portuguese flag.

"We could have been killed." Xisco glared. "Carlos has a bullet!"

Wiesentrauser's eyes widened. "This incident is unforgiveable. I will report it to my superiors and see that the *kapitänleutnant* is disciplined. Monseñhor Carlos, on behalf of my comrades, I apologize."

He is trying to shut this down.

Carlos frowned, "Some enjoy the war too much, even in Portugal."

"I am sorry, Carlos. This should not have happened. They are anxious fools who don't know what is going on. They're all afraid. I am sorry this happened to you."

"What are you doing here?" Again, Xisco dug for details.

All looked to Wiesentrauser for his answer.

"Here? You mean on this dock?"

"Yes, were you waiting for us?" Xisco persisted.

"Nein. The idiots ran out of fuel."

"I see," Ardis nodded, "I'm going in to see what happened with our request for medical assistance."

Ardis went in and enquired when the doctor would be there. Then she explained the trawler belonged to the Technical University of Lisbon. She asked to use the telephone. She called Garcia. She explained the situation, and reported the location of the U-boat. He was on it right away.

"One more thing, we overheard German sailors say they were going to Setubal to find work on Portuguese trawlers to fish the Grand Banks."

"To have eyes on our convoys. Good work, Ardis."

Ardis came out as a truck pulled into the yard. A doctor in a white laboratory coat looked at the wound and took Carlos in the truck, leaving Ardis, Xisco, and Wiesentrauser standing in awkward silence, watching the truck lights ascend the hill into town.

"I would like to see Carlos tomorrow." Wiesentrauser wrote down the address of his pension in the town and passed it to Ardis.

***

"Sir, I think you should see these." The lieutenant handed over the latest communication from Roberto Garcia in Lisbon.

"What have we here? A U-boat out of fuel in Sagres and heading to Cádiz." Lieutenant-Colonel Skilbeck read the summary of events.

"As you know, sir, German U-boats refuel in Cádiz."

"Right. Send this to Mediterranean Command using priority protocol. Then come back."

"Yes, sir."

In three minutes, the lieutenant returned.

"Lieutenant, a Portuguese radio operator on a Portuguese trawler on the Grand Banks was reporting on the movements of our convoys."

"Yes, sir, we removed him from the trawler and are holding him."

"Ardis Lowney has uncovered a new twist." Skilbeck adjusted his pen. "The Germans are now putting their own people on Portuguese trawlers. We need to approach this quietly so we don't tip off Jerry."

***

By morning, the sky had cleared.

Ardis and Xisco caught a ride up the hill into town. At the clinic, they found Carlos in a wheelchair with one leg up on a brace. He looked sleepy. His khaki shorts covered only half the bandage on his thigh.

"He's going to be fine. A couple of weeks of rest and proper hygiene and his leg should heal well."

Carlos purchased a pair of crutches and the doctor lent him a wheelchair they could leave at the harbour office.

They wheeled him out of the clinic and went for a coffee.

Ardis focused her attention on Carlos, who smiled weakly with little to say. The events of yesterday had dampened their spirits, but Carlos's condition brought them to a grim awareness. This was more difficult for him than they anticipated.

Ardis found a café near the embankment, overlooking the harbour. Though the day was early, the sun was bright. Having been on the water for days, they were prepared for the sun. They wore sunglasses and hats with brims to shade their eyes from the glare. With his bandaged leg and bolero, Carlos lent the group a certain flare.

"Thank God you're alive. I was terrified when you lay on the deck."

"Yeah, there was blood all over your neck." Xisco mimed the streak he had seen. "I thought you were hit there."

"I thank God every day, Ardis." Carlos appeared distraught. "Today, in particular." He looked up at her sunglass-shaded eyes.

"We are the crew of the *Water Dog*." Xisco tried to put a macho face on the situation. "We look out for each other."

Ardis nodded in agreement. Carlos smiled.

Xisco wanted his friends to laugh. "It was amazing, I was just watching the dolphins."

Carlos perked up. "Then suddenly Ardis gunned the engine." He smiled, slurring his words. "And tried to outrun them." He paused for a moment as if he were trying to regain control of his tongue, lips, and mouth. "Why did you do that?" He looked at Ardis.

"I—I –."

"No really, why?"

It was uncharacteristically direct of Carlos to be so insistent.

Xisco knew what was going on. Ardis was afraid she would be taken by the Germans, and tortured to death. "I panicked."

"Why did they shoot me?" Carlos lived in a fairy tale world in which war didn't exist.

Xisco understood she would be executed if she were discovered.

But Carlos was adamant. "We didn't do anything to hurt them."

"Because my country is at war with Germany."

"But the U-boat was in Portuguese waters. You aren't supposed to shoot each other when you're in Portugal." Carlos frowned at her.

"I believed they were going to kill us. Every one of us. What bothers me more than I can say is that I endangered your lives. I'm truly sorry, Carlos. You too, Xisco. I brought you here and I'm responsible for your safety. I'm not going to let harm come your way—not without a fight."

They watched a squat, grey and brown sea bird with a long beak totter from the nearby sand to their table. "Hey old girl." Xisco sat up. "I like this one. She looks like a gentle caregiver."

"It's a pelican," Ardis offered.

"You cannot sacrifice yourself, Señhorita." Xisco said to the pelican.

Ardis smiled. *His comments are for me.*

"I came here of my own desire," Xisco added.

Carlos watched the pelican.

"So let's decide about Wiesentrauser." Ardis changed the subject. "Are you going to call him?" She looked to Carlos.

He nodded. "I sense he would like to join us."

The idea of having a German diplomat on board the *Water Dog* made Ardis anxious to the core—despite how nice he had been to her. "Why would we do that?"

"He is my friend," said Carlos.

"I see." Ardis shook her head slowly.

It all feels all wrong. Yet Carlos has suffered so much already because of me. How can I say no? On the other hand, Garcia wants me to obtain intelligence on the German wolfram supply. As the saying goes, keep your friends close and your enemies closer.

Carlos didn't have any idea of her concerns. "Would it be okay if he joined us?"

"How can you even ask that?" Xisco put his arm out in front of Ardis, like a shield.

Xisco didn't trust Carlos because Carlos had helped the same Nazis who killed Sam.

Carlos looked at Xisco with narrowing eyes. "You have nothing to do with this. May I remind you, Xisco, we are all guests of Ardis."

"Their countries are at war, Carlos. That's not fair to Ardis."

Carlos did not look well. "I apologize," he replied.

"It's ok, Carlos." Ardis patted his hand, then turned away as if looking for an out. She nodded to Xisco, her confidante. "Thank you, Xisco. I owe Carlos a favour." Since the shooting, Ardis could not deny Carlos anything, including this.

They set out. Xisco pushed Carlos in the wheelchair. Wiesentrauser's pension was nearby so they went there and asked for him. They waited on a terrace beside the pension.

Within moments, Wiesentrauser joined them. He was dressed in his usual uniform, looking very formal compared to his visitors in their casual clothes.

With no hesitation, Carlos stated the reason for their visit. "Will you join our expedition?"

The invitation made Wiesentrauser smile. "Now, you mean? I would love to—I will be right back. Just need to pick up my things.

Ardis had watched him closely. *Wiesentrauser didn't even flinch.*

When he returned, he was wearing shorts and a short sleeve cotton shirt, just like them.

The Algarve

29. Break Out the Riesling

Ardis eased the *Water Dog* out of its berth. Carlos was on his mattress in the wheelhouse. Manfred and Xisco stood at the stern, looking at the boats along the pier.

Ardis rounded the jetty, pointed the Water Dog to the open sea, and pushed the accelerator control to the max.

Returning to open water injected positive energy into captain and crew alike. Despite her exhaustion, Ardis bore a smile that was infectious. Her blood pumped with the excitement of a yacht captain heading out to a regatta. She welcomed the warm sun on her skin.

Below the surface, though, a different story was playing out.

"I can feel our joie de vivre." Manfred clapped Xisco on the back.

Ardis regretted her agreement to give Manfred a chance. She recalled Major Brooker's advice in such a situation. *Stay alert at all times. Anticipate. Prepare. Trust no one.*

She quietly identified tools she could use as weapons. There was a wrench below deck, a gaff beneath the gunwales on the starboard side, a coil of rope in the cabin behind the wheelhouse, a net on a long pole on the port side, and she had her knife in the sleeve of her jacket hung in its place on a nail in the cabin. She took out the handgun she had been issued. In the loo, she tested the moving pieces. She loaded it and locked it. Then she tucked it into an inside pocket of her vest that she would have to wear at all times now.

Manfred moved ice into the cooler of food.

"Putting our drinks on ice is our most important work today."

He's cheerful enough. No one wants to be stuck with a mope.

Ardis asked Manfred to search for sea turtles and had Xisco steer the *Water Dog* along the shore. Then she joined Carlos in the wheelhouse.

***

"What is Germany like, Manfred?

"Germans are an orderly people." Manfred spoke with admiration. "I spent a few years in der Universität Mannheim where I studied German. I had completed an undergraduate degree in Romance languages at Strasbourg University. Mannheim was clean and structured. If a schedule said a train would arrive at 6:06, it arrived at 6:06. Elsewhere in Europe trains typically are late. In Alsace, we tend to be more relaxed but in Germany everything runs like clockwork. This is what they are like. Trust me, I know. Methodical. Organized. Disciplined."

Xisco noticed Manfred referred to the Germans as "they."

"They don't sound like they have too much fun, if everyone is so tightly wound." Xisco adopted Manfred's distant "they."

"Ja, the people in Mannheim are hard workers, and they know how to have a good time, too. They love to sing and dance. The thirties were tough times. We didn't have the food you take for granted here."

"I am surprised. Germany buys rocks for escudos and invades other countries. I expected Germany to be super rich."

"It may appear that way on the streets but not in the homes. Germans need to worry about where their next dinner comes from, too."

"It seems like it doesn't fit."

"Yes, our personal needs are irrelevant."

"But why is Germany fighting wars if its people don't have food?"

Manfred conceded, "One's diet is not as high a priority."

"That is not right."

Manfred was an educated intellectual and a member of the diplomatic corps of the preeminent European hegemony. "No, it probably isn't. But who am I to say anything?"

"Did you like growing up in Germany?"

"I am an Alsatian, born and raised in Ribeauvillé, Alsace, when it was part of France. Now of course it is back in the hands of Germany."

***

Like Xisco, Ardis noticed Manfred spoke about the German people in the third person—"they" and "them" as opposed to "we" and "us." Lexically, at least, he was on the same side—her side.

Ardis went out of the wheelhouse for fresh air. She checked for possible threats and the "weapons" she had identified.

Then she stopped.

The drama she had been enacting in her mind was silly. She had to let it go before it drove her crazy. Instead, she focused on her handgun.

Ardis returned to the wheelhouse cabin and saw that Carlos was in a deep sleep. Without thinking, she relieved Xisco as pilot to continue their exploration of the shore. Xisco went out and claimed his favourite spot on the bow, leaving her alone with Manfred.

"I enjoy talking with Xisco, although he has a lot of sensitivities."

"Ha." Ardis laughed. "He's just getting warmed up."

"Ardis." Manfred took a deep breath. "I want to thank you for allowing me to join you here on your vessel—*merci beaucoup*."

Ardis nodded, wary that a *compliment came with complements.*

"Meeting you with Carlos at the Tivoli, Ardis, was my good fortune." Manfred sat next to her, port side, in the wheelhouse. "I was surprised to see the Monseñhor with a woman friend. I was happy for Carlos—but I was confused."

"What do you mean?"

"Well, as a priest –"

"It's not like that." She steadied the wheel.

"I did not understand your relationship."

"Oh, I see." Alarmed, Ardis conjured up his next move. *A gun? A knife? Major Brooker's three moves to repel an attacker: Disarm. Disrupt. Dispatch.* "What is it you want to know?"

He spotted the silver necklace; the sea turtle pendant dangled free from beneath her shirt. Manfred laughed. "You really are a marine biologist, aren't you?"

Their eyes met. "Well, of course I am. What did you think?" She laughed politely. *Too close to him; too close to Berlin.*

She couldn't tell how he felt about her reply. She had dodged him gracefully enough. "I noticed you use a lot of French," she added.

"Oui, le français est la langue de la diplomatie et ma famille est française."

They were approaching Lagos; east of the river she saw the beach and pointed to it. They could see kilometres and kilometres of sandy beach. "Marvellous," she said.

The late start out of Sagres that afternoon left them little time to dally. There really wasn't much point to press ahead beyond Lagos. Ardis was tired. She wanted to get the boat off the open sea and in a safe harbour. She needed rest; Carlos needed rest.

She guided the *Water Dog* through the channel and took a berth at the Marina de Lagos. The evening came quickly upon them; they had a light, evening lunch on the deck. All were tired and talked out for the day. Xisco and Manfred went down to their bunks in the hold.

Ardis dropped onto her mattress in the wheelhouse. The shooting of Carlos and then her focus on his care and recovery had wreaked havoc on the rhythm of her days and nights.

30. Lagos *Ad Infinitum*

A rdis awoke early. Reassured that Carlos remained in deep sleep, she slipped into the galley. She made coffee and collected her log on her way to the foredeck. Witnessing a sunrise on the water was a delightful experience for Ardis; even with the *Water Dog* lashed to the dock, she welcomed the spectacle. She crossed her legs in a casual lotus position. She breathed in deeply and fully exhaled, happy to be alive. She was grateful that Carlos would be alright, and that all of them were still alive.

She opened her ship's log, and in the dawn light updated it with yesterday's events. She thumbed through the log. Her reports of sea life had thinned. Pushing on to Faro could quickly turn this around. The beaches and channels next to Faro—the rivers, lagoons, and harbours—all promised to be teeming with marine life. But she couldn't push ahead yet because of Carlos. They needed to take a break for the day.

In her mind, scenarios of treachery had played ruthlessly upon her sense of safety. She dismissed them. What was the point?

Ardis dangled, like an untethered sail on a hot and windless day.

***

Xisco came up on deck. "Oh, you're awake."

Seeing her cross-legged on the foredeck, ship's log in hand, he made a quick decision. "*Bom dia.*" His greeting was partly polite and partly an after-thought. Xisco moved astern.

Ardis turned her head. "*Bom dia!*"

Xisco decided to explore the marina and walk along the river to the beach. He would bring his canteen for water. In the galley, he found Carlos sitting at the table.

"You're up."

Carlos motioned with his crutch, under one arm. "It's beautiful."

Xisco looked at him with a mix of disdain and sympathy. Carlos was dishevelled and weary. What sleep he had had clearly wasn't enough. He winced when he tried to move his leg.

"Do you need morphine?"

"No, gave me nightmares."

Xisco brought him a basin of water and helped him wash. Then he fetched him clean clothes and helped him change.

Xisco handed Carlos his crutches and helped him go out on the deck. Carlos made it to the bench at the stern and sat down. He watched the seagulls waiting on the dock for scraps from fishermen returning from their morning trawl.

Manfred came up and got breakfast going for everyone. Over coffee, Ardis suggested they spend a day there.

Carlos quickly insisted they go to the beach. It was what everyone wanted. "I can do it."

They packed drinks and snacks, put on suntan lotion, sunglasses, and hats, and headed out across the low-lying dunes. Xisco and Manfred carried a cooler with the drinks, and food in a backpack. Ardis escorted Carlos, who advanced precariously across the sand on his crutches.

For Xisco, walking on the beach was a new experience. He wished he could share it with Céphise. He thought about his future, and what advice Sam would have for him. Sam would say make a list of what he could do well.

Xisco looked out over the sand at the long beach where sandpipers were running ahead of the surf and seagulls were everywhere. The foamy surf surged into the shallow water as children played with shovels and pails in the sand. Their parents peeked out at them from under their colourful umbrellas. He wished his brothers were here with him, too.

"Hey, what has made you so quiet?" Manfred set his load beside Xisco's on the sand.

Xisco glanced at him then returned his gaze to the sea. "I am thinking about my future. I don't know what I am going to do and I don't know anyone in my situation who can help."

"You're kidding. The three of us," he motioned to Ardis and Carlos, "know a thing or two about deciding what to do with our lives. We've all had to do it at some point."

"Yes, but you are professionals. Each of you has a lot of education."

"That's true. We had to commit ourselves to learning."

"I didn't have such opportunity."

"I think you do, and you haven't found a way to make it happen."

***

Carlos lifted and placed the one leg more slowly with each step.

Ardis wanted to help him out of the dreary, drug-induced state of inaction he had been in for the past few days. "This isn't a race. Let's stop for a rest."

They stopped and he put his weight on his good leg and in so doing lost his balance. Ardis pulled him back toward her and hung on to him tightly. "I've got you, Carlos."

Their predicament in close quarters reminded her of their dance in Sonim. *Holding him now is not what it was then. Though he might disagree.*

"Don't let go!" Carlos laughed. "I never would have guessed I could say that, Ardis."

She laughed with him, a polite gesture required by the situation. *I'm comforting him, that's all, and expect him to think no differently.*

She gave him a friendly pat on the arm as she made certain he had his balance once again. *Things are going to work out fine.*

She needed a break. The sultry breeze and the sand in her toes had activated her childhood memories of Sauble Beach and those lazy days of summer.

***

Manfred rented beach chairs and Xisco placed them in a row and set up a beach umbrella to protect Carlos from the sun. Manfred poured everyone a cup of chilled Riesling.

"*Pour votre santé.*" They touched their cups and drank.

"Mmm. That's nice." Ardis didn't drink white wine but liked it on a day like this. She was glad Manfred had good taste.

Manfred put his nose in the brim of his cup. "Good Riesling smells like gun metal oil."

Ardis did the same. "Oh yeah, it does."

"And the finish in your mouth is like slate."

"It really is." Ardis gained a new appreciation for Riesling.

Carlos sipped on it lightly. He made no comment. His tongue

couldn't taste the wine.

"We have pretzels." Ardis passed around the large, doughy, salt-encrusted bun.

As the others tasted their pretzels, Xisco spoke up. "I'm glad I have you together, Manfred and Carlos. Can I ask you something?"

"Yes, of course, ask away young man." Manfred smiled weakly.

"Manfred, are you Carlos's wolfram connection?"

"Ja, we became friends in Lisbon."

"Does he attend your church, Carlos?" There was a twinkle in Xisco's eyes.

Carlos smiled.

Ardis nodded and chuckled.

Carlos smiled. "Yes, Xisco. Manfred is my contact at the German consulate."

Xisco turned his attention to Carlos. "On the evening Sam opened the chest of gold, Sam told you he figured you were involved because of the payment from the Vatican bank."

"That's right," Carlos confirmed.

"Carlos, this means you bought wolfram from the Baron and sold it to Manfred?"

"Yes, it's a little more complicated than that."

"How so?"

Carlos expelled his air as if he had been holding it a long time. He took another deep breath and answered truthfully. "I helped arrange the purchase of three wolfram mines. The Baron was my contact in Sonim and his mining advisor was Sam Meyer."

"So that's what brought Sam to Sonim." Xisco was familiar with only parts of the story. "You sold the production from three mines to Manfred?

"Actually four. The Baron owns another."

"Manfred, I understand Carlos arranged for you to send three chests of gold to Sonim."

"Yes, he did and I conveyed his request through my channels. I understand the gold was delivered as expected."

Xisco leaned forward. "What did you know about the gold?"

Manfred sat back in his chair. "I heard in Lisbon the gold was not bullion as expected."

Xisco, too, sat back.

Carlos leaned in. "Did you see it?" Carlos asked. "I did. The image haunts me."

"*Nein*." Manfred looked startled. "I did not."

Xisco pressed him further. "What Carlos means is, did you realize the gold in one of the chests was personal items? Hundreds of wedding bands. Spectacles. Even gold fillings."

"They were all personal items. Gold teeth." Carlos let his anger show. "Can you imagine? We believe it was all stolen from Jews."

"Oui, I heard." Manfred could not look Carlos or anyone in the eye. He looked out to the Atlantic Ocean, closed his eyes, and dropped his chin. Perhaps he didn't want to taint his memories of the ocean. He remained like that, shaking his head as if he were saying nein, nein, but he could not deny it. "I heard rumours; it was something we didn't dare talk about. No one acknowledged this kind of thing for fear of the SS or the Gestapo. It was hideous. We all cowered, afraid of these monsters."

"Think of how the Jewish people in the ghettos feel." Xisco displayed no emotion.

Manfred turned to Xisco. "How do you know about the ghettos?"

"Sam Meyer was a Jew from Poland. He saw things. He received that chest of gold in payment, and he wouldn't have anything to do with it. He said it was evil."

"Manfred," Carlos leaned forward in his chair again, "when I heard about the stolen gold, my world stopped and time stood still. I saw those people and their cries of mercy came to life in place of my own. I am a priest who wants to help people. My goal is to serve God, our Church and people everywhere who are poor, hungry and suffer injustices. Yet, I played a role in helping the Nazis commit such barbaric crimes. I am ashamed of myself. God punished me when the U-boat attacked us and shot me. My wound is small God's justice."

As Carlos spoke, Manfred lifted his head and watched Carlos, meeting his gaze. He accepted Carlos's words in silence, nodding occasionally, sucking in air.

Manfred looked down at his hands. "*Pardonez-moi*, Carlos. I am afraid now that if I wore that uniform again, I would be a monster, too."

"Manfred," said Xisco, "Nazi leaders are the monsters. Not you."

"No one can say, 'I was doing my job,'" said Carlos. "But what else can we do?"

"Exactly," Manfred joined in. "Following along, makes me guilty, too. The truth is I am an imposter—it is how I survive as a diplomat."

"That's not a great concern, is it?" Ardis tested him. "We all must live with challenges and deal with them as best we can."

Carlos sat back in his chair. "The point of talking about this is not to push anyone into a course of action that would threaten their lives or the lives of others. There has been enough killing in this war. It's time we worked together. We could do so much more to improve our world. Wouldn't that be amazing?"

Carlos looked pleased with himself for raising a positive idea. "Here's to you, my friend." Carlos held up his glass to Manfred. "For honesty and bravery in dealing with your issues."

Ardis, Xisco and Carlos toasted their new friend.

"If it were up to us, there wouldn't be a war," said Xisco.

"You're right about that, Xisco." Carlos encouraged him. "I'm sure Manfred doesn't want this war and nor do any of us."

Ardis, Xisco, and Manfred walked the beach. Xisco was the first one to go in the water. Eventually, the three of them were playing in the surf.

Carlos watched children play in the water and build sand castles. He dozed off in his chair under the beach umbrella.

They stopped for dinner at the restaurant next to the marina. During dinner, Manfred excused himself from the table. When he came out, Marguerite was in the hallway.

Manfred's eyes bulged.

"What are you doing here?" As the Abwehr agent assigned to the wolfram file, Marguerite knew what Manfred's purpose was.

"Look. I'm here because my principal supplier of wolfram is here."

"I am confused about who you are with." Marguerite had a sly way of taking charge.

"The priest! The one we nearly killed."

She nodded for him to follow. They went out a side door and down the stairs into the shadows at the side of the restaurant.

"You had orders to report your movements."

"I've been on the water in tight quarters. I haven't had a chance."

"You are lying. You were on the beach."

"Besides, I didn't have anything to report."

"Here's the way it is, Manfred." She lit a cigarette and exhaled. "The Gestapo would kill me; the SS would kill you; but before we get to that, the Abwehr will talk. That's why I'm here."

"Ja. I'm listening."

"You are watching this *Kanadischer*. You had enough time to confirm she is a spy. *Nein?*"

"She's not a spy."

"We believe coded reports over radio from her reveal our naval movements."

Manfred couldn't deny the possibility. Damn, she is a spy. His feelings for her have clouded his own analysis.

"Here, you'll need this." She handed him a Luger. "Kill her. Send her body into the deep. We don't want a diplomatic embarrassment in Lisbon, do we?"

***

Since Sagres, Ardis had a growing fear her expedition was at risk of becoming farce; its results would not amount to anything of value and her career would nosedive into obscurity. Her failure would be unstoppable. Carlos's shooting had given her reason enough to end the expedition. She had decided to give it a day or two to see what might come of it. They were dealing with the situation and proceeding as best they could, and thankfully, they got through the first few days, which were challenging. Carlos was getting better. Now, she feared she had been unwise to proceed, and would have to account for it.

The last few days were not enough to make a decision about the expedition. Nothing had changed. There was no pressure but her own frustration and impatience to accomplish something with her research.

What made Ardis so irresolute was the weather. It was gorgeous. There wasn't a cloud in the sky and the sea was transformed into a bed of shimmering Aquamarine. At night, the stars stood out in relief, each a beacon of hope representing someone's dream. She searched this parade of dreams in the sky to find her own. But it wasn't up there; it was happening—this was her dream. Why would she ever want it to stop?

She let the party go on. She led it.

They visited beaches at Portimão, Albufeira, and Faro, where their days on the water proved to be a wholesome tonic for all. Carlos was getting better, and she was doing what she loved to do most.

On their return, they took a direct route, stopping only at a secluded beach between Lagos and Sagres. Ardis anchored the *Water Dog* in the cove as she had seen the yachts do, even though her chain was not as long and her anchor not as heavy.

The heat of the day lingered in the stillness of summer. There was no wind to speak of, and the water was calm and smooth as glass.

On the *Water Dog*, they smelled the aromas of myrtle and junipers that grew beyond the sandy beach. They were so close that they could hear a high, piercing buzz in the air. Xisco smiled. "Cicadas!" But this brood was clearly on a different cycle than the cicadas in Sonim, which he had heard the year before.

It was a lovely evening but the crew were exhausted from their long day. First Carlos and even Xisco said he was exhausted and heading to bed earlier than usual.

"Hey, guys," Ardis said, "if you are awake during the night, check the anchor. Have a look to make sure we're okay."

It proved to be an uneventful night, in that regard.

Manfred appeared at the top of the stairs holding a bottle loosely at his side. "I have been saving this." Manfred tilted the label on the bottle in her direction, then poured a couple of fingers in a glass for her.

A peace had settled between them. A stiff drink was exactly what she wanted after a long day. She accepted it.

"*Merci beaucoup.*" She mimicked the way he said thank you.

"You know *mademoiselle*, I could never hurt you."

"Now I'm worried."

"It is unfortunate that our countries are at war. If this were any other time, things would be very different."

"I would have to agree."

"Toast?" He held out his glass.

"Here's to peace in our time." She echoed Neville Chamberlain's pre-war sentiment. They clinked glasses. Ardis tilted her glass all the way. She shook as her tired system attempted to reject the repulsive but effective tonic.

He laughed. "If there wasn't a war going on around us, the drinks would be sweeter, the breeze would be warmer, and we might have time to appreciate this experience on water."

"Mmm. I wasn't expecting that."

"Good, I want you to know I have enjoyed this voyage very much."

"I'm glad. That shows you are a gentleman."

She held her empty glass out in his direction.

"*Pardonez-moi, s'il vous plait.*" He recovered the bottle from the deck and poured a refill.

"Thank you, Manfred."

He leaned in close and stopped; she looked into his eyes. He kissed her; she tasted the cognac on his lips.

He pulled her to him. Water lapped under the *Water Dog* on the calm surface.

It dawned on her this was where she and Roberto had nearly kissed not so long ago. She pulled away. She put a finger to her lips and smiled.

Manfred acknowledged her wish for discretion.

He appeared pleased with the situation, nonetheless. She had to smile. She would survive this close encounter with the enemy, after all. And what did it cost but a kiss.

31. Arrival En Masse

A rdis joined Xisco at the gunnel nearest the shore. Something in the water excited him.

"There's one," he pointed, "There's another."

Ardis could see their heads and shells poking out of the water all around them. Hundreds of them.

"Here's one by the boat." Xisco was excited enough for everyone.

Ardis scanned the horizon for intruders.

She got her first close look at one of the sea turtles. "Oh my god, they are Kemp's ridleys!"

It had meant everything to Ardis, but now she took the unexpected event in stride as if it happened every day. "Finding a large gathering of turtles does not mean we found their rookery." Ardis didn't understand the situation and until she did, she would be cautious.

"Then why are they here?"

"I don't know. Let's watch them and see what we can learn."

They watched the turtles all day. They put up the tarp they had rigged over the deck for protection from the scorching sun. The song of the cicadas in the trees along the shore eerily reached out to them. Nothing happened, except the number of turtles kept growing exponentially.

Ardis told them to be ready. "They're going to hit the beach tonight. Turtles nest at night." But the enthusiasm had fallen away from her voice. Part of her was unable to express her surprise and excitement, and part of her was unimpressed by a discovery that no longer meant the world to her. She was nonplussed.

The activities of the turtles seemed to subside in the evening.

By the time it was dark, Ardis was worried as she scanned the beach. Have they gone to another beach? But she saw they remained there, all around them in these waters. There were many more of them now. What were they doing?

That night, the crew took turns napping. Nothing changed.

At 3 a.m., Ardis had a clear view of the beach in the moonlight. She saw nothing. She returned to the stern and kept an eye on the open water, worried that the Gestapo would pick up their position. At some point before dawn, she fell asleep wrapped in her coat and a blanket on the bench at the stern.

***

"Ardis, wake up, Ardis." It was Xisco. "You're missing it."

She bolted upright. "Missing what?"

The sun was just peeking above the eastern horizon.

"Look."

She scanned the shore, squinting. The Kemp's ridleys were going ashore in an endless wave of turtle after turtle. They dragged themselves up the beach, flipped sand aside to create a spot to lay eggs, roughly covered them again with sand, rocked back and forth to pack the sand, and then avoided the incoming turtles as they pulled their way back to the surf.

The commotion she saw stunned her. "I believed they nested alone in the dark. I didn't expect sea turtles would do this all at once like this—and during the day."

"Apparently they do."

The tsunami of Kemp's ridleys was a mass laying of eggs.

"Look at this!" Xisco was going bananas.

Ardis sprang to get her camera equipment, but she didn't feel the excitement like she thought she would. She felt as if she was going through the motions.

Xisco scurried to retrieve her equipment—camera, tripod, and canisters of film. His experience handling the camera and equipment really showed. He had everything ready to go in the dinghy in minutes. Ardis brought her "still" camera.

When Carlos and Manfred joined them, Xisco was beaming. "Oh boy, eh?" Xisco mimicked the animation Ardis displayed during the first days of their voyage, making Carlos laugh. She laughed, too, but the fervour had gone out of her.

Everyone helped put the dinghy in the water. There were so many turtles, it was a challenge to find a piece of shore not already taken. After a minute, the traffic had diverted around them and they could proceed in.

"This is way beyond my wildest dream," raved Xisco. "I want to get some photographs on the shore." Xisco jumped into the water in his bare feet and pulled the dinghy up. He hurried ashore, almost in a panic, and Ardis pressed hard to keep up.

Xisco and Ardis walked around the females and found a high point at the back of the beach to set up the camera. Xisco checked the camera on the tripod and started the camera rolling. He slowly panned the beach, first one way and then the other.

Xisco captured the frenzy of sand throwing and eggs flying through the air amidst the steady stream of the Kemp's ridleys coming ashore. The beach was too small to give all the females a unique place to lay their eggs.

"No other turtles nest en masse like this," said Ardis. "This is extraordinary."

"Did you not already know this?"

"How could we? No one has documented this. We didn't know where Kemp's ridleys were nesting. Period. This is a discovery of three things. Where they nest, how they nest in one synchronized mass, and that they nest during the day and not at night like other sea turtles."

"It is quite spectacular, Ardis. Stand over here so we can see the turtles on the beach in the background while I take your picture."

Since a silent film could not capture her words, Ardis smiled, talked, and pointed as if she were having a conversation. "My name is Ardis Lowney. I teach marine biology at the University of British Columbia in Canada. Behind me on Praia da Figueira, a beach on the south coast of Portugal in a popular area known as The Algarve, is one of the most amazing spectacles of nature I have ever witnessed. What you are seeing is a mass nesting of Kemp's ridleys, one of the most enigmatic sea creatures of our time. This sea turtle was first identified by fisherman Richard Kemp off the coast of Florida more than 60 years ago. However, their nesting grounds have remained a mystery. Until now."

Ardis stopped and smiled, signalling she was finished. Xisco stopped the film.

They gazed on the spectacle before them. The turtles rocked back and forth on their nests to pack the sand down. There were so many; they were digging up each other's nests.

"We'll have to come back when the eggs hatch, it will be a whole new show."

"We can't miss it."

Ardis scanned the horizon, half-expecting another U-boat suddenly to appear.

An ancient ridley paused on its trek down to the beach and looked Ardis in the eye. "You shall not. See my brood. This time."

Ardis looked over at Xisco.

Xisco didn't hear or notice a thing. The turtle spoke only to me.

The turtle continued to the sea.

32. When Demons Leapt Out

It had been a long day and everybody was tired and hungry. Unloading the dinghy, Carlos tried to cheer everyone up. "This has certainly been an eventful day for the Captain of the *Water Dog.*"

On hearing this, Manfred slipped down into the hold to get a couple bottles of the champagne he had been saving for just such an occasion. He heard the commotion on the deck move toward the wheelhouse, then voices at the top of the stairs and footsteps. "I will be up in a minute," Ardis hollered over her shoulder as she descended into the hold.

Manfred leaned into a dark corner as Ardis passed directly by him to reach her berth and pulled out a case. He wanted to surprise her. He watched as her hands flew quickly, experienced. Her fingers tapped fast.

Before his eyes, Manfred saw the proof of Marguerite's claims. There could be no more denying it.

Ardis finished up and returned the inconspicuous case into the bottom of her duffle bag of personal, mostly feminine, things. She returned up the steps.

Manfred let out his breath, deciding how to handle this. He grabbed the champagne he had gone down for, then grabbed Marguerite's Luger.

***

Ardis came up the stair and joined Xisco and Carlos in the wheelhouse.

Ninety seconds later, Manfred appeared at the stop of the same stairs from which Ardis had emerged.

The blood drained from her face.

"I have champagne to celebrate," Manfred burst into the wheelhouse.

"Ardis will be famous." Xisco understood the implications of the marine biology event they had witnessed and was excited for Ardis.

"What an incredible discovery," Manfred declared. He looked into her eyes.

Ardis looked away. Feeling awkward, she lost time, yet resolved to stay in character. "My supervisor will be ecstatic to hear about it."

"And here I thought you were *ein Spion*." Manfred let his sarcasm hang naked in the air.

She froze. She knew what *ein spion* meant.

In an instant, Xisco shot back a thoughtless comment. "Yeah, but so are you." Xisco could be guileless in the company of his friends.

"What do you mean?" Carlos did not understand what was going on.

Xisco's eyes met his. Xisco winced the way one does when making a mistake. Carlos had seen the moment on Xisco's face when Xisco realized what he had revealed.

What Carlos saw didn't matter, really. Manfred saw so much more.

Standing beside the table in the middle of the wheelhouse cabin with Ardis trapped on the inside and Manfred by the door, Carlos looked first at Ardis, then Manfred, then back at Ardis. "You're a spy?" he said to Ardis.

Both Carlos and Manfred looked at her accusingly.

No longer able to conceal what he had known all along, Manfred pulled out the gun and pointed it at Ardis. "You lied to me."

Ardis recoiled. Having a Luger levelled at her and seeing Manfred's white-knuckled fist gripping the handle would not have been worse if Manfred wore the black uniform of the Nazi SS. Ardis recognized this for what it was; the enemy attacking her face on. The gun gave him the upper hand. The only thing she had on her side was the trace of a nascent friendship she thought she shared with Manfred.

Yet, she no longer was afraid.

"Me, a spy?" She glared at him. "I don't go in for whispering secrets like half the people in Lisbon are so fond of doing, and I'm definitely not into killing anyone. I am a marine biologist. I am fascinated with sea turtles. Sure, I talk to the people I know and tell them what I see when I'm out on the water and that ain't much. So if you call that being a spy, then I am a spy, but a lightweight one at that. Did I see a U-boat? I did! Did I report that? You bet, I did. Once the doctor was called, I went into the marine office and I used the phone to call my superior in Lisbon and report the incident. And do you know why I did that? I did that because we were attacked by that U-boat—in Portuguese waters. They were shooting at my boat and they hit Carlos, one of my crew, who, as you know, is a Portuguese citizen."

"I can see you were upset by that." Manfred spoke from behind the barrel of his Luger.

"You're damned right I am." She scorned the chance he could squeeze the trigger and her life would be over. "I'm angry you have the gall to call my actions into question."

Xisco stepped in front of Ardis. "Manfred, Ardis is not a threat to anyone. The Nazis are the ones who threaten you."

"Move aside, Xisco. I don't want to kill you, too."

"I don't think you want to kill anybody, Manfred." Xisco stood his ground at the centre by the table.

Carlos took a step back and didn't say anything.

Unexpectedly, Ardis pulled out her gun and pointed it at Manfred.

Alarmed, Manfred fired, aiming intentionally high.

Ardis ducked with eyes closed, and fired wildly.

Carlos pressed against the wall and Xisco remained beside the table despite the shooting.

"Oh no," said Manfred. With his good hand, he held his arm where he was bleeding. His Luger cluttered onto the floor.

That was when pandemonium broke out in the wheelhouse cabin. Everyone was talking at once. The little demon in each of them leapt out of their souls and demanded attention and control. But none of them was listening to the other.

"Stop, please." Carlos looked shaken, yet he brought sanity back into the room.

Ardis and Manfred looked at each other with fearful eyes. He looked ridiculous standing there, wounded. He could still pick up his Luger and kill her in a second—a thought that crossed everyone's mind.

"For so long," Manfred's voice carried a tremor that Ardis hadn't heard before, "my goal has been to stay alive. Nothing else."

"Is that so?" Ardis spoke sarcastically as tears spilled from her eyes.

"Since the start of this war, I have feared the Nazi leadership. Their war. It made me numb." He grimaced.

Ardis felt guilty; all along he had been trying to be her friend. "I had no idea."

"It is something I dared not share with anyone."

"Then why now?"

"I trust you. You're all good people."

"Yet, you waved that gun around."

Manfred smiled—a horrible grin under the circumstances. "It is okay, Ardis. Here, you take the gun." With his foot, Manfred pushed the Luger toward her.

She bent to pick it up, but Manfred set his foot on it. "I want it back."

Ardis nodded. "Ok, I'll just set it on the table."

The level of tension in the room dropped as the embarrassment of what had just transpired gripped each of them with a gawky silence.

"Well, that was interesting." Xisco breathed a sigh of relief.

Carlos sought at once to cover up the tension. "Let's have some wine."

His suggestion to have wine irked Ardis. He was the one who had initiated this mess. "Not yet." She brought the chill back into the room. "We have unfinished business."

Manfred collapsed on the floor.

***

Bubbles floated to the surface and popped, soft-like. From darkness to unfocused light; from blur to definition. Consciousness fighting for some grip. An unending, irritating parade of floaters (his). Dust particles hanging in angled beams. An occasional fly of one sort or another. The passage into the wheelhouse bleached in sunlight like an overexposed photo.

Pain sliding away.

Eyes squinting open in harsh white, faces blurred together with sudden movement nearby; forgetting what had compelled eyes to open in the first place.

Choosing the shaded softness, limiting disappointments to one at a time, an unhappy, uneasy understanding pervaded conscience.

Rewinding. Facts raced by. A threat. Muffled shots. Sudden sting (intense). Beatific images of an event that henceforward would be a defining moment. But the why left a reeling, caterwauling of illusions, howling.

Sensing assistance close by, he was grateful. A wave of well-being flooded his conscience. His eyes welled up with tears. Happy tears. A voice and unrecognizable meaning comforted him. Her tears joined his. A hand held his. Wiped his face. It could not have been just any woman who nursed him and his wound. It was Ardis.

***

Ardis nursed Manfred through a rough twenty-four hours of a drug-induced nightmare. She arranged for a doctor to look at him. The doctor redressed the wound, and replenished her supply of morphine.

Ardis, too, re-enacted the sequence of events, the before and the after, and when she napped, she dreamed that she held him captive, and had to talk him down. He raged, then begged forgiveness. It was nonsense, of course.

She should have been the one begging—the irony didn't escape her. The wrongfulness of shooting him clung to her. She would always feel ashamed of her action, and to her surprise, grateful to Xisco for bringing them all back to *terra firma*.

"Neither of you are threats!" Xisco had yelled to calm things down. "You were trained to serve your countries. Neither of you caused this war."

It was true. Ardis had been caught in it. Manfred was caught in it.

Still, Ardis was unforgiving of the fact that he resorted to pulling out his Luger in the first place. Why did he do that? Why didn't he try to talk, first?

"Neither of you wants to kill the other," Xisco had said in the heat of the moment. He fought hard in those moments to keep them alive. "You should help each other," which makes sense. "Each of you wants to live."

True, but if someone is going to die, it wasn't going to be her. Of course, she mistrusted him. She had built-in radar that guided her to avoid the obvious traps and low-odds gambits. She wanted to stay alive. And yet . . .

Ardis noticed how the lines on Manfred's face relaxed as he looked at her.

"There's something happening between you. You could be really good friends," Xisco had declared, showing he understood both of them.

A couple of days evaporated in this fog of recriminations. Finally, when Manfred came to on the third day, he barely glanced at her, he looked at Xisco and then Carlos. He looked as if he wanted to reconnoitre a connection; his focus returned to her.

"Xisco is right," were his first words to her. "You are special."

"Good, then you should be sorry," Ardis replied. "And if you are not sorry, you shouldn't be here with us."

She regretted saying that. It seemed so hard-hearted although she understood why and how she had arrived at that. He had found her out.

"I saw you using a radio," Manfred didn't disguise the situation. "We know you've been sending encrypted messages."

That in itself had been enough to digest. She needed an out. But Carlos, who had been quiet up to that point, pressed her. "What's really going on here, Ardis?"

She had looked away, pulling her thoughts together. And she came right back at Manfred.

"I came here to research sea turtles. My government asked me to report what I saw on the water, so I'm doing my bit to help. Which I did when your U-boat attacked us."

Manfred had a question. "What is your business with Carlos?"

"I helped Carlos by filming his sermon."

"Yes, we met on a beach." Carlos concurred. "It was a chance meeting."

His support in that moment redeemed him. It gave Ardis the boost she needed to take charge of the situation.

"Manfred, everything changed for me after our encounter in Sagres when you came onboard my boat. Everything would have been fine but your presence put my safety in jeopardy. My supervisor didn't want me there at all because of you. Can you imagine? The highlight of my career as a marine biologist and I was being told I had to stay away because of you? What are you doing here? That's what I'd like to know."

Manfred looked flustered. Ardis had turned the tables on him, cornering him. He lit up. "Look, I'm the one asking the questions here."

Carlos didn't accept this. "No, Manfred. Tell us what you are doing here. It can't be your interest in sea turtles. So tell us."

Now the three of them were looking to Manfred for an answer. He had no choice.

Manfred stuttered. "I—I'm here because your radio messages got picked up and flagged. I've been ordered to kill you."

Ardis felt a chill run down her spine. "Then why don't you?"

"I didn't want to do that. My life has been in stasis, not going anywhere, not accomplishing anything. Since we met at the Tivoli, Ardis, you have been the one bright point in my life. I couldn't do anything to harm you."

It was an honest and logical answer, but it touched a nerve for Carlos, who turned only his neck to look at him. "You just want your wolfram."

"Yes, I suppose I do." Manfred shrugged.

Ardis held out her hand, palm up. "War interrupted our lives—and brought us together.

Xisco folded his arms, and smiled. "What are we going to do now?"

Part Three, Fall 1942

The Intrepid Ever After

33. The Current

A rdis heard the motor, a low rumble in the distance, coming in her direction. Was this the Gestapo coming for Manfred? She hoped they wouldn't see the *Water Dog*.

She asked Xisco to hide Manfred below and to make sure he stayed there. It took several tense minutes to get him safely down the stairs and into a bunk in the hold. She concealed her handgun and knife in her vest.

Ardis recognized Garcia on the approaching trawler's deck. He waved. The vessel came alongside; men tossed ropes over to tie up, then came aboard. In the waning light, Ardis recognized Kim Philby and Ian Fleming from Camp X.

She glanced at Fleming's Royal Navy blazer. *So much for a low profile.*

"I'm the Navy man," he said.

"I can see that." Her sarcasm was not wasted; Philby chuckled.

"These chaps will forever want their sea legs," said Fleming. "They're lousy landlubbers."

"Never mind him, he's a lady's man." Philby dismissed Fleming.

"Excuse us, gentlemen." Garcia took Ardis aside.

Ardis alerted Garcia of Manfred's presence. "I offered to help Manfred to desert."

"That's fine, but I don't want Manfred able to identify Philby, Fleming or me."

"Yes, sir."

"Ardis, I am modifying your plan. We're all going."

"Tonight?" Ardis was not surprised.

"Yes, tonight."

The Nazis had killed Sam, and Manfred led them right to her. Her identity was long blown. If they weren't there already, the Nazis would come very soon . . . for her.

"Your orders are to get out of Portugal."

The fact that she presented no objections caused Garcia to pause. He looked at her for a reaction. Seeing none, he continued.

"Who shot Manfred?"

"I did."

Garcia nodded and gave a shrug. "He should have known better."

***

Garcia found Xisco at the prow. "Xisco, do you mind if I borrow your BSA?"

"Please do."

"Thank you. I made a plan for us to split up. You will drive Manfred and Carlos to Lisbon in my car. Take the road along the Alentejo coast. Ok?"

Garcia and his group returned to their boat. Philby and Fleming would drive east, then north to Lisbon. Garcia would drive west to Sagres.

***

Ardis and her crew cruised their final leg together.

She immediately set a course to the east, then south, and once out of sight from shore, changed course in a wide arc westward to Sagres. Then she had Xisco and Carlos bring Manfred back up to the mattress in the wheelhouse.

Ardis wanted a moment with Manfred. She asked Carlos to give them the wheelhouse.

"I'm awfully sorry, Manfred. I've never shot anyone and I don't plan to do it again."

"Good." He frowned. Manfred shook his head as if he wanted to ward away any heavy, complicated thoughts. "I think you are a fine lady."

Ardis saw Manfred was an uncomplicated man, after all. She looked into his eyes. *He really meant every word.* She felt a tightening in her throat. Her lips quivered. But tears would not spill down her cheeks, she swallowed her happiness whole.

"Ardis, are you ok?" With forefingers, he tilted her chin up. "I'm so glad things turned out the way they did. Will you go back to Canada now?"

"I expect soon."

"I hope we have a chance to meet again someday under better circumstances."

"I hope so, too."

"We will find each other." He looked content. "I will be in Ribeauvillé, Alsace," he said.

She burst out laughing. "Thank you for telling me." She laughed a nervous laugh, then embraced him.

"I will be in Vancouver, at the University of British Columbia."

They hugged.

The repetitious splashing of water off the hull had a calming, hypnotizing effect. There was no doubt Manfred was in her sway and she in his.

"The stars are out." Manfred saw them through the windows in the wheelhouse.

She dreamed of what they could share together in some distant tomorrow. A terrible ache made her feel it could well be a lost opportunity.

***

In the darkness, Garcia was waiting for them on the wharf at Sagres.

Xisco and Carlos said their goodbyes. Ardis hugged each of them. Although Xisco could have been a risk to Ardis, he had turned out to be a godsend. "Xisco, I am leaving Portugal." She whispered, not wanting to say it aloud.

"I see. This is good-bye then."

"Yes, it is. You've been great, Xisco." In fact, he had turned out to be her most loyal defender, which she would have liked to express, but there was no time.

Ardis turned to Carlos and gave him a hug, too.

He stepped back and smiled. "Thank you for everything, Ardis. We accomplished some important things together."

Ardis had shot film of his sermon, hired students to edit the film into a newsreel, added titles, narration, made copies, and distributed them, including several to Cardinal Cerejeira.

"What will you do now, Carlos?"

He frowned. "I'm in no rush. I like the idea of making my Cardinal wait."

"Then what?"

"I will find Laurenza and decide whether to be with her or accept the promotion."

"Really? You haven't decided, yet?"

"On the one hand, a life of love would be sweet, sweeter than I deserve; and on the other, the promotion would be an affirmation of everything I've ever stood for."

"Not so long ago you were dead set against serving the Church."

"I believe my role is to act in the name of God with truth, compassion, and tolerance."

"But what about Laurenza?"

"I know, it breaks my heart to think of her."

"Have you considered how you will break her heart?"

He stood with his head bowed. "It is not an easy choice."

"No, it isn't." She felt he was grasping at air with no consequences at all.

Garcia started the BSA. Ardis took her place on the makeshift seat Sam had rigged.

Ardis waved goodbye; she and Garcia disappeared in the darkness.

Everything had happened so quickly.

***

Xisco, Carlos, and Manfred left the *Water Dog* in a berth and drove up the hill.

Once the doctor had redressed Manfred's wound, Xisco and Carlos loaded him into the back seat and took the coastal road to Lisbon via

Milfontes.

In the dark, Xisco got into the feel of the road, which was rough. He needed to proceed slowly to avoid all the bumps. He expected they would arrive in Lisbon by noon if all went well.

***

Garcia and Ardis sped north along the Alentejo coast. At a dirt road, they turned left and continued on through sand dunes for a stretch of ten minutes before arriving at a beach, where they stopped. The place was deserted. There were no structures. No sign of civilization. They were alone. The night was pitch black and a steady din of roar, the Atlantic Ocean, commanded the atmosphere.

Garcia shut off the motorcycle and the lights. "Now we wait."

"What will happen?"

"A submarine will take you to Ponta Delgada in the Azores. On board, they will give you a new identity. Build on the profile. You will board a passenger steamer for New York City."

"Why do I need a new identity? Aren't I finished spying?"

Garcia shook his head. "You are known to them. If you are intercepted between here and America, you could be in danger."

"I see." She wasn't out of the enemy's grasp just yet. She needed to blend in.

He suggested she dye her hair and change her clothing. "You will be a displaced American, who is just another refugee fleeing Europe on a steamer bound for America."

Garcia pointed out that with her training and observation skills, she could provide eyes on the water and other passengers. She had, after all, proven herself.

"Looks like I am still working."

"To save your life, definitely." Garcia practically glared at her. "Are you upset you won't get to see the hatch?"

"Why is everyone so concerned about the sea turtles? Don't you know, Lieutenant, there's a war going on?"

"That doesn't sound like you Ardis. Are you okay?"

Ardis sighed. "I just hope everyone gets through this." She worried most of all for Manfred.

In the dark black of the sea, they saw a speck of light. Garcia flashed the motorcycle lights on and off a few times.

"That's your cue." Garcia helped her with her bag that was tied onto the back of the BSA.

"I'll see you in Canada." She placed her hand behind his neck and pulled him close for a hug. "Come home safe, Roberto."

"You too, Ardis."

"Garcia, I forgot to tell you, Xisco has the canisters of exposed film. There's enough footage for a few more newsreels. Xisco can help identify what's there."

"What about the sea turtle footage? Do you want your grad students to work on that?"

"Oh yeah, I guess that, too."

The dash from shore to a dinghy through shallow water was exciting. Someone gave her an overcoat, which she appreciated. The rising and crashing as they rode into the waves on their way out required everyone to hang on.

The current was strong; she knew she could never go back. In that moment, she understood her life.

Ardis climbed the hull of the smooth submarine, following the chain of men up into the conning tower and descending the ladder into the command room. The captain greeted her. They were Americans—professional, polite, and focused. The captain conveyed her new orders.

> Tail to NYC. Do not make contact. Dangerous.
> Male, age 38, named Reimer. Thick set. 6 feet.
> Short brown hair, blue eyes. Gestapo.

The officer handed Ardis a second communication, this one from Dean Ellert.

> Congratulations on your discovery, Prof.
> Lowney! Amazing! Let's get you back here to
> write this up. Perfect for your PhD thesis.

As per protocol, Ardis returned the paper to the captain for destruction. He located her assigned bunk and she lay down for a moment. The vibration of the submarine was subtle, virtually nonexistent. She listened closely and within seconds was sound asleep.

***

Around 2 a.m., Xisco, Carlos, and Manfred approached Vila Nova de Milfontes. A kilometre before the road forked, they came upon a road block. At this hour? Naturally, Xisco slowed down, then stopped when an officer stepped out with his hand up.

A woman in black leather approached the car.

"That's Marguerite. She is an Abwehr agent." Manfred identified her to Xisco and Carlos.

Manfred told Marguerite that Carlos was his wolfram contact and the boy was a helper. She didn't harm Xisco and Carlos, and to their surprise, she didn't kill Manfred.

She led Manfred away into a large sedan and drove north toward Lisbon.

Xisco didn't know who the Abwehr were. It would have been useless to return to the *Water Dog* because everyone had left that day. So they, too, continued north.

"I was never afraid of what Manfred would do to Ardis," he said to Carlos. "I fear what his superiors will do to him."

In Lisbon, Xisco gave Carlos the address of Céphise's house, where he was now living.

"When you see Ardis or Garcia or any of those fellows, please give them my address."

Carlos looked at Xisco's uneven scrawl on the paper.

Their adventures on the *Water Dog* left a hole in Xisco's life. "Come and see me."

Carlos nodded, looking at the paper in his hand. "I will."

34. Above Her Love

A cold spirit blackened his heart as he entered the Cardinal's *palaceta* on Campo Mártires da Pátria.

Carlos had come to settle his future once and for all and was told the Cardinal could not see him. Instead of waiting, Carlos walked in with indomitable strides and the help of a cane.

There was a gentleman with Cerejeira but Carlos didn't care nor wait for introductions or permission to speak. "Your Excellency –"

Cerejeira threw up his hands. "Your manners, Monseñhor."

His guest interceded. "Let's hear him. I'm interested." It was the Prime Minister.

"Prime Minister –" Carlos was tongue-tied.

"Monseñhor Silva, say what you came to say. First, please tell us what happened?" Salazar gestured to the cane.

Carlos appreciated that Salazar was capable of caring enough to ask about his injury. His concern was personal and relevant. The embarrassment Carlos felt after learning he had interrupted a meeting with the Prime Minister fell away. "A sniper aboard a German U-boat in the Atlantic Ocean . . . off Sagres."

The Cardinal jumped in. "That's absurd. You are not feeling well."

"You are right." Carlos knew he was out of his depth, but he would make the best of it. "I'm not happy with our wolfram dealings. It is unethical." With no prepared introduction or explanation, he would be foolish to say anything further.

The Cardinal smiled. "I understand. My job is to manage our resources. It costs money to build and operate our cathedral and the hundreds of parishes across the country. We also contribute to the Church in Rome. Where does all this money come from? Donations by the parishioners?" He laughed, a short, brittle laugh. "The people are poor as Church mice."

"I recognize that, which is why I wanted to help in the first place."

"Then what is your issue, Monseñhor?"

"Selling wolfram hardly seems an appropriate role for servants of

God because we are supplying the wrong side. The Nazis are aggressive agitators that wage war, steal from our neighbours, profit from the losses of others, and have no concern for the suffering they cause."

"Monseñhor, I appreciate your concern for the nation's affairs." The Prime Minister rebuffed him. "Rest assured, the Nazis are not our kind of people. These matters of state beguile us in their infancy then torment us as they ripen and we see them for what they are. We stand to gain nothing by opposing this aggressor when not even our strongest ally, Britain, can do so. It took a war to bring everyone to a fulsome realization of these truths."

"Yes, a church—our Church—plays a different role, I expect." Carlos turned to the Cardinal. "Wolfram is used to build weapons. Why does the Church of Lisbon own a wolfram mine? Why is the Vatican involved in wolfram at all?"

"That is not your concern. It isn't public." The Cardinal glared.

"Because it isn't ethical." Carlos stood his ground.

"I told you we invested in the commodities of our country. We need to use our resources to deliver the best return." The Cardinal was resolute in his position.

"How is it appropriate? The Church should be helping people who are poor and need education and opportunities to build their lives."

Salazar leaned in. "Why were you shot by a sniper on a U-boat?"

"It was a mistake. The German envoy apologized for the incident."

"Wiesentrauser?" Salazar knew the diplomat, too.

Carlos nodded.

Cardinal Cerejeira was curious about this incident, now, too. "May I ask what you were doing on the Atlantic Ocean off Sagres?"

"I went to the Algarve to reconsider my roles. I saw things that sickened me. I've been meaning to tell you, Cardinal."

"Yes, Carlos, go on."

"The Germans paid for wolfram with gold stolen from the Jews."

The Cardinal was surprised. "You are certain of this?"

"I am. We are selling wolfram to a warring country that pays for it with gold stolen from Jewish families, who are being held in ghettos against their will. The Jews might as well be in a prison built and owned by the Catholic Church."

"That's not our business, is it?" Again, the Cardinal was firm.

Salazar sought to soften the blow. "There have been rumours like this trickling in. I am not surprised. A war costs money."

"Cardinal, I can no longer perform my roles. I understand if you demote me. I do not need to be a Monseñhor to serve God."

"I could hardly demote you under the circumstances, Monseñhor. You see, Carlos, your accomplishments have come to the attention of the Vatican. I sent them your newsreel in Trás-os-Montes about Fatima. The reception by the Holy See has been remarkable. Even the Pope was impressed with your short film."

"The Pope? He saw it?"

"Yes, he has directed me to nurture you as a leader in the Church of Portugal. I have news, Monseñhor. You are to be ordained a bishop."

"Bishop?" Carlos came there to withdraw, expecting admonishments and instead he was being promoted?

"Yes, that is so. Congratulations, Carlos." He shook Carlos's hand.

"Congratulations, Monseñhor Silva." Salazar shook his hand.

"With your bishopric comes a new assignment. I have a district that needs a young man like you to tend to a remote and dispersed flock. It is the north, Carlos, from Gerês to Bragança and it includes your new friends in Trás-os-Montes. You will be Bishop of Braga."

"Ah, Gerês is a lovely area, both scenic and historic." The Prime Minister approved.

"Braga—the first, the oldest, and the seat of saints." Carlos recounted this as if he were reciting facts from an exam on Church history in Portugal.

"Carlos, you are a good person. I respect your judgment."

"Cardinal, there is a community of Jews in the north of Portugal that has practiced their religion in secret since the days of the Inquisition."

"The Marranos? There have been rumours. They will be part of your new diocese. I look forward to hearing how you work with them, too."

Carlos appeared distracted. He wanted to succeed and participate at such a level, but there were so many issues to tame on such short notice. He stepped to the door.

"I don't know," Carlos said. "I must reflect on this."

"Wait!" Cerejeira shouted. "Take a few days off. I will take care of the mines. You take care of yourself. Think about it. If you are to be bishop, you need to be in a good space."

It was up to Carlos.

"Carlos, I need a bishop to develop a shrine at Fatima." Cerejeira looked up at him. "If you're interested, you can have first choice."

Carlos had one more decision to mull over. He had to go to his special place.

***

In his cassock, white collar, and hat, he wore his sandals with his pants rolled up to mid-calf. He walked with determination, leaning on his gnarly old staff.

He trudged through the deep sand with vague recall of the issues he had dealt with here in the past. His memories were tuned to Ardis, who cared for him when he was shot. It felt like love, though he couldn't say; he didn't have anything to compare it to. He hoped she would be safe at home in Canada soon.

There was Laurenza. He pushed aside thoughts of her for now.

True, he had no formal training about women nor even informal conversations with guys. Everything he knew about women, he discovered on his own. As an orphan, he never knew the love of a mother. He resented this fact of his life more than anything; he managed the disadvantages, he nurtured his own self-assurances and denied there were any emotional impacts. Like old news, these considerations came into his consciousness like clockwork.

He created a new mantra, "I am a rock." He wanted to be like Peter, upon whom the Church was built.

Carlos gazed long out to sea, thinking of Laurenza. He believed he loved her. But a relationship with her was the stuff of myths. To himself, he admitted that he didn't know how to convert feelings of lust or love into an action as ordinary as a hug or a kiss even though he already had made that conversion with her at the orphanage in Rome.

His progress across the beach was slow. For a change, he hardly noticed; he had people on his mind, decisions to make.

Carlos was troubled by many things and having a conversation with Laurenza was one of them. He wanted to avoid her urgency; he wanted to avoid her. Though he loved her and wanted to be with her, he couldn't. Not just now. He had let himself down for his part in selling wolfram to the Nazis, which was unforgiveable, especially because of their payment with gold stolen from Jews. He needed to make amends, but how and to whom? To the Jewish people? To God? To himself? Or to all three? He was angry he let himself be put in that situation. He had been a patsy for the Church, and he was done with that. And yet, it wasn't good enough. He now had an opportunity to be involved and make amends in a major way.

Laurenza had come to find him. Surely that meant she loved him.

Carlos was now in a position to leave it all behind and start a new life with her. Someplace abroad, away from the war. In America. His vision raced ahead of him.

If he chose to go away with Laurenza, he could escape all of this. It would be easy. It would be heavenly, he could think of no better word. Heavenly. He was aware of the irony that a word and a concept such as heaven, that stood for so much he believed in, could also be the panacea for all things that were difficult for him in this world.

He took off his sandals and left them on a rock at the top of the beach. He wanted to wash his feet. He waded knee deep in the surf clutching his cassock up around his waist. He fancied his past was out there lurking like a spectre beyond his reach in deeper waters. There it would always remain, ready to rise with any storm and become a force larger in size and momentum than it had ever been. It would flatten him on the beach someday if he weren't careful, or throw him on the rocks and wash him out to sea.

He thought little about the money now growing in his bank account. It had grown, without his having paid any attention to the sum. Manfred shocked him that day in Rossio Square when he left him a box-like carrying case with two hundred ounces of gold. Carlos sold it immediately and stashed the cash away. Also, when he settled the trades, he found he had a chunk of money that wasn't owed to anyone. He resolved to deal with this money later when he had more time, but he never had that kind of time or, in truth, the inclination to address the matter. Other sums such as sales commissions also went into his account. Blindly, Carlos had become moderately wealthy.

Carlos had begun to doubt the Cardinal's purpose and the mysterious other party. He was ashamed he hadn't even considered whether or not getting involved in wolfram as the Cardinal had directed him to, was morally right or even legal. He had accepted the Cardinal's judgment at face value, as if it had been God's will. Surely it wasn't. Profiting from war that killed so many people? The truth was awful. It was never too late to back out of a wrong endeavour. His career was on the wrong path.

The fault for this mistake was all his own. Yet, he resented the Cardinal whom he had trusted. This, coupled with the betrayal he felt after he was shot, pushed him to a point where the objective truth was the obvious and only option.

Keeping the money in his bank account wasn't wrong. A diocesan priest brought his wealth with him into his vocation to buy a home and to fund his living. Some used it to leverage their careers as deans, bishops, or cardinals. Carlos had not aspired to rise to the level of bishop, but now that he had the opportunity, the money he had accumulated would become useful, if not necessary. It occurred to him that the money he now possessed was an act of Providence: God's will.

Carlos had to decide whether he would honour God through faithful service to people or whether he would continue to pursue his ambition to serve the Cardinal and the Vatican.

He was overwhelmed. Using his crozier, he drew a line in the sand.

Did he want to serve the Lord God as a priest? "Yes, I do." He spoke aloud to the wind and rocks. One checkmark on the left.

This would mean total commitment to a meaningful life, which, though tough, would give him great peace. Could he make a difference in helping people find their way to God? "Yes, I can." He put another mark beside the first one.

Did he care whether people he didn't know were saved and went to Heaven? He didn't need to ponder this idea at all. "Yes, I care." He placed a mark on the left.

Did he think it was okay for people, who stole bread to feed their family, to go to Hell? "No, actually." He put a mark on the left. He believed people should not be damned for being weak, hungry, or poor.

He reaffirmed his belief in the need to help the poor.

Did he want to serve the Vatican and the Cardinal as a bishop? "No, I cannot." A checkmark on the left.

Could he do all these with faith in God? "Does He even care?" He wondered this aloud. He placed a mark on the right then circled it.

There was injustice and inequality in the world. The strong get ahead and the weak are cast aside. Did he believe in social justice? "Yes, I do." He placed a mark on the left.

Did he want to assist people who were poor, sick or unable to care for themselves? "Yes, more than ever." Left.

A more pertinent matter came into mind—he dismissed it but it came back, again and again. Did he believe in God?

He leaned on his wooden crozier staring at the sand, remembering his conversation with Xisco on the *Water Dog* before he was shot. He was about to make his mark on the beach when a rush of surf flooded his sand tablet and soaked the parts of his cassock that had slipped his grip.

"Damn." He turned to the ocean wanting to see God Himself. But instead another even bigger wave struck him and nearly knocked him down. His cassock was drenched thoroughly. Fortunately, he had tightened the chin strap and his hat wasn't lost in the ocean.

Carlos knelt on the beach and prayed. He began by asking God to forgive him for his role in helping the Nazis in the war and in their persecutions of the Jews. As an afterthought, he asked God to forgive the Cardinal and the Prime Minister for their roles and to give them strength to face the aggressive Nazis.

He should not take the promotion.

He stood and commenced his return journey across the beach. What saddened him was a deep and enduring sense that nothing really mattered. Ever. The good and the bad come to exactly the same end. No matter what he did or how he lived his life, his existence as a human being would amount to the same—utter emptiness.

Wet and covered with sand, Carlos looked back along the beach to the spot where he had knelt in the sand.

He wanted a say in matters vital to the Church and to him personally. If he didn't take the promotion, he would lose this opportunity to have such a voice. And if he did take the promotion, he would betray himself and everything he ever believed in.

All Carlos wanted as an orphan was to be loved in a family. He longed for the love of a mother, and the guidance of a father. Yes, the seminary had given him structure, but it could never give him the enduring love and commitment that only a family could give him. The Holy Mother Church provided all of this and more, and a career as a priest was the only path that promised him the love of a family he craved so much.

Now he spoke aloud as much to the cliffs above the beach as to himself. "I will never know all the answers. There are and must remain mysteries. I have accepted my vocation based on my faith alone or I have no vocation. But why Lord, why, do you test me so?"

At that moment, he was struck by a third wave. He was a mess.

***

Carlos looked for Laurenza. He thought nothing of the fact that he had left her until last, focused as he was on his own issues before him. He found her where she said she would be. She looked happy to see him. He had been away far longer than expected, and he was certain she would be disappointed with his decision.

Normally, Carlos would have suggested they walk along the waterfront. It was flat; no hills to run their breath ragged. But he had a feeling she wouldn't take what he had to say so well. He had to be away from the crowds. She told him about Estufa Fria, one of her favourite places she had discovered while he was "convalescing" in the Algarve.

They took a cab up the Avenida da Liberdade past the statue of the Marquês de Pombal that he saw the day he returned from Sonim with Ardis and Xisco.

Laurenza led him, limping, up the hill. Tucked into the top corner of Parque Eduardo VII, Estufa Fria was a tropical garden that had been built in a former quarry and was kept cool from the ravages of the sun by bamboo screening. To Laurenza, it was a lush jungle of trees with a meandering stream, waterfalls and bridges, and deep foliage in which to wander. She didn't mind the refugees who, like her, enjoyed visiting Estufa Fria to pass the time.

Being there relaxed her, she told him.

He felt she wanted him to declare himself to her.

"We have experienced many things together," Carlos pronounced. He leaned on his cane.

Laurenza was searching his eyes, looking for a sign.

How he felt about her now didn't feel like love the way it did in Rome, where he had been so enchanted with her wholesome beauty. Now, the enchantment was gone. He wondered whether it was lust that he had felt which was more than likely. Now, his feelings for her left him confused.

This was it. This moment would define him forever.

Carlos did not initiate conversation, but observed her. She exuded a now-or-never air of courage. Her confidence astounded him.

He took her hand, a naïve gesture against the emotional depth that had been building inside her. He hadn't considered what he ought to say. He just blurted it out. "I want to thank you, Laurenza, for giving me the most beautiful moments of my life."

"Carlos, I would do it all again—and more." She looked at him as if she were waiting for him to just come out and say something like 'I am not prepared to give you up again, Laurenza, not ever.' But he couldn't.

"It doesn't have to be right away." She was trying to make it easy for him.

"Yes, when the war is over, we can all go back to being normal people again."

Laurenza was unable to contain herself any longer. "And be together."

There, she had opened a door for him and he very nearly stepped through the opening she had presented to him so he might join her.

Carlos withdrew his hand. "What are you saying?"

"This is our chance to set our future. We have to decide now. Are you going to leave the Church to be with me?"

"But Laurenza, you know I'm a priest! I can't!"

"How could you, Carlos? After all we've been through? I thought you loved me." Laurenza looked fiercely into his eyes.

He looked away to the horizon and reoriented himself.

"I guessed as much. No matter, I am emigrating. When I heard there was a long wait for passage, I put our names on a waiting list. I got berths on a ship for South America. I am scheduled to leave first thing tomorrow—on the *Serpa Pinto*. It is unlikely I will see you again."

Carlos was strangely cogent. He had played with Laurenza, and lost.

"I thought you cared for me differently, Carlos, but I understand. You have no intention to be with me. It is just as well."

It was if she were speaking to herself.

He wasn't even looking at her.

Laurenza turned abruptly and walked. She didn't say good-bye.

Carlos had been lucid, but in fact, he was comatose. Leaning on his cane, he watched her walk the long decline of Parque Eduardo VII, around the Marquês de Pombal, then lost her as she disappeared on the Avenida.

35. The Hatch

The run from Lagos to Praia da Figueiro went quickly. Xisco captained the *Water Dog* and Céphise put her feet on his lap. On arriving, Xisco identified Garcia's vessel. Teachers and students from the university would be on it. He steered in alongside.

Xisco waved to them. "We didn't miss anything, did we?"

The lone graduate student remaining on board to tend to the boat greeted him. "Your timing is perfect, Xisco. The hatch is beginning." The student pointed to the shore. "It started with a few early this morning and if you look closely, you will see them. Based on your film footage, we believe these are only the first of a great number to come."

"Excellent."

It had been be eight weeks since the eggs were laid. Xisco recorded this information in Ardis's journal, which he safeguarded for her.

Xisco dropped anchor about twenty metres away. He and Céphise put a dinghy into the water, loaded the film gear, and went ashore.

Garcia shook Xisco's hand and gave Céphise a hug. "I'm glad you could make it. This is really something to see!" He motioned to the scene on the beach.

The hatch was underway. The sand was crowded by hatchlings making their way to the sea. Only a couple of centimetres long and wide, the hatchlings were delicate and vulnerable.

Xisco took it all in. "There were a lot when they came into nest, but this is crazy."

Céphise was enchanted. "They are so cute."

Though the hatchlings were only a tiny fraction of the size of their mothers, their enormous numbers compensated, making their presence on the beach a compelling spectacle to the party of biology teachers and students. To their horror, all kinds of land and sea birds, from falcons and hawks to seagulls and albatross, feasted on the young turtles and grew instantly fat, unable to even move much less fly.

Following Ardis's instructions, everyone selected a five-metre square space and recorded the number of turtles that hatched as well as the number taken by predators in ten minutes.

A couple of foxes found the hatch and gorged themselves beyond healthy proportions. Wild dogs converged on the scene and wreaked havoc on the hatchlings until they could no longer move. One dog died right there on the beach.

Other predators, including all manner of fish, sharks, and dolphins greeted the new turtles when they reached the water. In only a matter of minutes, even the sharks receded into deeper pockets, uninterested in any further kill and the dolphins swam away slowly at the surface. Schools of over-fed fish drifted away. All predators on land and in the sea were sated.

The hatchlings continued to pour off the beach and into the pools where they were met by the juveniles of their species—the scouts of new nesting grounds and the shepherds of the flock. They guided the horde to shallow water shelves and shoals that provided the best feeding opportunities for the young turtles.

Céphise filmed Xisco standing in front of the scene and pointing. Later, in the studio, the graduate students would record his voiceover, explaining the scene he was witnessing. As all the action died down, and people settled into counting hatchlings, Xisco and Céphise each found a place to sit cross-legged out of the way at the back of the beach where they could take in all the action and count hatchlings.

***

For two days, they walked up and down the beach, completing their ten-minute counts. During this time, Garcia's team also monitored the shoreline in both directions.

The hatch finally dwindled to an end.

Garcia joined Xisco and Céphise on the beach.

"As you suspected, Xisco, the nesting was not confined to this section of beach. The hatch extended in both directions on the beaches between the rocks."

"I expected that."

Garcia showed his calculations. "We estimated there were at least forty thousand hatchlings."

"Enough to survive." Xisco took a sip in his coffee. "That's what cicadas do. My Papai said the cicadas overwhelm their predators. There aren't enough birds to take their fill, so more survive. Ardis called it one of Nature's brilliant survival strategies, and she wondered whether the Kemp's ridleys adopted this strategy, too."

"What do you mean?"

"Ardis theorized that they may shift their nesting locations to throw off their predators. Which would make them nomadic, moving across earth's oceans possibly spanning the globe."

A local couple walked down the beach. Xisco greeted them and they stopped to chat. Both the man and the woman appeared elated. "*It is the chegada maciça das tartarugas* . . . the mass arrival of the turtles." They had seen them here when they were teenagers. They made love in the sand and she conceived.

"Our son is seventeen now."

Like cicadas, they returned in seventeen years. "It is good luck."

"*Isso foi a verão que as cigarras cantou. E eles estão cantando agora.*" That was the summer cicadas sang. And they are singing now.

***

Roberto brought Xisco up to date with news. Carlos had been appointed bishop of Braga and Fatima, responsible for the north and for developing the Holy Shrine of Fatima.

Xisco responded with a laugh. "Looks like he got everything he wanted." He told Garcia that Carlos had to choose between a promotion to bishop or a girl.

"I would have taken the girl."

"Well, yaa-aah!"

Then they got down to their business—the hatch and the follow-up.

Xisco told him he was uncomfortable standing in for Ardis in the film shot on the beach. "That moment belonged to Ardis."

He was quite right. It was her burning motivation and her dedication to find answers that had propelled this discovery.

Garcia assured him she would continue to be involved. "Her work on the project is just beginning. She will have plenty more work to do."

Top of her list was writing a paper for publication, followed by final production of the film and then promoting the film. It would consume her efforts for years.

Garcia officially wrapped up Ardis's project in the Algarve.

"It is such a shame Ardis did not see the hatchlings."

"I agree, Xisco. She would have loved it. One day, Xisco, you can hand-deliver the film to Ardis."

"What do you mean?"

"She asked me to send you and Céphise to Canada."

"No, thank you, Roberto. We have a job to do here in Lisbon."

"I see. Well then, perhaps you will consider staying on with us." Garcia didn't want to lose Xisco's services. He saw him as a viable replacement for Ardis, providing eyes on the water.

Xisco accepted on the condition that Garcia would aid him and Céphise in their operation to assist refugees in departing Europe safely. To this end, Garcia promised Xisco lots of room to use his position for the benefit of the people he was already helping.

***

Xisco's role on the *Water Dog* came at a good time. He had no intention of returning to live in his village. Xisco and Céphise assumed the mantle of Sam's responsibilities as cavalaricos of a people in search of freedom. They operated Sam's safe houses, and although the numbers had diminished to a trickle, their involvement was still important.

Xisco took Céphise to see his village. On the way, they stopped in Vila Real to visit Benjamin Pedra de Campo. Xisco asked him to transfer the deed of the Sonim property to his parents, and to sell another property in Alvara, and give him the proceeds.

Next, they stopped at the By The Way Café, where Harratt led Xisco to Sam's truck in storage behind the restaurant. With Harrat's help, Xisco put the BSA in the back and covered it with a tarp, just as Sam used to do.

Xisco gave Sam's truck to his father. Xisco kept the motorcycle, which he brought out from under the tarp to show Armando. All his little brothers needed to have a ride on it, of course. He took Céphise on a walk through the village, with brothers in tow. He showed her the square and the fountain, Bartolo's Padaria, the school, the wall and gate around the Montalvão yard. He pointed out the stable. They walked out to the cemetery and looked back on the village. He considered taking her down to the river but a forgotten memory of swimming with Cristina jumped up out of the past, confusing him. He left that for another time.

Xisco gave the keys to Sam's house to his Mamãe, who asked him why he didn't stay in the village and live in Sam's house himself.

"I considered this, Mamãe. Perhaps one day, but for now, there are places I want to see."

"But how will you have a family without a house?"

"I don't know, Mamãe. Whatever happens will be an adventure."

"Your good fortune cannot last forever."

"You are right, Mamãe. I have been fortunate."

***

Eugenio, Xisco, and Armando left the village in the dark, well before any rooster went up on a rooftop to greet the rising sun.

Eugenio took the back way—through the village, around the fountain in the village square then onto the old lane that ran past the cemetery and the fields to the Rio Rabaçal. Just before the river, the road branched to the left and he took that branch.

They got part way when Eugenio pulled over. "I can't do this. I can see it now. We will show the elders. After their shock and dismay have settled down and after their distrust is exposed, the issue of whether or not to accept the gold will divide them."

The chest of gold from Eugenio's stable was under a tarp in the back of the truck.

"One of them will say, 'The people who died would want it to honour Yahweh and serve our families. Then one of them will say, 'We do not want our Holy of Holies desecrated by any connection with such evil.' The divisions will disappear. Not one will want to accept this gold. With an ounce of dialogue, the elders will reject it. As we should now."

Xisco nodded in agreement. "It would embarrass and shame us for the rest of our lives. Let's return it to your stable."

"I have a better idea. Let's bury it."

Xisco laughed. "That's why you put the shovels in and brought Armando?"

"I had a hunch. Armando is here because we need another witness from your generation to provide vigilance over this vile hoard that it may never be resurrected."

They buried the wooden chest where they first met Sam, in the depression where Sam lay in the cover when his gun didn't fire and Eugenio dropped the boar with one shot.

"This is all best forgotten, *filhos*."

"I'm with you on this one, Pai."

"Good. Now let's go hunting."

***

Xisco had deliberated long on the meaning of renewal; he pictured the village fountain he had gazed upon so often which had mesmerized him with the way the water gushed up and fell in on itself only to gush up and up and fall again.

This was how he conceived the pattern for his life. Starting over, repeatedly.

So very often he had felt the rise and gush in his life only to fall in on himself. And then the rise and great gush up and continuing up that he was feeling now. He could find his purpose in life and actually make his life meaningful. Before too long, though, he would fall in on himself. He was prepared for this. He would ride the ups and downs of the fountain of life ongoing, a series of renewals and fallings, renewals and fallings.

Such was the nature of youth and the way he existed still. He would always be in such a state. The smile in his eyes spread across his face. This was the Fountain of Youth! Though Prester John was nowhere in sight, he was there in spirit. Of this, Xisco was certain.

But would he feel young forever?

36. Refugees of the *Serpa Pinto,* 1943

Ardis located her cabin two levels below on the port side, miraculously away from all mechanical and human disturbances. *Perfect.* The engine vibrations emanated from deep within this ship, soothing her; she had found safe haven in a tempest. *Two beds, mmm.* She lay down on the one in the corner, breathed a sigh, and let her chin sink into the crook of her arm. She closed her eyes. The deep rumble didn't remind her of any ship she had known; this one was so much bigger than anything on which she had sailed.

She wished with all her heart the Gestapo *had* boarded a ship bound for New York City. But Rio de Janeiro? This was not in her plan. She considered Dean Ellert's plea for her to come home and write up her discovery as a PhD thesis. *Screw that, I have a Gestapo to follow.*

A light hand tapped on the door.

Who wants me now?

The door swung open. A woman and her boy looked in. The woman checked the number on the door against her ticket.

It was obvious. They would share this cabin.

"Hello." Ardis sat up. *Good thing I kept it together.*

The woman smiled before she spoke, signaling her intention to obtain cooperation, not permission. "In Lisbon, you no come. Day before now the man from ship tell us you come now."

Ardis boarded at Ponta Delgada, in the Azores.

She's my age. Looks somehow familiar. I don't know any women with little boys. Not in this part of the world. Not anywhere. Would look more closely but don't want to stare.

The woman spoke to her son and Ardis recognized very few words; it wasn't French or Portuguese. Italian maybe?

The woman looked at Ardis. "You have no one?"

Ardis stammered, "I left my life on an Alentejo beach."

The boy fussed; the woman gently calmed him; she was good with children.

Ardis was glad for the boy's presence for he commanded his mother's attention, granting Ardis some privacy. She remained a few minutes then went out to get some air.

Ardis walked the deck. The *Serpa Pinto* was an eight thousand-ton passenger liner with one hundred and sixty crew and six hundred passengers. Though the passengers around her looked battered by deprivation and loss, Ardis blended in. For some, their clothing no longer mattered. They had survived. Their few possessions that did matter were emotional and emblematic of a love they once had, a parent, or a child. Some looked delighted to be there and were clearly looking forward to their future in the New World. Others carried the sadness of their losses on stooped shoulders and in downcast eyes.

Ardis cast anxious eyes on open waters, scanning for U-boats. Portuguese neutrality no longer protected them. Anything could happen. She walked around the ship in so many different directions that she lost track of the number of circuits she had completed.

Ardis selected a spot near the stern where she could lean against the railing and gaze across the sea. From high on the deck, Ardis gained a perspective that was remarkably different from the one she had been accustomed to on the *Water Dog*, where she could reach over the gunnel and scoop up the ocean in her hand.

Although those experiences had happened only days ago, her experiences on the *Water Dog* were quickly becoming fragmented, as if they had been torn from another life. What was real? What did she only imagine?

She pictured the hordes of turtles crawling ashore, and no longer looked forward to returning one day to see a hatch or writing up a report. *What is the sense of any discovery that has so little impact on the world?*

Her time in Portugal stood out over and above everything she had ever done. She missed her friends on the *Water Dog*. Yet, she wanted to go home.

She shuddered to think of Manfred, looking at her down the barrel of his Luger. She dispatched that memory to a corner of conscience. There was a war going on, and as Roberto said, she needed to put these memories away. *It is a price I have to pay.* Now she worried that no one would pay more than Manfred.

She feared for Manfred's safety. She willed herself to remain connected with him and the life she was leaving, but it was futile. The last of Portugal, the Azores, was a speck on the horizon and slipping away fast. The last fragment would burst in a flash of light just as the sun did when it set, before disappearing into the place where the ocean meets the sky.

A deep voice arose behind her. "It is the last you will see of land for ten days."

Startled, Ardis turned swiftly to see a black man, older than most, wearing a navy jacket with faded gold brocade on the forearms and epaulets.

"Captain Charon, Ma'am." Bushy, white hair framed his peaked white hat and dominated his chin. Ruddy lines ran like rivulets from his eyes. "I am the ferryman who carries the souls of survivors across this sea."

A smirk is on his face and in his eyes.

Americo Charon was the captain of the *Serpa Pinto*. He would have known Ardis as the woman who boarded at San Miguel.

"Hello, Captain. You do us all a good deed to ferry us on your ship, sir."

The humour she first detected melted into neither a laugh nor frown.

Is he irked about something? Grouchy?

"When winds blow hot from the south, crossing this sea can be a Hell worse than Hades, but we'll be fine this week. We will arrive in Rio de Janeiro safely, I assure you."

"I'm glad to hear this, Captain."

The big black man with white hair gave her a cold glare that made her shiver inside. "War consumes our world," he said. "Despite our best intentions, events and circumstances conspire to thwart us. You have to let go. Let Random Chance wander a bit through your mind. Let Truth peek at your soul. But do not let Chaos unload any disturbing memorials in your heart. And Deception, the monster that steals fleeting glances? Do not let him become a common visitor."

Has Captain Charon lost his mind?

He bid her adieu with a nod and resumed his stroll around the deck.

"Good evening, Captain." *He isn't mean at all; he's just an oddball.*

Ardis felt compelled to do as he instructed. For all the days and nights on the *Serpa Pinto*, Captain Charon presided over a battle she waged between her recent past and her imminent future. She was no longer the person she had been.

Ardis changed the route to her cabin. Mid-ship, a group of women from Third Class, coming up for air *en masse*, blocked her way. The men—what few were travelling—would soon follow and bring a degree of boisterousness to the deck. Rather than retrace her steps, Ardis chose to blend in, off to the side.

She had learned to identify the differences between passenger classes. First Class kept to themselves in the stack of drawing rooms and lounges on the foredecks behind the wheelhouse, which was the command centre ruled by the Captain and two officers. Those from Tour Class like herself roamed the deck midship and in the stern. In the hold—Steerage—were reputedly the rowdy ones, who danced and caroused into the night, happy to have a holiday from work; for when they landed they would surely return to their labours from which there would be little reprieve no matter where they went.

Ardis scanned them from a distance. One in particular, stood out. Ardis was surprised—shocked, actually—to recognize Laurenza.

Ardis ducked out of the way and receded into the shadows. Away from the scene, she second-guessed herself. Laurenza looked different; it wasn't her.

But it was.

And the crazy thing was, she was the woman with the boy who shared her cabin. In Praça do Comércio, Ardis had only seen her from a distance. Seeing her up close in their dark cabin wasn't the same. Still, what were the odds?

Though the coincidence angered her, she entertained herself by expressing it the way Bogart would . . . *Of all the cubbyholes crawling with bugs, on all the decks, on all the ships, she walks into mine.*

She set out to walk off her emotions, but ran into another roadblock, literally.

A group of passengers brought a woman to the Captain at the stern, where he usually mingled with passengers. The woman was wailing incessantly, grieving her losses to passers-by, and upsetting people who were dealing with their own issues. The Captain spoke to the woman and her objectors as a preacher to his flock. "You are grieving about the past. On my ship, there is no room for ghosts. My ship carries living souls to the other side."

He turned away from the woman to address the others around her. "How many of you have lost someone dear to you? Show me your hands."

To a person, everyone in his audience, including Ardis, raised her hand.

"Leave behind your dead and your wailing, woman. That is the Old World. My ship is for survivors who look ahead to the New World, the land of the living."

The Captain governed the lives of his passengers with a straightforward Realpolitik, acting in the interest of all over the interests of any individual, minority group, moral ideal, or ethical consideration. And he did it with aplomb.

Ardis found comfort in this no-nonsense approach of the Captain's. The objectors drifted away. The Captain nodded to Ardis and resumed his stroll around the deck, mingling with passengers. She trailed along nearby where she could observe his interactions. And she came face to face with Laurenza on the deck.

As her cabin mate, Ardis was obliged to pay Laurenza due respect. She smiled openly, and held out her hand to shake. "My name is Ardis."

"That is a one-in-a-million name."

For a woman dressed so plainly, Laurenza was more beautiful than Ardis deemed possible. She had freckles across the top of her nose and cheekbones. Her green eyes were bright in the sun. Ardis pictured Laurenza in a dress for the ballroom. She would look stunning.

"My name is Laurenza Bianchi. " Then she presented her boy. "This is Paulo."

One glance at the boy told Ardis what she needed to know. He had Carlos's complexion.

"Hello, Paulo." Ardis crouched in front of the boy. "How do you do?" She offered her hand, which he took after a quick glance to his mother confirmed it would be ok.

Little Paulo smiled.

He had the same grey-brown eyes. "How old are you, young man?"

Laurenza translated into Italian; and Paulo replied in Italian. "Doo-eh."

"He will be two in April."

Laurenza bore a son she conceived with Carlos. If Carlos knew, he hadn't mentioned it, which would have been uncharacteristic of him. Uh-uh, this would be news to Carlos, too.

"That's right, Paulo," Ardis got close to the boy.

Laurenza had let Carlos go on with his life and she accepted all the consequences.

"It must be challenging to have a child on your own." Ardis complimented Laurenza.

"I'm very content with my responsibilities," Laurenza replied evenly, revealing neither great difficulty nor pride and joy. "Speaking of which, it is Paulo's bedtime."

Ardis had an urge to swap stories with Laurenza, who knew Carlos well and was possibly aware of Ardis. Laurenza was intelligent and well spoken; she possessed character.

***

Ardis returned to the cabin later, quietly entering so as not to awaken Paulo and Laurenza. And as an early riser, she was able to slip out before they stirred.

As if they didn't have a cubby mate.

Later, she saw Laurenza and Paulo on deck, when they came out for air.

Honesty would be the best approach if she wanted to be a true friend. Ardis spoke out. "May I tell you something? But I need you to promise not to tell anyone."

Laurenza looked her full in the eyes and nodded. "Yes, of course."

"My name is Ardis Lowney. I am from Canada. I took Carlos Silva with me to the Algarve, as well as Xisco, a boy from the village of Sonim."

Laurenza's eyes widened as she surveyed Ardis for the first time.

"I thought you had blonde hair; that's what threw me off. Carlos talked about an Ardis when we last met. He said he will be forever grateful to you." Laurenza looked down for a second, then directly at Ardis. "I imagine you know of me, as well."

"I do, I do." Ardis nodded. "I saw you with Carlos in Lisbon, from a distance across Praça do Comércio. It appeared there had been a confrontation."

Laurenza nodded. "Before he went to the Algarve, he said he needed time to reconsider whether or not to leave the priesthood and join me. We never spoke of it in so many words."

Ardis knew he had been leaning toward accepting the promotion to bishop. "Yes, I knew. What did he decide?"

"Carlos accepted the promotion. The Cardinal needed a new bishop in Braga. He also needed a new bishop in Fatima, to develop facilities to serve large crowds on pilgrimage. Carlos took both assignments. Fatima is his passion, as I'm sure you know. He will have staff to oversee construction of various projects."

"That is a lot of responsibility."

"The Cardinal actually views Carlos as a possible successor."

"You are not angry?"

"Not in the least. Ardis, I am excited to meet you. Finally, I have someone with whom I can talk about Carlos."

Ardis had the impression that Laurenza had a kind soul and meant well.

"Carlos couldn't handle a life outside the Church. I needed to adapt to my changes fast. I did what I had to do."

"He doesn't know he has a son?"

"No, I didn't tell him. Carlos has to follow his ambitions. Otherwise, he would have regrets and be of no use to himself, much less anyone else."

Ardis wanted to hug her, so she did. Laurenza held a very kind view, Ardis saw; her own was remarkably different. "I arrived at a different conclusion," Ardis said. "In the community, Carlos represented the epitome of all good things about a Christian life, but his character was riddled with wilful blindness. By accepting the promotion to bishop over your love, Laurenza, he became the epitome of hypocrisy. That's how I saw it."

"We live in glass houses. None of us need throw any stones," Laurenza gently admonished Ardis. "I saw he had struggles. He served others all his life. Not everything he did was appropriate. I was involved with him of my own free will. I was in love. I'm sure he was, too, and that's why I had to go to Lisbon and check."

Ardis nodded, taking it all in.

"Ardis, I do wish Carlos well. It frustrated me, but I do not hold it against him. He had been under a lot of stress, and then on your boat he had time to reflect. He didn't make his decision easily. He wants to impact on the views and matters of the Church in Portugal. His career is a noble calling."

"I am surprised you didn't tell him about Paulo. Why didn't you?"

"Wanting me was a requirement, make no mistake. I will only be with someone who wants me. Plus, I wanted him to make a decision based on what was right for him, not what was easier or more convenient for me."

That was how their friendship started.

***

On the third day, Ardis located the man she believed to fit the description of the former Gestapo she was assigned to tail. The fellow was tall and thick set, for sure. Blue eyes. Ardis recognized him. He had exited the Aljube just before Sam was released, and looked at her from the car as they drove past. She didn't detect any acknowledgment that he had recognized her. The advice to change her hair colour and style may have saved her. If he did recognize her, she would be in grave danger. He could be here to remove her from the board like an irritating pawn that she was.

The war had forced Ardis to make a life-and-death choice: either fight for her family, her country, her way of life, or lose everything and everyone she knew and loved. The choice was that easy. Becoming a team player had been the pragmatic thing to do.

Now, Ardis was realistic. She understood why the Allies were fighting this war: to protect their freedom from the fascist Nazis. When the Nazis invaded countries, killed people for no reason, and left their children starving and orphaned, she saw that she needed to do her part to help stop the brutality that had swept over Europe before it could come to Canada.

Ardis thought long and hard on what she might do about Reimer. She didn't share the specific details of her decision with Laurenza, only the philosophical elements.

"I was just thinking, it doesn't make sense to risk life and limb during a war to make the world free if we let things go to hell later."

Laurenza nodded. "I'll leave saving the world to you; I've got a hungry boy to feed."

***

Ardis needed to get things off her chest and Laurenza was a good listener who could be trusted. Ardis told her about Manfred, meeting him, how things got out of hand in the Algarve, how Carlos was shot, and how Manfred aimed his Luger in her face before she shot him.

"Carlos pulled us into a confrontation. Pressed to act, I did something I regretted. Manfred aimed his gun at me. I turned away and closed my eyes. As he shot, so did I. He aimed high intentionally, I think; I fired in response to the threat and nearly missed."

"When you had to, Ardis, you shot the gun. You were trained to do this. If you had not, you would have failed. You were not trained to fail. Not only was it your patriotic duty, it was a covenant you made with yourself as an individual to be true to yourself and survive. You had to give up your career, your life. You had to be brave and you had to take risks. You need to be gentle on yourself."

Laurenza helped Ardis file away the events that were overwhelming, so that Ardis was able to deal with them.

"He consumes my thoughts and I send good thoughts out for him."

"You mean you pray."

"Well, it is a type of request to a superior being who may be in a position to intercede. I asked for his life to be spared, not taken."

The worst-case scenario for Manfred now was a terror-stricken death in the hands of the most wicked and vile humans that ever walked the earth. Manfred's prospects enervated her spirit, her ambition, and her will to live. She had to walk off the negativity daily, which she did on the deck in every kind of weather except pouring rain.

Laurenza taught her to say, at least in her mind, that she was sorry and ask forgiveness. She told Ardis to open her heart to love and be grateful for the people in her life.

Ardis confessed she was truly sorry for shooting Manfred. She thought of Carlos, too; she had nursed both men on the mattress on the wheelhouse cabin floor.

"Forgive me." She spoke aloud as if to the men who had been in her care.

Ardis also told Laurenza about the last evening aboard the *Water Dog* when Manfred had revealed his feelings for her.

"He expressed an idea I had known for a long, long time—that life was something to treasure and to value for what it is, something that needs to be lived, in action, not in one's imagination. After all the tension earlier that day, I was amazed. I had never heard anyone express the meaning and purpose of one's life with such clarity. It was entirely disarming. My training and my instinct was to distrust this man with every fibre of my being. Instead, I fell for him. I fervently hope Manfred has escaped. If he was taken alive, he would be tortured until he babbled out of his mind, and then he would be killed."

***

A raven accompanied the ship. It was the most massive raven Ardis had ever seen.

"It is a lost soul, a strong one, finding its way to the afterlife." Captain Charon looked wistfully at the black bird gliding beside his ship. "Many believe a crow is a harbinger of death. Some say its presence actually means the opposite: the beginning of all things new and good. It is odd, is it not? Every living thing, including a crow, presents change, that is, life."

***

Ardis focused on the Nazi she was tailing: Reimer, the Gestapo who killed Samuel Meyer in the Aljube.

Xisco held Samuel as he died, his swollen face all bloodied and bruised. When Caroline, Max, and Pete died in a London bombing, did they suffer like that? Reimer turns my stomach. Makes me want to scream in his face.

Ardis observed Reimer. She learned his routines. She noticed how he laughed.

He tilted his head back and closed his eyes. God help him. How could such a vile man feel so light? So happy? The devil may let this man be happy, but I will not.

My orders to follow him to New York City did not include anything about killing. Perhaps there would be someone waiting at the pier in NYC, but how likely is that to happen in Rio de Janeiro? It is not likely at all. Really, it is up to me now.

To make sure, Ardis didn't take any risks. She avoided him.

So glad I changed my hair colour and style. Reimer will not recognize me.

On this evening, the ocean was calm. A rising moon reflected far across the surface. A few people like her who could not sleep, had come up from below to mill about and fortunately, they seemed to favour the foredeck. She was alone. Reimer emerged from below. She kept him in her peripheral vision, looking further away as he came closer. She let him stand beside her.

With both arms on the railing, she pushed the handle of her knife into the palm of her other hand, a move she had practiced a hundred times before.

„*Guten abend,*" he offered.

Her German was worse than her Portuguese. „*Guten abend,*" she replied.

Seeing him take a nip from a flask, she took a chance. "The problem with the world is everyone is three drinks behind." It was a Bogie quip; she leaned toward him as if sharing a laugh, a gesture of familiarity that she intended as a distraction, just as Major Brooker taught her.

He laughed, throwing his head back and exposing his wide, fat neck.

Her arm flew through the space between them. He didn't see it coming.

A jet of blood spurted then gushed.

As Brooker said it would.

Reimer clutched his severed carotid artery. His Luger clattered onto the deck. He looked at her, aghast, and immediately felt woozy from the sudden drop in blood pressure. He collapsed forward onto the railing and was still conscious.

The gun had been in his hand. I could have been dead in seconds here, too.

She leaned over him. "You killed Sam Meyer and now you're going over for it."

Captain Charon saw what she had done.

Ardis had one more thing to say to Reimer. "The best goodbyes are short. Adieu."

Both good Bogie lines to remember for a time like this when you really need them.

The Captain came to the railing and bent to pick up Reimer's gun. Ardis set her foot on it.

"That's mine now." She looked him in the eye.

Captain Charon smiled, exposing for the first time his oversized and very white teeth, and nodded approvingly.

With her foot, she slid the gun closer and picked it up. "Any bullets on him?" She padded the jacket and found a case that she pocketed at once, along with the Luger.

Captain Charon grinned wide and his teeth glowed white in admiration for a job well done. The assassination of Reimer had completed Ardis's induction into the underworld.

Sure feels good. Damn.

Adrenalin flowed in her veins . . . *for Pete, for Caroline and Max, and for Sam.*

Reimer's bodily fluids pooled at his feet. The smell of piss pervaded the still night air.

"Not all souls get to the other side." Captain Charon spoke as if the murder was a natural event. "This one is food for sharks; his parts will be shat across the oceans. No evil can withstand the certitude of such demise."

Charon patted the body. He handed Ardis a small envelope with one word on it: Brazil. Then he pulled two large, flat packages from Reimer's overcoat—one from each side of his chest, which probably helped to make him look thicker than he actually was. Charon set them on a dry area behind them.

Ardis wanted the body out of sight. She pulled on an arm, trying to heave the heavy Reimer over the railing. The Captain hoisted Reimer by a leg and together they dumped him overboard like a bleeding pig.

Firing a gun at Manfred had filled her with regret. Slicing open the throat of Reimer filled her with a self-loathing she had not anticipated. The awful smells along with the disgust she felt about what she had done and what she had become, sickened her. With no warning, the contents of her stomach heaved into the air and splashed onto the blood and piss on the deck, where she bent over to prevent her puke from landing on her clothes. Coughing and spitting up spew, her turtle pendant dangled down in front of her face and caught her puke. "Dammit!" She ripped it off and flung it to the deck. The trajectory of her anger was too acute. With unexpected momentum, the silver chain bounced on the deck and slid under the railing. Ardis saw the opal carapace of her tortoise catch against a railing post and she lunged for it. But the weight of the chain and the vibration of the ship shook it loose. The turtle pendant slipped from Ardis's fingers into the sea.

"Nooooooo," she wailed, her arm reaching under the railing. Everyone she ever loved and everything she ever stood for had broken loose and slipped away from her. In her grief, she wept for Pete, Caroline and Max, and Sam Meyer, though mostly for herself.

Captain Charon picked up the packages and led Ardis to his cabin and to an adjoining room with a bathtub full of hot water he said he was about to use, but it was hers now. He gave her clean clothes to change into. Then he went back out and had crew throw pails of seawater on the deck to wash away the mess.

In the wee hours of the night, Ardis slipped into her berth in the cabin she shared with Laurenza and Paulo.

A predawn rain shower cleansed the *Serpa Pinto*. The rhythm of its engines didn't skip a beat.

That afternoon, she returned the clothes Captain Charon had given her and picked up her own, cleaned and dried from hanging in the breeze on the Captain's private balcony.

Before she could leave, he put his hand on her arm and looked into her eyes. "The evil spirit that possessed that Gestapo has moved into you, Ardis. I can see it plain as day, just as clear as I can see the good in your soul. That spirit torments you. That spirit will never die. It will do battle with you for your soul. Remain strong, Ardis, and you will win."

Ardis nodded. "Ok."

Charon gave her one of the packages.

"It's a mix of currencies. Plenty, no matter where you go."

***

They sighted land. The *Serpa Pinto* continued on course away from the coast. Ardis stopped counting the days. Her demeanor darkened and she remained inside the cabin and feigned sleep. Laurenza checked in on her. "What is the matter, Ardis? Why are you so sad?" But Ardis would not respond. She didn't dare breathe a word to Laurenza of what had happened. She couldn't bear the disappointment that Laurenza would feel for the woman Ardis had been and for what she had become—a rabid killer. Ardis felt enough disappointment on her own. Now, it was Laurenza's turn to slip out early with Paulo and return late.

Ardis had succeeded as a spy. As Laurenza had pointed out, Ardis did the job for which she trained. She contributed to the war effort. She fought to protect the people she loved. She fought Fascism to preserve Democracies so people could live free.

But her heart was no longer in marine biology. She had become more concerned with spying, wolfram, the war, and ultimately, killing. This was crazy, just as the sea turtle had said that day on Burrard Inlet with Pete before he left for the war. As long as fighting senseless wars distracts humanity, humanity would never save sea turtles from extinction.

War is the path to extinction. In a flash, she saw the outcome and recoiled into her own shell. The turtle had introduced concepts she had yet to consider.

Ardis had failed to heed her spirit guide.

***

Her depression lasted three days, and for both women those days and nights seemed to last an eternity. Ardis had too many thoughts and feelings to process; meantime, Laurenza's spirit lifted as they drew closer to the new world where she would make her home.

Word spread among passengers that they were approaching their destination. Ardis seized on an overwhelming urge to embrace this new destination, even if only for a brief time. This idea created an opening for her to break free of her depression. She visibly brightened; she joined Laurenza and Paulo.

"Addie," Paulo called to her. She lifted him to see the city among the mountains.

"In time, you may return to the realm of the living, Ardis." She turned to see Captain Charon, whose wide smile of big, white teeth warmed her like sunshine.

"Captain," Ardis breathed deep with closed eyes. "I cannot thank you enough." She was grateful they had survived the voyage—an outcome she no longer took for granted. Paulo squirmed out of her arms and back to his mom.

"Ardis, the end is only the beginning." The Captain understood very well that for his passengers, the end of a voyage meant new beginnings, especially in a new world. "Where will you go in South America?" Charon posed the quintessential question to them both.

Laurenza held Paulo's hand. When she shrugged, she lifted his tiny arm with hers.

"Will you stay in Rio?"

"Little in this place resembles Italy, yet nothing changes, everything remains the same." Laurenza looked into the water with Paulo. "I will use my head and my hands to make work, and see how it goes."

"Oh, I see." Ardis understood just how difficult Laurenza's life could be, and yet how capable she was to make her way prosperous.

"What about you, Ardis? Where will you go?"

"My plans have changed. I will go to New York City then home."

Ardis had accomplished her mission and believed she could now return to her former life.

Captain Charon told her the *Serpa Pinto* would carry on to Montevideo, and return in ten days. Then he returned his attention to Laurenza.

"Do you know I am a *Brasileiro*? I can help you get settled."

Where to live was Laurenza's next challenge. She juggled Paulo in her arms. "Really?" She peered at him. "You are a life-saver, Captain."

She spun Paulo to make him titter and laugh.

Ardis had one important matter to resolve. What would she do with the package of cash that Charon had salvaged on that terrible night? Laurenza was the one who needed it most, but telling her where it came from was not an option. Ardis had to take a chance and hope that the circumstances left Laurenza little time to piece together details.

While Laurenza danced, Ardis slipped the tightly bundled package into the single bag in which Laurenza carried her few possessions. She would find it, sooner than later.

The gate at the top of the stairway opened and things happened fast. Passengers surged onto the gangway, ensnaring Ardis and Laurenza with Paulo in her arms, all the way onto the wharf. Ardis turned to look back at the *Serpa Pinto* and saw Captain Charon following the crowd, descending the gangway to the wharf. She waved to him. Like an old friend who would see her again soon, he returned an affable wave along with a big smile, and continued towards them. He carried a duffle.

"I am taking a break here, too."

The Captain had removed his jacket and hat, and changed into a cotton shirt, shorts, and sandals.

"I will help you get settled in."

The women welcomed him. Charon pressed ahead to the street to hail a cab.

"Hola, Rio!" Laurenza and Ardis hugged, with Paulo in their midst. Ardis surveyed the surroundings in Centro, the five-hundred-year-old heart of Rio de Janeiro.

"You and Paulo will make out alright; the Captain will see to it." Ardis tussled Paulo's hair, kissed his cheek, and breathed in the tropical air. Amidst palm trees and lush greenery, the abundant neoclassical and baroque architecture of Rio surprised her—it was not unlike Lisbon, only more beautiful.

Captain Charon secured a cab to take them through the city of mountains beyond Botafogo, Copacabana, and Ipanema—close enough to the centre and its opportunities yet near to the sea and its openings. He arranged for Laurenza to use a small flat in Vidigal, a favela located next to the ocean by LeBlon. It was a temporary solution. Vidigal would be Laurenza's stepping stone.

Ardis nodded with satisfaction. To her surprise, the bungalow near Jericho Beach, the one with the garden and the cottage-style screen door like the one at her parents' cottage at Sauble Beach, came to mind. All she had experienced taught her that life in all its beauty and grandeur—in, on, or near the water—was a miracle. She surveyed the Atlantic, the arc of Ipanema, and the forested mountains beyond, so full of life, commanding her awe.

The Earth is a garden of masterpieces.

CR

Epilogue

D uring 1942 and 1943, Ardis Lowney's activities in Portugal culminated in the following achievements.

The creation and distribution of newsreels, with the support of the Technical University of Lisbon:

- Refugees and Nazis Crowd Lisbon Cafés
- The Lingering Effects of the Fatima Miracles (Adopted and promoted by the Vatican)
- Nazis Pay for Wolfram with Gold Stolen from German-Jewish Citizens
- Nazi U-boat Fires on Research Vessel Cão de Água
- Nazi U-boat Captured!

Contributions to confidential Navy reports:

- Catholic Church in Lisbon sells wolfram to Nazis
- Nazi payment for wolfram comprised of gold stolen from German-Jewish citizens
- Nazi naval activity in Rio Tejo and coastal waters stable, 1942
- Nazi U-boat fires on *Research Vessel Cão de Água*; Portuguese national shot
- Nazi informants on Portuguese fishing vessels on the Grand Banks
- Nazi U-boat captured in Sagres Harbour, November 1942
- German diplomat shot in neutral Portugal on November 28, 1942
- Gestapo agent disappears from the *Serpa Pinto*, January 1943

An academic report, prepared by her colleagues in her honour:
* Ardis Lowney, MSc., managed and led the project that produced "The *En Masse* Daytime Nesting of Kemp's Ridleys at Praia de Figueiro, Algarve, Portugal, November 28, 1942," a report to the Faculty of Marine Biology, University of British Columbia, 1945

Marine biology commendations, awarded in absentia:
* The Prince Albert Award from the Society of Marine Biologists, 1946
* Dom Carlos I Award in Marine Biology from University of Algarve in Faro, Portugal, 1947

An Honorary Doctorate degree, awarded in absentia:
* For her role in discovering The *En Masse* Daytime Nesting of Kemp's Ridley, Ardis Lowney was awarded an Honorary Degree of Doctor of Marine Biology by Johns Hopkins University, Baltimore, Maryland, 1947

File Status:
* Inactive. Subject went missing in February, 1944
* Permanently Classified. Strictly Confidential. Archived: 1946

About the Author

Timothy Paleczny

In 2022, Tim published *The Tale of Indigo*, a book of poetry that explores our most-enduring myth and the great issues of our time—greed, war with pathogens, and climate change.

Tim co-founded and led *Blood & Aphorisms*, a Toronto fiction magazine, from 1991 to 1997. According to the Canadian Magazine Publishers Association, *Blood & Aphorisms* was Canada's bestselling fiction magazine. He edited *Stories from Blood & Aphorisms*, published by Gutter Press in 1993.

Tim studied English Literature, earning a Master of Arts degree at the University of Waterloo and an Honours Bachelor of Arts degree at St. Jerome's University.

Tim has a son and a daughter, and he lives in Barrie, Ontario.

Tim's author page on Amazon: amazon.com/author/timpal
His website/blog: timpaleczny.com
His newsletter, "About That Life": timothypaleczny.substack.com
Links to his social media: bio.site/TimPaleczny

Thank You!

I would like to recognize my family and friends who assisted me along the way. Thank you for your help and encouragement!

- Aidan gave me comments on later drafts; and he continues to be a great support, providing practical advice ongoing.
- Olivia inspired me to work into the evenings. In the summer before Grade 12, Olivia provided my second draft with detailed and demanding comments that gave me a welcomed boost.
- Barbara helped me clean up my grammar and encouraged me all along. Barb painted the Kemp's ridley that is on timpaleczny.com.
- Ray & Sally facilitated my experience of life in and on the ocean. As a well-read sailor, Ray helped me with boating details; and both Ray & Sally supported my efforts with enthusiasm.
- Jack imparted the meaning of God's *immanent* presence. His reference to the "downtrodden" inspired the title for Chapter 20.
- Betty-Anne worked with Barb on a painting of the *Water Dog*, a U-boat, and dolphins that is also on timpaleczny.com.
- Deb joined me in Lisbon to tour the Algarve, Alentejo, and the Azores; and she supported my efforts with enthusiasm.
- Jean provided two drafts with detailed critiques, full of lessons.
- Helen Doner created the map and cover illustration to great acclaim.
- Valéria suggested the name Xisco, and helped to identify the protagonist. "It was her mission and her boat," she observed.
- Lois asked to appear in my novel as a marine biologist whose specialty was sea turtles. And Faith suggested the name Ardis.
- Laurie Kelly commented on a draft and inspired a bigger picture.
- Hannah F. commented on an early draft, drawing on her History MA, interest in WWII, and familiarity with Portugal's neutrality.
- Maria & Manel brought me to Santa Cruz to see Praia das Amoeiras. The dinners they hosted on their terrace in Lisbon were my favourite part of my 2017 visit. Marvellous!

To all my readers & reviewers, thank you for joining me!

Acknowledgments

This is a good opportunity to provide some background and trace the origins of *A Life on Water*. I also want to acknowledge anachronisms in the story and discuss aspects that differ from facts.

Well-known public figures, events, and settings in the story reflect historical facts. Other characters and the plot are fictional, including Ardis Lowney. I tried to ensure every detail of her character was plausible. Yes, the Epilogue is fictional.

Xisco of Sonim

I visited the village of Sonim in Trás-os-Montes, Portugal, in 1998 with my former wife and her father, Fernando. He grew up in Sonim and became a stable boy at nine years of age. His love of history and Portuguese explorers inspired the schoolroom chapter—the kernel from which this story grew. Over time, the character acquired a life of his own. To mark this distinction, I changed the character's name to Francisco, also known as Xisco. But nothing will change the fact that Fernando inspired this novel. As I wrote this, in July, 2023, Fernando was 92 years old.

Ardis Lowney

In August of 2015, I told Lois I was working on a novel, and she asked me if she was in it. I told her no. Six months later, I reported I was still working on it, and she asked again. This time, I said "yes, Lois, you are in it, what do you want to be?"

Without missing a beat, she said "A marine biologist."

"What is your specialty?" I needed to know.

"Sea turtles."

"Okay, you're in it." I was kidding of course.

Around this time, Fernando told me his father and the men in the village collected rocks for which foreigners paid cash. This clue led me to learn of the Nazi's need for Portuguese wolfram during World War II.

At that time, Lisbon had been a hotbed for spies. My story would benefit from having a character who was a spy, and even better, a female character. My research led me to Camp X and the rest fell into place.

Unfortunately, Portuguese speakers pronounce Lois as Louis, so Lois became Ava.

Then I noticed spies in movies named Ava, which wouldn't do. To come across to readers as authentic, a protagonist needs to evoke original impressions. I looked for a name that was unique.

I mentioned my hunt for an authentic name to Faith, who suggested her mother's name, Ardis Downey. I had never heard of the name Ardis. It reminded me of Artemis, the Greek goddess of the hunt combined with the insect, a Preying Mantis. The name Ardis was so different it didn't appear on a list of 150 unique names. Plus, it fit my character seamlessly: Ardis means "ardent" or "fervent," and Lowney means "warrior." These names met my search criteria perfectly.

Kemp's Ridley

The Kemp's ridley was identified by Florida fisherman Richard Kemp off Key West in the 1880s. But it wasn't until 1947 that their nesting grounds in Tamaulipas, Mexico were documented on film. The discovery remained unknown to marine biologists for another five years.

Mexicans refer to the *en masse* nesting as the *arrabiada*, the arrival.

Although a nesting of Kemp's ridleys in Portugal is inaccurate, the consumption of baby turtles by many predators on land and in the sea fits the feeding frenzy theme in *A Life on Water*.

The feeding frenzy theme features cicadas on land being devoured mostly by birds. It also features small fish in the sea being herded and consumed by blue fin tuna, dolphins, and other predators.

The World Wildlife Fund has identified the Kemp's ridley as the most endangered species of sea turtles. I hope readers' encounter in my story with this endangered species helps to raise awareness and efforts to protect them. For this reason, I don't mind being inaccurate about the Portuguese location.

University of British Columbia

The marine biology program at the University of British Columbia (UBC) was not instituted until years later. However, its Royal Officer Training Program and the letter read by the Dean are historically accurate. Captain Grant was a commanding officer in Vancouver.

Fran's Restaurant

Fran's Restaurant on College Street in Toronto wasn't opened until 1960. However, the first Fran's Restaurant in Toronto opened in 1940 at Yonge and St. Clair streets. I used the College location because of its proximity to the former Eaton's across the street, where Ardis shops.

Camp X

Camp X was located in Oshawa, Ontario. Its purpose was to train American operatives before the United States formally entered the war. My story implies that Camp X was operational in 1940, but it didn't exist yet. According to the Camp X official site (http://www.camp-x.com/officers1942.html), Lieutenant-Colonel Arthur Terence Roper-Caldbeck of Scotland was appointed the first official commandant of Camp X in December of 1941.

Nazis were guilty of war crimes, not the German race

Nazism was an extreme nationalist, fascist, and totalitarian political movement that not all German people supported. German people also suffered from Nazi brutalities, including police state persecution, murder, and starvation. The text avoids labelling Nazi actions as German actions.

Ardis's Flight to Portugal

An account of Gertrude Stein's first flight in 1934 became a model for my presentation of Ardis's reaction to flying in the opening of the fourth chapter. (Google "Gertrude Stein first flight.")

Wolfram and the Vatican

Did the Catholic Church ever own wolfram mines in Portugal?

I wasn't able to confirm whether the Catholic Church ever traded in commodities. I couldn't find any information on this topic. What I did find, though, shocked me.

In 1987, the chairman of the Vatican bank, Banco Ambrosiano, went public with the news that $1.5 billion had gone missing. A week later, he disappeared. His body turned up in London, England, hanging from the Black Friars Bridge over the Thames River.

Churches of various denominations invest in commodities. Just ask the right people. Don't be surprised if you learn such commerce helps to offset the maintenance costs of many houses of worship.

Samuel Meyer

My inspiration for Samuel Meyer was an Orthodox Jew from Poland named Samuel Schultz, who discovered the Marrano Jews in Rebordelo in 1925. Like Samuel Schultz, the fictional Samuel Meyer is a mining engineer, too.

That is where the connection ends. The actions of Samuel Meyer are fictional in their entirety.

In my story, Sam Meyer is not Orthodox and not even a Conservative Jew, although he was raised that way and knows the Shema and other prayers. An Orthodox Jew would not engage in hunting, especially for wild boar, an unclean species that is not Kosher.

Early on, I believed the Rebordelo that Samuel Schultz visited was the village located about 10 kilometres from Sonim, where there is an active Marrano community. Later, I learned there are four villages in Portugal named Rebordelo.

The Miracles of Fatima

Sam Meyer expresses his theory that the miracles of Fatima were perpetrated by Cardinal Cerejeira and Prime Minister Salazar to leverage the fear of their Catholic audiences and cow them into compliance. Sam claims this deception constitutes a hoax against Portugal's people.

Fatima Events promoted during late 1930s

- Our Lady appeared at Fatima in 1917
- Miracle of the Sun on October 13, 1917
- In 1938, the Fatima Storm, an aurora that appeared across the globe, was predicted at Fatima as a sign that God was about to punish the world
- In 1939, the world plunged into World War II

Captain Americo Charon

In real life, the captain of the *Serpa Pinto* was Americo Dos Santos, who was a hero in his own right. In *A Life on Water*, I maintained the first name Americo for the captain of the *Serpa Pinto* and I borrowed Charon as his surname.

In Greek mythology, Charon was a spirit who piloted a raft in Hades that carried the dead across the River Styx to the final judgement in the afterlife.

I couldn't resist.

In this context, the life that Ardis had lived is over. She has changed and she is crossing over to a new world. This is a setup for what happens in the sequel to *A Life on Water*, which I am working on now.

Final Thoughts

Portuguese author Fernando Pessoa wrote: *"Boa é a vida, mas melhor é o vinho. O amor é bom, mas é melhor o sono."*

Life is good, but wine is better. Love is good, but sleep is better.

Did you enjoy this book?

Reviews are vital to help me reach new readers.

Please leave an honest review on Amazon at

amazon.com/author/timpal

And tell your followers on social media about *A Life on Water*.

I really appreciate your help. Thanks!

My Writing Venues

I talk about what is going on in my fiction and poetry,

and I share what I am learning about publishing.

My website/blog: timpaleczny.com

My newsletter: timothypaleczny.substack.com

THE CAVALARIÇO

Cavalarico Books

. . . are available in ebook and print formats here:

amazon.com/author/timpal

For more information, visit cavalarico.com

Made in the USA
Las Vegas, NV
28 December 2023

83650224R00208